THE IMDALIND SERIES

Kiss of FIRE

-THE IMDALIND SERIES-

REBECCA ETHINGTON

Published by Imdalind Press

Copyediting by Annette Skoubye, Dragon Fire Edits, C&D Editing
Cover Design © Sarah Hansen, Okay Creations
Cover Photography © Regina Wamba
Formatting by Inkstain Interior Book Designing

Production Management by Imdalind Press

ISBN (print):   978-0-9884837-0-5
ISBN (e-book):   978-0-9884837-1-2

Printed in USA
This Edition, November 2012

To My Grandmother—
Who loved to read and loved to hear my stories.
You always told me I could write, and strangely enough it turns
out I can!

-

To My Papa—
Who taught me what true love really is.

CONTENTS

PROLOGUE

*E*VERYTHING CHANGED ON MY FIFTH birthday while my parents were in the backyard hanging the "Happy Birthday Joclyn" banner that was surrounded by yellow and blue streamers. The colors danced through the trees as the wind blew them around. My parents laughed and joked as they decorated while I danced in the doorway as I waited for my friends to arrive.

I stopped to watch a brilliant blue trail of glitter as something small flew around me. I only caught a glimpse of wings before a sharp stabbing pain shot into the right side of my head. It left me feeling like I had been slammed against a brick wall. The sensation burned like acid that spread quickly through me. I dropped to the ground as the pain coursed throughout my body. The hot current flowed under my skin like boiling water in my veins. My vision faded to black as the sensations grew into a torrent that split my bones apart. A buzzing silence filled the world around me until the sounds of my own screaming filled my ears.

I remember my mother panicking alongside me; my father on the phone with 911. I remember the sound of the ambulance siren, my vision a never-ending black, and my body filled with the stabbing agony that incapacitated me. Trapped in my prison of

1

unrelenting tortures, I drifted in and out of consciousness. No matter what the doctors did, what medicines they pumped into me, the pain didn't go away. I couldn't move past it; sometimes I couldn't stop screaming. Eventually, I slipped into a coma.

The first thing I saw when I woke up was my mother's face filled with worry. My father looked sick with fear. Even at five, I knew something was wrong. I had been in the coma for months, and no one knew what had happened. The only signs of anything having changed were a change in my eye color, from green to a colorless silver, and a small mark that appeared right below my right ear. It was the size of a penny, the skin vivid red and raised like a brand, while in the middle a small indistinguishable figure stood out in vivid black. I ran my finger over it for days. It didn't hurt, but it was ugly. The doctors assumed that I had been bitten by some sort of bug and had an allergic reaction, but deep down, I knew that wasn't right. Besides, something like that wouldn't have affected my eye color.

I wasn't the only one to doubt the doctors; my father doubted them, too.

I went home the next day where my mother covered me in blankets and provided enough ice cream and cartoons to last me a month. She got time off work and took care of me like she had never done before.

I almost believed the mark didn't really matter... until the fighting started. It was weird to hear them yell. I had never known my parents to fight before; they had always loved each other so much. My father had become obsessed with the idea of the mark, convinced that the mark I now had on my neck was something different, that it meant something. He rambled and yelled about it. He spent hours at the library and days on the Internet. The grinding noise of the modem dialing-in wound on my nerves; some nights I couldn't sleep. The fearful face he had the day I woke up never left him. He wasn't the same man, but I still loved him. My five-year-old self would crawl up on his lap and plead for everything to be okay; I would promise him that I didn't hurt. I thought he believed me... until the day he disappeared.

I heard them screaming for the last time from the security of my bed with my blankets pulled high over me. I cried as they screamed at each other and gasped at the crashing that rocked the doors in the house. That night, I cried myself to sleep. When I woke up, my father had gone, and it was all because of me.

My mother didn't talk about it for months. Her heart had broken; I think my heart broke, too. Even at five, something inside me had changed; I knew I was different. Part of me knew that my father was right and that the mark did mean something. It was also the reason he left; the reason my mother and I were alone.

At five, I hid that part of me away.

CHAPTER
1

My LONG BOARD CLICKED RHYTHMICALLY down the sidewalk as I moved. The warm wind of early summer tugging against my dark hoodie, pulling at the long strands of black hair that had fallen out of my hood. I didn't like traveling in front of the houses in this part of the neighborhood. I normally took the back alley, but today, some road crews were working on pot-holes and I had to make my trip in front of the giant mansions that littered the hills of the east side of the city.

The rich ladies, with their upturned noses, liked to look out their windows at me as if I were somehow infecting their perfect little world with a contagious disease. They looked at me like I was poor—which I was—a menace—which I wasn't—and like there was something wrong with me—which I wasn't even sure of. Normally, I would laugh at their response to me, but I didn't like them taking so much notice. Chances were, they would complain to my mother's boss, and she would get in trouble, again. It wasn't my fault the road crews decided to work on the alley, but it's not like "His Grace" would care.

My mother had worked as Edmund LaRue's cook for almost ten years now, having taken the job after my father took off. Mr. LaRue—or King Edmund as I called him—was an arrogant, greedy, self-righteous man who kept to himself. He probably had more secrets than rooms in his house, if that were even possible. However, as much as I despised him, he paid my mother well, so I didn't complain.

I jumped off my long board as I approached his house. If he heard the clicking of it against the sidewalk, he might throw another fit; that is, of course, if Mrs. Nose-Against-The-Window hadn't already put in a call. I looked up the long driveway as I stepped in front of the gate. Only the gray Rolls-Royce lay parked against the side of the house, causing my heart to fall—no bright yellow Lotus. Ryland wasn't home yet.

I hopped back on my long board to roll down the side of the house; my somewhat good mood dashed by the absence of my best friend. Who cared if King Edmund got mad at me for making a racket?

I crashed into the kitchen, the slam of the door disrupting the 70s music that my mother and Mette, the LaRue's baker, were listening to. Plopping myself onto one of the many bar stools surrounding the long work surfaces, I placed my head on my arms and covered my face as much as I could with my hood.

"Happy Birthday, Joclyn!" my mom said. I only grunted as I attempted to cover my head with my hoodie. "How was school?"

"Fine," I answered into the countertop.

"Fancy that," Mette said in her rich, Irish accent. "She can almost disappear into the table. Must be a trick learned when one turns sixteen."

I grumbled nonsense at them again and covered my head with my arms, trying to ignore the laughter of the two women.

"Not funny," I growled.

"Hello, in there! Joclyn, can you hear me?" My mother lifted the side of my hood as she called into it, and I tried not to smile. "Well, I think she's done it! She has melded into the sweatshirt and become one with it."

"That will make it easier to wash her, that will."

"Not funny." I tried not to sound amused, but I don't think it worked. My mother snorted so loudly it reverberated off the pristine marble countertops.

"I'll just throw her in the washing machine, then a little bleach, *lots* of detergent, and the skateboard can go in the dumpster."

"Hey! It's a long board, and it's the only way I get around! Unless you bought me a car. Did you buy me a car?" I shot up like a light, my face breaking out into an eager grin.

"There she is," Mom laughed, throwing a present at me. "Happy Birthday, honey! Sorry, no car this year."

"She lives. She lives. Praise the Lord! I thought for a second we would have to call a priest to exorcise her from the sweater," Mette laughed, her red bun bobbing on top of her large, round head. "Happy Birthday, dearie."

My mom nudged the present at me again, prompting me to open it. Her eyes were sparkling with that eager anticipation she always got about gift-giving. The package was a good size, but lumpy and squishy. Clothes. Clothing had been an issue with my mother and me since that darned mark showed up on my face and chased my dad away. I preferred to hide the mark, and myself.

She thought I should show the world how beautiful I was. I guess she might be right; I could be seen as the epitome of the fair-skinned, dark-haired beauty with some form of ethereal features. My mom fawned over my bone structure and perfectly-formed eyebrows that just grew that way. But, when I looked in the mirror, I only saw a skinny girl who wasn't quite good enough. My mom obviously saw something different. She liked to give me blue shirts to highlight my black hair, or green belts to set off the silver of my eyes, or so she said. All I saw were vivid colors or an obvious lack of fabric that would make me stand out.

For years my mom kept trying to convince herself that my choice of baggy, dark-colored clothes was a stage that I would outgrow. I always found a way to hide myself; I kept my black hair long and falling in a sheet around my face, my clothes always dark and at least a size too big. It was all done in a way to help me blend in so people wouldn't notice me. I felt comfortable inside my safety shield, hoping that no one could see me or figure out what was wrong with me. When the Goth kids showed up at school, it worked to my advantage. My mom, for once, thought I was trying to be cool, but I wasn't overly emotional or narcissistic like they appeared to be. I just wanted to disappear.

"Go on," Mom prodded. "Open it."

I sighed before ripping off the paper. It was a deep red shirt, embroidered with some beads and fabric flowers. There was no denying it was pretty. It even looked like one of the things I wished I could wear, if only I felt comfortable doing so.

"Just try it on, Joclyn." My mom danced around in her white kitchen shoes. How in the world could I say no to that?

I dragged my feet all the way to the bathroom with the red shirt sticking out of the arm of the hoodie my hands were hiding in. I put on the shirt, cursing the fact that my mother could tell what size I was even through my purposely too big clothes. It was snug, but not too tight.

I stared at myself in the mirror for a second, looking through the tunnel of dark hair. I looked so different in the shirt, almost pretty. Without thinking, I pulled my hair up into a pony tail, just to see what it would look like, but the mark stood out so vividly; its ugly shape stuck out right behind and below my right ear. I twisted my hair and pulled it around the side, twisting it down the side of my neck. The low twist covered it easily, but I still didn't trust it. Part of me wished I could dress like this, but I could never tell my mother that.

I looked in the mirror a second too long, trying to figure out a way to get out of this. Even if I said it was too small, my mom would insist I show her anyway. Best to get it over with. I sighed just a little bit before leaving the bathroom, knowing that Mette and my mom would fawn over me. I closed my eyes so that I wouldn't have to see my mom dance around with excitement again. The door clicked open, and I stood there, eyes closed, waiting for it to come.

"Oh, Joclyn," my mom said, "it's beautiful." I didn't need to have my eyes closed, I could hear the soles of her non-slip shoes squeak against the floor as she danced in joy.

"Mom, don't..." I pleaded, but I knew it was useless.

"That color... with your hair... Oh, please wear it to dinner tonight, without that darn sweatshirt," she added. I could feel her tug on the hoodie, but I hung on to it for dear life.

"Mom. No." My eyes snapped open in my attempt to retort, and I froze. Ryland stood right in front of me, a huge grin on his face. My jaw dropped as my heart went into overdrive.

Ryland LaRue was the son of my mother's boss. Ry was two years older than me and stood a good head taller. We had been friends since my mother first started this job when I was five, playing together in the kitchen and hiding on the grounds of the estate. Ryland would always be my very best friend, but lately, it was hard to see past his dark, curly hair, crystalline blue eyes and "private school Rugby muscles" without feeling like my heart was getting restarted. This heart-slamming was for a different reason though: he hadn't seen me wear anything other than a hoodie since I hit puberty. I felt uncomfortable, and Ryland's appreciative grin wasn't helping matters much.

Mette and my mother broke out into huge bouts of laughter at their little joke. The look of surprise on my face must have been hysterical. Rather than join along, as part of me wished to, I squeaked and moved to put my hoodie back on. I slid into it as quickly as I could without revealing my scar. I had kept it hidden from Ryland for this long, thanks to Band-Aids and carefully-placed hoods or hair; I didn't need him seeing it now. It would only give him a reason to run away.

"Ah, come on, Jos... It's pretty," Ryland pleaded.

"No," I spoke as sternly as I could, turning to repeat the word to my mother who was in stitches with Mette against the confection mixer. My mother's laughter stopped.

"Joclyn, you have to wear it tonight," she pleaded. "Your grandmother bought you a matching skirt."

"Skirt?" I gasped. There was no way they were getting me into a skirt. Although, I could tell by the look on my mom's face that I was trapped. My birthday dinner was the only time of the year I saw my father's parents. It would break their heart if I said no.

"Ugh. Fine. Fine!" I snapped, ignoring my mother's look of triumph before rounding on Ryland, one finger pointed into his face. "One word of this to anyone, even mentioning it to me, Ry, and I will kill you."

"Uh huh," he laughed, his blue eyes rolling. "What are you going to do, Jos? Hide from me? It does look very pretty on you, you know."

"Ryland LaRue, so help me..."

"Yeah, yeah, I got ya." He smiled, grabbing my hand that still pointed in his face. "Come on. I'll have her back in an hour, Mrs. Despain."

"Better make it two, Ryland. I don't need her moping around while I try to get the chicken broiled." My mother smiled so brightly that I could have almost guessed what was on her mind. More gifts.

"No problem, Mrs. D."

"Oh, and Joclyn," my mom's voice called after us. I turned back to her, halting Ryland's departure. "Please try to avoid Edmund and Timothy. I think my job has been threatened enough for one week." She smiled, but it was half-hearted. She was always the first to get in trouble over my friendship with Ryland.

I nodded in understanding before Ry pulled me out of the kitchen and into the servants' quarters. We gained the usual snickers and side-glances as we scampered past the many rooms occupied by the live-in staff, heading to the back corridors that the servants used to move around the massive house.

At first, our friendship had been tolerated by Edmund, but a few years ago that had started to change. For a year or so, it had been labeled unacceptable and then last year, we were told we were not supposed to be friends at all. Ryland had been warned and threatened by his father to stay away from me, while my mother had been under constant "warning" of losing her job. I wasn't surprised. To *King* Edmund I was nothing more than a dirty peasant. We probably should have taken it seriously, but Ryland insisted everything was okay, so my mother and I followed his lead.

We entered an upper hall where Ryland's bedroom sat, the door just ahead of us on the left. I kept my eyes looking straight ahead, smiling until an unusually short man in a three-piece suit with a thick, neatly-trimmed beard turned the corner to face us. I jumped behind Ryland, not needing his arm to move me there. I knew that man, and I hated him.

Timothy Vincent was the Vice President of Ryland's family's company, Imdalind Forging. He was responsible for the metal-forging method that had made them their millions. Timothy was also the man who reprimanded my mother on a weekly basis about my continued relationship with Ryland. He caught sight of us and moved forward quickly, an even angrier scowl than usual carved into his face. Timothy always made me uncomfortable, even on his best days.

"Ryland, we have been looking for you." My heart sank. *We.* That could only mean one thing.

A deeper gait entered the hall, and I moved further behind Ry. I didn't have to see Edmund LaRue to know what he looked like. In many ways, Ryland could be described as his father's clone, but instead of the mop of loose curls Ryland had, Edmund kept his hair short and slicked back in a gentle wave. Where Ryland's eyes were the warm and welcoming color of the depths of the ocean, Edmund's were as cold and distant as the polar icecaps. They always cut into me with a frigid, poisonous edge that made my insides repulse.

I sank into Ryland's back, my face pressing against his polo shirt in an attempt to hide. His muscles were tensed and strained.

Ryland's hand reached back and found the tips of my fingers that stuck out from the cuff of my hoodie. He squeezed my fingers between his in an attempt to reassure me. As always, his touch warmed my body, the tingling warmth shooting right to my stomach.

"Ryland! I am so glad we found you. I would like to move our lesson to an hour after dinner." Edmund's voice was laced with a false endearment that shook my bones. His statement was not a question, but a command.

Ryland had been taking lessons with his father since he was twelve. Ry had always insisted it was some fencing thing, but the way they talked about it always made it seem so sinister, like they were going to take over the world. Who knew? Maybe they were. Corporate drama was a little out of my league.

"Yes, Father, that's fine. I will meet you in the court." Ryland's voice was distant and diplomatic. When he talked like this, he reminded me of the heir to the multi-million dollar company he was, not my energetic, fun-loving best friend.

"Ryland," Timothy spoke slowly, dragging out his syllables, and I knew he was going to address our friendship. I shifted my weight, cursing the dark hoodie that stuck out from behind my hiding place. "I am so glad to see you have taken our advice about your choice of friends." Timothy's voice seemed hopeful, odd, seeing as how I stood right here.

I attempted to draw the fabric closer to my body. Being so close to both of them made me almost, dare I say it, scared.

"I have expressed my opinion on this multiple times, Timothy. Please do not make me repeat it." Ryland stood a little straighter as he attempted to end the conversation.

"Now, now, Ryland. We don't need any of that." Edmund's voice lacked any warmth. "After all, I would hate for your attitude to be the cause of a downfall."

I cringed. Was he talking about me, or about my mother? Edmund had never before said anything so bold when I was within ear-shot; it was almost like he couldn't see me. That, in itself, was a ridiculous thought; Ryland wasn't enough to hide behind, even with all his muscle.

"You know my terms in regards to that, Father." I could see Edmund's expensive penny loafers slide against the white carpet. I shifted my weight, scared he was moving to get a better look at me.

"So it would seem. Well, at least now I won't have to dismiss her mother, or worse. We just can't have anything spoiling my perfect son, now, can we?" I saw his body shift as if he were moving closer. Ryland's fingers pressed harder against my own.

"No, Father." There was a pause and then Edmund's shiny leather shoes stepped away from us down the hall. Timothy's shoes followed Edmund's hesitantly, like they were waiting for something else to happen before he turned the corner.

We moved the last few steps quickly, darting into Ryland's spacious room before either of them had a chance to return.

Ryland's bedroom was roughly the size of my entire apartment. The giant rectangular space was separated down the middle on the left side by a long wall that housed a kitchenette on one side and Ryland's massive entertainment system on the other. The right side of the room contained his oversized bed that still sported the colored blankets we had used to make forts when we were little kids, while the entrance to his bathroom lay beyond the bed. Behind it all was a closet the size of a small motor home, containing far too many clothes for someone who went to a school that required uniforms.

I went to the high cabinet next to the entertainment center where he kept the chocolate before plopping down on his bed to enjoy a Mounds Bar. Ryland locked the door behind him, just in case his father or the servants decided to get nosey, and turned on some brainless TV show as he went.

"I hate them, you know. Hate," I spat sourly, ripping the wrapper off the candy.

"That's a strong word, Jos."

"I know, but don't you think they deserve it? Saying all that about how I am going to ruin you, talking about me like I was not even there. It's like they couldn't even see me."

"Maybe they couldn't," Ryland said almost inaudibly.

"Ha, ha, ha, very funny, Ry." I paused at the curious glance Ryland gave me. "They wouldn't hurt anyone because of me, would they?"

"I wouldn't put it past them," Ry grumbled as he leaned against the wall his TV was mounted to.

My head jerked up. "They would?" Not cool.

"Don't worry so much, Jos. I wouldn't let them, even if they tried. If I could get them to be nice to you, I would, but I can't. Either way, I won't let them hurt you. Besides, you don't need to worry about it. You only have to deal with them for the rest of the year. I get him for my entire life."

I could only roll my eyes, but then the candy bar fell untouched to my lap. I didn't like the daily reminders that Ryland was leaving overseas for college in just a few months' time. Oxford, a huge giant ocean away. I tried to push the information to the back of my mind. I would be lucky if I ever saw him again.

"So, did you get the role?" Ryland asked eagerly, plopping down beside me, his obvious change in subject managed as smoothly as possible.

"No, of course not. The role went to Cynthia McFadden, not that anyone was really surprised."

"What? You read the role perfectly!"

"Well, I did here in your bedroom. In the school gymnasium, I'm not sure the drama teacher could hear my monologue over the catcalls about my lack of hygiene..." I hoped that didn't sound too bitter.

Cynthia had brought half the football team with her and they had quite a fun time jeering at anyone who auditioned for the same role as the cheerleader. I thought I had done a good job, even with the jocks yelling at me to bathe or brush my hair, but Ms. Flowers didn't think so.

"What role did you get then?" His silky voice calm and eager.

"None."

"None? You would have been cast as Ophelia without question if you had auditioned at my school."

I couldn't help but laugh. "Of course I would have. You go to an all boys' school!"

"I guess you're right. But Michael Aliente has been eyeing that role for years now; you might have had your work cut out for you."

"Well, I don't think I could beat Michael; he's way too good at those monologues." We laughed, the thought of tiny Michael in a long Shakespearean gown bringing tears to my eyes.

"Do you want me to do something? I could make a phone call..."

"No!" I snapped. He had said it with only good intentions, but his face moved from concern to shock. My fast-beating heart plummeted; I didn't mean to offend him. "I mean, no, thank you. Cynthia will be great in the role, though she may come off as more of a floozy than a crazy girl, but, whatever."

"That's not what I meant, Jos. I meant about the guys teasing you. I could always pick you up from school in the Lotus; that would stop them in their tracks."

"They would only say I paid you." I smiled at him. I loved Ryland when he got like this; he was an incredibly caring guy.

He didn't return the smile. Instead, he looked at me as if I had just sold his precious car, to buy a long board made of solid gold. "Joclyn, I don't like them making fun of you, especially when they say things that are not true. I mean, really! *You*, not bathe. I can smell your shampoo from a mile away."

"How do you know that's not just the perfume I use to cover up the almighty stench?"

"Joclyn."

"Ryland." My glare was no match for his; his blue eyes cut into me. "It's all right, really. It's not like there's anything you can do."

"I have a full Rugby team who would gladly fight for your honor."

"What, do we live in 1740 now?" I laughed. He didn't. Strangely enough, he was serious. "You would fight the Eagles' Landing football team for my 'honor'?"

He nodded.

I was beginning to feel uncomfortable. "Why? I mean, no one cares about me. I disappear in that school. They only said those things because they couldn't even remember who I was."

"I care about you, Jos, and I don't want people talking about you like that." My heart sputtered for a moment before I turned to him, making sure the mark below my ear remained covered.

"That's why you're my best friend, Ry, because you care. You are the only one who knows me." I smiled at him in a desperate attempt to convey that I was okay, that the name-calling didn't hurt, even if it did. I could tell he wasn't buying it. He could always see through my looks. "I'm fine, Ryland. Honest." I waited, but he didn't say anything. I could just see him barging into my school with a dozen other guys in dark blue blazers. Ugh. "Ry, I am asking you as nicely as I can manage to not do anything. I can handle it; you don't always have to protect me." I tried to put as much energy into my voice as I could. I am not sure it worked.

"All right, I won't do anything. It's just a crappy way to spend your birthday."

"That's okay. I got a great shirt, soon to be skirt-combo out of it, which I will never wear. So, no harm done."

"You know, you really should wear..."

"Don't start, Ryland," I said, falling back on his bed.

"You just need the right accessories, is all." He spoke quite calmly as he placed a small wrapped box on my chest. I sat up, letting the box fall into my lap.

"What? Are you asking me to marry you?" I scoffed the words, but I still couldn't take my eyes off the box.

"Hell, no! I have been engaged to Cynthia McFadden for years. Didn't you know?" He pushed into my shoulder, almost knocking me over. "Just open it."

I moved back to a sitting position like a weeble toy. I couldn't say anything; the richest guy in the state had just given me a jewelry box. Part of me didn't want it, but the girl inside of me forced my fingers to rip the paper off.

The box was back velvet, soft to the touch. I caressed it like the box itself was the gift before opening it to reveal an inside of soft black silk. Nestled into the shiny silk was a teardrop-shaped ruby the size of my thumbnail. The beautiful jewel was suspended from a fine silver chain. A beautiful silver wire wrapped around the Ruby in swirls and spirals that joined it to the chain. I could only stare at it. I knew without asking that the ruby was real. The necklace was worth more than my mother made in a year.

"Do you like it?" Ryland's voice was soft, entertained by my reaction as he chuckled at my solitary head-bob of a response. He grabbed the necklace out of the box and then moved to place it around my neck.

"Sorry it's not a car," he laughed, "but your mom wanted to give you a full new outfit for your birthday and forced—eh, recruited me to help. I thought this would set off the diamonds in your eyes. I think she will do anything to get you out of those hoodies and jeans."

I looked down at the necklace that now hung around my neck, my voice coming back. I moved my hair out from under the chain careful not to show that dreaded mark.

"Besides," Ryland continued, "you can always wear your new outfit under a hoodie and then your mom can still feel like she won." I couldn't help but laugh, though, I also felt like crying. I had never received anything so beautiful, something that I instantly loved. Darn my girl emotions! One tear had leaked out.

"Thank you, Ryland. It's beautiful. I love it." My voice did not get above a whisper.

"You know, Jos, you're more of a girl than you let on. I'm just glad I am the one who gets to see it." With that, Ryland kissed my forehead. I thought my heart might explode.

I hadn't had a birthday this good, ever.

CHAPTER 2

THAT ALL ENDED WITH DINNER.

We always met my grandparents at the same place; a little Mexican dive called La Fea Gato. La Fea Gato was in between our two houses, so we each had to drive an hour to meet for dinner. After having done it for eleven years, it wasn't a big deal. I even had a favorite on the menu and spent the majority of the hour drive dreaming of Chile Verde rather than listening to my mom dote over how pretty I looked, and how big the rock Ryland had given me was.

At first, she had attempted to pull my hair up, but I had put my foot down, startling poor Mette with a wail she had never heard come out of me before. I didn't care how much my mom promised that the mark was barely noticeable, or that scars were fashionable; mine was staying hidden. In the end, I had brushed my dark hair out until it hung around my slender face like a sheet.

We arrived at the restaurant late, rushing to the table to allow my grandmother her obligatory time to ogle over how much I had grown or changed. We all knew it was an act; my grandparents only came out of respect for my mother's wishes. I never saw them any other time.

My grandmother was a round woman with gray hair that she always wore in a bun. Her appearance suggested that she would be wearing a flowered apron, smiling and selling butter rolls rather than wearing business suits with the severe look she always had. My grandfather had always been quiet and somewhat reserved, but today he seemed downright cranky, and greeted my mother and me with a curt head-nod. My grandmother didn't seem to notice and looked me over quickly before shoving a bright pink parcel into my hands.

I tried my hardest to smile at the impending skirt, but I was not sure it worked. My mom's iron grip dug into my arm as she prompted me to open it. Even though it was obvious no one wanted to be there, my mom was still going to try her hardest to make this work.

The tape came off easily, as if it had been rewrapped, and an atrocious red and black plaid skirt tumbled onto my lap, followed by a small black bag that would hold only a wallet, if I was lucky. I looked at them both as happily as I could before being shooed off to the bathroom where I held the skirt up to me, against my new shirt. They didn't match. I was going to look like a style-defunct school girl. Of course they all declared I looked wonderful anyway. I could have worn a stuffed chicken and it would have received the same reaction. My frustration and irritation were turning into uncontrollable laughter.

Once the food came, I bowed out of the conversation, and my grandmother seemed to lose her lackluster interest in me. I focused on my food as my mother and grandmother chattered away about work and neighbors, and aunts, uncles and cousins I had never seen. I caught snippets of information about Uncle Robert's new wife and Cousin Becky's new—scandalous—tattoo, not taking anything in. The taste of chilies and guacamole consumed me so much that I was unaware of my grandmother's question until my mother tapped my leg.

"Joclyn?" she asked, repeating her question, "how is school?"

"Fine," I said, hoping I didn't have to elaborate. There wasn't much more that I could say about school, so we sat in uncomfortable silence.

"Excuse me." Mom spoke as normally as she could, although it was obvious she left in order to give us all time to talk. "I have to go to the restroom."

My grandparents had nothing to say without my mom there, so I sat staring at the last of my empanada and listened to the clink of dishes and bits of conversation around me.

"Don't open the bag until you get home." My grandfather's rough voice made me jump.

"Excuse me?" I asked, taken back.

"The bag. Don't open it until you get home. There's a letter from your father in it." I think I may have leaped a few inches out of the booth. The words "your father" were never spoken, least of all by his own parents.

"My father?" I spoke much louder than I had anticipated, my heart beating a million miles an hour. "You've seen him?"

My grandfather leaned forward, but my grandmother looked at him so sharply, even I felt uncomfortable with her gaze. My grandfather shrank back against the booth.

"Yes, dear." Her voice was falsely sweet. "Your father asked us to give that letter to you. And we agreed."

"You've seen my father," I repeated again, although I wasn't sure if I felt joy, anger or excitement at this. Each emotion was there, but they didn't stop swirling around each other; my stomach turned into a bowl of butterflies.

"Yes," my grandfather supplied, ignoring a second look from

Grandma. "He came by just the other day wanting to see you. He had a birthday gift for you, so we put it in that bag so you could have it. But don't open it here; I don't know if your poor mother's heart can handle hearing a single word from him."

"He wanted to see me...?"

"Yes, followed us here, no doubt. Poor lad seemed desperate..." Grandma cut Grandpa off with one stern look and he sank back in his chair, looking crabby again. I didn't notice, though; I had begun spinning around in my chair in a futile attempt to look for my father. I knew it was pointless. I didn't even know what he looked like anymore. Any man here could be him. That one had his eyebrows, another had his nose. Of course I had pictures, but they were from so long ago. Besides, it was hard to recognize someone from a twelve-year-old photograph.

"You might want to make sure his gift has been properly paid for, dear. I wouldn't be surprised if he stole it. I am not sure my poor son has had more than two coins to rub together in a while."

I stopped my frantic search to face my grandmother. Her face was somewhat hard and disappointed now. I wanted to hear more, to ask her what she meant, but my mother slid back into her chair, announcing herself to be full.

The car ride home was quiet, unlike either of us. The little black bag sat on my lap as if it were a dead weight or a bomb waiting to go off. I didn't want to look at it, but couldn't keep from stealing glances. I tried counting the stars, the fence posts, the houses; but nothing worked, and so, my eyes kept floating back to the bag.

"So, Joclyn...?" My mom's voice came out of nowhere. "Did you have a good birthday?" I looked down at my mismatched clothes, at the beautiful necklace, and smiled.

"Yeah, Mom. I did. Thanks for everything."

"You should wear that outfit tomorrow."

"Not going to happen, Mom."

"Why not?" she whined, offended.

"Well, I would get mugged for the necklace and tortured for my mismatched clothes." My mom looked down at my outfit as I gestured toward it, her face breaking into a gigantic smile.

"It does look bad, doesn't it?" she sighed. "I thought your grandmother would have more style sense—"

"Well, if you limit her to pencil skirts, she does great," I scoffed.

"At least the bag is cute." Her comment was innocent enough, but it stopped me dead in my tracks, the smile draining from my face. All I could do was nod and stare at it.

It was cute, but I couldn't stop thinking about what could be inside. Any other person who had been abandoned by their father would throw it away without a second thought. Yet, I was drawn to it.

He had left because of the mark. Maybe the letter would tell me something about it, maybe he had found something out, or maybe it was a plea for us to let him come home. I couldn't stop thinking about the possibilities, my heart beating uncomfortably at each one. If I was smart, I would have just thrown it away.

When I got home, I ran to my room with only a hurried goodnight to my mom. A shower would have to wait, changing would wait. I ripped open the bag and dumped the contents on my white bedspread. A small dirty package and a piece of paper fell out, each one leaving gray grease marks on the spots they hit. I looked at them—the package or the letter? I opted for the package; get the gift out of the way so I could focus on the letter.

I grabbed the small crumpled paper and began un-wrinkling it into a flat mass. There, amongst the dirty folds, sat a pure white marble; it almost looked like a pearl. I looked at it in disbelief. How could my wayward, possibly homeless, father afford to give me a pearl. It must be fake. I knew there was something to do with teeth to be able to tell if it was real and so I reached out to grab it with the full intention of biting it in half. However, the second my fingers came in contact with it, a shock of white-hot heat seared through my arm. I jumped back, cursing, wondering what my father had sent me.

I stepped closer to my bed, stopping as my head spun on my shoulders, my vision tracking and my stomach heaving a bit. I steadied myself, waiting for the spinning to slow and cursing whatever food poisoning I had gotten at the restaurant.

I looked everywhere for the bead, but the white pearl no longer lay in the dirty wrapper; instead, one of deep purple had taken its place. I moved the dirty paper around, and I searched over my bedspread, but no other pearl—of any color—could be found. Luckily, when I grabbed the purple pearl, no shock shot up my arm, though the small marble was very warm. I couldn't help but be a little mad; it seemed like a cruel joke for a renegade father to send his daughter something that zaps her.

I placed the purple bead back on the wrapper and picked up the letter. Silly really, whatever was going to hurt me the most was going to be written on the page. I opened it, a shaky breath flowing out of me.

My Dearest Jocelyn:

Great, he doesn't even know how to spell my name right.

My Dearest Jocelyn:
I write this letter in the hopes that my parents will deliver it to you, and find you well. Happy Birthday!! I can't believe that eleven years have passed since I last saw you. I am sure you have grown into a beautiful young woman. Do you have a lot of boyfriends? Tell them to be careful or your dad will get them.

I was torn between laughter and frustration; it seemed odd for a man I hadn't seen in so long to be giving me advice on how to threaten boys. I almost put the letter down; maybe I should have.

I hope you are doing well in school and not giving your mom much trouble.

I know I have not been a good father. I would apologize, but I know I would not gain your forgiveness, and in truth, I do not want it. I would have taken you with me if your mother had not hid you from me. You probably don't even remember that day; I suppose it is better that way.

I do need you to know what I have found, and why I left. I knew there was something more to your mark than the doctors could tell us. When I was in college, a young man by the name of Thom, who was in one of my classes, had something similar; and one day we found him gone, his dorm room trashed.

I was so afraid that the same would happen to you, that you would be taken from me, my precious daughter. And so, when your mom would not listen, I left to find proof. And I found it, Jocelyn!

Your mark is special; it is magical. Your mark means you can do magic. They call it Koosa! It took many years, but I found a group of people who find those with marks such as yours and save them from the people who took my friend from college. I do not want you to disappear. I only hope that those who would harm you haven't already found you.

The people I found gave me a rock to give to you. They call it a birthstone. It will help them find you. All you have to do is touch it and it will call to them, and lead them to you. Isn't that wonderful? I found a way to save you! I am told it may hurt when you touch the stone, so please be careful. But, touch it as soon as you can so you can be saved, and I can see you again.

Love Always,

Your Father, Jeffery Despain

I read it once, then again, and again. Then I cried for at least twenty minutes. My poor father! The smart, beautiful man that my mother had fallen in love with had lost his mind. He was talking about magic like it was real and referring me to cults so that I could be saved. I think I cried myself to sleep, clutching the necklace Ryland had given me in one hand and the cursed bead my father had given me in the other.

CHAPTER 3

NOTHING COULD HAVE STOPPED THE nightmares I had that night. They began the second I closed my eyes and did not leave until the moment my restless night ended. Every aspect of the letter came to haunt me in one terrifying race for my life. I moved from being chased by a homeless man with sharp jagged teeth who was covered in rags, to being surrounded by extraordinarily tall people dressed all in white. No matter how fast I ran, I couldn't get away from any of them. I ran through the silent dream in a trance, my body tense and terrified.

When I woke up, I felt like I hadn't slept at all. My body was heavy and numb from emotional and mental exertion. My chest hurt with every breath, each movement straining sore muscles. I lay in bed for a long time, drifting in and out of sleep, having decided that I wasn't going to school that day. The nightmares didn't return, but I slept fitfully, my subconscious afraid of being haunted.

By about three in the afternoon, my body felt better, like I was recovering from a small head cold rather than feeling like I had been hit by a large load of bricks. Not being able to ignore the call of nature any longer, I trudged to the bathroom. It was odd how ill my body felt, almost like I had caught some strange body-ache bug. As much as I wanted to blame food poisoning for my illness, I wasn't sick enough, and blaming body-aches on a pearl-like bead was downright silly. I tried to convince myself my problem wasn't physical, only emotional. Who would have thought that a delusional letter from my father would have affected me so much? I collapsed back on my bed, my head throbbing with the collision.

My phone buzzed as a call came in. I reached for it, assuming it to be my mom checking in on me. I was shocked to see Ry's name and a picture of us on top of his car on the caller ID. Ryland never called. Of course, we saw each other every day so there was never a need, but it was still odd. I stared at his name until the ringer stopped and the system sent him to voicemail. I could have answered and told him I was sick, but knowing Ry, he would be able to hear the lie in my voice alone, or even worse, he would rush over to check on me.

I sighed, my chest aching with the movement. I hadn't changed since the birthday party; I had fallen asleep wearing the odd outfit I had been provided during dinner, the necklace Ryland gave me still hanging from around my neck. The ruby lay against my white sheet, looking like a drop of blood. I touched it with my fingertips, surprised by its warmth. The sincerity of the gift still surprised me, and staring at it stirred up a whole range of emotions that clashed with the bone-crushing depression I felt. I rolled over and lost myself in my thick comforter, falling asleep again.

I woke-up a few hours later, the light of day leaving my room, my mother's hand pressed to my forehead.

"What hurts?" she asked, her hand moving to feel my glands.

"Everything," I whispered.

"Hmm. Well, you don't have a fever, so it's probably just a head cold. Can you eat?"

I shook my head no. Even if I had wanted to eat, I doubted anything would stay down. Mom clicked her tongue at me, a sure sign she didn't believe me.

"You'll need to get liquids down, though. I wouldn't want you to get too sick."

I mumbled something in agreement.

"You're just lucky it's a Friday, that way you have the whole weekend to recover." She stood and headed to the kitchen of our small apartment.

I could hear her banging around in search of cups. My mother spent so much time in the LaRue's kitchen she often forgot where things were in our home. I guess that's why I spent so much time there as well. When I was here, I was always alone. You would think I would be used to it, but it just made me feel more forgotten.

"Mette had to go out of town for some family thing," my mom yelled from the kitchen. "I have to pick up her shift tomorrow, but Edmund and Ryland will be out tomorrow night, so I should be home early."

I shifted my weight and my torso filled with deep tissue pain again. I mumbled at her and rolled over, hearing my phone buzz again.

"You better get that," Mom sighed as she sat next to me, my body rolling into her.

"It's just Ryland. I'll see him on Monday."

"He's worried, Joclyn. It's not like you to avoid him." The parental scolding was dripping off her voice.

"Just tell him I'm sick."

"You're not sick, Joclyn."

I knew she didn't believe me.

"Now, are you going to tell him or am I?"

I didn't move to the phone. I heard the click as she picked it up and began pressing buttons. I jumped up in anger, my body protesting my sudden movements.

"Mom!" I shrieked, "Give it back!"

"Not until you tell me what's really wrong." She continued to click buttons, staring me down out of the corner of her eye.

What could I tell her? I couldn't tell her the truth; the truth would break her heart. Besides, how does one say "Dad's gone crazy, thinks I am a witch, referred me to a cult, and sent me a rock that hurt me" without both of us breaking out in tears? Our eyes locked together as my mind scattered around, trying to find something to tell her. She snapped my phone shut, handing it to me as she sat back down next to me.

"Are you going to tell me what's going on now?" she asked, draping her arm across my shoulders. I leaned into her, the soft parental contact relaxing me.

I had to decide what to tell her. I hesitated, a frustrated breath shaking my chest as it left my body. I braced myself for whatever would come—yelling, screaming, crying—and prepared to tell her a limited form of the truth.

"It's Dad," I said. I felt her arm stiffen around my shoulders, and her eyes glossed over and looked straight forward.

I sighed, regretting my decision.

"He came and saw Grandma and Grandpa," I rushed on, "but he didn't want to see me." I knew my voice would betray the lie, but hoped that her stunned silence would cover it.

My mom's arm was rigid and stiff against my shoulder; it felt like a dead weight holding me down. I knew I was wrong to say anything, but now that I had begun, I couldn't take it back. I didn't know what else to say. We sat in silence for much longer than felt comfortable, my mom's arm relaxing around me as she came back to herself.

"At least he's alive." She spoke barely above a whisper.

"What?" I said, loud and accusatory.

She turned to me, her eyes glistening with threatening tears. I felt my stomach tighten. I had spent the last twenty-four hours in a paralyzing depression caused by my psychotic father, and here my mother sat, crying for his safety. My blood began to rise in a slow boil as frustration mixed with disappointment in a way I had never experienced before.

"He left us, Mom," I said. "He doesn't matter."

"Oh, honey." I could hear the longing in her voice, and I shied away from her. "I know it must be so hard for you to understand; you are still so young."

"I understand he left us. What more is there?" I could feel my anger rising in me. Most of the time I could squash down my outrage, but this time, I didn't want to. This time, I wanted to feel it. I wanted to yell, and I wanted everything that had been balling up in me to come crashing out. I needed it to.

"There is a lot more, sweetheart; more than I think I could ever make you understand." Her voice was pleading, and it only set me off more.

"Try me," I growled.

She hesitated, our eyes locked onto one another in some sort of death match. I could tell she was trying to gauge how much she could tell me and how I would respond, just as I had done to her a few moments ago.

Her arm moved back around my shoulders, pulling me into an awkward side-hug. "When I met your father, we were in college. We were young and he was dashing." She sighed and looked away, lost in her memories.

"Some people say young love is fleeting, but I think that's wrong. I think young love is perfect. It's pure and full of hope and desire, but it's more than that. Young love—true love—changes you. It's like something deep down inside you grows and becomes part of the other person. It only takes a moment, but in that one fleeting glance of space and time, you change. You want to be with that person, and with no one else."

My fuming began to lessen. I had never heard my mother talk like this before, her voice so soft and light. The way she spoke, I could see my parents meeting, the love she would have had in her eyes. All of a sudden, my anger began to lull.

"That's how it was when I met your father. I couldn't be without him, and in that one moment, when he first kissed me, I knew I never had to be. He was mine, and I was his. I know it sounds crazy, and you don't have to believe me, but I still feel that way for him. I love him, Joclyn. Even though he left us, I still love him. I think you do, too. That's why it hurts so much that he didn't want to see you." She scanned me as she pleaded for me to understand.

I knew she was right, but at the same time, she was so very wrong. He did want to see me. He had sent me a gift and tracked me down. What hurt so much, and what had broken my heart, was that he had betrayed me. He had used my blasted mark against me, told the world, and created some fabricated story that turned me into a science project.

"So, you're happy he's alive, and not mad because you still love him?" I could feel the bile rising in my throat.

"Honey, I—"

"No! That's not okay, Mom. He left us. He left *you*. He saw his broken daughter and bailed so he wouldn't have to fix her. He didn't even care enough to try! Where was his love for me? Where was his commitment to either of us?" The bottled emotions of eleven years returned and came flooding out of me in a rush, my tongue barely able to form words through the threatening tears.

"Joclyn! Don't say that. He thinks he left out of love—"

"Which only proves that he didn't love us! That he didn't care."

"But he does," she pleaded. "Don't you see? He came to your grandparents; he asked about both of us, I'm sure. It only proves that he does love us; he does care."

This time, I kept my anger in check. This time, I slowed my heartbeat. I had to; I couldn't tell my mother the truth. Her words were so desperate. The truth that she had somehow been waiting for him to return all this time made me sick to my stomach. I glanced toward the garbage can where the ripped-up letter laid, the weight of my lie feeling like lead in my gut. I stood up, the forgotten cell phone tumbling to the ground.

"I need to take a shower." I felt numb as I walked away. My small breakthrough had opened up a chasm of forgotten pain and heartache that I didn't want to revisit. Before I even hit the bathroom, I felt the tears fall. They splashed down my cheeks in warm trails that welcomed more.

I turned on the hot water, hoping my mother wouldn't hear my sobs, hoping the tears would take away all the pain. I stepped into the overly-hot water, burning my skin before I could turn it down and then curled up on the floor of the tub, the water from the shower pouring over me. Only then did I open my hand. The tiny purple bead still sat in my palm, glistening as the water ran over it. It shimmered and sparkled as the color danced and changed. I clenched my hand over it, not wanting to see it again. No matter how much I wanted to throw it down the drain to be lost forever, I knew I couldn't. This stupid thing would always serve as a reminder of what I had lost, and what my mother had so foolishly let slip away.

I WOKE AROUND MIDDAY ON Saturday to the rhythmic knocking that Ryland had used as his signature since he was fourteen. I sighed in frustration. He had been here a few times before, and his visits always made me uncomfortable. Ryland grew up in a two hundred thousand square foot mansion; I grew up in an apartment that was smaller than his bedroom.

I listened to the incessant knocking for a minute more before grumbling and rolling out of bed. My body didn't hurt as much now, but it still felt stiff and heavy. I straightened out, cursing beads, Mexican food, and useless fathers for my endless illness.

I had fallen asleep right after my shower last night, meaning my hair had dried as I slept, resulting in an endless tangle of black hair. I flattened it around my right ear as much as I could, making sure the mark was covered, then threw a hoodie on over my cami and shuffled to the door with Scooby-Doo pajamas dragging on the floor around my ankles. I yanked the door open and walked away, leaving it ajar so he could let himself in.

"Good morning!" Ryland's voice was loud and happy, as always. He bounded in, slammed the door and threw his arms around my waist, lifting me up in an attempt to tackle me to the ground.

"Put me down!" I pounded on his hands, trying not to smile. It was no use; his grip only tightened around my mid-section. "I'm going to hurl!"

He dropped me and came around in front of me, inspecting the probability. He smiled at me impishly, sending my stomach into a pattern reminiscent of a roller coaster.

"Doesn't look like it to me." His blue eyes sparkled, his smile widening to a grin. He was enjoying this game too much.

"I'm sick, remember."

"Not according to your mother, you little faker." He smiled wider and tweaked my nose. My stomach did another flip at his touch.

"Traitor," I mumbled as I shuffled to the kitchen. Ryland bounded behind me, full of more energy than usual.

"Well, I had to get my information somewhere, seeing as someone wouldn't return my calls." He raised a brow at me as he settled into one of the two kitchen chairs, crossing his legs regally and looking out of place sitting at the tiny table at the end of our galley kitchen.

"Yeah, sorry about that. Sick or not, I did sleep all day yesterday." I pulled down a box of Fruit Loops and a bowl, carrying them and the milk over to the table where he sat. I could feel his eyes on me the entire time.

"People only sleep like that when they're sick. You okay?"

"I'm fine," I lied. His eyes widened in disbelief.

"Do you want some?" I shook the box of cereal at him, trying to break his gaze.

He shook his head and continued to look at me. "You know, when I was ten, I snuck into the kitchen and had some Fruit Loops from the box your mom used to keep in there for you..."

"And?"

"They were disgusting!" He made a face like he still remembered the sugar-sweet taste and it revolted him. I couldn't help but laugh; the idea of Fruit Loops being disgusting was funny to me. Of course, Ryland had been raised on a whole higher class of food, so it made sense.

I looked up to find him studying me.

"I'm worried about you. Are you okay?"

"I'm fine." I stuck a spoonful of cereal in my mouth, making it clear I didn't want to elaborate.

Ryland leaned forward and exhaled. "That's obviously a lie, Jos."

I ignored him, and continued to scarf down my cereal at an inhuman rate.

"I was worried," Ryland continued, his voice low, "that after I gave you the necklace, you thought I was looking at you differently, that you thought I wanted to be more than friends... that I scared you..." His voice trailed off and I dropped my spoon into the bowl. We stared at each other.

I had no idea how to respond. I felt hollow at his words. Somewhere, deep inside, I knew he was right; I did feel that way. It was obvious he was trying to make it clear that we were friends and nothing else. I sighed, realizing that I did, in fact, feel something more for him, but now I felt guilty, too. I should never have let myself feel that way. Ryland was my best friend, and somehow I had let my feelings change without even realizing it. It almost seemed like a betrayal of trust.

"No, Ryland, it wasn't that at all!" I tried to force a smile. "I love the necklace, but I know we're... I mean, I understand..." I looked up to him in a desperate attempt to find the right words and felt my heart sputter again.

He was looking at me, bright blue depths boring into mine with a look I had never seen before. His face screwed up in a heart-stopping half-smile that revealed a tiny dimple. I could feel my face fall again.

I grabbed the necklace from underneath my sweater and tried to screw my face back into a smile rather than the shocked disappointment I was sure I displayed. "I can give it back, Ryland. It's okay."

Ryland's hands shot across the small table to land on mine, hindering my intent to remove it. "No, Jos," he whispered, "I don't ever want you to take it off. Can you promise me that? That you will never take it off?"

I nodded, and his smile widened. He kept his hand on mine, his gaze smoldering me before I broke away and went to staring at my bowl of ever mushier Fruit Loops.

"So, what *is* wrong?"

I chanced a glance at him before returning to stare at my Fruit Loops. I didn't know what to tell him, or even how much. After my mother's reaction, I worried he would blow me off, too. I sighed and poked at a mushy red ring of cereal in my bowl.

"Joclyn, you can tell me," he said, his voice low and comforting.

I felt that familiar wave of relaxing warmth I always got from Ryland, my resolve returning.

"My father," I said.

"Your father?" His confusion was understandable. We never talked about my father, just as we never talked about his mother. They were both kind of taboo topics.

"He sent me a letter for my birthday." I decided that I could be more truthful with Ryland than with my mother. I still had to keep some key details from him; he had no idea about my ugly mark, and I didn't want him to find out. "But don't tell my mother," I added. "I only told her he made contact with my grandparents."

"What did the letter say?" Here, again, was something I couldn't answer with the full truth. I focused on his dark curly hair, not wanting to look at him again, worried I would lose myself in his eyes for yet another time.

"He referred me to a cult." I dropped my head into my hands as the desperation over everything that had happened since Thursday night came crashing down on me. I needed to pull it together.

"Oh, Jos, I am so sorry." I heard his chair scrape against the linoleum as he rushed over to me and gathered me in his arms, moving into my chair and sitting me on his lap. His strong arms wrapped around me, pressing me into his chest.

I buried my face in his shirt, the smell of a million bonfires and a million rugby practices consuming me. I could hear the steady thrumming of his heart as it echoed through my head, the rhythm calm and soothing. It did more than mend my frayed emotions; it told me it was okay to feel them. His arms held me tightly, his rough hands moving over my back. He moved his head down to rest on mine, surrounding me with a blanket of warmth, love and comfort. Only, that blanket was Ryland.

My heart rate didn't increase; instead it steadied as my

emotions evened out. Ryland's touch was some sort of perfect drug that took all my pains and worries away. We stayed like that until my Fruit Loops had become a rainbow mush. Even though my frayed emotions had calmed, I didn't want to move; I felt so comfortable in his arms. I could tell he didn't want to move either; his arms held me against him, his tense muscles making a comfortable pillow. I sighed into him and he rotated his head to kiss the top of mine.

His lips brushed against my hair, his hot breath sending a warm tickle of joy down my spine, and I shivered. His chest heaved as he laughed, the sound echoing through my ears. My stomach tensed into a tightly wound basket as his lips began trailing across my head toward my temple. He breathed against the skin there, and the basket inside of me snapped. I jumped up out of his arms, leaving him looking lost, sitting alone in the chair. Necklace or no, he had just made it clear that our relationship had to be purely platonic, and I didn't like the summersault my stomach was now doing.

"I have to get dressed," I sputtered as I fled from the room, my head spinning.

I moved the few steps to my room and shut the door behind me. I stood there, my back to the door as my heart rate steadied. I wasn't sure what had just happened. Okay, that was a lie; I knew exactly what had happened. Had I not jumped up, Ry would have kissed me. My stomach did a joyful swoop at the thought. Did I want him—Ryland LaRue, my best friend—to kiss me? I pictured myself kissing him, his hands against my face, his soft lips pressed against mine. I slid to the floor as my legs forgot how to support me. Obviously, I did. I really, really did. This was bad.

"Are you okay in there?" I jumped to my feet at Ryland's voice right outside my door.

"Yeah, I'll be just a minute."

"Can I watch Demo TV?" Ryland asked, his reference to my lack of cable making me smile.

"Yeah."

"Cool."

I grabbed one of my few pair of jeans, some ballet flats, and a different cami before rushing across the hall to the bathroom. After taming my bed-head, and brushing and scrubbing my teeth and face, I stood still, looking in the mirror. I needed to make sure I didn't let this get out of control.

I stared at myself in the mirror, once again caught with that fantasy of us wrapped in an embrace, arms and legs tangled together from head to toe. I shook my head, wiping the image from my mind. He was leaving in a few months; best to keep him as my best friend.

I dressed and left the bathroom to find Ryland perched at the end of the couch, his legs bouncing up and down.

"You're wired," I pointed out.

"State Rugby finals tonight. My nerves are displaying themselves in some sort of super-charged state." I couldn't help but smile at him, his legs didn't seem to stop moving, even though he was sitting.

"Save it for the field, 'kay?"

"That's the plan, but it doesn't seem to be working."

I walked over and sat next to him on the small couch, intending to watch whatever he had engrossed himself in, but his leg spasms were vibrating the whole couch.

"Knock it off. I feel like I'm in a blender." I pushed him sideways with all my strength, but he hardly moved. He only started shaking more, making odd buzzing noises in an attempt to mimic a blender.

I laughed before sliding off the couch to get away from him. His buzzing sounds grew as he followed me onto the floor, his large form toppling me over to smother me in his weird body-blender. I screeched through my hysterical laughter and slammed my elbow into his side in a desperate attempt to get him off me. He stopped shaking as he rolled away to lie beside me. We laid on the floor, side by side, our arms and legs pressed together as our laughter died out.

"Will you come with me tonight?" he asked, his voice sounding nervous for some reason.

"To your Rugby game?" I asked, my voice still chuckling as the last of the laughter escaped me.

"Yeah, you can be my lucky charm. Maybe I'll score the winning goal. Besides, it'll be good for you to stop moping around this place." He turned his head and winked at me. I was hit with the same vision again: his hand against the small of my back, his face pressed against mine. I sighed, nodding my head yes in defeat. I was in big trouble.

CHAPTER
4

RYLAND DROVE US TO THE Rugby game a few hours later—after making me endure two hours of infomercials that he found hysterical. To the standard middle class, things like Oxy-Clean and exercise videos were practical; to Ryland, they were hysterical ideas that no one would ever utilize. I just rolled my eyes at him. Sometimes, his innocence of everyone's normal existence was irritating, not endearing. Watching infomercials, he learned about rotisserie roasters and paint sprayers, and almost bought a leopard print snuggie, insisting that I needed one.

It wasn't until we pulled into the parking lot at Whittier Academy that I began to second guess my decision to come with him.

Ryland pulled his Lotus into a spot close to the locker rooms where a variety of other expensive cars were clustered. His canary yellow car looked a bit out of place next to all the black—while equally-expensive cars—surrounding us. I got out and leaned against the back of the car while Ryland extracted his duffle bag from the small shelf behind the seats.

The campus of Whittier Academy was acre after acre of tall broadleaf trees with large flagstone buildings tucked among them. From the parking lot, I could see the large stadium, a few tennis courts and a neatly cut field next to a stable. Set away from the sporting arena was the first of what I could only assume were academic buildings or dorms, but nothing was labeled, so I couldn't be sure.

The whole campus had been taken care of with absolute perfection. The trees were groomed, each hedge squared. The ivy growing up the side of the building trailed through the stone with eerie precision. Even the long stretch of cobblestone road we traveled seemed to be cared for with extreme diligence. The whole facility screamed wealth and privilege. I felt like a blob of dirt on its sparkling floors.

I shoved all of my hair into my hoodie, making sure my right ear and the mark were covered, and then smoothed out my dirty jeans as I tried to cover up my flaws. Somehow, growing up with Ryland, being with him every day, I never felt out of place; but, being here at his school, I could feel the gap between us widen.

He walked toward me with his rugged strut, and I sank against the car, trying for the first time since I was five to disappear from Ryland.

"What's up, Jos?" he asked, wrapping his fingers around my elbow. "Are you okay?"

"Yes... I mean, no... I mean..." He smiled at me and I felt my insides melt. "I don't belong here, Ry. This isn't my world."

"What do you mean, this isn't your world? You are part of *my* world, so you do belong here." His grin widened as he led me away from his car. My giddy, high-school-crush butterflies came out of nowhere because he had referred to me as belonging.

"You going to sit on the front row and cheer me on?" he asked, although I could tell by his tone he already knew the answer.

"Ha ha. No. I will, however, give you the loudest feminine yell from somewhere near the middle."

"That's my girl." He reached over and rumpled my hair like a dog's, ruining my perfectly placed hood. I gave him a spiteful look as I fixed his handiwork, but he only grinned at me before running off to join his team.

I watched him before turning around as some of the other boys began asking about me. Although I couldn't stop their ogling, at least from a distance I could pretend to ignore it.

I had moved about halfway up the stadium seats when a large, inclined roof caught my attention. Without even thinking about it, I changed directions toward the enclosed announcer's booth. It was covered in the same smooth flagstone as the other buildings, but it was the roof that called to me. The deeply angled slope extended high above the field.

I jumped up about three feet and hoisted myself onto the red asphalt tiles. I loved being so high for the same reason I loved that our apartment was on the third floor with a big open window where I could sit for hours. From up here, I could watch over everyone; I could see what was going on and feel a part of it without the worry of someone else thinking something was wrong with me. What I loved the most, though, was the way the wind moved across my face, tickling my sun-starved skin. The powerful energy of the wind pushed against me and moved into me. It was lucky I was sane, because part of my soul wanted to take off into the air and soar away.

I sat perched on top of the booth; legs dangling on either side of the A-shaped roof, watching both teams run drills on opposite sides of the field. Ryland's team wore deep blue shorts and matching shirts, each shirt emblazoned with a giant dragon spewing a perfect line of fire. The dragon wasn't the school mascot, however; it was the logo of Ryland's father's company, Imdalind

Forging. Being around Ryland so much, I often forgot how large his family's company was and how much it had a hand in everything Ryland did.

After about an hour of drills and prep, the crowd began to file in. When the slow trickle became a more steady flow, I decided it was time to leave my roost, so I wouldn't get in trouble. I moved my way down the steep slant of red asphalt shingles, freezing in place when a hot trickle moved up my spine. I looked up, afraid some bird had decided to humiliate me, but stopped halfway at the sight of Edmund strolling into the stands.

He wore all black, his good looks accentuated by a heavy leather jacket and diminished by his usual scowl. I glued my body to the roof; I knew I shouldn't be there.

Edmund was accompanied by a shorter boy who appeared to be about Ryland's age, but given his height, it was hard to tell. His features were rough and rounded, giving him an odd boy-like quality that didn't fit him at all. He had unkempt, deep-red hair and eyes so dark that, from my distance, looked almost black.

I sought out Ryland, fully prepared to glare daggers at him, only to find his face panicked as he looked back and forth between his father and me. I guess Edmund's appearance was a surprise for him, too.

Ryland looked at me one last time before he turned away and began signaling his father down. I took Ry's distraction at full value and dropped the remaining six feet before rushing to find a seat that was, hopefully, far enough away.

I dodged through the growing throng of people, my femininity becoming apparent. I was one of a sprinkling of girls surrounded by the over-rambunctious boys of Whittier Academy, most in their bright blue blazers, even though it was a Saturday. I dodged through them, trying to avoid the catcalls that had started the second I had been noticed in the stands.

Oh, the joys of being among boys stuck in an all-boy school. Any time they even got around a girl, the hormones came out like crazed tiger cubs surrounded by fresh meat. Luckily, Tyler Brand, one of Ryland's friends I had met a few times, found me as I darted around, inviting me to sit next to him and his friends. I was still noticed far more than I was comfortable with and part of me wished I could sit alone; but with Edmund so close, it just wasn't safe.

I slid closer to Tyler and his group, attempting to make polite conversation; all the while, I kept looking around to find out where Edmund and the mysterious boy were going to sit. I had forgotten how hard it was to keep up a conversation with anyone other than Ryland. I tried to interject as much as I could, but I kept tripping over my words and making awkward comments. Before long, the group began to look at me with the expression I knew all too well: the look that said they knew something was just a bit off about me. Eventually, I gave up and sat back, making sure my hair covered my mark so it wouldn't give them another thing to dislike about me.

Edmund had chosen a seat in the front row about two sections over, the red-headed boy still right beside him. The boy looked almost protective, like he was supposed to be Edmunds's bodyguard. I had never seen him before, so I guess he could be. What bothered me the most about him was that he kept standing and looking at the crowd. It wasn't the casual glance for trouble; it was the deep stare of someone who was searching for something or someone. Several times his look lingered in my direction, and I felt my spine stiffen uncomfortably.

Even with the mysterious boy's continued stares, the game went by quickly, and I found myself enjoying it more than I had thought I would. I couldn't help but join in with the crowd's excited screams and cheers; their excitement was infectious, and before long, I was smiling from ear to ear. Ryland was right; a good Rugby game was the pick-me-up I needed. The Whittier Academy team made a scramble toward their line and I got swept up in the screams and hollers of hundreds of boys, anticipation of another goal resonating through everyone.

Ryland's team had the ball, passing it from teammate to teammate as they ran down the pitch. The ball got to Ryland, only for him to be tackled roughly by the opposing team when two players lunged at him, sending him backward into three more. All five members of the opposing team and Ryland went down in a spectacular heap of bodies. The ball continued on; however, it took a moment before Ryland stood again, a bit of blood dripping from a cut on his lip.

I stood in worry. I must have looked ridiculous because I heard Tyler laugh beside me.

"He's fine," he yelled over the roar or the crowd. "It's normal."

I nodded as I looked back to the field to see that Ryland had already run to rejoin the play. I had seen a few of these tackles during this game alone, but it still seemed rough, given that the players wore no padding. I sat down; aware that Edmund's bodyguard was staring in my direction.

Ryland jostled back into place among the running bodies. The ball quickly passed to him, but this time, he avoided all of the other players as he weaved around each of them. Once he passed them, the wide expanse of field lay before him. He took off in a dead run toward the goal line, his strong legs pumping him forward until he reached the other end of the field for a glorious goal. Our side of the stadium erupted as Ryland turned around in a sort of victory salute.

"26 – 19, with one minute left. We are State Champs!" Tyler yelled, drowning out the voice of the announcer who tried in vain to say that Ryland had scored the winning points.

Ryland continued to dance and move about as the members

from his team surrounded him. He sought me out before blowing a kiss in my direction. I looked around for who his gesture was aimed at before turning back to him in shock. What a dangerous thing to do with his father right there. I wasn't sure if I should be overjoyed or scared. My eyes locked with his, as my heart stuttered to a stop before he turned and ran back onto the field. I couldn't bring myself to move.

"I didn't know you and Ryland were like that," Tyler yelled suggestively in my ear.

My mind clicked back into action and I turned to face him. "What?"

"You know. I didn't know he loved you." He stretched out his vowels in a taunt. I stared at him, unsure of what to say. I looked away from Tyler, not wanting to give him the glory of an answer, confused about what I would say anyway.

The finality of the game explained the excitement level of the crowd. Everyone was yelling at the top of their lungs, jumping up and down. Banners of blue and silver waved all around me as the boys began the deep booming war-cry that was the signature of their team. I couldn't help but join in, knowing my petite voice would not even be heard among them.

The ending whistle sounded and the stands emptied as the occupants rushed the field. The banners multiplied, and the screaming and yelling increased in amplitude—if that was possible. I was swept up with them in the excitement, forgetting that Ryland's father was still in such close proximity. I didn't care, though; I wanted to find Ryland somewhere in the crowd and throw myself in his arms and congratulate him.

I made it about halfway to the field before a sharp pain shot into my chest, causing me to stop short. It felt like I had been burned. My hand moved to the pain, shocked to feel Ryland's necklace red hot under my sweater. As soon as my hand made contact with it, the heat left it, taking the pain away. I looked at my hand and sweater, expecting to see welts or scorch marks, but nothing was there. I continued to stand in place as the crowd jostled me around in their attempts to pass my stationary form.

One perfectly placed shoulder was all it took to take me down. The force of the jolt sent me down hard. I threw my hands out in front of me, but not in time. My knee hit first, meeting the hard asphalt of the track that surrounded the field, a jolt of pain surging through my leg. My hands hit next, sliding against the asphalt in a deep grind that rattled my wrists. I winced with the pain that moved through my joints, waiting for my brain to catch up with me. A warm, stinging sensation spread across my knee, a telltale sign I was bleeding.

The bodies flowed past me in a steady stream I could barely see through. Knees, feet and legs jostled me around, digging my injured joints further into the ground. I looked around for some form of safety from them.

I had just caught sight of the home team's benches when a giant tug grew out of my chest; it felt like someone had grabbed the necklace in an attempt to pull me toward safety. I followed the inward pull, my hand fluttering around my sweater to shoo away whatever was pulling at me.

I pulled myself onto the bleachers, the changing angle sending a sharp sting through my knee. My jeans had ripped, revealing a couple of bleeding cuts. My mom was going to kill me; I only had a few pair of jeans and we couldn't afford to buy a new pair right now.

I winced as I removed the loose bits of asphalt from my knee and the palms of my hands; my hands had small scrapes, but no blood was drawn. With the asphalt gone, the cuts on my knee didn't look so bad, but they still stung. I screwed up my face in irritation, resigning myself to sit there until the crowd thinned out and Ryland found me.

I had only sat still a moment before Ryland burst through the rambunctious crowd in front of me, his brow furrowed in worry. His chin was dribbled in dry blood, his battered lip now swollen and blue. He looked at me before catching sight of my knee and dropping down to inspect it.

"Are you all right? I got here as quickly as I could." His hands hovered around my knee for a bit before deciding the jeans were a lost cause. He reached out, obviously intent on ripping them more.

"No, don't!" I pleaded.

"What?"

"I need these jeans, Ry." I hoped he would catch my meaning without my having to profess my poverty.

"I'll buy you some more." He smiled shyly at me before pulling his hands apart, ripping the jeans down to the seam.

Great, my mom was definitely going to kill me now. They weren't even patchable. I highly doubted she would let Ryland actually buy me a pair of new jeans, either. The cuts weren't even that bad; they just liked to bleed a lot.

"Did you see me fall?" I asked, wondering what he had meant before.

Ryland looked up at me, a confused look on his face.

"You got here 'as quickly as you could'?" I asked, repeating his phrasing.

He still sat at my feet, trying to find something to stop the bleeding.

"Yeah, I was standing over there," he said, jutting his chin in the direction he came from.

He looked around a bit, as if he were looking for someone rather than something. Seeming not to find anyone specific, he sighed and removed his Rugby jersey.

My heart stopped. His muscles rippled as he removed the shirt, sweat glistening off every part of him. I should have been disgusted, but I couldn't tear my dumbfounded stare away from him. His muscles were more spectacular than I would have expected: large defined shapes—dare I say—chiseled into his skin. He had a large ace bandage wrapped around his right shoulder, as if he was nursing an injury. I didn't know that he had been hurt, though; he normally told me about these things. The whole image of him standing before me was like a bad cover on a romance novel. I forced myself to look away as he wrapped the shirt around my knee.

"It's not the most sanitary, but it will work for now." He tied the shirt before sweeping me up in his arms, careful to hold me away from his sweaty body.

"Ry! Put me down! I can walk!"

He looked at me out of the corner of his eye, a small smile playing at the edge of his lips as he carried me out of the stadium.

I looked behind us, seeing the horde of people jumping and cheering, and felt a pain of guilt.

"You're going to miss your party," I whispered, knowing the pleading was evident in my voice.

He didn't slow his pace, but his jaw hardened and his hold on me tightened.

"Don't worry about it." His voice was controlled.

"Ry, it's your senior year; you just won State. *You.* You scored the final points. You need to be there!"

He didn't respond as he set me in the passenger seat of his bright yellow Lotus.

"Okay, how about I take you home and then I'll come back? I just want to make sure you're all right."

"I can stay, Ryland," I pleaded. "It's just a little cut."

"It's not safe for you here." He shut the door behind me and walked around the car. I turned my head toward the party. I wanted to stay, too, whether it was "safe" or not.

"What do you mean, it's not safe? Is it because your dad showed up?"

He threw the car in reverse, ignoring my question.

"Ryland?"

"It's just... Private school guys tend to drink a lot and I don't want you to get hurt."

It seemed like the lamest excuse I had ever heard. My forehead must have wrinkled in surprise, because Ryland laughed and then reached over to smooth my forehead with his thumb.

"You think I can't fend off a bunch of drunken brats?" I was affronted. I may come off as timid, but I could defend myself. Or, at least, I hoped I could.

"I know you can't," he replied.

"Have some faith in me, Ry." I don't know why, but my pride bristled.

Ryland looked at me with obvious concern. "Drinking, drugs. We are all just spoiled boys. You shouldn't be around that."

"We?" I asked, hoping he wasn't counting himself among them.

"Just trust me, 'kay? I know it kinda sucks, but I want to protect you." His comment was odd; it still made no sense why I couldn't stay.

"Protect me?"

"Yes, Jos. There are just some people that you shouldn't be around." His voice seemed distant and far away, as if he were thinking about something different. I opened my mouth to say something, but I blew off the idea of asking any more questions. He was set in his thoughts and not likely to respond.

He drove far too fast, his car weaving in and out of traffic in a mad rush to get back to my tiny apartment. We didn't go to my house though; we went to his. He pulled through the large wrought-iron gates, speeding back to the door by the kitchen. His sporty Lotus looked ridiculous next to my mom's rusty station wagon, and I couldn't help but laugh out loud.

I moved to get out of the car, but Ryland rushed around and picked me up before I could stand. The car ride had rid his skin of the glistening sweat, and he now held me close to his chest. The warmth from his skin seeped through my sweater and spread over my skin comfortably.

"I can walk, Ry," I protested, albeit half-heartedly. He smiled down at me as he walked across the parking lot and into the kitchen that was empty except for my mother.

"What happened?" my mom asked, her eyes bugging out of her head.

"She fell on some asphalt and cut her knee. I need to get back, but wanted to make sure she was okay first," he explained to her, his eyes never leaving mine. I heard my mom exclaim and rush out of the kitchen, presumably for a first-aid kit.

Ryland lowered me to the barstool I usually sat on. His movements were slow and controlled, his face lingering near mine for longer than was necessary. I was overwhelmed by his smell as he moved away from me, yet keeping his face inches from mine. My mind filled with images of our interlocked lips; I didn't push them away this time.

Ryland lifted his hand to my face, resting it against my jawline as his thumb caressed my cheek. I was so confused. Wasn't it just this morning he had worried that I had gotten the wrong idea from the necklace? Wasn't it just this morning that he told me he just wanted to be friends? Wasn't it? My heart beat uncomfortably in my chest as he moved his head toward mine, his eyes darting down to my lips before returning to capture my gaze. My mom cleared her throat behind me, and we both jumped.

"See you on Monday, Jos," Ryland smiled at me before turning and rushing out the door.

I sat still, in shock, feeling like I was robbed of something important to me. I stared at the door as I tried to wade through an endless sea of confusion.

My mom huffed and came over to me, first-aid kit in hand. "You can't have him, you know?" Her voice was a calm whisper. She didn't even look at me; her focus was on my cut knee.

"I know," I answered, surprised at the sadness in my voice. "Just this morning he was saying the necklace meant nothing, and he was just my friend. I don't know what's gotten into him."

"Him?" my mother asked. "There seemed to be a lot of you in that equation."

I sighed in response. I knew she was right. Whether he was the one to initiate something or not, I would not be the one to stop it. What had happened to us in the past few days? Couldn't we go back to playing Conquer the Castle and destroying monsters on his PlayStation?

"What's going on?" I threw my head into my hands.

"You love him," she replied.

"What?"

"Well, you do; you always have—both of you. Now, it's just grown into something a little bit more mature."

"But I still can't have him." It was a statement, not a question.

"No, honey, no matter how many amazing, rippling muscles he has," she laughed. "Your being with him is like a serving girl marrying a king; it's not going to happen. Life is not a fairy tale."

"What do I do?"

"Leave him alone, make new friends, and forget about him."

My heart plummeted at her words. I didn't want to do that. Forbidden romance or no, he was still my best friend. Not to mention that soon, he would be leaving me forever.

"I can't do that, Mom. He's leaving for Oxford in just a few months. Then... then, I'll never see him again."

My mom sighed at me. I could tell she didn't approve. She wanted me to walk away from him, but she couldn't stand to see me hurting either.

"Weren't you telling me just a few days ago how love changes you? How wonderful love is?" I couldn't keep the accusatory tone out of my voice, no matter how hard I tried.

"This is different."

"How is this different, Mom? It doesn't feel different."

"You will be able to tell the difference when you experience the real thing… when you experience something you can keep."

I looked at her for a long time. The way she had talked about Dad before, I could feel that same desperate longing in me now, and it kind of scared me.

"How many times have you been in love, Mom?" I asked her.

I saw her hesitate, her chest heave.

"You need to remember that he is your friend, Joclyn, not a boyfriend." She avoided my question. "Give your heart to someone who can take it and not break it, honey; because in all honesty, I'm not sure what Edmund would do if he found out."

And that was the real reason anything between Ryland and me could never work.

Edmund would kill me.

.

CHAPTER
5

I HAD BEEN PICKING AT the remains of my cafeteria pizza for about the last ten minutes, my eyes unfocused and looking off into space. I could hear the ebbing noise in the cafeteria, a sure sign that lunch was almost over, but I wasn't going to move until the bell rang. I sighed as another piece of pizza crust fell away from the whole and onto the plate.

I had been lost in thought for most of the day, my mind jumping back to my roller-coaster of a weekend. No matter how many times I revisited each event, I still couldn't make sense of it. Crazy father, awesome best friend who keeps trying to kiss me, and a mother who—although she is right—wants me to stay away from Ryland forever. I sighed again, in hopes that some of the stress would leave my tensed body.

"You must be new, too."

I looked up from my decimated pizza as a girl plopped down across the table from me.

She was small for a high school student, her frame appearing almost delicate and breakable. However, her large, brown eyes did not seem young; instead, she almost looked like she had seen and experienced too much of life. She had shoulder length, auburn hair that gently curled around her heart-shaped face. When she moved her hand onto the table, about thirty hard plastic bracelets clinked against the melamine surface. I had to smile at her choice of clothes; the "Styx" t-shirt was obviously vintage and looked like something my mom would have worn in high school.

"What makes you say that?" I asked, recovering from my shock.

"Well, you're sitting alone."

"Ha," I laughed humorlessly. "You are the new one. I always sit alone."

"I'm Wyn."

I took her extended hand and she shook it over-enthusiastically, plastic bangles clinking together. "Joclyn."

She grinned as if my name had made her happy.

"I just love your name!" she squealed, her joy was either infectious or nauseating—I couldn't decide. "It's like something out of 17th century literature. Who were you named after?"

"I don't think I was named after anyone." I lied. I was actually named after my dad's favorite aunt, but I wasn't about to share that with the obnoxious girl I just met.

"That's lucky. My full name is Wynifred, and my mother named me after some ancient relative who is supposed to be a queen," she chattered.

I began to wonder how I could get rid of this girl. At first, her over-exertive happiness was fun, but now she was starting to sound like a cheerleader. I looked around, wondering if I could find a quick escape away from her.

"I'm sorry," she said, her quiet voice losing its hyperactive quality. "I'm coming on too strong, aren't I?"

I just stared at her, unsure of what to say.

"Hi, my name is Wyn. I just moved here with my brother, Ilyan, who has taken care of me since my parents died," she said in a deeper, slower voice that seemed more natural for her. "I turned sixteen in January, but don't have a driver's license yet; I prefer to get around on my skateboard. My favorite band is Styx, which I know is way before my time; but I can't help it—I love them. I like rice pudding with raisins and think ice cream is too sophisticated for me. I like to read, but not so much that my brain turns to mush. Oh! And I love long walks on the beach with handsome men with rippling biceps."

We laughed together; it was the strangest introduction that I had ever witnessed.

"Well?" Wyn asked when the laughter had died down. She was staring at me, waiting for me to introduce myself in the same way.

"I'm Joclyn," I began, my nerves swimming in my legs. "I live with my mom; my dad took off when I was little. I turned sixteen last week, and I prefer a long board to a skateboard."

She grinned from ear to ear when I said that, glad for a connecting tie.

"Ummm... I love Fruit Loops and late-night British comedies. I don't have a favorite band, but I like to listen to music when I'm doing homework," I ended lamely, as if asking her a question.

"And the guy?" Wyn prompted.

My insides turned to jelly as an image of Ryland flashed through my mind.

"Oh, you know: tall, dark and handsome, and all that jazz," I answered, flipping my hand to the side.

"Well, I guess you'll do."

"Do?"

"Seeing as it's my first day, I need a friend, and I like you the best out of all the irritating cheerleaders and pompous nerds I have met today." She smiled, and I couldn't help but reciprocate.

I had always purposefully ostracized myself; however, there was something about Wyn that made me want to know her better. Of course—in the back of my mind—I wondered how long it would take for her to figure out something was wrong with me. Everyone always did, even without seeing my mark. I had always been just a little bit "off".

"What class do you have next?" she asked, jumping to her feet when the bell rang.

"Advanced Drama."

"Oh, goodie! Me, too!" She grabbed my hand and towed me out of the now empty cafeteria, jabbering about how lucky she was to have found me on her first day. It wasn't until we had left the cafeteria that she realized she had no idea where she was going and opted to follow rather than lead.

I led her down the hall as she continued to jabber about how her first day had gone and all the irritating people she had met. I smiled at her description of our very eccentric American History teacher. "Small, withering, Mardi Gras attendee" fit him.

I hesitated outside the door of the drama room. I had been placed in the advanced drama class by mistake this year, and as such, it was a class filled with seniors, meaning that the notorious Cynthia McFadden was in this class. While it was unlikely that most people would mention anything about the cast list for Hamlet, I knew her kind. The probability that she would say something was high, and I preferred to steel myself against it.

The drama room was a large sunken performance space, surrounded by tiers of carpeted risers that rose up from the center of the room where you entered. Ms. Flowers, the drama teacher, always kept the room dimmed during performance time with stage lights blaring; but during class time, we were treated to fluorescent lighting that made every soda stain on the carpet pop out. A large thrift-store couch sat right in the middle of the lowest tier, looking out on center stage. Most of the students lounged on the different levels as they prepared for class to start, leaving the couch for Ms. Flowers's use. Wyn ran off to find Ms. Flowers while I went to my usual alcove.

"Well, if it isn't Smelly MyHoodie," Cynthia McFadden's voice echoed around the large space, causing several heads to turn. I crinkled my nose at her poor attempt at name-calling, waiting for the deeper onslaught.

"We missed you on Friday, at rehearsal... Oh, wait, I forgot. You didn't get a role." If anyone had read a book on how to be the quintessential high school diva, it was Cynthia. She had mastered this role better than she would any other. From perfectly plucked eyebrows and hair—hours of preparation—to overpriced shoes and backpack, she looked like a snob. It was more than her looks though. How she spoke, how she talked, it was all done to be anyone's high school nemesis or hero. If I had to pick, I would have to say she was my nemesis, although the term is a bit dramatic.

Even though Cynthia was a year older than me, she had been one of the first in elementary school to realize there was something wrong with me. I hadn't always hidden behind hoodies, and in first grade, Cynthia had seen the same thing in me that had made my dad take off. Maybe it was the way I held myself, how I never talked too loudly, or the fact that I liked to climb to the top of the baseball fence. Something just bugged her, and she made it her business to get everyone else to see it, too.

I attempted to let her taunt roll off me, sealing my lips together to prevent a rebuttal. I growled to myself as I attempted to walk past her; I wasn't one to create confrontation.

"Hey, I'm talking to you." She grabbed my arm hard, hindering my escape, and then jumped back as if I had shocked her.

I turned toward her, keeping my jaw shut tight, ready to take whatever cruel punishment she had ready for me.

"You stupid, little girl. I'm so glad my graduation is a month away and then I won't have to smell you anymore. Too bad everyone else has to put up with you for another year." She looked at me, expecting a reply, but I couldn't think of what to say without my entire face turning red and a string of expletives pouring out.

"Why don't you just go hide up by the stage lights, pretend you're flying and casting magic, or whatever it is you do up there, you little freak." She flipped her long, bleached-blonde hair and turned away from me, only to come face-to-face with Wyn.

Tiny, little Wyn had her hands balled up in fists at her side, her face flushed red. Even though Wyn's full height only came to Cynthia's chest, the look on Wyn's face caused Cynthia to take a step back. I was concerned Wyn would say something stupid that would cause criticism for the both of us.

"At least she can get up there *and* keep her clothes on," she said, "or is that too much of a challenge for you?" Laughter and whistling sounded throughout the large room; even my jaw fell in surprise at her forwardness.

Cynthia stood still as Wyn pushed past her, grabbed my hand and pulled me to sit front and center in the room.

"Thanks," I whispered as we sat.

"No problem, anything for my friends." Wyn flashed me a wide smile before turning to face Ms. Flowers who was now beginning her lecture on the senior showcase, in which Hamlet would be featured.

I was not sure how much I heard of what she said; I kept looking toward Cynthia who was still fuming. Ms. Flowers caught my attention as she began to prepare for the show by separating everyone into groups: the cast of the show, costumes, set and props. Each group sat together, the cast with their noses upturned. I rolled my eyes at them and moved to stand by Wyn in the "set" group.

We spent the rest of class reading through the script and making a list of set pieces. No one in our small group was excited about our task, and with five minutes to go, we had broken off into different conversations.

"Thank goodness school is almost over. I have about a season worth of Castle to catch up on," Wyn moaned as she threw herself back onto the rough carpet we sat on.

"Castle?" I asked.

She raised her eyebrow at me as if I had committed some form of heresy by not knowing what she was talking about.

"Yes, Castle. The TV show. Crime drama, starring Nathan Fillion, only the yummiest man to grace the screens of the television." She gasped at my obvious lack of understanding.

I had no idea what she was talking about.

"At least tell me you know what 'Firefly' is?" she pleaded.

"I don't watch TV, Wyn. I mean, I turn it on sometimes, but I never really watch it."

"I'm going to educate you. You need a good dose of several of life's necessities. Besides, Nathan Fillion is *really* nice to look at."

I laughed, the bell drowning out the sound of it.

We left the room and retrieved our boards from the office. By the time we got outside, word of Wyn's confrontation with Cynthia had spread, and students were giving her thumbs-ups and high-fives as they passed. All the attention went into Wyn like energy from a live wire, and soon she was bouncing up and down. I laughed as I watched her, her enthusiasm leaking over into me.

"I can't believe I did that," she repeated for the hundredth time.

"Well, it seems to have gone over well with the student body." I laughed as yet another student waved to her. Our school did not have a small campus, and word must have traveled faster than usual. I couldn't help but laugh as she bounced around yet again, adrenaline from her conflict with Cynthia still coursing through her.

"Oh, yes, well done." I could recognize that sneer from a mile away. "So, you and your foul mouth seem to have made you a few admirers."

We both turned to face Cynthia McFadden, who was surrounded by half the football team once again. The moment Cynthia spoke, an eager group of onlookers materialized out of thin air, hoping for some action. I took a step behind Wyn out of habit.

Wyn opened her mouth to say something, but we never found out what. All the football players gathered behind Cynthia began to point away from us; several of them taking off in that direction. Cynthia looked like an angry kitten at her posse's departure. When she turned, though, her little fit stopped and she began to smooth her hair.

I turned my head toward what everyone was staring open-mouthed at and my heart plummeted to my toes.

A bright, yellow sports car I knew all too well had pulled into the teachers' parking lot. Ryland leapt out of the car, his dark, curly hair bouncing. He pulled off his Whittier Academy blazer and draped it over one shoulder, revealing a tight-fitting, white V-neck t-shirt which showcased his strong arms. He looked like an ad for cologne or men's underwear.

My heart kicked into overdrive; I couldn't move.

"Oh, no. Oh, no, no, no," I groaned, causing Wyn's head to whip in my direction. "He promised he wouldn't..."

"Do you *know* him?" she asked, her voice laced with a combination of entertainment and worry.

I couldn't bring myself to answer her, only nod numbly as Ryland scanned the crowd for me.

"Well, I will leave you to it then," she said. "See you tomorrow, Joclyn."

I didn't even register Wyn's departure; I was still staring at Ryland as he searched for me. He glossed over most of the student body, giving them all a chance to notice him and his expensive car.

Finally, he found me and began moving in my direction. The second his eyes met mine, my shock melted away, leaving me feeling blissfully numb, my heart calling out in sheer joy to see him. It took a moment, but even that melted away as I registered everyone looking between us, and my joy deteriorated into a half-hearted anger.

He waved at me, and to my horror, Cynthia McFadden waved back, her blonde hair flipping in an obvious attempt at flirting. Ryland moved past her without seeing her, pushing her to the side, and my anger melted away into laughter. He rushed to me then, sweeping me up in his arms and spinning me around as if this was some strange scene from a chick flick.

I couldn't help but laugh at his actions, the movement sending my stomach into cartwheels. He pressed his cheek against mine as we spun, his deep chuckle echoing in my ear.

"I'm in so much trouble, aren't I?" His warm breath tickled my ear as he whispered to me.

My heart sputtered. "You have no idea."

"Then, I might as well do the thing thoroughly." He set me down again and kissed my jaw line. His lips lingered for a second longer than they should have, freezing me into place. I just hoped I didn't look too much like a deer stuck in the headlights.

If my heart had been having troubles before, it was nothing to how I felt now. I couldn't move as my head began to swim around me, my legs feeling like Jell-O.

Ryland wrapped his arm around my waist and pulled me beside him. My body melded into his as he led me forward, towing the long board behind us. He kissed my temple before placing me in the passenger seat, his lips burning against my skin even after I lost contact.

Ryland walked around the Lotus much slower than he usually did, as if he were giving everyone one last chance to see me in the car and him with me. Most of the football team stood together, staring the car down. Cynthia McFadden stood in the middle of them, her face flushed red with anger, her arms folded across her mid-section. It wasn't her face that caught my attention, though, it was Wyn's.

She stood behind the crowd, hiding behind a large conifer tree next to the red brick school. Her mouth moved as if she were talking to someone out of sight. Her face was screwed up with what could only be described as a furious worry. The combination of anger and concern did not sit well with her and only made her look like she was about to catch fire.

I looked toward Ryland as he hopped in, a huge smile on his face. By the time I looked back to Wyn, she had disappeared.

"Let's get out of here!" Ryland sang, kicking the car away from the curb and speeding down the street well above the speed limit.

IF IT WEREN'T FOR THE yells of excitement that echoed around the school hall, I might have been punched. I swerved to the side at the noise and saw the angry, little fist whip through the air in front of my face. My quick movement upset my balance, and I tumbled to the ground, my hood falling off my head as I landed hard on my tailbone.

One, little punch and the crowd gathered around me. I saw the eager faces jostle over each other in their attempt to get a better view, many of them yelling "catfight" over and over again. I looked away from them, unsurprised to see Cynthia pacing in front of me, her face screwed up in furious anger.

Seeing her fuming form made me cringe. Hell has no fury like a woman's scorn. Ryland's dismissal of her yesterday was going to cost me big.

"So, you thought you could show everyone how popular you are by paying some rich stripper to come pick you up?"

"He's not a stripper." The words escaped me without warning. While I should have been surprised that I had chosen to stand up for Ryland before myself, I was more surprised that I had responded to her taunts; I hadn't done that in years. That fact didn't escape Cynthia's notice either; her face lit up in joyous expectation for the coming fight.

"Prostitute, stripper; it's all the same." She walked up to me, her high-heeled foot swinging wide in a poor attempt at a kick.

I swung out of the way, sliding against the floor and into the crowd who stood me up and pushed me toward Cynthia. I rammed into her hard, the push from the crowd giving her the perfect opportunity to slam a tiny, angry fist into my stomach. I cringed, but it didn't hurt much. I had been sucker-punched harder by Ryland when I was eight and we were fighting over Ninja Turtles.

Without any warning, Cynthia began clawing and slapping at my face, the only exposed skin on my entire body. I yelped in a panic and tried to fight back as best I could, but it was no use. She was hell-bent on turning me into her scratching post. I pushed her away from me before her attack could get any worse, the palm of my hand slapping hard against her cheek.

"Leave me alone; at least I have friends who will stand up for me." It was a lame retort and I knew it, but I couldn't think beyond the burning in my face.

"Well, he sure isn't your boyfriend. After all, who could love an ugly, useless, insignificant, little nothing?" She hit me hard in the stomach, and this time, I doubled over, the wind knocked out of me. I heard the crowd around us yell as I fell to my knees, my eyes watering.

Cynthia walked up to me and lowered herself down to whisper

in my ear with her bottom stuck out precariously, causing several of the boys to whistle. "Your own father didn't love you, why would anyone else?"

My blood boiled under my skin. The truth of her words dug into me and fueled the intense pain and anger I always kept hidden. I could feel the necklace grow warm against my skin, the warmth fueling my intensity. Without thinking, I slammed my hand into her stomach in a pointless attempt to hurt her, to get her away from me, to humiliate her somehow. Instead of her scuttling across the floor on her ridiculous heels like I had hoped, she flew ten feet straight into the air. Her back slammed against the ceiling tiles before she fell like a rock to the ground.

The crowd went quiet.

I stared in horror at Cynthia's motionless form. My heart thumped wildly as I desperately tried to make sense of what had just happened. I didn't know what had happened, but I did know I needed to get out of there.

I didn't even bother to meet any of the curious stares that were trained on me, and I didn't stop to check if Cynthia was all right. I just grabbed my bag, shoved the few things that had been scattered around the hall back into it and took off.

I held the bag against me as I power-walked away, my head down in my normal attempt to blend in. I hadn't lost control like that in a long time. Okay, I hadn't lost control like that ever. Throwing someone ten feet in the air? That didn't just happen, right? I had heard of women lifting cars off injured people and defending themselves in times of danger; it didn't seem likely, but that must have been what had just happened to me.

I could feel the angry warmth leech out of me as I walked; my skin, less persistent in its attempt to crawl away. The necklace that always seemed to echo my moods so perfectly faded from a white, angry heat into a warm, calming sensation.

I turned into the hall that housed my locker, unsurprised to see Wyn leaning against the locker next to mine, her eyebrows about as far up as they could get. Had news of my superhuman feat spread that fast? I just ignored her and caught my breath; I had no intention of discussing what had just happened.

"Tall, dark and handsome, eh?" Obviously, she hadn't heard yet.

"Don't start, Wyn," I snapped.

"Who is he? Why didn't you tell me you had a boyfriend?" she spouted out her questions, but even I, the new friend, could tell she was restraining herself; she was dying to ask a million more.

"His name is Ryland and he is my best friend, not my boyfriend."

"Didn't look like a *not* boyfriend to me," she said cryptically.

"He was trying to piss off Cynthia, just like you did." I snapped my locker door shut.

"Oooo, a kindred spirit." Wyn smiled as she fell into step beside me. "I like him more and more."

"Not my boyfriend," I reminded her.

"Yet," she said pointedly. "See you at lunch!" She waved at me before running down the math hallway, leaving me to walk alone to English.

I slid into my seat just as the bell rang, my heavy book slamming into the old wooden desk. Mr. Heart hadn't arrived yet, so I smoothed my hair and wiped my palm against my face to check for blood.

Even before Cynthia's little catfight, I had been the recipient of taunts and insults all morning; all ranging from asking how much he cost to wondering how I did it. I didn't give anyone answers and had kept my hood up more than usual. My carefully crafted "disappear into the walls" routine had been broken wide open. I sighed and slammed my head onto the desk as Mr. Heart walked in, silencing the class immediately.

Mr. Heart got right to business, one of the few teachers to take the end of the school year seriously. A little more than half the class were seniors, and so, their minds had already moved to graduation, but a few others of us—myself included—had a whole other year of high school education in front of us. I pulled out my notebook and began to take notes in preparation for the final exam in two weeks.

"Pssst."

I heard the noise, and I could already tell whoever had made it was trying to get my attention.

"Pssst."

Still going to ignore you.

"Pssst, Joclyn."

Great, now they want to get me in trouble.

"Joclyn."

I looked up to the whispered voice. One of the seniors on the football team had turned all the way around from two rows away to face me.

"You and that LaRue kid, eh? I always knew you was a gold digger." The hairs on the back of my neck bristled. I brushed my frustration aside and stuck my tongue out at him like a child.

"I bet he likes that, too, doesn't he? You dirty little minx." He licked his lips hungrily, and I ducked my head.

This is why I hadn't wanted Ryland to come and pick me up; I knew this would happen. I chewed on my tongue for a minute before returning to take notes.

That's when I saw him.

An unbelievably tall, lanky man stood with his back against the wall, not far from my desk. He stood tall, with long arms folded across his chest. A thick curtain of stark, straight blonde hair hung to his shoulders, framing his narrow face. His features were sharp and defined, but they suited him rather than making him look like a villain.

If I hadn't been so taken back by his piercing gaze, or even dared to get another look, I might have said he was handsome. However, he was staring at me. I had glanced at him before looking away, a blush rushing to my cheeks at the sight of his deep-blue gaze boring into me.

I wondered why no one else noticed him; he was so foreboding and his stare so piercing. I couldn't be the only one who felt uncomfortable with him being there. Then again, I was the only one that he was staring at.

I fidgeted before trying again to focus, but it was no use. I looked straight forward, note-taking forgotten, trying not to continue to steal uncomfortable glances toward the figure who leaned toward me. I dropped my head, letting my long, black hair fall between us to take away the temptation to look back.

The minutes on the clock ticked by at a snail's pace, my whole body aware of the continued stare I was getting. My skin prickled with an uncomfortable energy that kept my nerves on high alert. I kept shifting my weight to see if he was still there, a chill going up my spine every time I caught a glimpse of his unmoving figure or ripped designer jeans in my peripheral vision.

I ran out of the room when the bell rang, desperate to get away from the penetrating stare, as well as from any new taunts from the football team. My next class was empty of tall, blonde men and open catcalls, giving me time to focus on the material and catch up on what I had missed last week. When the bell rang, I ran from that classroom, too, my nerves still on high alert from blonde men, and angry girls.

The news of my fight had now traveled through the school. As I made my way to the cafeteria, I was treated to the open catcalls as well as looks that ranged from curious to terrified. I can't say I blamed them; I was scared of myself.

I pulled my hood up over my head and attempted to disappear

behind the long overhang of fabric. I let the catcalls wash over me and focused on the feet of the students around me. I walked down a tunnel of shame; everyone turning to look, everyone saying something. What I wouldn't give to have said something back, but the fear of a repeat performance plagued me. My progress was stopped by two large, worn, dress shoes.

"Hood down, Ms. Despain."

I pulled down my hood and looked up to the old, withered face of Mr. Ray, our Assistant Principal.

"I hear you had an altercation earlier today. Do I need to remind you what our policy is, about fighting?"

I swallowed slowly and shook my head, waiting for the yelling or suspension or whatever usually came with these things. It did seem a little odd that we were doing this in the hall, however.

"You will be glad to know that Ms. McFadden is fine, but if you begin any more fights with any other students, we will be forced to place you under suspension."

"But, I didn't..." I opened my mouth to rebut—after all, I hadn't started the fight—but stopped dead in my tracks. His face had changed; his eyes were panicked and drifting, like he was afraid of me, too. "Yes, sir." I said.

Mr. Ray didn't say anything else; he simply nodded his head and walked on past me.

I didn't wait long before I ran down the hall in an attempt to get away. Great. Everyone thinks I am crazy, or possessed, or something. I entered the cafeteria and headed for my usual place, not bothering to get any food. My stomach wanted to turn itself inside out already; I was afraid of what it would do if I put food inside of it.

I slammed my bag down on the table and pulled out my ancient phone, flipping it open to send Ryland a few choice words.

You owe me. BIG!

I snapped the phone shut and placed my head on the table, wishing more than anything that I could just disappear.

"You look terrible. I thought you would be happy after your PDA yesterday," Wyn giggled as she sat down.

"Not my boyfriend," I reminded her, not bothering to lift my head.

"Well, everyone else thinks so, so you might as well ride it for all it's worth."

I had to remind myself that Wyn didn't know me, no matter how much we hit it off yesterday. "Going with the flow" was not my thing, neither were PDA's for that matter. My phone buzzed and I snatched it up.

What happened? Do I need to come and set some minds straight? ;)

I could feel the scowl creep into my forehead.

No! Stay away from me! You're ruining my reputation!

"So, what's wrong then?" Wyn asked.

"Just what happened earlier," I whispered, not wanting to elaborate.

"Why? What happened?"

I looked at her skeptically. How could she not have heard? My attention pulled from her as my phone buzzed again.

No! People are talking to you! Acknowledging your existence! Scandal! I say, scandal!

I was torn between laughing and scowling more, his jokes wriggled under my skin even over text, but it wasn't in a bad way.

"How's Ryland?" Wyn asked, looking up at me from over her soda straw.

"What?"

"Ryland," she continued, gesturing to my phone. "You're obviously texting him; you are grinning from ear to ear."

I shook my head, wiping the smile from my face. I hadn't even realized it, but I was. This whole thing had become a weird, tangled mess of trouble, irritation, and entertainment.

Jos, I'm sorry. I thought it would help, and I was wrong. Tell me what I can do to make it up to you. Are you okay? His text was followed by a picture he had taken of himself, his face twisted into a pleading puppy-dog face.

I laughed aloud, his face wiping away a bit of my stress.

I think you owe me a movie.

"He's fine," I answered her question a little late, snapping my phone shut.

I looked up to Wyn, grinning widely and then stopping short, the smile disappearing. Directly behind her, the blonde-haired man stood, leaning against the window-lined wall.

I must have jumped because Wyn shrieked and dropped her soda. The dark liquid began spreading across the table, threatening another one of Wyn's vintage band shirts. I grabbed a wad of napkins and began throwing them on the soda.

"What's up with that, Joclyn? You scared me to death; I thought you saw a ghost!"

I moved my head to look around her, but the man had disappeared.

"I don't know. I think maybe I'm being stalked."

"Stalked?" I could hear the disbelief in her voice.

"Yeah, there was this guy in my English class. He just stood there, staring at me. It's creeping me out." I knew I sounded crazy.

"First, you're dating the hottest guy I've seen in years, and now you're being stalked. You're one lucky girl."

"Not my boyfriend," I growled through gritted teeth.

Wyn just sat and smiled at me. Ryland always told me I was fun to tease; I guess he isn't the only one to think so.

"So you've said. Maybe your stalker was just a teacher's assistant, or even a janitor, who thinks you're cute," Wyn offered.

"I don't know. The way he was staring at me; it was creepy, like he was trying to see inside my soul."

Wyn raised her eyebrow at me. "See inside your soul?"

"Yeah, that sounded a bit crazy," I said.

"Ya think?"

My phone buzzed and I picked it up, ignoring Wyn's over-emphasized eye roll.

How about hamburgers from Sonnies, movie, my room, Saturday night. I found the perfect grade B movie – you're going to love it! The Evil Dead.

I couldn't help the smile from creeping back onto my face.

Sounds perfect, but you better throw in ice cream.

"Well, if you see any more soul-eating monsters, let me know and I'll take care of them for you."

"Seeing, not eating, Wyn."

"Oh yeah, 'cause that makes more sense."

I knew it didn't, but I still couldn't help but laugh at myself.

"Darn it! We are going to be late!" Wyn jumped to her feet as the bell rang, throwing books and pencils into her bag. "Hey, do you want to come over tonight? I got a new movie in the mail, and my brother's going to be out. We can pretend to do homework, too." She looked at me so eagerly, I couldn't say no. Besides, spending time with someone other than Ryland might help my mom say yes to our new plans for Saturday.

"Sure."

"Great." The tension dropped from her shoulders as if she were worried I would say no.

My phone buzzed one more time as we ran out of the cafeteria, Ryland's message lighting up the screen.

Anything for you, sweetheart. I'll even splurge and get Superman ice cream :)

Sweetheart? When did things get so complicated?

CHAPTER 6

*I*DON'T REMEMBER WHEN I'VE laughed so much. That's not to say that I have never laughed with Ryland, I have. Somehow, though, playing and joking with a girl—a girl my own age—was different. We could joke about things I would never bring up with my mother and never even dreamed about sharing with Ry. For the first time in my life, I regretted not seeking out a girlfriend; I had always felt complete with Ryland. Now, with Wyn, facing Ryland's departure in a few months seemed bearable.

We lay back on her bed, legs draping off the side, as we caught our breath from laughing, small chuckles still escaping. Just being here had made me forget all about the stress of the day, and we hadn't even gotten to the movie, yet. *Night of the Living Vampire* was sure to suck as Wyn had said so poignantly.

"So, I know he's not your boyfriend," Wyn began, a smile on her face, "but how the heck did you become friends with the heir to Imdalind Forging?"

"What did you do, Google him?"

"Yeah."

I couldn't help but laugh, her voice sounded like a cornered child.

"My mom has been their in-house chef since I was five; I practically grew up in their kitchen."

"Really?"

"Yeah, Ry and I have been friends since day one. It drives his dad and Timothy crazy; I am a little below their status." Saying it out loud made the whole "falling for a prince" situation more real.

"Timothy?" Wyn asked with something akin to recognition.

"Yeah, he's kind of the head of the company and Ryland's wrangler. He *hates* me." As I did him.

"And they still let you two be friends?"

I was just as shocked as she was. "Not by choice. Ryland kind of makes them."

"And they don't just fire your mom?"

I almost laughed outright. "Oh, they threaten to, but I don't think they want to lose such a great cook. Besides, Ryland's leaving for school in a few months, so I guess they don't think it's worth the fight anymore. It's not like I can follow him to Oxford."

I hated talking about this stuff; my heart felt so heavy and broken, like part of me was leaving with him.

"You love him," she said.

"More than I should," I whispered. I knew I sounded ridiculous.

"It's okay to love."

"Not when they don't love you back." I sighed again; it felt like I was trying to get rid of all my stress through my lungs.

"Especially then. I think it makes you a better person. At least then you know what it feels like to love instead of living without ever knowing. I love a lot of people that I know will never love me back, but I am happier because of it." I could tell she believed what she said; her voice was so deep and heavy.

"You sound like my mom."

"I've never heard that one before!" she laughed.

"And who do you love?"

"Talon," she sighed.

The sound of desperate love made me giggle; I wondered if that's how I sounded when I talked about Ry.

"I'll introduce you to him when he comes to visit."

"So he loves you back then?"

"Yeah..." Her voice was so airy I couldn't help but smile.

The song on the oldies station we were listening to changed. Wyn jumped up, squealing in delight. She leaped onto a pile of boxes that sat at the foot of her bed, pulling me up with her. She continued to jump and squeal as she danced around, the corners of the boxes heaving as she danced and moved.

"*I'm so tired of losin', I've got nothing to do and all day to dooo iiiiiiit! So, I go out cruisin', but I've no place to go and all night to geeeeeet theeeeeere!*" Her hair swished around her face, heavy plastic bangles jangling and clanking. Her joy at the Styx song was infectious and I found myself singing and dancing along, even though I didn't know the words.

"*Too much time on my hands!*" We sang together, our loud monotone voices clashing against each other. "*Too much time on my hands!*"

Wyn jumped off the boxes, hair and arms flying, to land on the plush carpet in an air guitar solo. Her arms swung and wiggled in an attempt to play the nonexistent instrument she held in her hands. Her short, auburn hair flipped around her face as she swung her head in an attempt to "rock out".

The guitar solo ended. Wyn jumped up again and grabbed my hands to push me into her crazy dancing. We jumped around the floor like clowns, pulling out dance moves that our parents must have done, in our rambunctious attempt at dancing.

"Please tell me you've been to a Styx concert," Wyn yelled

between verses.

"Do they still have concerts?" I asked, jumping around alongside her.

"Yes!" Wyn grabbed my hands and began to spin me around as she continued to yell verses and choruses full blast. And, quick as it had come, the song ended and we both collapsed on the floor, laughing at ourselves.

"So," Wyn sighed after a moment. "You gonna show me your scar?"

Her question was so innocent, but my reaction was anything but. Time seemed to stop. My heart stopped. My breathing stopped. The only thing that didn't stop was my stomach, which flipped as my head screamed at me to run.

"What scar?" Maybe if I played dumb, I could deter her. I had already checked that my hair covered the right side of my head, and the dreaded mark. It didn't. I was always so careful; I don't know how I didn't notice.

"Oh, come on," Wyn sighed as she sat up beside me, draping her arm over me and hindering my escape. "That one, right there below your ear. It almost looks like a dragon. That is *very* cool." She leaned forward and looked at it. "I'm kind of jealous."

"A dragon?"

"Yeah, here's his tail and his head." She traced a shape through the darker portions of the brand, her fingertip tickling the skin that never got touched.

I jumped up from under her arm and ran to the mirror that hung above her dresser. My hair naturally fell over the mark, so I pulled it back to get a better look. I had never really looked at it, but Wyn was right—the dark lines that moved through the raised skin did look like a dragon.

"How'd you get it?" Wyn asked, coming up behind me and leaning on the dresser. "Accidental maiming, fell off a stage, helicopter rescue gone wrong?"

I hesitated. I didn't know how much I trusted her. I just continued to stare at it in the mirror, part of me wanting to touch it; the other part continuing to scream at me to run.

"Nothing as cool as that," I managed, making it clear I wasn't going to elaborate.

"Have you shown it to Ryland? Boys love scars; I bet he would love this one." Her voice had taken on a strange quality that made me a bit uncomfortable.

I spun away from the mirror to face her. Her eyes were wide and eager.

"No! I would never show Ryland! You're the first person to see it, besides my mom." *And my dad*, but I wasn't going to get into that.

"Really? Wow, now I feel special." She slugged me playfully in the shoulder. "But you should totally not hide that away, that thing is awesome!" She bounced back over to the bed, landing in the center, springs creaking.

"Not to me," I mumbled.

Wyn continued to look at me, as if she expected something. I wasn't going to give her the benefit of an answer, not today anyway. Besides, what could I say that was believable? My life could be considered normal until it came to that mark and then it was full of mysterious illnesses and disappearing fathers.

The way this evening had turned out had become very confusing and complicated. Why did the past few days have to be so... weird? I just wanted to hide and forget that Wyn had ever caught a glimpse of the ugly thing, forget that odd men were watching me, forget that I could throw girls into ceilings, forget that Ry kept trying to kiss me.

"I gotta go." I was sure the disappointment in my voice was not missed. I grabbed my bag and started heading toward the door.

"Hey, Jos." Wyn caught up with me, catching me before I disappeared through the door. Her inadvertent use of Ryland's nickname for me sent a shiver up my spine. "I'm sorry I brought it up. I didn't know it was a taboo thing. I'll pretend I never saw it." She smiled at me, her voice sincere.

"Thanks, Wyn, It's just—" I hesitated; I had to tell her something. "It's just that, that... thing... has kind of ruined my life."

"Don't let it anymore, 'kay?"

I nodded and her face brightened.

"So, don't go. I won't mention it again, and we still have a stupid movie to watch."

"Thanks, Wyn, but I do have to go. I actually *do* have homework to do." I tried to sound indifferent, but I wasn't sure it worked.

"Oh, okay. I'll see you tomorrow then?"

I just nodded in agreement, shutting the door to her apartment behind me.

I STOOD OUTSIDE WYN'S APARTMENT complex for about ten minutes, trying to decide where to go. I needed to talk to my mom. I didn't know what I would say to her that wouldn't end in a fight, but I felt so naked and exposed after Wyn's innocent discovery of my mark.

I made sure my hair covered the right side of my face before I turned my long board in the direction of the bus that would take me into the wealthy district of town. There were still about forty-five minutes until dinner would be served in the LaRue's dining hall, meaning my mom still had about two hours or more of work. Rather than wait at home, alone, for her to get there, I opted to face the hustle of the big kitchen at dinner time. Spending forty minutes alone on the bus was still better than waiting alone for two or more hours before she would get off.

The bus stopped and I quickly boarded. The neon lights were already on, illuminating the plastic seats and metal floor with a strange, blue glow. I made my way to the middle and sat with my hood up, backpack sitting on my lap and my head leaning against the glass. As the blue sky deepened around me, it felt like everything inside loosened up, calming down and becoming brighter.

Wyn had said I had let the mark ruin my life. At first I wasn't exactly sure what that meant. To me, my life seemed to be pretty okay. I had a great best friend, a mother who really cared, and I did well in school. On the other hand, I also hated school because it meant that I had to be around other kids—that I had to hide.

I didn't "have to" do anything, though. I didn't "have to" cover myself up. I didn't "have to" pretend to be invisible. Maybe Cynthia only saw something off in me because I made her see me that way.

I had been hiding myself because of the mark, not letting anyone get too close. I wouldn't let myself make any friends. The only reason I let Ryland in is because he had been persistent. He had held my hand as I got over my insecurities and had promised, from a young age, to always be there. So, without Ry, I was friendless and alone.

My mother worked upwards of sixty hours a week, my best friend wasn't really allowed to be my friend, and I was picked on at school.

My life did suck, and all because I allowed a stupid mark to destroy me.

I laid my head against the back of the seat and watched as the city lights of old-fashioned neon and new-aged fluorescent blended together in a rainbow blur of colors until the city laid far behind and ever-expanding houses laid before me.

There had been a reason I let the mark control my life, and as much as I rationalized my behavior and my loneliness, the fact still remained that I was broken, that my dad didn't want me. Mark or no mark, the outcome would be the same.

Their last fight still haunted me. I would still revisit it in monthly nightmares; the screaming more intense, more audible, more of the blame placed on me. I would wake up covered in sweat, only to turn over and cry into my pillow in the desperate hope that my mom wouldn't hear. She never did.

I exited the bus, grateful for the evening air that swirled around me. My long board clicked loudly as I traveled the last five minutes of alleys and side streets until I arrived at the door to the kitchen.

The click-click of the long board ricocheted around my head as the fight replayed again. It still rattled me, it still hurt, but it wasn't as bad. And through it all, I realized something. My dad left me; he ran away from me. He ran away because of the mark, and I didn't want anyone else to run, too. So I hid. I just didn't want to get hurt anymore. All this time, and I hadn't realized how broken I was inside.

I arrived in the kitchen of the LaRue's just as dinner was being served to the family. As I had expected, the kitchen was in a frenzy of activity as the maids and wait-staff rushed around with trays of food and decanters of who knows what. My mom was busy rushing around and yelling different instructions to different staff members.

I dodged and weaved my way through the activity to find my usual barstool. It always surprised me that so many people were needed to serve only Ryland and his father. After a few minutes, the staff disappeared, leaving my mother and Mette to clean and prepare for the dessert course.

"How was your friend's house?" Mom asked, setting a large bowl of leftover soup in front of me. She looked at me eagerly, excited I had taken her advice so seriously.

"Wyn," I provided. "It was fun. She likes Styx," I added, causing

Mom's smile to widen.

"A girl after my own heart," she said.

"Yeah, I really like her."

Mom smiled and moved away from me, back to her cleaning. "And the movie?" she asked, spooning a strawberry puree into a crystal dish.

"We didn't get around to the movie; we mostly just talked."

"Girl talk? You?" she asked in disbelief.

"I know."

Mom wiped her soapy hands on her apron and came over, stealing a spoonful of chicken dumpling soup. "Mmmm, I do make a good soup." She licked her lips in enjoyment.

"The best," I agreed.

The platters began returning, most picked clean either by the family or by the staff on the way back to the kitchen. The trays and dishes clanged as they threw them, one after another, into the sink. My mom rushed back into action, as she directed the huge number of tasks with ease.

I remembered when she had first started. She had come home in tears after she had forgotten to serve an appetizer course, and the roast beef had been served lukewarm. The next morning, we had arrived in the kitchen to a very uncomfortable Edmund who explained what had gone wrong, while also offering his compliments on her pear gelato. He had left after that, leaving behind a small, freckled boy with blazing, blue eyes and an absolute mop of dark, curly hair.

I had been hiding behind my mother's legs, and when I saw him staring at me, I buried my face into the back of my mom's thighs. He had come up to me, tugging on my arm in an attempt to get me to play with him.

"What's her name?" he asked my mom in his innocent voice.

"Joclyn."

"Hey, Joclyn." He tugged again. "Do you want to come play with me? I made a castle in my room; do you want to come see?"

I had turned my head to look at him. He smiled at me, and I felt more comfortable. I took his hand, my mom still prodding me along to go with him.

"You have very pretty eyes. They look like diamonds."

He was always charming, right from the start.

I smiled at the memory, the way I had when he had first said the words to me. Somehow, even all these years later, it still made me feel warm and fuzzy inside. I had been so uncomfortable about my newly-changed eye color, and he had taken all that fear away.

"You ready?"

I looked up. My mom was standing by the door of the now empty kitchen, hand perched on the light switch.

"Come on, honey; it's time to go home."

I stood slowly, my body stiff from sitting in my daydream for so long.

"Glad you're still with me," Mom said. "I thought I lost you for a little bit."

"Sorry. I was just thinking, I guess."

"Something good and not involving rippling muscles, I hope."

I ignored her obvious jab at Ryland before stepping into her old station wagon. "No, Mom," I grumbled as I closed the door behind me and shut us into the small space. "Wyn saw my scar." Better get it over with right away; it was what I traveled out of my way to talk to her about after all.

The mood in the car changed immediately; stressful energy dripping into the air. I wasn't sure who was more stressed about my statement, me or my mom.

"Mmmmhmmmm." My mom's non-committal grunt prompted me to continue.

"And I think I know why I'm so scared to let people see it."

She didn't respond; she just drove, waiting for me to continue. She was always so good at that, just sitting and listening without interjecting.

"I'm afraid that people will think I am broken and leave me, just like Dad did." It felt good to say it aloud, to let my deep-rooted fear free for the first time. Somewhere between leaving Wyn's and entering the bright lights of the city, I had started to let that shy little monster of fear out from where he had been dwelling, hidden inside me for the past eleven years.

"I'm sorry, honey. I never knew... I didn't realize that everything had affected you so much."

"Neither did I. I figured it out on the way over," I sighed. "The way Wyn talked about it, how she asked me not to let it ruin my life anymore... I don't think I realized that I was doing that until that moment."

We sat silently, lights flashing in the dark, the sound of the over-worked engine buzzing in my ears.

"Not everyone left you because of the mark, you know," my mom said, her hand patting my knee in a comforting way.

"Just Dad."

"Yes, just Dad. He left because he couldn't handle it."

"And because he was paranoid." I knew I was being a little too honest; I just hoped Mom didn't read too much into it.

"Maybe a little of that, too." She smiled, but it was a sad smile, as if she knew the truth, but didn't want to admit it.

"But not everyone left, Joclyn. I didn't leave; Grandma and Grandpa Despain didn't leave and Grandma Hillary didn't leave. Ryland didn't leave."

"That's not fair, Mom. Ryland doesn't even know about the mark."

"True, but if you were broken, he wouldn't have stuck around so long."

"I guess that's right." I knew it was; from the beginning it was. Even when he had found me crying in the bushes behind the kitchen when I was eight, he just smiled, handed me a rose and dragged me back to his room to play video games.

"So tell me..." Mom's voice cut through my memory. "Did Wyn run away?"

"No."

"Did she scream in fright?"

"No."

"What did she do then?" I had seen the trap from the beginning and had to smile at my mom's obvious attempt to make a point.

"She thought it was cool, and told me I shouldn't let it ruin my life anymore."

"I like this Wyn more and more. Maybe she will help me to get you out of those hoodies."

"Don't start, Mom," I pleaded.

"Well, I've got to try. We do have that shopping date on Saturday. You would look so nice in that brand new, red shirt."

"Okay, I'll make you a deal." An idea had come to me out of nowhere, although I knew it might not work, it was worth a try.

"Now, I am worried."

"I won't wear a hoodie, no hoodie all day on Saturday, if you let me hang out with Ry that night and watch a movie."

"Joclyn, we talked about this." She was stern.

Stupid Ryland, having to take off his shirt! I don't think my mom would have ever started to take this stance if he had kept his shirt on. Oh, and if he hadn't tried to kiss me in the kitchen... I stifled a sigh at the memory before rebutting.

"I know we did, but I can't just walk away from him, Mom. He's my best friend, and he's leaving for Oxford in a few months and then he won't be my friend anymore, anyway. He will have other friends, and girlfriends, and a fiancée, and run a huge company. He won't just be Ry anymore. He will be Ryland LaRue, heir to a fortune." I spoke very fast. Even though it hurt to say it, I knew it was true. No matter how many fantasies had entered my mind, it could never happen.

"He already is that."

"I know," I whispered. It took me a moment to find my voice again. My heart thudded around my chest in a desperate plea not to make this compromise with my mom. "Mom, can I just have him as a friend for a little while longer? Then I will leave him alone forever. I'll have no other choice."

"It's not just that, Joclyn." She sighed again, frustrated.

"Then, what is it?" I held my own though, my eyes digging into hers.

"Okay," she conceded, "you know how Timothy is always warning me to keep you two apart?"

"Yeah." I was hesitant; I didn't like where this was going.

"Well, it used to be a half-hearted warning. Now, it feels almost... dangerous." She looked away from me, the subject making her uncomfortable.

"Dangerous? Like 'Keep her away from him or else'?"

"It's more than that. Timothy made mention of your safety and how dangerous ovens are. I don't know. It just made me uncomfortable."

Edmund had said something similar in the hall a few days ago. It was such an odd thing for him to say that I had just dismissed it, but hearing it again from my mom was weird. Forget corporate drama, this bordered on super-villain.

"Anyway, I've started looking for a new job."

"What?" Panic, sheer panic, gripped me. I felt my chest get tight and uncomfortable. Not only was change not good for me, she was ripping my best friend away from me. "Mom! You can't."

"I have to, Joclyn. I have to keep you safe. You are my number one priority."

"Then, you have to let me go on Saturday, if you are going to take him away from me anyway," I pleaded with her, trying to ignore the earth-shattering pain that centralized in my chest.

"I don't know, Joclyn. A movie?"

"We've watched plenty of movies before." I was begging; I had to go now.

"Yeah, but alone, in his room."

"Done that, too." We had even watched a movie with the lights off, but it still wasn't as much of a scandal as my mom made it out to be.

"Yeah, but never with overactive, crazed, teenage hormones trying to stick you two together like magnets."

I paused. She had a point.

"Don't worry, Mom. Nothing will happen. I can't let it. I just want to enjoy the last little bit of time I have left with my friend."

"I'll think about it."

"Okay, but just remember, if I can't go to the movie, I am wearing the biggest hoodie I own. If you let me go, I will leave the hoodie at home, and I might even wear the skirt. Well, not the skirt; I'd look like a moron."

CHAPTER
7

$\mathcal{I}$ TIPTOED THROUGH THE HOUSE on Wednesday morning, trying not to wake my mom. Wednesdays were the only day in the week my mom got to sleep in, having to go in for dinner service and the late-night weekly board meeting that night. Of course, letting her sleep in meant that I had to leave for school about twenty minute before usual. That, coupled with the fact that I had slept in, meant that I was running far later than I was comfortable with. The problem with living in such a small apartment was that trying to be quiet was impossible when you were in a hurry.

I brushed my teeth in a rush, attempting to run a comb through my hair at the same time. The dark circles under my eyes had taken on a whole new shade of ugly, so I rubbed some of my seldom used concealer on them, vowing to eat a piece of fruit for breakfast. I brushed my hair, letting the sleek black strands hang low down my back.

I rushed out of the bathroom and into my small bedroom, throwing on one of my two, un-ripped, pair of jeans and a fluorescent green tank top. I looked at myself in the full-length mirror that hung behind my door. Everything fit my small frame snuggly, something that would be hidden when I put on my hoodie. Of course, if my mom agreed to my compromise, I would have to spend all day Saturday like this. Not that that would be a bad thing, my arms and face could do with a little sun. I sighed, trying to figure out if I was ready to throw the hoodie aside. Although I could feel myself changing, I didn't think I was ready to change that much.

I grabbed a dark green hoodie as I walked out the door, locking it behind me. After my father had left, my mother had moved us as close to her new job as she could, which landed us in a tiny, overpriced apartment in a very upper-middle class neighborhood.

Most of our neighbors made six figures and tended to look down on those that lived in the complexes. Some of them were nice and tolerable, but every once in a while, you ran into someone who thought that we shouldn't be allowed to socialize with them.

It was amazing how much I dealt with financial stereotypes every day. My mom was personal chef to a gazillionaire and I went to school with kids who get new Lexus's for their birthday.

I hopped on the school bus that stopped right outside my apartment complex with a few other kids and made my way to the middle, finding a bench to take up all on my own. We arrived at school about five minutes to the first bell, pulling up to the bus stop in front of the large, red brick building.

The school grounds were bathed in patches of sun from the rays that broke through the white, puffy clouds lining the sky. An unnaturally warm breeze wrapped itself around me as I stepped off the bus. The wind caught and pulled my hair in odd directions, so I pulled my hood up in an attempt to hide myself. The steady gusts kept pulling at my hood, causing me to hold it in place.

The large expanse of grass in front of the school filled up with last-minute stragglers as the morning bell prepared to ring. I walked toward the main entrance, wanting to get out of the wind as fast as possible. I had gotten about halfway when a tall figure distracted me, causing my feet to stop in shock.

The same, tall, blonde man stood just off to the side of the front entrance to the school. He leaned against the building with his arms folded across his chest. He wore a tight fitting, light blue, button-up shirt and another pair of strategically ripped designer jeans. Even with the wind whipping against his clothes, he stayed still. His head was bowed and I could just make out closed eyes amid the masses of his blonde hair blowing in the wind. I knew he wasn't looking at me, but I couldn't shake that tormented feeling like I was being watched, or as I had put it earlier, stalked.

I looked away from him and picked up my pace, eager to get into the school. I had forgotten about him after everything else that had happened last night; however, seeing him there again brought all that anxiety back. I felt jumpy and nervous as I walked into my first class, French.

I looked over the room before sitting down, worried that the blonde man had followed me here. My irritation shivered up my spine, making me wonder if my paranoia level was becoming unhealthy. I settled in before Madame Armel could begin her instructions in French. I was only in this class for graduation credit, meaning the class was filled with a bunch of freshmen and sophomores, so I tended to sit at the back and blend in more than usual.

Madame Armel began her lesson on advanced conjugation, while I opened my book in a futile attempt to follow along. It was hard to stay focused however; my mind kept wandering. My thoughts jumped from checking to see if the blonde man was around, to worrying about what I was going to say to Wyn when I saw her, and ultimately, to thinking about Ryland. My mind jumped from lip-locked fantasies that made my heart swim and pound, to the thought of his arms wrapped around mine in an intimate embrace, sending a pleasurable shiver up my spine. I couldn't think that way, though. I had promised myself that we would just be friends and that I would leave him alone. I was left with a hollow, empty feeling as I shooed the fantasies away.

The bell rang much sooner than I expected and I rushed out of class, my mind still overtaken by thoughts, worries and fantasies.

WYN SAT DOWN NEXT TO me, cafeteria tray and plastic bangles clanging. She didn't say anything at first. I didn't blame her; I didn't know what to say either. How could I start a conversation after what had happened last night?

"I'm sorry," I whispered, much softer than I had wanted to.

"I'm sorry, too," she responded, her bright voice sounding off against my strained whisper. "If I had known it was such a big deal, I wouldn't have brought it up." She paused and bit her lip, as if contemplating whether or not to say something else. I looked at her in expectation, but she had decided against it, looking back down to her food.

I sighed and went back to my food as well. I was glad we had moved beyond it, but the awkwardness still wasn't over. I hoped I could think of something witty to say that would strike up a bright conversation, yet nothing came to mind that I wanted to share. Every thought in my mind was an over-dramatic problem, so I kept them all to myself.

We sat in a very strained silence through all of lunch, each of us eating our greasy cafeteria food as if we sat alone. I felt an odd gnawing at my heart that I wasn't sure I had ever felt before. I had ruined everything and all because of the mark. Wyn was right when she told me not to let it ruin my life anymore, except this time, I was doing it intentionally. It wasn't like Wyn had tried to leave; I sat here trying to push her away, not knowing how to stop myself.

I turned toward her just as the bell rang, surprised to see her already looking at me. Her dark eyes stared into me, pinning me in place with a look of mingled excitement and fear. She looked like she was expecting something from me. I opened my mouth to answer her unasked question, but closed it again, realizing I didn't know what she was going to say.

"I better get going to English," Wyn said without looking away from me.

I watched her as she turned to leave, ratty shoulder bag draped across her back. I wanted to run after her, to explain why everything upset me and all about Ryland, and my dad, and everything. I just couldn't make myself move.

Wyn took a step to the side, leaving a break in the small group of students leaving the cafeteria. That small movement gave me a clear view of the door, and the blonde man standing next to it.

I looked away from Wyn's retreating back to meet the stare of bright, blue eyes. My stomach clenched in fear as his gaze bored into mine in a glance so intense, I felt the blood drain from my face. All the times I had seen him, I had felt uncomfortable, like I was being stalked, and this time was no different. Except now, I knew without a doubt that he was following me. My frantic and panicked heart felt like it was going to beat right out of my chest.

In the back of my mind, I began to rolodex through every possible reason for being stalked. Everything from child predator to long-lost relative went through my mind in rapid succession. All the while, his eyes never left me; they kept me locked in place with their wide, eager expectation.

The man leaned forward, his back arching him toward me. His eyes narrowed as he continued to stare into me. A shiver wound its way up my spine, causing me to inhale for a breath I hadn't remembered holding. At my sudden intake, a coy, little half smile spread across his face as if he enjoyed it. My stomach clenched in even further terror, my mind casting away any thoughts of what that smile could mean. I didn't want to know. He continued to stare into me before releasing me as he turned to walk out of the cafeteria.

I didn't dare move, even though class had already started. I was left alone with the janitorial staff and the smell of ammonia. I continued to stare at the vacant door as the edge of fear ebbed away and my spine started to relax. I shouldn't be so worked-up over one random man staring at me, even though he had been following me. It could be anything, right?

I shook my head in frustration as I gathered my belongings and headed out the side door of the cafeteria that led to the back of the school. I knew I would get in trouble for skipping classes, but right then, I didn't care. I didn't want to be there, didn't want to risk being seen by either Wyn or the blonde man.

I turned around right outside the door and placed my fingers in the grooves of the deep red brick that covered the school. I lifted myself up, my worn sneakers gripping the brick as I began to scale my way toward the roof. My backpack bounced against my back as I moved up. With so little to cling onto, I was surprised I could do this at all, but something about heights and climbing had always drawn me in.

I smiled as the wind pulled my hair out of my hoodie and snaked it around my face. The feeling of the warm air made my skin tingle. With one more pull, I reached the top and sat on the edge of the building, my legs dangling over the side.

I sat, just looking at the tops of the houses and the small field where the freshmen were playing soccer. Before long, the fear of being stalked and the anger at the tension between Wyn and me came back and I sank down a bit.

I wanted someone to talk to. I needed to figure out what was going on, what I was supposed to do. I needed Ry. I needed his strong arms around me and his soothing voice telling me it was okay. I knew I shouldn't. I shouldn't indulge myself.

I reached into the pocket where I kept my phone, surprised when my fingertips brushed instead against something small and round.

I pulled it out, expecting to find a wrapper, but instead found the small purple marble in my hand. It rolled around my palm as the wind tugged at it. Watching it shine against the flickers of light clicked something together in my brain. The man, the bead, my dad.

My dad had referred me to a cult, and the cult had obviously found me.

CHAPTER 8

FOR THE SECOND TIME IN a week, I woke to the sound of Ryland's knock echoing through my tiny apartment. I fought the urge to yell when I looked at the clock, 5:15 a.m. My alarm wasn't set to go off for another forty-five minutes. I rolled out of bed and landed hard on the floor.

"I'm coming," I said loud enough for him to hear me.

"About time," I heard his happy voice yell back. Great, he's wide awake.

I crawled toward the door, grabbing a sweater I had discarded last night and threw it on to cover the light-weight cami I wore. I continued to crawl until I reached the front door where I pulled myself upright and threw the door open.

"It's five in the morning, Ry," I yawned, my hair falling around my face.

"Yeah, sorry about that." He ran his big hand through his dark curls, looking away from me. "I was just worried about you."

"You were worried about me?" My voice sounded more hostile than I had meant it to.

"Yes, Jos." He looked down, his eyes smoldering and I felt my heart sputter. "Why aren't you wearing my necklace?" He reached out and trailed the tip of his finger against my neck, his touch leaving a shivering trail behind it.

I grasped toward my collar bone, shocked to find the fine silver chain missing. "It must have fallen off while I slept." I looked back toward my room, as if just expecting to see it sitting on the fold of my comforter.

"Why don't you go get it? I'll get breakfast ready." He smiled and held up a bag full of greasy doughnuts. I couldn't help but smile at the look on his face; he was so adorable. I let him in before turning to retrieve the necklace from within the mass of pillows and blankets that was my bed. The necklace lay warm in my hand, as if I had been lying on it all night.

"See, not lost." I walked up behind Ryland as he searched for plates in the kitchen.

"Good." He took the necklace from my hands and went to put it around my neck again. I moved my hair for him, so as not to reveal my mark. For a split second, I almost didn't. I almost wanted him to see it, to see what he would do. That risk was too much for me, though, so I kept it hidden.

"Please don't take it off, okay?" he pleaded, his deep blue eyes boring into me.

"You act like I'm going to go hock it and buy a car." I laughed at the thought, but he didn't. My laughter died off as I sat the milk and some glasses on the table.

"Relax, Ryland, it's not like I could, even if I tried."

Ryland looked at me menacingly from beneath his long lashes.

"I couldn't, could I?"

He chuckled at me.

"I could?"

"More than likely, but please don't, Joclyn," he pleaded, coming to kneel in front of me and gathering my hands in his. His hands were warm and soft; the warmth radiated up my arms and through my body in a comforting way that enveloped me.

"Please don't, Jos. Don't take it off, don't sell it, don't lose it, don't give it away. Think of it as a piece of me," he said and looked down at our interlocked hands. "You know I am leaving the country soon, and it may be a while until I see you again. I may... I may never see you again. Please keep it close. That way I will always know you are safe."

He lifted his head to look at me, and I was shocked to see his eyes brimming with threatening tears. He lifted our hands together and placed them over the necklace, right next to my heart.

"Promise me, Joclyn, please."

I didn't know how to react. Was this goodbye? I didn't think I could handle anymore. It had been a week, one week since my birthday, and everything had flipped upside down. Ryland's thumb began to caress the back of my hand that he held against my chest, waiting for an answer. The action sent my heart and stomach tangoing through my body in pure pleasure.

"I promise," I exhaled, hoping that this wasn't goodbye. Not already. It couldn't be; there were still four weeks until graduation.

Almost as soon as the words left my lips, my mom's bedroom door creaked open and Ryland left my side, sitting back in his own chair before my mom could even exit her room.

"Why, Ryland," her voice was laced with parental venom, "was that your knock I heard at such an ungodly hour this morning?" She wrapped her robe around her as she made her way to the kitchen in search of a coffee mug.

"Sorry, Mrs. D." Ryland slipped right into his normal voice, as if nothing had happened over the past few minutes. "I wanted to provide breakfast for my two favorite ladies." He winked at my mom as he shook the doughnut bag, causing me to almost choke on the maple bar I had just bit into. My mom looked between us in some sort of amused frustration. I wished she would just laugh; it would make everything go a lot smoother.

"Joclyn, I have given some thought to what we talked about in the car on Tuesday night."

I sat up straighter, swallowing my doughnut. I couldn't believe she was going to do this in front of Ryland, but, oh well. I chanced a glance at him to see that he was just as attentive as I was.

"I will let you two have your movie night on one condition."

I sat forward more; she had my full attention—this had to be good.

"No hoodies for the rest of the week."

Not good.

"What?" I shrieked. I looked over at Ryland. He was smiling ear to ear.

"Thursday, Friday, Saturday. No hoodie." She was firm.

I was doomed.

"Good one! I knew you'd get her out of those hoodies somehow!"

I rounded on Ryland; my face must have been terrifying because he flinched away from me.

"Please tell me you had nothing to do with this, Ryland." My voice was a growl.

"Not a bit." He winked at me and I felt my resolve lessen. Stupid hormones!

"Mom!" I pleaded with her like a child. This was not a compromise; this was torture.

"Take it or leave it, Joclyn."

"Mom, this is so not fair! I can't go to school without a hoodie. Do you know what will happen?" Yes, I was begging. I didn't care. I couldn't lose Saturday night, but this was unacceptable.

"People will see what a beautiful young lady you are. Oooh!

Maybe you'll get asked out on a date!" she said triumphantly.

I felt Ry tense behind me. I just wanted to melt into the kitchen floor.

"Whatever, Mom."

"Joclyn, if you want to go with Ryland Saturday night, you need to do this for me."

I felt the last of my resolve slip away. How many times was I going to get guilt-tripped this morning?

"Fine." I think I sounded like a beaten kitten. "I'll see you later, Ry." I waved to him as I tromped off to my room. If I had to put some thought into my clothes, this was going to take a while.

"Actually," Ryland began, stopping me in my tracks, "I am going to take you to school today. That's what I came over to tell you."

I swear my heart just shot right down to my toes. I was not sure if my mother laughed or gasped; either way, the sound that came from the kitchen was not very good.

Ryland looked at me with this heroic glee, like he had just won the best prize in the world.

"Fine!" I snapped and ran to my room, slamming the door behind me. I put some mindless music on a little louder than normal in an attempt to drown out the voices from the kitchen, and set to work.

I pulled out a pair of darker jeans that would fit snug, but still had enough room in them that I wouldn't look like I was trying too hard. That left shirts. Okay, so brand new red shirt was out—I had to save that for Saturday. So that left a gray one with ruffles I never wore and a green one with fabric roses near the hem. Seeing as they would both get a turn, I grabbed blindly, draping the green shirt over the jeans. Grabbing the rest of the stuff I needed, I ran across the hall to the bathroom and took the world's quickest shower.

Without the hood to help keep my hair in place, I had to do something to it to guarantee that ugly mark didn't peek out. I brushed my hair before lifting the hair up above my right ear. There it was, the dragon, peeking out from beneath my ear to look at me. I dropped my hair and pulled it to the side into a sleek side braid, guaranteeing that no one would see it.

I shoved my clothes on, not bothering to look at myself in the mirror. I didn't want to see myself and lose the forced confidence I had tried to rattle to the surface. I sprinted across the hall to my room, slamming my door behind me. Even my music couldn't drown out my mother's joyous laughter.

It was like my birthday all over again. I liked the way I looked; I just wished I felt more comfortable. I dabbed on some concealer and lip gloss before turning to the door, my hand freezing on the knob. It wasn't just my mom out there; it was Ryland, too. Beyond that, what was I going to do when I got to school? My false confidence morphed into a full-blown panic attack and I found myself hyperventilating behind the bedroom door. The skin on my chest grew hot, as if my panic had ignited the necklace that was hiding underneath my shirt.

The knob twisted under my fingers and was jerked out of my hand as the door flung open in front of me. Ryland grabbed me around the waist and pulled me to him, burying his face in my hair. He cradled me against his strong chest, his hand wrapped around my waist as the other smoothed my hair. As his hand moved its way up and down my back, I found my breath slowing, the panic melting away.

"Shhhhh... it's okay, Jos. Just breathe. I'm here." I wrapped my arms around him as I came back to myself.

He moved me away from him; his hands never left my shoulders as his thumbs moved over the skin on my arms. I looked up at him in nervous anticipation, but his eyes didn't leave mine. He didn't look at what I wore. He didn't appraise my uncovered body. He just stared straight into my eyes with a passion I had never seen before.

"You're beautiful." His hands trailed down my arms, their warmth leaving a trail of goosebumps behind them. He intertwined his fingers with mine for a brief second before leaning down, his lips brushing against my hair. "Your eyes, they are just like diamonds."

I shivered at his whisper, his voice lingering in my ear. He squeezed my hand before dragging me off to the kitchen where my mom sat, still in her robe. At the sight of me, she dropped her doughnut. Her face screamed pure joy; it almost felt like she was sending me off to my first day of kindergarten.

"Oh, Joclyn, it's beautiful." She cupped my face with her rough kitchen hands. She was crying, and I felt like crying, too. I had given her what she wanted, her dream. If only for three days, I was giving her that beautiful, little girl she had always wanted. Deep down inside, I knew I wanted to be that, too.

CHAPTER 9

I DIDN'T WANT TO GET out of the car. Who would? It was nice and warm, and the leather of the seats, soft and cozy. Ryland had turned the radio down low and he had his hand on my knee, thumb caressing me in a comfortable way. I scowled at the large red school in front of us.

"Maybe I didn't think this through enough," I said.

"What do you think they will do; more than just notice you, I mean?"

I turned to glare at him. I wasn't in the mood to go over my fight with Cynthia just yet. His hand moved from my knee to trail up the pale skin of my arms, leaving another row of goosebumps behind.

"That would be enough to ruin my day." I tried to laugh, but it didn't come out right; my panic made it sound more maniacal than I had intended.

"Honestly, Jos, did you think I would feed you to the wolves?" His eyes sparkled as he reached behind my seat for a large wad of fabric.

I recognized the fabric as a hoodie, and I couldn't help the smile that spread over my face. I untangled the mass of fabric to reveal a bright blue jacket with a small stamp of Whittier Prep's crest on the chest.

Ryland shifted in his seat and began to help me pull the sweat shirt over my head, careful not to let it run against my sleek braid. As it moved over me, I caught the strong, pleasurable smell that was so Ryland; grass from endless hours on the Rugby field and some sort of heavy smoke, not like the smoke of a drug user, but that heavy wooden smell like a million bonfires or fireworks.

"Thanks, Ry." I looked up at him and gave him my biggest, goofiest grin; all the while chanting in my head. *Only friends, only friends...*

"Anything for you, sweetheart."

Only friends, only friends...

His hand moved up to cup my face, his thumb trailing along my jaw and I froze, my mind went blank. It was only when he began to move closer that my brain went into overdrive.

"I've got to go." It took all my strength to pull my face away from his touch and move out of the warm comforting interior of his Lotus. My heart screamed at me as I pried myself away, desperate to get back to him. I closed the door behind me and leaned against it longer than would have been natural until I heard his dark chuckle from inside the car. I jumped at the sound and moved away, speed-walking toward the school.

"Hey, Jos."

I turned to his voice, his body leaning over the passenger seat and out the window so he could talk to me.

"Ryland." That came out a bit stiff.

"I'll be here to pick you up right after school."

I nodded at him and began walking again. I only made it about two steps before he stopped me again.

"And, Joclyn, the sweater's a gift, another piece of me, okay?" He winked at me, his blue eyes flashing. My eyes were glued to his for a minute before he tore away, speeding off in his car.

I continued toward the school, my head buzzing in an odd swarm of happy mosquitoes. Nothing made sense; Ryland had sat at my kitchen table less than a week ago explaining that the necklace didn't mean anything, but since then, he has been trying to kiss me. Then there were all the gifts, like he was saying good-bye.

My heart thudded as I crossed the street, making a beeline to Wyn who was in a heated conversation with someone tall who stood with their back to me. I was determined to get over the weirdness so we could keep working on our friendship; after all, I would need her after Ryland left.

Wyn's voice rose a bit, the frantic tone increasing as I moved closer to her. She was so engrossed in her conversation that she didn't even see me step right up next to her.

"I'm not going to do that! Can you imagine how that would ruin everything? You would be making me start all over again." I ignored her comment and looked toward the man standing across from her.

My heart seized in an uncomfortable fear. The man who had been following me around campus stood right there, his bright blue eyes burning into mine. Now that I was close to him, I couldn't help but notice how familiar his eyes were, like I had seen them somewhere before. My mouth just hung open in a sterilized panic I couldn't quite bat away.

"You know him?" I rounded on Wyn after my brain clicked back into place. She knew him. I mean, she stood here talking to him.

"Who?" Was she joking? He stood right here.

"Him! My Stalker." I motioned toward him, my heart falling into my stomach to see him staring at me with an amused smile on his face.

"Hello, Joclyn." He spoke smoothly, his voice laced with some deep, throaty accent I couldn't place. His deep rumble vibrated through me, sending a shiver up my spine.

"Oh, great! You could have at least told me she saw you. I told her you were a janitor!" Wyn's voice sounded almost hysterical as she shrieked out. The tall man turned toward Wyn, staring down at her. Wyn bowed her head, her lips moving in some form of apology I couldn't understand before lowering in an unmistakable curtsy. That wasn't normal.

"Will someone please explain to me what's going on?"

"Joclyn, Ilyan. Ilyan, Joclyn," Wyn introduced. "Ilyan is my brother, Jos. And, apparently a big jerk. Sorry; if I knew it was him you kept seeing, I would have told you."

Ilyan turned on her again, but this time, Wyn stood her ground. They stared daggers at each other for a minute as if engaged in some form of silent conversation. Definitely brother and sister.

"I'm so sorry if I scared you," Ilyan began, his accent rolling his vowels in odd ways. "I am working on my thesis concerning high school peer groups and how they affect the grades and future outcomes of children and adolescents. I have been conducting my research here."

"Ummm." I didn't really understand all that just came out of his mouth. "So, not a member of a cult then?" I spoke my thoughts aloud without thinking, and my hand flew to my mouth in embarrassment.

Wyn and Ilyan only burst out laughing.

"No, no cult," he lilted with a curious half-smile.

I let out a big sigh of relief. Good, maybe my dad hadn't acted on his craziness yet. I couldn't stop looking at his eyes; they were just so familiar. I kept staring, expecting their mystery to jump out at me. I guess I had been staring for far too long as Wyn cleared her throat beside me.

"So, what are you named after? Ilyan isn't a very common

name." I spoke the first thing on my mind, hoping to end the rather awkward silence. "Are you named after a king or something; I know Wyn is named after a queen."

"I guess you could say that," Ilyan laughed with a rich, happy sound that seeped through me. Even Wyn joined into the joke. I must be missing something.

"What?" I asked, looking between them. They shook their heads in unison; the joke, one they didn't want to share. I looked away in irritation to see the school grounds devoid of inhabitants.

"Oh, gosh! We are going to be late!" I whisked Wyn away from her brother without even bothering to say good-bye.

We parted ways at Wyn's locker and I kept running, thankful that it was an A-day and to have gym, instead of French with Madame Armel, who would notice my tardy. Hopefully, I would have time to dress down before class began.

I ran into the locker room, my heart plunging to see it empty. Even if I dressed and went in, the teacher would make me run the mile. No, thank you. I sat down on one of the many metal benches. I was not having a very good track record—first, two classes yesterday and then, gym today. My mom was going to kill me.

I leaned against the locker, intending to sleep through the hour long block. For some reason, sitting still caused the smell from Ryland's jacket to increase. I didn't move, letting the delicious scent waft around me. What was I going to do about him, or even about me, for that matter?

Without any warning, a vision of our bodies intertwined together filled my mind. His heavy muscular form pushing against me as he wrapped his arms around me in a passionate... what was I doing? I shook my head in frustration, emptying the fantasy from my mind. It was obvious he wanted to kiss me, and I knew, beyond a shadow of a doubt, that I wanted to kiss him. My mom was right; we were both hormone-driven teenagers. What harm could one kiss do, though? He was leaving after all; I might as well make the most of it.

I slammed my head into a locker. Even with all my rationalization I still had made my mother a promise. As much as my heart broke, and as many times as I would have to repeatedly convince myself of it, I had to keep that promise. Until Heaven and Hell broke loose and we could somehow be together, no matter what, I would keep the promise.

My mind jerked out of its heart-breaking reverie as my phone buzzed in my pocket.

How's the jacket?

I couldn't help the smile that spread across my face.

Large, warm, and very hideable. Thanks.

I tucked the phone in the pocket of the hoodie and leaned my head back again. He must be ditching class, too, because the next message came right away.

Hideable?

It's a word! I knew it wasn't, but it should be.

Uh huh... I guess it's good you are a junior, because you obviously still have some leprosy to deal with. ;)

Leprosy? My loud laugh echoed around the walls of the locker room. I covered my mouth, scared I would get caught ditching gym.

Spell check! I meant learning.

Right; and I'm the one who needs extra 'learning'? It took a long time for him to reply, and by the time he did, students were already making their way back into the locker room, so I stood and made my way out of the room before I was discovered.

Be warned, we are doing pie tonight.

Pie.

We hadn't done pie for months. Although it wasn't as cool as it sounded, "pie" simply involved taking a chocolate crème pie—my favorite—up the canyon and hanging out at the fire pit. Normally I would be excited for pie, but right now, it just seemed like a bad situation that would end in forbidden kissing. My heart sputtered and my stomach swooped. I would keep my promise to my mom. I had to.

I can't, there is no way my mom will let me. I typed as I slid into my desk in my next class.

I'll take care of your mom. She will let you; don't worry.

It had taken quite a bit of compromise to get permission for the movie on Saturday; I doubted it would happen. Then again, she had already gotten me into a regular, old t-shirt.

I can't. I have lots of homework. I lied, knowing he would see right through it.

Why are you avoiding me, Jos?

I stared at the screen, knowing that class had already started and I wasn't paying even a scrap of attention. What could I say to him? It wasn't like I was doing it on purpose. There was just so much I couldn't tell him, no matter how much I wanted to. There were so many times I wanted to kiss him, to let him kiss me, but I couldn't. Just being his friend was going to be harder than I thought.

Fine. We'll do pie.

I put my phone away and attempted to focus on class, ignoring the continual buzzing from my pocket. My next classes passed in quick succession, and I worked hard to finish as much of my homework as possible.

My phone finally stopped buzzing as I slipped into my normal spot in the cafeteria, content to disappear for the rest of the day.

"I am so sorry about my brother," Wyn said as she dropped into the seat opposite me, her tray laden with enough food to feed a group of girls. "He's an idiot," she continued without waiting for me to respond. "If I had known it was him you thought was following you, I would have told you. He's an idiot," she repeated and then bit into a French fry.

"Hey, I'm just glad to know I'm not going crazy anymore."

"Nope, not crazy. He is, though." She rolled her eyes. "Speaking of crazy, what's with that cult comment?" Wyn raised her eyebrows at me, but I just waved her off.

"Just something my dad said once." She kept waiting for me to elaborate, but I kept staring at my food, hoping she wouldn't pry.

"Well, anyway," Wyn began in an odd attempt to break the silence, "can you come over tonight? We never got to watch our movie from Monday, and Ilyan will be home so you can see how non-freaky he is."

"I can't. I'm doing pie with Ry," I said. I was sad I couldn't go. As much as I was looking forward to the evening with Ryland, I was still terrified at what might happen.

"Pie? Is that code for something dirty?"

My voice rang out in noxious laughter at Wyn's comment. I was so happy we were in the middle of the lunch room where no one would notice the noise.

"No!" I said through giggling. "It's just pie."

Wyn stared at me in confusion.

"You know," I prompted, "we get together, we eat pie, and we talk."

Wyn sighed as if that was the stupidest thing she had ever heard.

"We have done it for as long as I can remember. When we were little, it was just a way for him to get away from his dad, and we would hide in the bushes behind the pool."

"How romantic," she grumbled.

"Not my boyfriend," I reminded her.

"So you hung out in the bushes with a boy who may or may not be your boyfriend?"

I decided to let that one slide.

"I was six and bushes were cool."

"Well, if I ever see a cool bush, I'll point it in your direction." Wyn gobbled up a handful of fries in an obvious attempt not to laugh at her bad joke.

"Gee, thanks. Anyway, once he figured out how to drive, we started going up the canyon, which is where I'll be going tonight." *Not to have a make-out session with my best friend*, I reminded myself.

"So, you're going up the canyon to have pie with your boyfriend..."

"Not my boyfriend," I grumbled.

"Whatever. So you're going up the canyon with Ryland to eat pie. What a romantic date."

"It's not a date either, Wyn." She stared at me as if waiting for me to admit it.

I shook my head at her in frustration. No matter what she thought, this was not a date; it was only pie, which was still part of the problem.

"Well, how about tomorrow night then? We could even make it a sleepover!" I had never had a sleepover before, and the idea got me excited; but, I knew with all I had to barter for to get permission for Saturday, and now pie, a sleepover was out.

"I can't do a sleepover, but I can come over for a movie."

"And dinner," Wyn added.

"And dinner. We better get going," I said. "They are supposed to run through Act Two today with the set pieces."

"Do you think if we write 'Cynthia McFadden wears boys' underwear' on the side of the castle, she would get offended?"

"I doubt it, but all the boys might get in a fight trying to figure out whose underwear she's sporting."

"So, still worth a show then?" Wyn wagged her eyebrows at me in excitement. I knew she wouldn't, but part of me hoped she would. I could do with the laugh today.

It was the first time I would be seeing Cynthia since our bizarre altercation in the hall. After the first day, the terrified stares and catcalls from the students had died down. I hadn't seen Mr. Ray since then either.

I opened the door, expecting the worse. Class had already begun. The actors were already in their costumes, so Wyn and I went right into action. Wyn, Jamison and I moved set pieces on and off the stage as the cast worked through their lines and blocking. At least once in every line, Cynthia would forget something, giggle like a maniac, and then proceed to mess up the rest of the line. It wasn't even worth it to mention that I knew to whole show by heart. Hamlet had always been one of my favorites.

I had thought I was in the clear; the show was almost over and the last of the royals were dying rather poorly-acted deaths in the middle of the stage.

"I know what you did, you little freak." I spun around to face Cynthia, her face almost maniacal in frenzied excitement.

"I don't know what you're talking about," I said with as much confidence as I could muster.

"I think you do. You're a freak. I'm going to find out why, and make sure everyone knows."

I just froze, her acidic voice washing around the space.

"Knows what?" Wyn bounced into the conversation. I could have kissed her for arriving with such perfect timing.

Cynthia flinched a bit, her resolve lessening at my added support.

"Freak," she repeated before strolling off to join the cast for the curtain call.

"Ugh. She bugs me," Wyn spat. "It's like she thinks she owns the world."

"Yeah, well, maybe she does," I whispered to myself before

going to remove a large wooden throne.

When the bell rang, the cast and the rest of the class stormed out of the room, leaving Wyn and me to finish putting the set pieces away. Even the teacher had disappeared.

"You were right, by the way," Wyn spoke out of nowhere. "Cynthia McFadden is an atrocious Ophelia. How do you think she got the part?"

"No one would pay the price of admission if there were a whole bunch of nobodies in the cast." It was honest, that's how all high school shows were cast, no matter how much I practiced in Ry's room.

"I bet you know every speech by heart, don't you?"

I paused, holding a large foam block in my hands and looked around me.

"Do you think everyone is gone?"

"Ooooo, yes!" Wyn's eyes glittered as she dropped what she carried and ran to the first tier of the audience space.

My confidence shuttered for just a moment before coming back tenfold. Wyn's excited face super-charged me. I moved to center stage and dropped my head. I ran through the entire piece in my mind before I began. I knew how I wanted to hold my hands, how I wanted my voice to sound. I just hoped it came out right.

"O, what a noble mind is here o'erthrown! The courtier's, scholar's, soldier's, eye, tongue, sword, Th' expectancy and rose of the fair state, The glass of fashion and the mould of form." I recited each line with all the purpose and emotion I felt, my body and hands moving as I pleaded to myself and the invisible characters around me. Even though I was no good, my body still felt alive.

"That unmatch'd form and feature of blown youth Blasted with ecstasy. O, woe is me. T' have seen what I have seen, see what I see!"

I finished as I was taught, head down, arms to the side; but I was jolted out of my closed position by not one but, two pair of clapping hands. My head jerked up just as Wyn's hands stopped their furious applause to see Ryland. My heart calmed for just a moment, glad that it wasn't Cynthia or some other irritating senior, before going into turbo-drive at the sight of Ry standing in the doorway.

"See! I told you! You were amazing!" He rushed in and swept me up in a giant bear hug, his arms crushing me against his chest. "Wasn't she amazing?" He turned enthusiastically to Wyn who only nodded at him.

"You must be Wyn." He dropped me before rushing over to her, his big hands outstretched.

"How did you know about Wyn?" I asked, interrupting the enthusiastic handshake Wyn had been sucked into. I hadn't mentioned her to him at all.

"Well, see, someone has been avoiding me all week, and I have to hide from my father somewhere, which means that your mother and I have become the best of friends. And, I know where the cups are kept in the kitchen now."

"No!" I shrieked, my hand flying to my chest. Wyn stuffed her hand to her mouth in an attempt to stifle a laugh.

"Yes, it's true. I can now tell you where cups *and* plates are to be found in my own kitchen. I know it's a shock, but soon I may even be able to locate a bowl." Ryland spoke seriously, like he was announcing a death, his voice causing Wyn's laugh to come unplugged.

"It's a scandal," Wyn said between laughs.

"Not about that! Have you really been talking to my mom this whole week?"

A wide smile spread across his beautiful face, verifying the truth. My mom knew that Ryland had been calling me without even looking at my phone. She was up late this morning on purpose, knowing that Ryland was going to take me to school. I don't know why this bothered me so much, but it did.

"No," I whispered. "What did she tell you?"

"Absolutely everything! She even showed me your naked baby pictures." I yelped in horror and did what any other logical girl with a crush would do; I slugged him in the shoulder. Unfortunately, my hand was weak and his shoulder was very strong. My hand exploded in pain as the muscles and bones separated from the rough impact.

"Ouch! Darn it, Ryland! Not fair." I shook my hand, waiting for the sting to go away, stomping my foot in the attempt to distract my mind from the centralized pain.

"Oh, you're such a baby. Come here." Ry grabbed my hand and placed it in between his big, warm ones. The warmth of his hands grew and moved into my hand as the pain melted away. It was comforting to have him hold my hand so tightly, his warmth moving through me like it was something tangible.

"Better?" he asked. I could only nod.

"So, Wyn," he didn't release my hand from his grasp as he turned to her, his wide goofy grin back in place, "are you coming with us? Pie in the mountains?"

"I take it my mom said yes?" I asked, perfectly aware that my hand was still clasped inside his.

"Of course, she did." He flashed me a wide, perfect smile before turning back to Wyn, waiting for an answer.

"I probably shouldn't." I could see the reluctance on her face triggered by Ryland's false invitation, but I also saw a way out of being alone with Ryland.

"Please come, Wyn! It'll be fun!" I removed my hand from the warmth of Ryland's grasp to move toward her. I tried to make my eyes as pleading as possible, but having never done it before I wasn't sure the attempt worked. I stared her down for a few moments longer, pleading until she sighed in defeat. I jumped in the air in celebration as she nodded her head in agreement.

I led the way out of the drama room, now eager to get up the canyon and enjoy some time with both my friends. Wyn breezed past me, texting something on her phone to her brother, I was sure. I followed her until I felt Ryland's large hand on my back, his warmth spreading through me.

"Something tells me you're scared to be alone with me." His breath buzzed through my hair as he spoke; he was that close.

"It's not that," I began. "It's just..." He moved in front of me, placing his hands on my arms and stopping me in place.

"It's okay, Joclyn. I know. It took me a while to realize you were worth more than my father's commands, too." His face filled with a happy light that made my heart spin in pure joy. Ryland leaned down before I could stop him and placed his lips against my cheek.

I was overcome with his smell as his lips lingered there, the warmth of them spreading throughout me and making me dizzy. Far before I was ready, he ran away from me, running to catch up to Wyn and leaving me sputtering alone in the middle of the hall.

CHAPTER 10

THE FIRE PIT WAS IN a large clearing that you could only get to by parking off the side of the road and hiking for about twenty minutes through uncut forest. Some time ago, someone had dug a giant hole in the middle of the space, giving people a reason to call it the fire pit. I never knew how Ryland found this place, but I knew we weren't the only ones who came here. Every once in a while, we would come across crumpled chip wrappers or beer cans.

Ryland led us as we trudged our way through the undergrowth, pie in hand. I could smell the delicious chocolate fragrance drifting back to me, and it made my stomach jump in anticipation.

I stayed back by Wyn, thankful for her company. After what Ryland had said to me as we were leaving the drama room, I didn't need to be alone with him. I needed to think—and somehow prepare myself for Saturday night.

We entered the clearing and I went to go look for firewood. The cool mountain air was already starting to get a bite to it and being this far up the mountains, it was sure to get chilly quickly.

The clearing was surrounded by what appeared to be a perfect circle of giant oak trees. They all had to have been planted at the same time because each one was about the same height. They towered over us as we walked through them, much taller than the smaller beech and brush oak that lay behind them. I couldn't help but touch the trees as I passed; just being this close to them sent a live current through my veins. I loved the way they made me feel.

Ryland was already working on preparing to start the fire when I dumped all the dried kindling and twigs I could find in to the make-shift hole. Ry smiled at me before turning back to the fire; he had always been amazing at getting the fire started. Even the first time we came up here, he had made a roaring blaze in minutes. He had tried to teach me once, but all I had managed to do was burn my fingers with his book of matches.

"1...2...3...4...5...6..."

"Why are you counting?" Wyn interrupted me.

"To see how long it takes Ryland to light the fire. Watch." We both turned toward him just as a blaze ignited in the pit.

Wyn's eyes widened in surprise and her mouth formed a giant O.

"How'd I do?" Ryland asked, wiping his hands on his expensive slacks.

"I don't know. I lost count," I admitted.

"Oh, great." His sarcastic voice echoed through the clearing. "Now how am I supposed to know if I beat my record?"

"What's the record?"

"Twelve seconds," I answered Wyn, causing her jaw to drop even further.

"Can you do magic or something, because that was wickedly fast."

Ryland balked at her question, his face falling pale to a ghostly shade of white like he had been caught at something.

"Ummm, no. I just like to light things on fire." He shook his curls, his uncomfortable face disappearing so fast I wasn't even sure if I had seen it.

"Too bad, that would be way cool if you could. You could pretend to fly and make things disappear!"

Ryland laughed at her. I guess magic wasn't cool to him. Then again, I couldn't see Ryland pulling rabbits out of hats with much flair.

"Well, for losing count, Jos, you owe me a race." Ryland leaned close to me, his face full of eager anticipation.

"You're on," I answered him, already standing tall; trying to meet him at his full height, which only brought me to his shoulders. I tried to look intimidating by squaring my shoulders, but it looked rather silly, and both Ryland and Wyn laughed at my poor attempt to psych him out.

"Oh, fine," I said, giving in and grabbing Wyn's hand to pull her over to the line of trees that surrounded the clearing. "You can play referee."

"You gonna cheat, Jos?" Ryland asked as he took his place at the tree next to mine, stretching his arms out in preparation.

"Nope, I am going to win." I gave him my biggest smile and then looked up to the tall branches above me. I knew I had a problem. Although I loved the feel and the smell of Ryland's sweater, it was way too big to be effective during a tree-climbing race.

"Oh, great," I mumbled.

"Losing confidence, Joclyn?" His taunts were pointless; he hadn't beaten me since the first time we had tried this.

"No, but I swear you're going to be in big trouble if I rip any of my clothes." I shed the large sweater and let it fall in a heap at my feet. I looked down to make sure my green shirt was lying flat before looking to Ryland who had fixed this strange look of happiness on his face.

"I like that shirt, Joclyn; it looks very pretty on you," said Wyn.

I turned to her and smiled in thanks. She gave me a big thumbs-up, which made me smile more.

"Don't worry, Jos. If you tear any clothes, I'll just buy you new stuff. I still owe you a pair of pants anyway; we'll have to go shopping."

"You wouldn't owe me anything if you would stop ripping my clothes off, Ryland."

Ryland's face blanched before spreading into a wide grin. Wyn laughed behind me. It took a moment for the reality of what I had just said to click into place.

"No! I didn't mean it like that." I rounded on Wyn, silently pleading, but she didn't even see me through the tears of laughter that rolled down her cheeks. "Ryland, tell her!" All my pleading was for naught, even Ryland laughed gleefully.

"All right, Wyn," I loudly interrupted the laughing, causing them to stop. "You tell us when to go. First feet to hit the ground again wins." She nodded in agreement, wiping the tears from her face.

I looked to Ryland, who winked at me before turning to his tree, still chuckling. My stomach twisted, whether with joy or nerves, I couldn't tell. I turned and faced my tree, nonetheless, stretching my fingers in excitement.

"On your mark," Wyn said. "Get set. Go!"

I lunged toward the tree, my hands pulling me up into the tangle of lower branches. The second my hands touched the bark, a fire ignited within me. It always did this every time we raced. I felt a strange energy surge under my skin as I vaulted up the tree, propelling myself higher and higher. The familiar feeling of flying took over me as I moved up, my arms propelling me faster and faster.

I looked to the side to see Ryland keeping pace with me,

although still behind. I grabbed the next branch and pulled myself up even harder, my legs kicking off to raise me up. I didn't look down; although I wasn't afraid of heights, I knew we were at least twenty feet up in the air now. I could see the deep notch we had placed in the tree all those years ago and knew it was almost time to make my descent.

"Goal!" I yelled as I pressed my palm to the large gash in the tree before turning to speed my way down the tree.

"Goal!" Ryland yelled from above me.

If I was fast climbing up trees, it was nothing to how fast I was going down. I knew Ryland didn't have a prayer. There was a movie I had watched when I was a kid, that had a man and boy climbing out of a tree as a car fell down on top of them. They swung and jumped and leaped in their frantic attempt to beat the car out of the tree and not be crushed to death. It had scared me senseless at the time; but in all reality, that's how I felt when I climbed down trees.

I continued to drop, not bothering to look at where Ry was beside me. Branches flew past me as I swung from one to another, dropping, only to catch myself on a large outstretched branch at the last moment. I could hear Wyn mumble below me, making me smile.

I released the branch that I had just grabbed, to fall to another one a few feet below me. I realized moments after I let go that I was going to overshoot and miss the branch I was aiming for. I looked down; there was still another ten feet to the ground. Wyn cried out in fear, which broke my concentration for a minute.

I pushed Wyn's panic from my mind as I twisted in the air to grab a branch that was next to me. I knew my timing was off because of the distraction. My leg slammed into the tree, and I felt a small branch poke into my skin through my pants. I continued my descent, gravity pulling me down headfirst. As I reached for another branch below me, I could feel the twig grind against the skin on my calf as it ripped through my pants. Great.

I grabbed the last branch before swinging my legs down all the way, my feet coming in contact with the ground. I let go of the tree, my burst of energy dissipating as I released the tree branch and dropped to the ground to pull my leg around to inspect the cut. My skin was slightly scraped, barely even bleeding. My pants, on the other hand, were a lost cause. The fabric was cut from my knee all the way down to the hem.

"Oh, my gosh! Joclyn, that was amazing!" I heard Wyn come up right beside me, her voice in awe.

"You think so?" It seemed so natural to me; to hear it described as amazing was kind of odd. I heard Ryland drop to the ground and then turn to make his way over to us.

"Yes!" Wyn squealed. "And, when you almost fell, I thought my heart was going to stop."

"You almost fell?" Ryland asked with something beyond alarm in his voice.

"Yes! She dropped from one branch to another, but missed the one she wanted, so she kind of twisted around to catch a different one. I was so scared." Wyn provided actions and everything like she was retelling the plot to an exciting action movie.

"Are you okay?" Ryland asked, while looking me over.

I ignored his appraisal and pulled the hoodie back over my head as I moved to stand next to him. It was then he saw my ripped jeans and the long scratch, his sharp intake of breath was a little exaggerated for the situation.

"It's a scratch, Ry," I said as he once again swept me up in his arms and carried me to a rock in front of the fire. "You're being ridiculous."

"I guess I owe you a new pair of pants," he sighed as he inspected the rip and the cut.

"Two," I reminded him.

Wyn plopped down on the rock next to mine and mouthed the word "boyfriend" with heavy exaggeration.

I scowled at her before turning my attention back to Ryland.

"Does it hurt much? We can go if we need to." His concern was evident in his voice.

"No!" I responded a little too loudly. I wasn't in the mood to be carried through the woods for twenty minutes. "I just need pie," I provided at Ryland's affronted look which turned into a wide grin.

"Boyfriend," Wyn whispered after Ryland went to the other side of the fire to grab the pie.

"Will you knock it off," I hissed.

Ryland sat on the ground between us, opening the top of the box that held the delicious chocolate crème pie and about five plastic forks. This was one of those times when his "grab a fistful" system worked to our benefit. I dove in, and smiled as the chocolate mousse hit my tongue. Mette made the best pies.

"So," Wyn began and I glared at her, terrified that she was going to start the boyfriend crap again with Ryland right in front of us. "How long have you guys been doing that tree-climbing thing? You both moved so fast; I couldn't believe it." I sighed in relief. At least this was something we could talk about.

"I think the first time we went up the trees was the first time we came up here. I was ten and you were twelve, right?" I asked Ryland who swallowed his bit of pie to answer.

"Yep. Two days after your tenth birthday. We stole Father's Vanquish and came up here. I don't think I'll ever forget that; it was the only time I have ever been able to beat you."

"You stole a car?" Wyn shrieked with her mouth full of pie.

I couldn't help but laugh.

"Yep." Ryland puffed his chest out proudly. "I had to sit on a phone book and could barely see out the window, so Joclyn had to steer most of the way."

I shook my head in irritation. I knew why Ryland was exaggerating. While I had driven most of the way—and been terrified, I might add—it wasn't because he couldn't see out the windshield; it was because he was crying.

That day had been one of the first days that Edmund had ordered Ryland to leave me alone. They had gotten in a fight and his father had hit him. He had run into the kitchen and pulled me with him into the large garage. We had left before anyone had even realized we were both missing. I still remember the bright red hand print on his cheek.

Without thinking, I reached out and ran my fingers through his dark curls near the base of his neck, wanting to wipe the memory from both our minds. He turned toward me and smiled, his gaze piercing into me.

"And you didn't crash the car?" Wyn asked, oblivious to our exchange.

"Well, we did," I provided, "but not that time. They didn't know we were taking the car for about a year."

"Jake was very nice to keep that secret for us." Ryland forced a laugh.

"Jake?"

"The butler," I provided.

"So... when you crashed the car...?" Wyn prompted.

"We more like cruised into a field..."

"And hit a cow," Ryland finished for me. We both laughed at saying it out loud.

"And you didn't get in trouble?"

"Oh, we got in trouble," Ryland answered. "I was confined to my room for a week."

It probably wasn't even worth mentioning that I had been grounded to school, my house, or the kitchen for a month. Even after Ryland was "released", I was still doomed to play fort under the staff table.

"Your father doesn't seem to be very hard on you; a week for crashing a car. I wish I was so lucky. My brother is ruthless."

"Oh, he punishes me, just not in the regular sense. He always expects me to be perfect, and accomplished, and make no mistakes." Ryland sounded so bitter and hurt. His father had always put him under so much pressure; I was constantly amazed he handled it so well.

"I guess it makes sense, seeing as he is raising you to run an empire." Wyn's logic made sense, but it was something we had talked through many times before. As much as Ryland wished to live up to his father's expectations, as much as he wished to meet his father approval, Ryland still struggled.

"I don't want to run his company," Ryland said dejectedly.

"What?" I flipped around to look at him, but he took another bite of pie, keeping his gaze down. He had never made mention of this to me before; it was always how he looked forward to becoming like his father. I looked up at Wyn who had a strange look of shock and surprise plastered on her face.

"I don't want to run his empire. I don't want to go to Oxford. I don't want to take his lessons. I don't want to be anything like him." He had turned to me, speaking only to me. I am sure Wyn heard him, but he didn't seem to notice or care.

"Ryland?" I asked.

"But I don't have a choice; I have to be everything he wants, and nothing that I wish." He looked so sad, so dejected; my heart broke in half for him.

I lunged into him, wrapping my arms around his neck, burying my face into the sweet smell of his skin. He held me against him, his large hands spreading their warmth throughout my back where they pressed against me. I tangled my hands through his curls as he held me tighter.

Right at that moment, I was grateful to have Wyn there, her eyes boring into us. Because, right then, I would have been the one to kiss him first.

CHAPTER
11

I STOOD ABOUT FIFTEEN FEET away from the fire. Wyn had assured me it was enough space to give me a running start. That was part of the problem. After Wyn had displayed her running feat and heroic jump over the fire, she and Ryland had spent the next twenty minutes taking turns leaping over the flames with decreasing running distances. They now insisted it was my turn, but my stomach flipped and my hands were sweating. I was not interested in this weird jump-to-my-death.

"You're making this out to be much more difficult than it is," Wyn whined. I had been stalling for the last few minutes, and although most of it had been spent giggling about my lack of nerves, Wyn had run out of patience.

"I've never done this before," I spouted back. "It's kind of scary."

Ryland gave me a small, sympathetic smile, but Wyn jumped off her rock and walked over to me, a mischievous grin on her face.

"Okay," she started, about eight feet from me. "You climb trees like you were born in one and fall thirty feet to your death without even—"

"It was about five, Wyn. Stop exaggerating," I interrupted her.

"Fine. But, you still could have died," Wyn said.

Ryland sighed behind her, which seemed to only fuel her fire.

"Either way, you're a tree-climbing genius! This should be a piece of cake."

"A tree can't burn me," I countered.

"But it can cut you and scrape you, and rip your clothes and break your bones," Wyn countered, motioning to the large rip in my jeans.

"But those heal." She had backed me into a hole and I didn't like it.

"Burns heal."

She was right, but it didn't mean that I wanted to jump over the fire anyway. I plunged my hands into the pockets of Ry's hoodie and hunched my shoulders.

"Not without scars," I add.

Wyn leaned in close and lowered her voice, "You don't want Ryland to think you're a chicken, do you?" she asked, her eyebrows wagging.

I just sighed at her. It almost wasn't even worth it to try to convince her I didn't care what Ry thought—because I did.

We both jumped when Ryland himself placed one of his large hands on Wyn's shoulder to get her attention.

"I think I can take it from here," Ryland said softly, dismissing Wyn with his sly smile.

Wyn seemed caught in headlights for a minute; I could tell when her brain clicked back into action and she slinked back to her rock without a word.

Ryland turned his gorgeous stare on me, and I felt my blood melt into my toes. It must have shown on my face because he smiled at my reaction, his straight white teeth glimmering in the firelight.

Just a friend, just a friend...

"Do you want to do this?" Ryland asked me, his voice soft.

"No," I said, "but, Wyn will never let me live it down if I don't."

"You know we have done some crazy things, and you choose to get scared over jumping over a fire?"

"Yep."

"Breaking into an abandoned hospital?"

"Not terrifying," I said. We had done that last year; even got chased out of the building by a decrepit security officer.

"Cliff diving?"

"Not terrifying." It didn't miss my notice that he was moving closer with each question.

"Driving a car at ten?"

"Nope."

"But jumping over a fire?" He reached out and grabbed both my hands, intertwining our fingers. Even with the size difference in our hands, holding onto him like this was still comfortable.

"I'm going to get burned." That sounded way whinier than I intended.

"I'll do it with you then." Ryland dropped one of my hands and turned me toward the flames; they swirled and flickered only about three feet above the wood and sticks.

I was being a baby.

"Do you remember the first time we raced up the trees?" Ryland asked me, his thumb tracing comfortable circles onto the back of my hand.

"The time you beat me?"

"Yeah. You were so scared. I had to prompt you to climb all the way up and then coax you all the way down while you cried."

"I didn't cry," I said. Well, maybe one tear had leaked out at the time, but it still didn't count as crying.

"The point is, after you got your feet back down on the ground, you realized how much you loved it. I haven't been able to beat you since."

I looked into his face for much longer than necessary. The firelight flickered in his dark hair and against his tanned skin, casting the light into weird mesmerizing shadows. He reached up to trace his fingertip along the chain of his necklace that hung around my neck, sending a pleasant shiver over me that caused him to smile.

"I'll jump with you," he whispered down to me.

I turned from him to look at the fire and tried to convince myself I was being stupid. Ryland's thumb continued to caress wide circles on my hand. His hand began to radiate the gentle heat that I was so familiar with; it filled me, traveling up my arm and through my body until I was filled with warmth that made me feel both comfortable and confident. Ryland's smiling eyes met mine as I looked up at him.

"One," his silky voice smooth and even, "two, three."

Our feet took off running in succession, his pace slower so as not to surpass me. As we reached the fire pit, we both took off in a flying leap and I closed my eyes. My heart fluttered as the air moved past me. For a fleeting moment, I felt like I was flying. I wanted the feeling to last forever.

My feet made contact with the hard-packed dirt and I stumbled a bit on the landing. Ryland righted me, placing his hands on my arms to steady me.

"You okay?"

"Yeah," I responded in a hyper voice.

"See? It's easier than you thought it was." He smiled at me before planting a swift kiss on my forehead and walking away toward Wyn. "And, that's how it's done."

I had a momentary flash of frustration at being used as a pawn between them, but the irritation dwindled as the warmth from

Ryland's kiss spread over me.

We left soon after that, leaving large amounts of dirt on the fire to extinguish it. We tromped through the forest in anything but silence. Wyn and Ryland jumped and pranced through the forest, singing various Styx songs I had never heard before. Their loud, out-of-key voices echoed off the trees, making it sound like the forest was filled with a cheap Styx cover band. They kept rushing up to me at different times, grabbing my hands in a desperate attempt to get me to sing along. Their bad singing had me in stitches, and it was all I could do to tromp through the underbrush without falling on my face.

We broke through the tree line to the side of the highway where Ryland had parked his Lotus. The alarm twittered in welcome as Ry approached it and inspected every inch for scratches or a break-in. I smiled as he caressed the hood in grateful appreciation at finding nothing. His affection for his car was a fine, debatable line between uncomfortable obsession and a deep love. Ryland seemed to read my mind and glared at me, his falsely affronted look deepening my chuckle into a laugh.

We all piled in, Wyn stretching herself horizontally on the storage shelf that Ryland liked to pretend was a seat. Ryland sped down the mountain doing at least ten over the speed limit. He put on an oldies station, in obvious tribute to their romp in the woods, and Wyn lay back to text on her cell phone again. I still wasn't sure what to say to Ryland yet, so I turned my head to look out the window, letting the song about some horse in the desert wash over me.

Ryland drummed his fingers to the music as he whispered the lyrics to the song. I fought the temptation to look at him; any conversation we could have would be forced with Wyn in the back seat anyway. Ryland had been acting out of the ordinary all night, and I don't think it was just because Wyn was here either.

He had always wanted to grow up and be just like his father; no matter how much the man had hurt him or dictated to him. It was always his greatest ambition to grow up and make his father proud. They butted heads and fought, but Ry had always sought his approval, except when it came to me. To have him say that he wanted no part of it made me wonder what had happened between them. I desperately hoped I didn't have anything to do with it; I didn't know if I wanted to be responsible for his throwing his life away, and severing his relationship with his father.

Of course, the first odd comment he had made had been back at the school. I still wasn't quite sure what he had meant, saying that I was more important than his father's rules. I could take a wild guess and make the assumption my heart wanted me to, but that was foolish. I had a sinking sensation that all of his revelations tonight were connected somehow. Part of me couldn't wait until Saturday night to find out what was going on with him. I needed to make sure everything was okay.

Before I knew it, we were winding down the canyon into the suburb where Wyn and I lived. I glanced up from the blackness of the window to look at the lights, their twinkling and shining dots looking like a million stars that had fallen from the sky.

Ryland reached out, grabbed my hand and squeezed, the action pulling me away from the lights. His eyes had a million questions behind them, a million thoughts, and a million words. I was lost in them, trying to figure out what he wanted to say to me.

He turned back to the road, his hand staying around mine, keeping them both in my lap. I knew why he was doing this; I couldn't say anything to him with Wyn here. I couldn't get my questions answered. I couldn't tell him what I wanted to say.

Before I could stop myself, my fingertips had moved forward to trace the lines of our intertwined hands. My touch shocked him and he shivered, giving me a knowing glance. I looked away from him and down to continue running my fingertips over his skin.

"So, Wyn, where to?"

I looked up to Ryland as his loud voice boomed through the quiet car. My mind froze in place. I hadn't thought about the time between Wyn's house and my own. I was doomed. Luckily, Wyn came to my rescue.

"My brother is picking me up at Joclyn's place," she said, her eyes never leaving her phone.

I saw Ryland's shoulders drop, while my heart eased just a bit. I wasn't ready to talk yet.

Ryland squeezed my hand, conveying some form of sorrow that I wasn't sure I reciprocated. In just a few minutes, he pulled into one of the few empty stalls at my apartment building. I looked up to the third floor where the obvious flicker of a television lit up the windows to my apartment. Ryland reluctantly let go of my hand as I exited so Wyn could climb out behind me.

"I'll see you tomorrow?" Ryland asked. Suddenly, I was relieved I had already made plans.

"Actually, I'll be at Wyn's house all night." My heart almost broke as his face fell.

I took off his hoodie and handed it back to him.

"What's this for?" he asked.

"My mom won't let me come over Saturday night if I walk in wearing a hoodie."

Ryland smiled in understanding as he took the jacket from my hands.

"Then, I will see you tomorrow morning." He smiled before bidding Wyn goodbye and sped off, leaving us staring after him.

Moments after he drove away, Wyn's brother pulled up in a sleek black Mazda, his body stiff and tough, as if willing himself to only look straight ahead and not toward us.

"I changed my mind," Wyn said as she climbed into the car.

"What?" I asked.

"He's not your boyfriend; he's your true love." She smiled before Ilyan drove off, her door not even closed all the way.

All I could do was look after her, knowing full well my heart was beating erratically in my chest.

CHAPTER
12

*N*IGHT OF THE LIVING VAMPIRE turned out to be just as horrible and sucky as promised. It was full of teenage humor that mocked the vampire craze with a nice splattering of cheesy gore thrown in. Wyn and I sat on the long couch in her living room with a bowl of popcorn in between us, while Ilyan occupied the overstuffed lounge chair. He was trying very hard not to laugh at the stupid jokes and dirty humor, but every once in a while a laugh escaped anyway, which sent me into further pelts of laughter, while Wyn chose to glare at both of us.

I pulled my hands into Ryland's bright blue hoodie that he had dropped off at school for me that morning and sank into the couch to watch the final fight scene of the movie. The lead vampire was running across a clearing after some girl he thought he was in love with; but instead, he decided she would make a better lunch. The whole thing was so over-the-top, it was ridiculous.

"Last minute, he decides not to eat her because he loves her, and they run away from the vampire horde together to live happily ever after." Ilyan's voice was bland, his accent rolling off his tongue.

"Ilyan!" Wyn shrieked, her hands going in the air. "You're ruining it."

"How am I ruining it? These things are so predictable. Besides, don't you want them to end up together?"

"Well, yes. But, I wanted to discover that for myself!"

Ilyan just sighed at his little sister.

"Joclyn," Wyn whined at me, "don't you agree?"

"I'm sorry, Wyn, but it is pretty predictable."

Wyn huffed, folded her arms and faced the television just as the vampire took the human girl in his arms and proclaimed his love for her. Wyn just pouted and huffed again.

"This should be romantic, but you guys totally ruined it for me."

Ilyan and I laughed together, drowning out the vampire's declaration of love. Wyn huffed more and rewound it so we had to sit through the whole ending over again.

"I'm going to go order some Chinese food," Ilyan grumbled as he headed for the kitchen. Part of me was jealous he had an excuse to get away from the mush I had to endure.

Wyn had her hands clasped together as she leaned forward, her face glossed over. I sighed as the credits finally began to roll again, and Wyn leaned back with a tear-streaked face.

Oh, bother.

"Wasn't that so beautiful?"

"Not really."

She looked at me like I had skinned her cat.

"But, I don't get into this stuff, Wyn," I amended to make her feel a bit better.

"But it was funny, and scary and gory, and romantic. It had something for everyone!"

I chose not to reply to her; the whole movie was just silly.

"What kind of movies do you like then?" she asked in slight frustration.

"Sci-fi, super-hero, action and spy movies," I rattled off, knowing full well I had just listed all of Ryland's favorites. If she had asked me what my favorite video game was however, I could have spouted off half-a-dozen racing games that I knew I enjoyed on my own. Ryland didn't like to lose.

"Super-heroes?" she said.

"Yes! They are brave and fight bad guys, and tend to look very nice," I said, fighting the blush that was rising to my cheeks.

"A woman after my own heart," Ilyan said as he fell back into his chair. "Which one is your favorite? I'm a Superman fan, personally."

"Iron Man."

"Really? I wouldn't have pegged you for a Robert Downey, Junior fan, or is it the comic books you prefer."

"Ugh. You don't read comic books, do you?" Wyn grumbled, sounding disgusted, but a smile still managed to creep onto her face.

"No," I said. Although Ryland had quite a collection, I had never touched them. "And, I don't think it's a Robert Downey, Junior thing. I think it's just the fact that he takes something difficult and something that could destroy him, and makes it into something amazing."

Ilyan looked at me with something akin to reverence, while Wyn stared me down with a knowing glance.

"It doesn't have to define you, you know."

I flushed at Wyn's comment, looking from brother to sister in panic. She had promised she wouldn't talk about the mark again. Luckily, Ilyan looked confused and had no idea what Wyn was referring to.

"Wyn," I begged, my heart thudding, "please don't."

Wyn huffed and sat back on the couch.

"Do I even want to ask?" Ilyan said.

"No." I buried my head in the sleeves of Ryland's sweater. Thankfully, the doorbell rang and Ilyan left to get the Chinese food.

"Wyn," I rounded on her the second Ilyan's footsteps left the room, "please don't bring this up. You promised."

"I don't know what you're talking about," she said stubbornly, spinning her plastic bracelets.

"Kung pow beef, anyone?" Ilyan said, handing out white containers.

I opened my box of Mongolian Beef and dug in; it smelled and tasted so good.

Wyn kept switching from staring at me to eating her food. Ilyan looked between us before flipping on another movie. I laughed out loud when he turned on *Iron Man 2*. Ilyan winked at me before turning back to his food.

"Ugh, really, Ilyan? You're going to make me sit through this?" Wyn whined.

"Well, we could talk, but you seemed quite content to be angry and stare off into space."

Wyn glared at him and went back to her food.

"I apologize for my sister," Ilyan began with an oddly regal air. "She can be quite stubborn at times."

Wyn sighed deeper at him. I laughed at her; she seemed irritated by him, and that alone was quite entertaining.

"So, Ilyan. Where do you get your accent from?"

He raised an eyebrow at me in obvious confusion.

"Seeing as Wyn doesn't have one... It's just odd. That's all."

"Oh!" Ilyan chimed, realization dawning on his face. "I lived in Prague for quite a few years before our father died. I left so I could help raise my sister." While he didn't sound sad because of the situation, there was something else in his voice that made the entire thing sound practiced.

"Wow. Prague. That must have been amazing."

Ilyan opened his mouth to respond, but Wyn's sharp tongue cut him off. "Don't let him fool you. It was all party-party, very little work."

"Work?" I questioned. "You must be quite a bit older than Wyn to have lived and worked there." I thought I had stated something obvious, but Wyn giggled like I had given a lead-in to some inside joke.

"Not really," Wyn provided. "His mother still lives there. Our dad just got around a lot."

"I was born in Prague in the 80s."

"So, still too old for you," Wyn taunted.

My head snapped to Ilyan who winked at me again.

"Oh! I didn't mean it like that!" I said, embarrassment creeping into my face.

"Neither did I, Joclyn," Ilyan said. "Don't worry so much."

I ducked back down to my Mongolian beef and tried to focus on the movie. Even though I had seen it a million times, it was still one of my favorites.

"You need to be nice to her, Ilyan; she's my friend, and if you scare her away, I'll never forgive you."

"Fine, fine," he said "Ne že by na tom záleželo, stejně bude za chvíli bydlet s námi." The words fell off his tongue like diamonds and pearls. I looked over at him, taken by the beautiful sound. It seemed familiar in my ears, even though I had no idea what language it was.

"Ilyan," Wyn pleaded.

Ilyan stood before walking down the hall to the bathroom.

"What language was that?"

"Czech; it's his home language."

"It's beautiful," I sighed. "Do you understand it?"

"Enough to understand when he's being rude," Wyn said.

I smiled and went back to the movie, sad that my food was

almost gone. I would have to ask where they got this from; it was delicious.

Ilyan returned a moment later, and I excused myself to the bathroom. The sun had gone down all the way now, and the first stars were beginning to twinkle from behind the frosted glass in the bathroom window. I sat down and grabbed the cell phone next to me without thinking. It wasn't until I opened it that I realized it wasn't mine.

The phone flicked to a text conversation. The name "Wynifred" covered the top of the screen above the thought bubbles of the conversation.

I think we are wrong about him
What do you mean?
Well, he says he wants nothing to do
with it, but it's more than that. He uses
kouzlo on her all the time to calm
her, help her, keep her safe. What
I thought was her is really him; it's
the residual that he leaves behind to
help her.
Are you sure?
100%
Hovno, tohle se Ovailia nebude líbit
Don't swear.
Respect, Wynifred
Sorry, My Lord.

I looked at the last bit of conversation; it just didn't make sense. *My Lord?* And who were they talking about? The whole thing was too much like something out of a Bourne movie. Besides, they didn't seem the types to be involved in some sort of role-playing game. I reluctantly looked away from the screen at a soft knock on the door.

"Joclyn," Ilyan spoke through the bathroom door, "I left my phone in there. Can you bring it out with you please?"

"Uh... yeah..." I answered, washing my hands before opening the door to see him standing against the door frame. His long, blonde hair hung straight and sleek around his face, his blue eyes sparkling. I was once again hit with the familiarity of them, like I had seen that exact color somewhere else.

"Everything go okay in there?" he asked, hand outstretched.

"Gross, Ilyan," I chided and placed the phone in his hand.

"Thanks." He flipped the phone open to look at the screen before turning back to me with a smirk.

A smirk like that would usually excite me and send my stomach swooping, but then again, a smirk like that was usually accompanied by Ryland. Coming from Ilyan, it made me curious; I felt like I needed to get to know him better. I shook the thought from my mind.

Ilyan crossed his arms over his chest as he continued to stare into me. I couldn't help but notice how nice his pastel dress shirt fit against him. He had a nice frame and the fabric clung to him in the right places. I could feel a blush rising to my cheeks, so I ducked my head to look at my shoes, unsurprised to see Ilyan sporting another pair of ripped, designer jeans. He must like the style.

"Do I need to leave you and your shoes alone?" Ilyan asked with a deep chuckle.

"No, I'm fine," I retorted, my head snapping up to meet his gaze.

"Well then, are you ready to go home? It's almost ten and I don't want you to get in trouble with your mom." He continued to lean against the door frame, trapping me in the bathroom.

"Yeah, I guess I better."

"Good, I'll go get my car," he said before jogging down the hall.

"Your brother is odd," I announced as I sat down beside Wyn.

"He's an idiot; don't let him fool you." She continued to bird peck at her food, not looking at me.

"Hey, Wyn," I ventured. I hoped this didn't give my spying away. "What does kouzlo mean?"

Her head snapped up in alarm, and her food almost slipped out of her hand. So much for being discreet.

"Where did you hear that word?"

I exhaled. Probably better to lie, even though Ilyan would give me away eventually.

"Just something Ilyan said to me in the hall."

She watched me, and I recognized the same look in her that I often had myself when I was talking about my dad. She was deciding how much of the truth to tell me.

"It's Czech," she said. "It means charm."

I guess that made sense. *He was using his charm on her all the time*; it fit anyway.

"Oh, that makes sense."

"What did he say to you?" Wyn asked, that same alarm lacing her voice.

"It's nothing. It was just an odd word, so I was wondering what it meant..." That seemed to pacify her, so I left it at that. Still. I knew that face; it gave me the nagging sensation that she wasn't being entirely truthful.

The sooner I got home and to a search engine, the better.

CHAPTER 13

I HAD STAYED UP WAY too late last night trying to find the translation for "kouzlo" on the internet. The closest thing I found for a long time was "koza" which meant "goat". Why someone would give someone a goat to protect them, I didn't know. I finally found the translation I was looking for, and it did say that "kouzlo" meant "charm", but I still felt like Wyn was keeping something from me. After all, why would she have that reaction to the word charm?

Due to my prolonged internet searching, I was nowhere near ready when my mom burst into my bedroom the next morning, fully dressed, breakfast in hand, ready for our full day of shopping. She set the breakfast down and danced out of the room, saying she would wait for me in the living room.

I ate my breakfast—Fruit Loops and toast—as I tried to wake up. I had finally gotten to sleep at three a.m., and now my mom had me up at ten. Seven hours should have been enough, but I still felt like I was dragging.

I set my breakfast on the kitchen counter across from the

bathroom, as I made my way to a nice, warm shower. The hot water did the trick, and after a few minutes my body felt alive and energetic.

I dressed in my red, birthday shirt and my only pair of jeans that weren't ripped before making my way to the mirror to figure out something to do with my hair. I slipped Ryland's necklace over my head and slid it into its normal place under my shirt.

I was reaching for my hairbrush when my eyes fell on the bright, purple bead. It looked so innocent just lying there on my dresser. I stared at it as something clicked in my mind. Kouzlo. Hadn't my father used that word in his letter?

I whipped around to look at the small wastebasket next to my dresser and cringed to see it empty, the letter long gone. My life was turning me into a lunatic. Crazy father, hopeless crushes, and bizarre foreign friends; no wonder I was losing it. I had made something out of nothing. I grabbed the bead and shoved it into my pocket before pulling my hair up in a half-ponytail, making sure to leave enough hair down to fall over my ears and cover the mark.

I blotted on some lip gloss, blush and a little bit too much eye shadow before leaving the bedroom and declaring myself ready. My mom turned off the TV and turned to face me. She brought her hand to her mouth, her eyes glossing over. Great, she was going to be crying all day.

"Mom," I said. I already felt out of place, and I didn't need to be cried over.

"Oh, honey," she said, "you are so pretty."

Her arms encompassed me in a big, motherly hug. I could feel her body shake just a little bit as she leaked out tears of joy. I returned the hug, my arms hanging awkwardly on her back.

"Thank you," she whispered in my ear before pushing me away from her. "Forgive your blubbering mom, will you? I'm just a little bit excited to show off my beautiful daughter." She smiled before grabbing my hand and dragging me out the door.

We drove straight to the biggest mall in the city and wandered first into one of the few main department stores, much to my disappointment; I always enjoyed the smaller boutiques more. She led me straight to the misses department and began loading me up with graphic t-shirts and peasant tops. It was then that I realized what this trip was. I had been trapped in Dress-Up-Your-Daughter Day. I groaned, but hoped that I could finagle at least one pair of jeans out of her.

After I came out in my first shirt, I began to wonder if my mom was going to be able to turn off the waterworks at all today. She gushed at me in a bright, blue t-shirt emblazoned with Hello Kitty in camo gear on the front. Not the shirt that would be one to induce tears. I ran back into the dressing room and ripped the shirt off. It was cute, but I would never forget her crying over Hello Kitty-Goes-Army.

"Mom," I begged from behind the door, "you can't cry over everything I put on, please?"

"I know," her sniffles breaking her voice a bit. "It's just... I have always waited for this day..."

"Mom..." I pleaded.

"I know. I'm sorry."

I tried to ignore her as I picked out my next shirt. I could hear her rummaging through her purse in the search for tissues.

"Oh! I almost forgot; Ryland sent this for you." Her hand appeared above the door, holding a small envelope.

I finished putting on an embellished tank top before reaching up to take the envelope from her. I ripped it open, trying to ignore the flip of my insides. A VISA gift card was inside with a small slip of heavy-weight paper rested against it. The paper that the card was attached to announced that there was an available balance of one thousand dollars. Leave it to Ry.

Please, ignore that this is a large amount of money.
I want to spoil you. Buy yourself a pair of pants (or two!) and
at least one hoodie.
See you tonight ♥

I shouldn't have smiled, but I did anyway; I couldn't help it. As a result, I exited the dressing room grinning like a madman. My mom took that to mean that I liked the shirt, and I just let her think that. It was a nice shirt, and I wasn't in the mood for a "stay away from Ryland" lecture.

I was pushed from dressing room to dressing room as my mom shoved shirts, pants and even skirts and dresses in my direction. I took it all in stride; what else could I do? She was so happy, and seeing her smile was addicting. I paid for most of our purchases with Ryland's card, ignoring my mom's prying to find out how much he had given me; probably the equivalent of a week's salary, but I wasn't going to tell her that. She would freak out.

We came out of the last store before our lunch break, laden with bags of shirts, dresses, skirts, pants and jewelry. I had purchased more pants than I had ever owned before. Mom made out with more than enough to compliment her stingy wardrobe, and I had even convinced her to buy shoes that didn't have non-slip soles.

We sat down to food court pizza and soda, setting all the bags to the side of us.

"How's school?" Mom barraged into her monthly question-and-answer session. One of the joys of having a mother who worked so often that I never saw her was every once in a while she would start in on the standard twenty questions. It drove me crazy.

"Fine," I said.

"Did anyone say anything when you showed up without a sweater on?" She was eager, making me feel bad for deceiving her.

"Not really. I got looked at a bit more than usual, but nothing big."

"Really?" she asked. "Any of them cute guys?"

"No, Mom. This isn't a good thing. I don't like being looked at; it makes me uncomfortable." I wanted to shiver at the thought.

"Well, one thing at a time, I suppose. At least we got you out of those hoodies." She smiled; I cringed at the thought of reminding her that the deal was up tonight. I let the thought fall.

"Sooo..."

Since this was going to keep going, I took another bite of pizza.

"Wyn's brother, he's quite the looker."

"Ew, Mom!" I cringed. "He's like ten years older than me or something."

"Really? He didn't look that old."

"Some people are blessed with good genes, I suppose."

"Hmmmm... Well, would it be considered cradle-robbing if I tried to hook up with him?" She grinned, so I knew she was kidding, but the thought still made me sick.

"Gross, Mom. I can't believe you even said that."

"Well, can you blame me? I am a tad bit lonely after all. I could use a—"

"Stop right there, Mom, please. Besides, I thought you were still in love with Dad."

Her face changed, her joyous smile slipping away to make room for an odd scowl. She looked almost, I don't know... mad.

"I am. And speaking of your father, why didn't you tell me that he sent you a letter?"

My face paled and my pizza crust dropped down to my plate. The empty trash can suddenly made sense; my mother never did household chores.

"I didn't want to upset you," I whispered.

"Well, at least I now know why you had such a hard time with it. Magic and cults... I wish your grandparents would have told me. I wish *you* would have told me. Maybe we could have gotten him some help."

"I know."

"I just don't know why you didn't tell me," she scolded again.

"I didn't want to hurt you," I explained.

"Ryland and I were so worried; I think we both could have helped you so much more if you had been honest."

I had been more honest with Ryland than with her, but I wasn't going to tell her that. I just nodded my head in agreement.

"That boy worries about you way too much. You should have heard him—"

"Mom," I cut her off, "why are you and Ry all of a sudden the best of friends?" She looked at me like I was being unreasonable. I didn't wait for her to reply; I just trudged on. "First, you tell me to stay away from him, and now you two are having heart-to-hearts in the kitchen."

"Well, we wouldn't be having heart-to-hearts in the kitchen if you hadn't been avoiding him all week." Her voice was calm and sweet, but her words still cut through me like a knife.

"You told me to!" I could feel myself getting hysterical. "You told me to go make other friends and start cutting Ryland out of my life."

"I was wrong." She spoke so softly I barely heard her.

"What?" I asked.

"I was wrong."

My head spun; my heart stopped beating. Was she saying what I thought she was saying? I didn't even dare to hope. My mind swirled in a steady beat of confusion.

"I don't understand," I admitted.

"It was something Ryland said the other day. I don't know; it just made sense." She paused and I waited. I watched her in eager anticipation as she chewed her pizza.

"Oh, come on, Mom," I whined when I couldn't wait anymore. "Explain, please."

"Okay. He told me he has had to fight his father for everything he has ever wanted, and ever gotten. Nothing has ever been handed to him, with the exception of money, of course. But with all his fighting and bartering, he has never been happy. And he would give up everything just to be happy and live the way he wants to live. It made me realize how wrong I was to dictate your happiness. When I told you to stay away from Ryland, I had your best interest at heart, but I don't think that staying away from him can make you happy." She paused. "I was wrong for that; I apologize. Can you forgive me?"

I nodded.

"But what about Timothy and his threats?" I whispered.

"I just got spooked, Joclyn. He can't do anything to me," she said, leaning forward over the table like she was telling me a secret.

"I guess that's right," I said.

"Besides, if he does fire me, I won't have any trouble finding a job. I've already received about four offers." She laughed and I joined in, although I wasn't laughing at her job hunting success; I laughed at my new opportunities.

I wasn't sure if this made everything easier or more complicated, but right at that moment, I didn't care. I could decide for myself. I could kiss him, he could kiss me, or I could tell him to stay away from me forever. My heart soared away in endless joy. I wanted to run into his arms right at that moment. I wanted every single body-crushing fantasy to come true. At the moment, though, we still had manicures to complete.

I don't think I had talked to my mother so much in my whole life. I told her everything. With the odd permission I had just received, I didn't need to hold anything back. I told her how I felt about Ryland and how he made me feel when I was near him. I sighed as I explained the look he always got when he thought about something difficult. I cringed as I retold the story of the first time I came in contact with Timothy, a story she had never heard before.

I didn't have to lie. I didn't have to hide. My mom listened and laughed and sighed in all the right places. And when my toenails and fingernails were painted a shocking shade of pink and hers a bright yellow, we both began to cry as I thanked her for giving me such a wonderful, entertaining life and for letting me be who I wanted to be. It was a little bit of an odd thing to say, but it felt right, and so I didn't hold back.

Before I knew it, I had texted Ry to announce my arrival, and I sat in the car, waiting for him to make it out of the kitchen door in front of us. I couldn't back out now; the time with Ryland had come—the time I had been half-dreading and half-anticipating. Now, with my mother's blessing, I needed only anticipate. I didn't even care about Edmund and his opinion. There was only one thing for me to work out: was it worth risking a relationship in the possibility of finding true love? As he stepped out of the kitchen door, dark curls hanging low on his smiling face, my answer was clear. Yes. Yes, it was.

CHAPTER
14

RYLAND STEPPED AWAY FROM THE kitchen door and right to the passenger side door. He opened it, letting the evening air and the fragrance of the rose bushes waft into the car. He leaned right in, his body hovering close to mine, so he could talk to my mom.

"Thanks for driving her here, Mrs. D."

"No problem, Ryland. Just make sure to have her home by midnight."

"You have my word. Home by midnight. Not harmed, scratched, or beaten. Perfect condition only." He held his hand up in the Boy Scout salute like he was making a vow to her then moved his head further in, stopping my progress out of the car.

"Oh, and, Mrs. Despain, thanks for everything." Ryland leaned even further into the car and pulled my mom to him, wrapping his arm around her shoulder. Her eyes grew wide before she registered what was happening and returned the hug.

This little moment brought a small, sad smile to my face. I had never met Ryland's mother, and we never talked about her. I had asked him about her once, a year or so after we had met. He had looked at me with this terrified face, threatening tears, so I had changed the subject. Even as we grew older it was something that we never discussed; so, to see him wrap his arms around a mother figure was heart-wrenching.

"Midnight," he repeated before moving out of the car and helping me out.

We both waved good-bye to my mom as she drove off, all of us with big, happy grins plastered to our faces. We watched the taillights disappear before we moved. Ryland grabbed my hand and intertwined our fingers before leading me into the kitchen.

Dinner service had just gotten underway, so the kitchen was a crazed mess of activity. Even though Edmund would be dining alone tonight, he still demanded a full service be presented. Chantal, the cook who swung shifts with my mom, was calling out orders to the hassled staff who barely noticed our trek through the kitchen. We moved through the usual corridors and stairways, but when we were about to burst into the main hall that led to Ryland's room, Ryland stopped and pulled me behind him.

"I need you to do something for me," Ryland began, a mischievous smirk playing around the corners of his lips.

"Okay," I hesitated, curious.

"I need you to climb on my back."

"What?"

"Please, Jos. Timothy has been stalking this hall tonight, and I can move quicker if I carry you."

I nodded at him. Odd request, but, whatever. I moved behind him and placed my hands on his shoulders, unsure as to what to do next.

"Jump," Ryland prompted; so I did, my legs wrapping around his waist.

He moved my legs up a bit, wrapping my body even closer to

his. His hands gripped my thighs as he ran down the hall. The door to his room opened the second we got there and closed behind us as Ryland shoved it shut with his foot. I moved to get down, but Ryland held my knees tighter.

"Wait."

I didn't move. My body stayed frozen on his back, waiting for something to happen, some sign that I could get down. His body tensed for just a moment before relaxing and releasing me. I found my feet, almost falling sideways into the large chaise lounge that sat by his door.

"You okay?" his voice strained as he fought a laugh.

"Yes. What was with that, Ry? You're acting like we're conducting espionage."

"Sometimes I feel like I am."

"Ryland LaRue, double O 4, Super Secret Agent." I put my hands in a gun shape and aimed around his room until I landed my sights on him, only to find him smiling before he turned around.

I could see his intentions, and I was in trouble. I turned and ran toward the closet where the Nerf guns were hidden behind his shoes. I only hoped I was faster than he was. I took a flying leap, dive-bombing into the shopping mall of a closet. I crawled on my belly to the Converse section and threw them to the side to find... nothing.

"What!" I yelled.

A monotonous chuckle sounded right behind me.

I flipped around, backing myself away from Ryland's large figure as he towered over me. It was no use; I had only moved three feet before his big hand wrapped around my ankle, pulling me out of the closet. The carpet rubbed against my back, grabbing my shirt and pulling it up to my bra-line. I tried to move it down, while desperately trying to keep my mark hidden. Why, of all days, did I not cover it with a Band-Aid?

Ryland had already dragged me back into the sitting area. His long legs straddled me as he looked down, his bright, blue eyes blazing.

"Thought you could get away from me, did you?"

"You stole my stock of guns, you menace! You wouldn't shoot a defenseless girl, would you?" I batted my eyelashes at him in a foolish and useless attempt to distract him.

"Your womanly wiles are no match for me," he laughed like a loud monotone villain as he pulled a bright, orange gun from behind his back. I cringed as he soaked me with stream after stream of freezing cold water. I sputtered and fought as he moved to crouch closer to me, his body prohibiting mine from getting away.

"Mercy!" I screeched from behind a curtain of water. "Mercy!"

Ryland chuckled and wiped the water that was dripping from my face with the palm of his hand.

"That was mean, Ry. You moved my guns."

"Yeah, sorry about that." His voice seemed sincere, but he still hovered above me, biting his lip. He stayed there, above me, our eyes locking a bit too long. I felt my heart pulse; I wasn't ready yet.

"Can I get up now?" I asked, pulling my shirt back down to cover my exposed stomach.

"Yeah." Ryland moved away from me. A moment later, one of his white, fluffy towels landed on my face.

I sat up and began to wipe and blot at my face and clothes in an attempt to dry off. I moved my now damp hair around my ear, making sure everything that needed to be covered was.

"Where's the sweater I gave you?" he asked as he fiddled with the large entertainment center.

"I had to leave it in Ilyan's car last night, so my mom wouldn't flip."

Ryland jumped and took a frantic step toward me. The look on his face froze me in place on the floor.

"Who?" he roared.

"Wyn's brother," I said.

Ryland relaxed a bit, but something still seemed off.

"He's a jerk, Ry. Like the epitome of a jerk older brother," I offered him the first explanation I could think of. Even though his reaction didn't fit with the protective crush theory I was going with.

Ryland studied me for a minute, his chest puffed and frozen in what...? Fear? Anger? I couldn't place it. Finally, he turned away from me, back to the entertainment center, and I made my way to the couch where a large chili cheeseburger sat waiting for me on the coffee table.

"Sorry, about that," Ryland said, his back still to me as he slid a DVD into the player. "I thought you were talking about someone else."

"It's okay, Ry. Don't worry about it."

Ryland sat beside me as the movie started, pulling his large burger onto his lap. The title of the movie came up in bloody, red letters, right before scary music kicked in and the camera panned over a lake.

"*The Evil Dead?* How scary is this? You know I don't do scary, Ryland."

"I think it's more like over-the-top scary."

I still looked at him skeptically as some lady from the 70s began to sing a song.

"It's supposed to be funny."

"Okay, but if it gets too scary, we're turning it off."

Ryland nodded at me and went back to the movie.

It was too scary; I didn't even finish my burger. To anyone else, it wouldn't have been that frightening; I was just a chicken. I wasn't even sure what was going on. There was something about a book made out of human skin, and everyone kept turning into demons and trying to attack each other. And there was blood, lots of fake, watery blood. By about halfway through, I ended up plastered next to Ryland, his arm wrapped around me as I kept hiding my face in the collar of his yellow polo shirt.

"It's over," Ryland crooned, his hand rubbing my back.

"That was cruel, Ry. You made me watch the entire thing." I didn't even want to move my head from his chest.

"Well, you didn't ask me to turn it off, either." My head vibrated as a deep chuckle moved through him.

I couldn't give a decent rebuttal. He was right; I hadn't asked him to turn it off. I just sighed and moved closer to him. In all honesty, I was comfortable, and I knew he had planned to watch that stupid movie for this reason. So what if he wasn't the only one who enjoyed it?

The minutes ticked by, but I didn't notice. Ryland's hand continued to trace the lines of my back, his heartbeat steady in my ear. The movie had returned to the menu, the light from the screen casting the room in a stagnant, blue glow.

"Can I ask you something?" I said, his hand still rubbing up and down my spine.

"Mmmhmmm?"

I heard his voice more as a vibration through his chest.

"Did you mean what you said?"

"I say a lot of things," he said, his voice almost a whisper.

"About not wanting to be like your father. About not wanting to run his company?"

He hesitated, and my body tensed. Was that not the right thing to ask him? I heard his heart rate accelerate and went to move away from him, but his strong arms held me in place.

"Yes, I meant it."

"But, you always wanted to be... I mean, you have always tried to be..." My words came out all jumbled. I paused; I wasn't sure how

I wanted to say this.

"Growing up, yes, I always wanted to make him happy. I always wanted to become what he wanted me to be." His fingertips stopped for a minute, tracing the skin at my neck before returning to my spine. My breath caught at the touch of his fingers against my skin; I could almost feel his smile at my reaction.

"What changed?" I asked.

"You have seen my father what... maybe a handful of times?"

I nodded in agreement.

"I see him every day of my life. He is a vicious, ruthless man, who uses people and throws them away, just to get what he wants. He used my mother to give him a son. He uses Timothy to make him powerful. He uses..." He stopped suddenly like he'd caught himself. "I don't want to be anything like him."

"Then what do you want to be?"

"I want to be good; I want to look back on my life and be proud of what I see and what I have done." His hand moved from my back to tangle through my hair, his fingers running down the long strands that fell down my back.

I felt my body tense for just a moment, but put it aside. I shouldn't be worried about a stupid mark right now.

"Well, that shouldn't be too hard. Just do it."

"I wish it was so easy."

"Why can't it be?" Our voices were whispers.

He paused. "I have to leave."

My hand tensed against his chest. *Leave?* What did he mean? Like leave the house, leave the state, leave the family? Where?

"Leave?" I asked in a panic, hoping for some clarification.

"Yes, leave. I don't know where to yet, but it has to be far away."

My heart felt like lead in my chest; a tense, un-beating mass, causing more pain than joy.

"I'm planning to tell him tomorrow. And, to be honest, I am

terrified." He laughed to break the edge in his voice, but his heart rate still hadn't decelerated.

"Why are you so scared?" I reached my hand up and placed my palm on his chest, right over his heart. His heart rate increased again before dropping. Hearing the change made me smile.

"I am afraid of what he will do to me. He has... a temper." His last word ended as if it was not what he had meant to say. The idea of Ryland getting hurt by his father in some way made my skin crawl.

"Then, just stay, Ryland. Don't leave."

"I have to go; it would be worse if I stayed."

I didn't know what to say. His voice was so calm, but the terror behind it was so evident; it made my heart hurt. I wrapped my arms around his torso and pulled him toward me; he responded to my gentle tug, pulling me into him further.

"Will you wait for me?" His breath caught on my hair as he lowered his head to whisper in my ear.

"Wait for you? What do you mean?" I turned my head up to face him, surprised to see his face only millimeters away from mine. My words got caught in my throat.

"Oh, Joclyn," he sighed. "You are the reason I want to be good. The reason I have seen the evil in my father. You make me good. You make me whole." He paused, studying me as his fingers moved over the skin of my cheekbone. "I need to leave; for you, for me." He paused again, his eyes searching deep into mine.

I could have stared into the endless depths of those eyes forever. I could have asked a million questions to dissect the mysteries behind them. He stopped me with three words.

"I love you." He whispered it, his voice weighed down with the deep emotion of the million times he had tried to tell me.

I couldn't move. I couldn't breathe. My heart caught in my chest as his eyes continued to search mine. They were so full of passion, of conviction, of love. I felt tears build beneath my lids as I looked at him; so overwhelmed at what he had just said.

"Oh, Jos. Don't cry, sweetheart." He reached up and wiped away a rogue tear that slowly trailed down my face. His finger trailed up the right side of my jaw, moving toward the mark. My body tensed for just a moment before I cast it away. He had told me he loved me; what did one cursed mark matter?

And then, his finger made contact with the raised mark.

It felt like a thousand volts shot through my body. I gasped in surprise at the sensation, shock whipping through me. My vision went white as the jolt encompassed me, my back arching in surprise or pain; I didn't know which. The electricity had gone as soon as it had come and my vision refocused on Ryland, but he didn't have the same look in his eyes as before.

He was terrified.

His body had tensed around me; his arms tightening as his eyes darted around the room. He stood up, taking my body with him, keeping me plastered against him.

"No," he moaned, and his voice sounded like an agonizing sob.

"No!" His yell of pain and fear echoed around the room as he tilted my head to the right side, his hands jerking my hair aside to reveal the mark.

"No," he repeated, but this time his voice strained into a sob.

He lowered his head to mine and pressed his lips to the brand, a smaller shock moving through me at his touch. He stayed like that, with his rigid arms surrounding me, his tender lips against my mark.

"I'm sorry." My voice was panicked. His reaction was so unexpected and fearful; I felt my body begin to shake.

"How long have you had the mark, Joclyn?" he demanded.

My body froze; my heart dropped. I wanted to kick and scream and hurt something. Why did this mark always have to ruin my life?

"Joclyn!" Ryland yelled in a panic. "How long?" He released my body and moved me away from him, his eyes meeting mine with the terrified look they held earlier.

"Since... since I was five," I whispered, my voice catching.

"You have hid it all this time?" He didn't wait for an answer; he just crushed me to him again. "Oh, Joclyn, sweetheart."

Sweetheart? Wasn't he mad, angry? Wasn't he going to cast me away?

He crushed me to him even further before releasing me, placing me at arm's length away from him. His hands held me in place, leaving me nowhere to look but right at him.

"You're the one. The one they have been looking for. And you were here... No! They have seen it by now."

"Seen it?" I asked, my confusion growing.

"The cameras, Joclyn; they watch me all the time. You have to get out of here."

And there it was. My heart sank to my knees and the tears started flowing.

"Leave? Ryland, why? It's just a mark—it's nothing. Please say it's nothing," I begged him, my hand clenching the front of his shirt in desperation.

"Oh, Joclyn, the mark means everything."

"Why? I don't want it. All it has done is ruin my life! I don't want to leave!" I screamed, my emotions and fear blending together in a boiling pot.

"If you don't go, they will kill you."

Wait. *Kill?* Was he serious? His terror started to seep into me, and as I watched his face, my anger melted into confusion.

"Ryland, what's going on? I don't understand."

Ryland pressed his forehead to mine, his eyes closed in agony.

"I don't know how to make you understand..."

The blue of his eyes pierced right through me as he looked to something beyond me. His eyes darkened with a heavy determination I wasn't aware he possessed. "They are coming."

"Listen very carefully, Joclyn. My father is coming, and if he finds you, he will kill you. I will head them off as long as I can, but you must run." He kept his head pressed against mine as he spoke, his words tumbling over each other.

"Your father?"

"Take my car and go straight to your mother. Take her and go... go to Ilyan."

"Ilyan?" I asked. Why were we talking about Wyn's brother now? What did he have to do with any of this?

"He is tall, has blonde hair and speaks with an accent, correct?"

I could only nod in surprise; how did he know?

"Go to him, show him the mark; he will protect you. I have to... I have to keep you safe, Joclyn. I can't lose you."

"I can't leave you." I knew I couldn't; my body screamed at me not to go.

"If we go together, they will hunt us down like dogs. I need to fight them to give you time to escape."

"Fight?"

"I will find you, Joclyn. I promise. Just go to Ilyan; he will protect you." He moved his eyes away from mine to press his lips against my forehead, the connection spreading his familiar warmth through my body. It spread through me, stretching to my toes; it filled every part of me with a calm determination, my fear vanishing behind it.

He dragged me to the door, his back straight and his muscles flexing. His hand held mine, neither of us willing to let go. He pressed a small key ring into my other hand.

"To my car, to your mom, to Ilyan," he repeated. "Say it."

"To your car, to my mom, to Ilyan." My voice was small and shaky despite my new-found determination.

"Good. And, no matter what you do, do *not* take off the neck-lace."

The door opened before us, without anyone having touched it. I could hear many running feet through the hallways, the sound getting louder as they moved closer. My heart beat faster in its attempt to escape my chest.

"Run, Joclyn," Ryland pleaded. "Don't look back. Run!"

CHAPTER
15

I RAN DOWN THE HALL, a man's voice yelling behind me. His angry shout ricocheted off the ivory colored walls, echoing in my ears. That one shout was followed by what sounded like a hundred others, but I knew that couldn't be right.

"Leave her alone!" Ryland's voice was like a magnet to my heart. It took all of my willpower to not turn around and to just keep running.

"What have you done, son?" Edmund's cold voice was a palpable thing; its mass, its anger, hitting my back with a tangible force.

I ran to the door of the servants' corridors and swung it open, slamming it behind me. I didn't stop to see if it closed. I didn't stop for one last look at Ryland. I just ran. My feet moved forward of their own accord, taking the steps two or three at a time as I fled down a level toward the garage where Ryland's car was parked. I had moved about halfway down the staircase when the whole building rocked under my feet.

I was thrown into the metal hand-railing as an explosion shook the building, the loud booming of who-knows-what resounding around me. I stopped and looked back. My heart begged me to go to him, to save him; but what could I do against all those men? What could I do against explosions? I clenched my fist around the key in my hand, the plastic cover pressing into my skin.

I couldn't go back and help him. I couldn't. I had to do what he asked. "To the car, to my mom, to Ilyan."

I burst through the final door into the large garage and looked among what appeared to be hundreds of cars for the yellow Lotus. I spotted it on the far side of the garage and began to move through the vehicles toward the expensive sports car ahead of me. I had only made it partway through the garage when another explosion rocked the space around me. This one was bigger than the last one. I screamed out in fear as I slammed into a turn-of-the-century Ford; pieces of plaster falling from the low ceiling above me.

I picked up my pace, trying to ignore the constant rumble on the floors above. I made it to the car and threw myself in, starting the engine. It roared to life and the garage door opened in front of me; the sound of the engine, its cue to rise.

I gunned it.

Ryland had taught me to drive this car almost a year ago, but I hated to because I could never keep the speed reasonable; being behind the wheel felt like I was in the middle of a video game. My heart rate sped up even faster as adrenaline added itself to my fear. I tore out of the garage and down the street, the odometer reaching one hundred thirty miles per hour in just the first few seconds.

I caught a glace of Ryland's house as I drove in front of it. The third floor was in flames. I wanted to stare. I wanted to call the police. I wanted to do something. However, Ryland's instructions echoed through my ears; his warning of what his father would do to me. I strengthened my resolve and turned the corner. If I stayed at this speed, I could get home in five minutes. The challenge would be to avoid traffic and the cops.

I struggled to keep my speed high, but once I made it into the city I was faced with traffic lights and other cars. It was maddening to move so slowly. I hit the steering wheel in exasperation as I stopped at a traffic light, again. I screamed my frustrations and fear at the red light just as it turned green and then I zoomed between cars in my eagerness to get home.

Moments later, I pulled up into the no parking zone in front of my apartment building. Out of habit, I looked up to my third floor window and my heart dropped. Even though it was night, my mom was sure to stay up to make sure I got home okay and share a play-by-play of the evening, but the window was dark.

I tore out of the car, leaving the engine on and the door open, to run up the stairs. With each step, the necklace bounced against my skin, its temperature steadily increasing. I reached the third-floor landing and froze; the door to our apartment was wide open. I just stared at the dark expanse of space beyond my apartment door.

Something in the back of my mind told me to turn around and leave, to just go to Ilyan, but I couldn't. The fluttering panic in my heart pulled me forward. I could taste the danger on my tongue. I could hear the voice of reason screaming at me to get away. At the moment though, I could only think of my mother.

I stepped into the apartment and waited for my eyes to adjust to the darkness. Figures and shapes began to emerge from the black that surrounded me. I looked from one out-of-place object in the room to another until my eyes rested on an arm protruding from behind the half-wall that divided the living room from the kitchen. The fingers of the hand curled softly; the bright yellow fingernail polish were all too familiar.

I screamed out in fear and pain as I made my way to her, my knees sliding against the linoleum as I dropped to her side. She lay on the floor of the kitchen, her body pressed against the painted wood cabinets. My hands floated above her, desperate to do something to help her. I could feel the racking sobs of my agony threatening to break through. I grasped for her wrist, trying to remember how to take a pulse. I thought I felt something, but could not be sure that, through my shaking hands and loud sobs, I had found her pulse at all.

"Mom!" I screamed. I could hear my own agony line my cries. "Mom! Answer me. Please be alive." I was still at her side when the door to our apartment slammed shut and two dark figures moved in front of it. I grasped my mother's hand as I turned toward the intruders, my wailing sobs dying down.

"Well, well, well," one of the two spoke with a light, mocking voice. "Is the little half-ling crying over her mortal mother? How disgusting."

"Don't give her any sympathy," the other said; a man whose deep voice made him seem much older than his body led me to believe. "After all, we were the ones who had to watch her in his room year after year."

"And all the while, she plotted to kill the prince."

"We would have done better to kill her as a child."

"If only we had known she hid the mark." The two chattered back and forth as if I wasn't there, their wicked voices making my skin crawl.

"Kill? Kill who? I wasn't going to kill anyone," I gasped, my voice breaking with tears. I clung to my mother's hand, desperate to feel her squeeze back. I needed her to sit up, to tell these wicked men to leave, and to just make everything better. In the deepest portion of my heart though—a part I was trying to ignore—I knew that it would never happen again.

"Oh, don't bother to lie," the man with the deep voice sneered. "We know all about the vile things inside your head." He took a step closer and I crept backward, my mother's fingers slipping from my grasp as my back pressed against the bathroom door.

"Cail," the first man spoke with a touch of boredom to his voice, "just get it over with and kill her. There's no use in playing with her."

"Kill me? I haven't done anything wrong! I don't know what you are talking about," I screamed at him in desperation as he continued to move forward.

I knew, in my heart, it was too late. I had failed Ryland. I had told him I would run, and here I was, trapped and about to die anyway.

"Could it be?" Cail's voice was soft, but I could hear the amusement behind it. "Do you really not know?" He took a step forward, letting the light that filtered in through the window illuminate his face. Cail—the bodyguard from the Rugby game, the one who had accompanied Edmund, the boy who had constantly looked in my direction, the one who had seemed to sense I was there.

His lips twitched as he watched me place the connection. I shrank away from him, lost in the pitch-black hatred of his eyes.

"Recognize me, do you?" he said. "Yes, I could feel someone nearby at the Rugby game. I never would have guessed it was you, though."

"Didn't you say you saw Ilyan nearby? Perhaps she doesn't know anything."

"Yes, and now, he has waited too long to come and collect his precious 'Chosen Child', so I get to kill her." Cail raised his hand to me in what could have been perceived as a gesture of help, but I didn't wait to find out.

I jumped to the side as the door behind me exploded in a shower of splinters. I scrambled across the slick linoleum in an effort to find a hiding place and scooted behind the counters to slam against my mother's limp form. I stayed still until the refrigerator slid across the floor. I scuttled under the kitchen table just as the fridge launched into the counters, causing them to explode in a shower of sparks, pinning my mother's legs underneath it. She didn't even react.

I screamed and spluttered as my breath came in short spurts. I could feel a panic attack coming on as my chest seized. Nothing made sense. Things were exploding around me, my mom lay unconscious on the floor, and two men were trying to kill me.

"The last of the 'Chosen Children', helpless and alone," the first man laughed from the other room.

I whimpered as I watched their feet enter my tiny kitchen, the first man still laughing. The table lifted itself away from me and slammed into the wall where the refrigerator had been only a moment ago. I wailed in terror and backed up to feel my feet come in contact with the wall. I was trapped. I stood, back dragging against the window frame behind me. If I was going to die, I would die standing, not cowering in fear.

"I'm sorry, Ryland; I failed. I didn't make it to Ilyan," I whispered to myself.

As I spoke, I felt a small tug in the pocket of my jeans. I looked down to see the small, purple bead wiggle its way free, and fly up to hover in the air between me and my would-be assassins. Suddenly, a bright light filled the room. The flash blinded me, and when I moved my hand from over my face, the bead lay harmlessly on the ground.

"No!" the men yelled together.

"Ilyan," the first man spat angrily. "Kill her now; he will be here any second."

Cail raised his hand, and I sank against the window, cringing away from him.

I love you, Ryland. I bid him farewell, expecting the blow to come at any moment. Before anything could happen, a comforting warmth began to spread over my body. It felt so close to the warmth I felt when Ryland touched me that I focused on it, happy for the last connection between us. Tears streamed down my face as I watched the man flex his fingers, a bright light forming in the palm of his hand.

Just as the light in his hand became the size of a softball, a burning heat seared into me from the necklace that hung around my neck. I called out in pain as it burned me, but before I could even reach for it, a flame of blazing, white light shot out of it, intercepting the one that the man had just shot at me. They collided in the middle of the kitchen in an explosion that shook the entire apartment complex. The men were thrown back into the kitchen wall just as I was thrown backward out the window.

The glass window shattered around me, the sharp edges cutting into my skin as I plunged through it. I felt the air swoop by me as I was thrown into the cool, night air outside, knowing that below me laid three stories of nothing before the hard asphalt of the alley.

Time slowed down as I fell, tears flying away from my face and into the air above me. I could have counted each star, each cloud. I could have given them names and danced among them. I watched them as my mind caught up to what was happening.

The wind whipped around me, but it wasn't the welcoming sensation I had felt on the tops of buildings or up in the trees. This time, the wind moved through me as it bid me farewell. The night sky watched me as I fell, the twinkling eyes of each star shining, as if to say "I'm sorry." I reached for them in frantic desperation, wishing they could reach out and stop me from the impact that awaited me.

Far too soon, I collided with the asphalt street. The alleyway filled with a resounding crack as my back snapped under the impact. As my body broke, a fire spread through me, burning me from the inside. It seeped and shuddered through me, consuming every part of me. I could feel its burning pain eat away at the nerves and muscles of my legs, igniting my hip bones. My body protested against the pain as my head added its own agony to the fold, the fire spreading into a resounding tension that shattered my skull into a million broken fragments, causing black spots and blobs to dominate my vision.

I opened my mouth to scream, but no sound came out. My mouth opened wider as it strained against the agony that consumed me. The rest of my body stayed still, even though my insides felt like they were writhing, twitching and contorting with the pain. My mouth continued to open in a silent scream as my vision began to fade in and out of blackness.

I could feel my body giving out, and sadly, I didn't mind the thought. The warmth I had felt before, the warmth that reminded me so much of Ryland, continued to move through me, the warm feeling intensifying into a numbing sensation that spread through my body like water. Although I could still feel the pain—the burning agony—I didn't care so much anymore.

Something around my neck pulled me, and I felt my body being dragged across the uneven gravel of the alley, my limp frame shaking and rattling against the ground. My shirt ripped and tore against the rough stones, pieces falling away to reveal skin that I was sure was getting scratched and cut against the sharp gravel.

My vision faded in again as I was dragged into the shelter behind a large dumpster. Something heavy crashed against my feet, the weight twisting my body at an odd angle that I was happy I couldn't feel. I looked around, desperate to see who or what had pulled me into the shadows, but found nothing.

My vision kept threatening to fade out again, but I fought it, desperate to see what was going on around me. The sweet-and-sour smell of garbage filled my nostrils and gave me something else to focus on in the effort to stay conscious.

The steady sound of footsteps on crunching gravel filled the alley, the thudding of heavy feet running along the broken surface of the asphalt vibrating in my head. I listened as the steps got louder, the angry voices that accompanied them becoming real. My head swam with sound and the vibration that I could not ignore; the agony within my head swelling with the new pain. My vision, and now my hearing, continued to fade as I fought against the blackness that was trying so hard to take me.

"He is going to pay for this!"

"...already is, mostly dead anyway..."

"If only... dead... get his car..."

Their voices faded in and out so fast, I could barely make out what the angry men were saying. I watched as two pair of shoes ran past the dumpster, the vibrations beginning to lessen as they moved away from me. My heart relaxed a bit at their departure.

Although they hadn't found me, I was still dying behind a dumpster.

I lay amongst the garbage for who knows how long, my body unable to move, my vision and hearing blacking in and out frequently. I knew I only had a matter of minutes left; I could feel everything giving out in an undeniable finality.

Suddenly, the weight on my feet lifted and I heard a sigh of relief behind me. I couldn't turn to see who it was, but I felt my insides tighten in stress and fear.

The dumpster that lay beside me moved to the other side of the alley, the heavy box making very little noise. I heard the soft crunching of feet move closer to me before carefully torn jeans kneeled down in front of me and a soft hand came to rest on my cheek. My vision gave way as I felt the person's warm hands move underneath my limp body and lift me to a hard chest.

"Don't worry, Silný," a heavily accented voice said. "I've got you."

Ilyan had found me.

CHAPTER
16

I COULD HAVE SWORN I was flying. I could feel the wind whip through my hair, the calm sensation of rising and falling evident as we moved. I could very well have been running, although being held while someone else ran tended to be a jostling experience. What I felt now was smooth and calming, like a gentle rocking.

The wind on my hair ceased as the rocking motion stopped and I felt a subtle drop as Ilyan sat down, lowering me onto his lap. I could feel the slight pressure of his folded legs under my body as he laid me against them. I felt as if my body had been attached to someone else's, and I was only getting brief explanations of what I should be feeling.

"Come back to me now, Silný," Ilyan crooned, his hand smoothing my hair. "I need you to see me."

Although I knew my eyes were open, I still wasn't seeing anything. My vision had blacked out shortly after Ilyan had found me, followed by my consciousness. I had come back to myself only moments before, but my vision still hadn't returned.

Ilyan moved my head gently, placing it in a more comfortable position against his leg, so that I could see him, I assumed. Still, the blackness consumed me. My body continued its attempt to drag me into death, but I didn't take notice of its attempts, thanks to the overwhelming numbness I felt. Perhaps, if I hadn't had the dull wash of pain to focus on, I would have gladly let it take me. I heard Ilyan exhale as he ran his fingers down my neck, tracing the silver chain of my necklace.

"Joclyn," Ilyan whispered reverently. "I need you to focus on my hand. Focus on my hand against your cheek. We have to do something, and it is really going to hurt."

Hurt? How could anything hurt? I felt so numb.

"Brother," he said, and for one fleeting second I was terrified that someone else had found me, but Ilyan's voice was smooth and calm. Who else was here?

"Brother," he repeated, "I have her now; I need you to release her." He paused as if waiting for a response, but none came.

"Listen to me, please," Ilyan pleaded. "I cannot save her if you don't let her go. I will protect her and keep her safe. But please, let her go. Let me save her life and give you the opportunity to save yours." Still he waited, but nothing happened; no one responded to his pleas.

"She is dying, as are you. You must trust me."

I felt my heart go into overdrive. Dying? Of course I knew it was true. In fact, I would have gladly chosen death not more than a few moments ago.

Ilyan waited before exhaling deeply, as if he had received a response.

"Focus on my hand, Joclyn." Ilyan had a panicked edge in his voice that jerked my mind right back to him. "I'm right here."

I couldn't understand why he was so panicked or what was so scary, until I began to feel it. First, Ilyan's concerned face swam into view as my vision returned, his hand plastered against my cheek. Soon after, the numbness began to dissipate. As it moved out of me, the intense pain of before began to come back. I felt it first in the tips of my fingers and toes then it moved up my arms and into my legs. A loud wailing began to fill my ears, the deep melancholy sound seeming to fully embody how I felt. It filled my ears with such sadness and heartbreak, it rattled in my bones. My eyes darted around, desperate to find the owner, but instead only found Ilyan, his lips a hard line.

I was the one making the noise.

It took me a moment to realize what else was leaving my body; the warmth. The warmth which reminded me so much of Ryland was leaving right behind the numbness. It sucked itself away from me, until I felt nothing but pain and loneliness. My mouth opened even further as my agonizing screams mixed with my tears. The pain, combined with the loss, created an emotional tidal wave that was too much for me to handle. I could feel my body begin to shut down.

My screams began to lessen as I let the endless nothingness that had stayed hidden off to the side of my consciousness cover me like a blanket. The blackness wasn't as nice as the numbness I had felt, but it still took the edge off the pain. It seemed to tell me to just give up, and I wanted to, so badly.

"My hand!" Ilyan practically yelled. "Focus on my hand!"

I forced my eyes back to his and tried to move my mind away from the comfortable blackness I had let take over and onto the hand I felt cupping my cheek. My screams decreased as I focused on him, finally coming out in panicked puffs.

A new warmth began to fill me; it radiated out from where Ilyan's hand rested on my cheek and began to fill my entire body. Although it felt the same as the warmth I always felt from Ryland, something was different and drastically wrong. My mind and body began to fight against it.

"Don't fight me, Joclyn," Ilyan pleaded. "You have to let me in."

I didn't know what he was talking about; my heart seized in panic as my cloudy brain tried to grasp hold of understanding.

"Let me in," he whispered.

Could he possibly mean that the warmth was him?

The warmth continued to spread throughout me, followed closely by the numbness I had only recently lost. I welcomed the numbing, glad that the pain was sweeping away into a loose memory. I kept my eyes on Ilyan as the pain faded; desperately wishing I could clutch myself to him and demand answers. I wished I could yell and fight, or simply disappear. Nothing in my body worked properly; nothing moved and no words came.

Ilyan moved his hand away from my legs and produced a cell phone, leaving my limp body to fall like a ribbon over his folded legs. He dialed a number and placed the phone to his ear, all the while his hand never left my cheek.

"Get me Ovailia." There was a pause after he spoke as he waited for Ovailia to take the phone. When she did, his voice transferred into his native language. The words were full of consonants and deep sounds that rolled off his tongue and into the night air.

My mind wandered off at the sounds, my fuzzy brain not able to understand anything that was being said. It was easier to not focus on anything and instead let myself drift off into the nothingness. I wasn't in pain now; it almost seemed like the blackness wanted me even more.

"Stay with me, Joclyn." Ilyan's voice broke off from his foreign chatter, the change in tongue bringing my mind back. "Focus on my hand. Focus on my voice." He stared at me intently while waiting for me to agree.

"Ovailia," he continued into his phone, "we will be returning home within the week. I need to get her body healed enough to travel." He paused as the person on the other side of the line spoke. I felt my heart soar at the talk of healing me. A hospital and a shot of morphine sounded just about right.

"Tell Talon I will keep her safe."

Talon? Wasn't that Wyn's boyfriend?

"No! Everyone needs to stay where they are. It is only going to cause problems if they empty the motel."

"Ovailia," Ilyan snapped, and his accent increased, making his voice difficult to understand. "I 'ave levt zoo in sharge, ind iv zoo canoot keep zings usser constrol for vun veek vifout my prezzanse ve vill haff to reffink zis arrangement. Iz zat clear?"

He snapped the phone shut and huffed angrily. Even through his angry rant, his hand had still stayed softly on my cheek.

"You're lucky you don't have a sister," he said, his accent lessened. I was confused. I thought Wyn was his sister; perhaps this Ovailia was their sister, too, and they just never mentioned her.

I felt an uncomfortable pain seize through my spine, and my body moved involuntarily.

"We have to move." Ilyan stated, looking away from me in expectation. He flipped open his phone again and dialed a number.

"Wynifred?"

Wyn? My heart beat erratically at her name.

"We will be there in about an hour. We are in Sunnyvale."

Sunnyvale? But that was at least a two hour drive. How did we get here?

"I took us here to break the trail, but we cannot stay here long. She is very greatly injured. I need you to draw a bath."

A bath? Wasn't he taking me to the hospital?

He snapped the phone shut and placed it back into his pocket.

"Joclyn? We are going to have to move. I know you probably really want to go to sleep right now, but you can't. Try to focus, all right? Focus on me; focus on my voice. You need to stay awake, for

Ryland."

"Ryland?" My voice came out like a sob; in fact, I was surprised I had even spoken at all.

"Yes, Joclyn, for Ryland. You need to stay awake for him. Can you do that?"

I stared at him intently, hoping my expression would display the yes I felt in my heart.

"Good girl, Silnÿ."

Ilyan shifted his weight and moved my rag doll form into his arms, his hand never once leaving my skin. He moved smoothly, his body rocking and jostling me around with each step he took. This sensation was so much different than before; I could feel every step, every time his foot hit the ground.

The steps and swaying increased significantly before the wind returned and the rough movements stopped. I watched through open eyes as stars, street lights and buildings soared past us, faster than I thought possible, the shining orbs becoming blurs in my line of vision. The wind in my hair relaxed me even further and I felt myself move into the ever-present blackness once again.

No! I needed to stay awake for Ryland... and for me. I would never be sure, but I swear my arm jumped uncontrollably as I tried to force myself out of the comfortable warmth that the blackness provided.

"It's okay, Silnÿ," Ilyan said, his accent rolling out his vowels again.

I did want to believe that, but everything was so confusing. Even in my foggy, hazy mind, I was having trouble understanding what was going on. I couldn't get the images of flying furniture, my aggressive attackers and my mother's body out of my mind. My heart shuddered at the thought of my mother's limp form. It sounded more like I called out to her. Ilyan looked down at me, shocked to see me looking at him.

"Your mother?"

My eyes grew wider.

"I'm sorry, Joclyn. I wish I would have gotten there earlier. I wish I could have saved her." He looked down at me again, and I saw the sympathy hidden in the chasm of his eyes.

My whole world had broken apart in one wild blow. The truth of Ilyan's words was a wrecking ball against my soul. I saw her frozen body in my mind, and I knew he was telling the truth; that she was gone. Even though my brain accepted it, my heart simply wouldn't. It fought and screamed inside my broken body. It begged me to hit and yell, and beg to know that Ilyan was lying. I could almost feel my body jolt as I attempted to act out what I needed to do.

"Calm, Joclyn. I need you to stay still. Try not to think about anything now." Ilyan exhaled sharply. The raw emotions that coursed through me boiled my blood aggressively, causing my body to jump and twitch. I wanted to yell, and cry, and demand answers all at the same time; but in the end, it was just another pain to add to all the others that encompassed me, and the numbness swept it away.

The wind stopped, and I felt Ilyan's hand run comfortingly against the bare skin of my back. The warmth inside me increased and my mind became fuzzy, Ilyan's touch taking everything away.

"I know things are becoming clearer, but you need to relax. We will have time for questions and answers when your body is healed."

The wind came back into my hair again, blowing it across my face. The sensation made me think of my many trips up the canyon with Ryland. I loved to roll the window down all the way and feel the air across my face, smell the scent of the trees, the water, the fresh mountain air; they all had a magic of their own. That's what this reminded me of—magic.

The wind decreased to nothing again as Ilyan's feet hit against something hard and brought us to a stop. I lessened the strain on my eyes and let them fall toward the light in front of us. I recognized the balcony door of Wyn's apartment immediately. The large couch and overstuffed chair sat exactly where they had been only yesterday.

"It's probably best if you don't see Wyn right now." Ilyan's hand covered my face and lowered my eyelids. "It may only upset you more."

I felt him take a step forward and then heard the click of the patio door as it shut and locked us into the apartment. Wyn's frantic steps came up in front of us. I tried desperately to open my eyes, but the lids wouldn't budge.

"Oh! Goodness, please tell me she is alive, Ilyan?" Wyn's voice was panicked and deep, but something else had changed. I could almost detect a hint of an accent, an accent almost identical to Ilyan's. I almost didn't recognize her voice.

"She can hear you, Wynifred; please watch your tones."

"I don't see how that matters anymore, My Lord. Your little cover has been blown wide open."

Ilyan grunted angrily.

My Lord? My mind flashed to the text message. "My Lord" was not a standard nick-name for a brother. And cover? I knew I had missed something, but my fuzzy brain couldn't place anything together properly.

"The bath is drawn," the distorted voice of Wyn continued.

"Seal the door," Ilyan commanded before walking away, his arms still holding me tightly to his chest.

"What happened, Ilyan?" I heard Wyn's strange voice come up from behind.

"I'm not exactly sure. All I know is that Cail and Drummond were trying to kill her." Ilyan's voice sounded like poison.

"Cail?" Wyn asked.

I heard a door open and we moved into a humid room, the air strong with a deep smell of lavender, lilac, sandalwood and mint. Ilyan bent down and laid me on the bathroom floor, the tiles hard and cold against my bare skin and through my torn shirt. He shifted his hand from my back to my face, his hand never losing contact with my skin. Another set of feet entered the room, the impact vibrating the floor.

"Close and seal the door, Wynifred. I don't want anyone to hear her screams."

Screams? What was going on? I tried to pull understanding through my fuzzy mind, but nothing came.

"How did they find out about her mark?"

"I have no idea. But if it wasn't for Ryland saving her life and Jeffery finding us, she would be in much worse condition."

Jeffery? My father?

"It's a miracle she is still alive."

"Ryland? How did he...?" Wyn spluttered.

A strong hand gripped my shirt tightly and gave it one sharp tug. I felt the few strands of fabric that remained un-torn from the alley give way as my top was ripped from me and the shirt cast away.

"That's how," Ilyan sighed, his voice oddly reverent.

I heard Wyn's voice sigh something in Czech I didn't understand.

"You need to be careful with the pants," Ilyan instructed her. "If you jostle her spine too much, it won't heal correctly."

I didn't even have time to think about lying in my underwear on the bathroom floor in front of Ilyan before he spoke.

"I'm sorry, Joclyn. I have to bring the pain back, but it's only for a moment. We will both be right here with you the entire time." Ilyan didn't even give me time to respond; he simply removed his hand from my face and the warmth and numbness disappeared instantly. It wasn't like before when the pain built into a rage; this pain flooded through me in an instant, and I found myself screaming in agony, my immovable body desperately trying to escape the torture I was trapped in.

"Lift her!" Ilyan yelled over my screams.

I screamed louder as their strong hands moved me, sending another violent flame through my whole body. My screams bounced around the tile of the bathroom, trapping us all in the sound.

They lowered me into the tub, the hot water folding over me to envelop my body like a blanket, its touch relieving the pain. The mass of the water was heavier than what water normally felt like, but perhaps it was just my broken body that made it feel that way. My bottom hit the base of the tub with a thud, the impact sending an uncomfortable jolt up my back that made me call out in pain. The water smelled strongly of the flowers I had originally smelled, but something else was mixed in. It almost smelt like an odd combination of burning wood and mint.

"I don't think this is moving fast enough, Ilyan; she is still weakening," Wyn whispered into the silence. "She is going to have to go under."

"I'll go get the drevo." The door opened and shut, leaving silence in the bathroom.

"Joclyn," Wyn's voice was hesitant; I couldn't help but notice that the accent had disappeared. "You'll need to go under the water. It is only for a minute, and Ilyan and I will be right here," she said, hesitating again. "We... we won't let anything happen to you."

The door opened and shut.

"Should we take the necklace off?" Wyn asked, her accent returning.

"No. Perhaps the kouzlo will transfer to him and we can save two lives tonight." He paused and I heard something heavy hit against the side of the tub. "Joclyn? Don't be scared, Silnÿ." His voice was too distant; I focused on it as it echoed around my brain.

I felt his hands pry my mouth open and something large and rough was placed inside. The large mass was coarse and uncomfortable against my tongue, the bitter dirt taste shocking me. I tried desperately to spit it out, but Ilyan's hand stayed tight around my jaw, not allowing it to open again.

"It's okay, Joclyn. It will help you."

My body twitched in panic as I continually tried to force the uncomfortable mass off my tongue. I fought against Ilyan's hand that he held against my jaw, and I fought against the invisible bonds that tied my body, but nothing responded.

What were they doing? Why wasn't I in the hospital? I didn't understand. I tried desperately to piece together what I had been told, what had happened. I knew the answer was right in front of me, but I couldn't see it; I couldn't piece it together.

My eyes snapped open to see the two faces peering over the bath at me. Ilyan looked down with something akin to worry and fear, but it was Wyn who was shocking. At first, she looked the way she always did—chin-length auburn hair and dark eyes—but her features had changed so drastically, she almost didn't look like herself anymore.

Wyn's eyes were darker than normal, but not only in color, the whites of her eyes were almost nonexistent. Her eyes were not the most shocking change; against the side of her face was a dark tattoo that ran from her hair line and disappeared down the side of her neck and under her shirt. The deep black lines swooped and spiked over her skin with jagged edges that were sharp like the barbed tendrils of a wire. My stomach clenched tightly, afraid the wire was going to cut into her fine skin and rip her apart. The marks looked like the swirls and flowers and thorns of a tribal tattoo, but turned so much more sinister almost, as if it were an infection.

She didn't look ashamed or embarrassed as I looked at her, even though I was sure the surprise and confusion was clear on my face. She just looked at me sternly, her jaw set, before she reached forward and shoved me down, holding me under the water.

I panicked and fought against her, but my body couldn't obey my mind. I could only stare at them from under the water as I tried in pointless desperation to move. I opened my mouth to scream, but it wouldn't obey; instead it stayed clamped shut around the wad of dirt that still rested on my tongue. My chest began to burn for want of air, my vision began to darken again. I felt the weight leave my chest as Wyn removed her hand, but it was too late. I willingly drifted into the blackness.

CHAPTER 17

THE LIGHT WAS SO BRIGHT I could see the veins in my eyelids. I looked at the thin, pink skin before opening them, blinking furiously in an attempt to preempt the pain that never came. My body rested against the hard, bright white floor of a huge, white space. There were no doors, windows, or even walls that I could see—only an endless white space.

I lay motionless in the middle of the expanse, searching all around me for something familiar. My eyes stopped on a small stretch of faded black that grew and throbbed off in the distance. Something about the black called to me, just like the blackness that haunted me in my pained body.

I sat up, surprised when my body obeyed my commands. I had been trapped in a pain-filled, motionless prison for so long that part of me was beginning to wonder if I would ever move again. I swung my legs around in front of me, my movement quick as I slipped on fleece pajama pants I had never seen before. I looked down at them curiously, trying to place them, but they weren't familiar at all. As I reached toward the pants, the long sleeve of Ryland's hoodie slipped over my hand. Unknown pajama pants and Ryland's hoodie; what odd things to be wearing in a dream.

I looked at them curiously, trying to think why my subconscious would place me in such odd clothing, and then I remembered Wyn holding me under the water. A flash of her tattooed face was all it took to incite panic in my chest. I gasped involuntarily, my chest heaving.

At my terror, a large comforting hand rested on my back. I turned toward the touch, surprised to see Ryland sitting next to me, his dark curls falling over his forehead. That wasn't right... how could Ryland be here? And, where was I?

My heart skipped a beat at seeing him there, right next to me. He sat still beside me, staring at me; his bright, blue eyes seeking into mine. He wore torn and stained jeans, but his chest was bare, his muscles defined and glistening as if he had just run a mile or two. I thought carefully over what to say, worried my hundreds of questions would topple over themselves in a jumble.

"Am I dead?" I asked, my voice sounding perfectly fine despite the burn in my throat as I spoke.

"No." Ryland's voice was low and comforting.

"Are you dead?"

"Anything but."

"So I am dreaming?"

"No." His answer was confident; it caught me off-guard as the question was mostly rhetorical.

"Then, where are we?" I could hear the desperate panic creeping into my voice.

Ryland leaned forward and moved my hair away from my face, letting his fingertips linger on the skin of my jaw.

"I think it's some form of shared consciousness," he whispered.

"I don't understand." This seemed more like a dream than anything else. It felt like a dream. It looked like a dream. Even through Ryland's confident answer, I still felt like I knew I was dreaming.

"That's all right. I wouldn't expect you to. Everything is so new to you. I wish I could be there to help you through it; you are probably very scared."

"Isn't it new to you?"

"No, Joclyn. I have known about this my entire life." His fingers continued to trail around my face, over the lines of my neck. The touch was warm and comforting; I was having trouble thinking straight.

"This?" I motioned to the white expanse around us.

"No, silly, not white spaces that lead into nothingness." His tone was exactly like Ryland; it was hard to believe that my dreams could be so accurate.

"Then what?"

Ryland exhaled deeply at my question and looked around him for something; or more like he was expecting someone.

"Tell me what happened to you." He moved closer to me, his voice soft. My previous question lay forgotten behind me as my memory of the evening began running through my mind in fast forward.

"I failed you, Ryland." I could feel the tears trying to burst out, my face growing warm as I attempted to restrain them.

Ryland leaned forward and pulled me into his lap, his arms winding their way around me.

"You didn't fail," he whispered into my ear, his lips rubbing against my mark. The touch of his lips against the mark sent a slight shock through me.

"But I went to my house, and my mom was... she was..." My voice caught, unsure if I wanted to face it, unsure if I could accept it. "And things were flying and then there was an explosion and... and I fell out of the window..."

Ryland pulled me to him tighter, my tumble of words instantly ceasing.

"I'm sorry, Joclyn, for everything. I never wanted you to be dragged into any of this. If I had remembered there was a window there, I wouldn't have made the blast quite so strong."

He made the blast? I looked at him, confused, begging him to elaborate; but he only smiled at the look on my face.

"Your back seems to be healing nicely, though." He ran his fingertips up my spine, sending a warm shiver trailing behind.

"Healing? How?"

"The same way you are healing me, Jos." He ran his fingers up my back again, through my hair, over the soft skin of my face. His touch seemed so real, I found myself leaning into the bare skin of his chest, breathing in his smell.

"Everything is so confusing, Ryland," I said. "I don't know what's going on."

"It's all quite simple, isn't it, when you think about it?" The small smile evident in his quiet voice.

I shook my head against him. I didn't know what was simple about explosions and flying and... and... my mother.

"How is it simple, Ryland?"

"Oh, Joclyn, you are so special, and you don't even know it yet." His fingers trailed along my hairline comfortably. "Don't reject what's inside you, sweetheart."

"But—"

"You are powerful, and amazing, and confident. You may be the one..."

"The one to what?" I pulled away from him to look at him, but he only smiled sadly at me before pulling me back into his chest.

"It's nothing," he whispered against my hair, cradling me against him until my body melded into his lap comfortably.

I could hear Ryland's heart beat through his chest, feel his warm breath run along my hair. I wished I could stay there forever, but instead, Ryland's body stiffened underneath mine, his shoulder twitching.

"I have to go." It was almost a growl.

"No." I clung myself to him like a child, desperate for this small sense of normalcy to stay with me.

"I have to." He pulled my face up to look at him, his blue eyes deep and worried. "My father is trying to perform a Vymàzat."

"Veemayzit?"

"Yes, he is trying to get inside my brain, control me. If he finds you here..." He stopped, the pain dripping off his voice. He pulled me away from him, just far enough away to see his face as a whole.

"Stay with Ilyan, Joclyn. The time may soon come that my father breaks in all the way, and when he does, I won't remember you anymore. When that happens, I will only be a danger to you. But just remember that I love you; I will always love you. And locked inside me somewhere, I will always be waiting for you." He spoke in an urgent rush; I could only stare at him.

His head twitched to the side, his face screwing up into a pained expression, like someone was stabbing him. As soon as the pain had come, it went; he grabbed me roughly and held me in place, so I had nowhere to look but at him.

"Promise me, Joclyn!" He twitched again, but his eyes never left mine.

"Promise what?"

"Stay with Ilyan. Remember that I love you." He stood, his whole left side twitching now. He looked at me in agony. "I love you." He held my hand tightly, the last contact we had, but even I could feel that slip away.

"I love you, too," I said, the truth of my words surprising even me. Ryland's face broke into a wide smile that lit up his whole face.

He leaned down, his hand instantly resting on the side of my face. He moved closer and my heart beat faster in anticipation of a kiss. Before he even made it halfway, his whole body twitched, sending him to the ground as he yelled out in pain.

"Ryland!" I moved to his body as he continued to twitch, my hands moving around him uselessly.

His body calmed quickly and without warning. He lay still, curled up on the floor. I tentatively went to place my hand on his shoulder, desperate to know he would be okay, even though it was a dream. My hand stopped halfway to him; it hung in the air as my fingers began to shake in fear. There, on his back, resting on the same shoulder he had wrapped during the Rugby game, was a mark; a small raised brand, almost identical to mine, even down to the dragon shaped squiggles.

"Ryland?" My voice was small. "What is this?" My fingertips touched the mark before pulling themselves away as a jolt spun through our bodies.

Ryland jumped up, his face coming only inches from mine.

"Still alive, are you?" His voice was a hiss and growl, the words dripping with venom and malice.

I jumped away from him. I knew it was Ryland, but nothing about him looked familiar. His eyes were wide and bloodshot, his face screwed up in a wicked grin. His eyes met mine, and I gasped. They were no longer the blue I loved so much, but a deep charcoal, almost a pure black. I stayed frozen to the ground, my mind sluggishly working through the shock to catch up to me.

"Not for long!" Fake Ryland lunged at me, and I leaped to the side, my fleece pants sliding me across the white space around us. My breath came in sharp bursts as my dream changed to a nightmare.

"Ryland?"

He only laughed at me, laughed at my panic. The sound was unlike anything Ryland had ever made before. It was deep and menacing; it ripped through me, sending a shiver of panic skipping through my heart.

Ryland began to twitch again, his body falling to the floor in yet another agonizing scream. He ran his fingers through his hair as he moaned, his white knuckles clawing through his curls. His hand jumped out, so fast I couldn't move my arm away before he grabbed me, holding on to me tightly, making my heart race. Ryland looked up at me. I breathed a little sigh of relief at his eyes, now back to their regular blue. Even through the relief, my heart still beat in fear.

"I have to go." His voice was strained between his deep breaths.

"Ryland?"

"I can't... my father..." He leaned forward, his shoulder and arm twitching more and more.

Ryland reached forward and ran his finger down the side of my face. His face twitched again before he pressed his lips against my forehead.

"Stay with Ilyan. I love you," he whispered against my skin, his lips brushing me softly as he spoke. He leaned into me again, his lips burning into my skin. I closed my eyes at his touch, and when I opened them again, he was gone.

I stared into the white space for a long while, trying to make sense of what was going on. Even though my mind was clear, I couldn't work through the pieces. Long before I was ready, before I had made any semblance of anything that had happened, the gray and black that had stayed at the edge of the white space rushed at me, sucking me into the darkness.

CHAPTER 18

I COULD HEAR THE TV. I heard the voices of some cheesy commercial chatter around me, almost like I was in the studio. I lay still, letting the sound wash over me as I replayed the dream in my mind, my face cringing at the lingering picture of Ryland's contorted face. I shifted my weight out of habit, surprised when my body obeyed my command. Unlike the dream however, the movement triggered a hundred aches and pains. While it didn't feel as bad as the last pain I remembered, it still was far from comfortable.

"Yes, Ovailia, I have felt them a few times, but nothing close as of yet."

At Ilyan's voice, I opened my eyes to a dark room. I lay in a curled position on the long couch, a huge pile of blankets set on top of me. It made my body seem overly large and lumpy.

Ilyan sat on the floor, his back resting against the couch by my knees, looking unfocused at the television directly across from me, the screen dim with some show about crab fishing. I watched it for a minute before Ilyan's voice spoke again, pulling my mind away from the flickering box.

"Her spine hasn't quite fused yet, but it is close. Once that has finished, we will be leaving. You need to keep him there; I will reunite them soon. Besides, I am not in the mood to babysit."

I looked away from Ilyan, feeling awkward for eavesdropping on his phone call.

"Manners, Ovailia, mrävy." Ilyan's voice was so stern it made my hair stand on end. The raised inflection must have awoken someone else in the room, and I heard someone gasp for air near my head. I rotated toward the noise, the movement sending an even sharper jolt of pain through my spine.

Curled up in the big overstuffed chair, Wyn still slept with a blanket over her legs. Part of me wished that the Wyn I had seen before—the Wyn who had pushed me under the water—was just a figment of my imagination. There she sat though, dark tattoos running down the side of her face and arm. Looking at them now, they didn't seem quite as sinister as they had before, but their presence still sent an unpleasant clench through my body.

"Finish setting your trails, and wait for my signal." I heard Ilyan click his phone shut and shift his weight.

I couldn't look away from Wyn. I didn't want to try anyway; my body had begun to hurt and I wasn't sure I could move.

"The marks were a gift from her father and brother when they kicked her out of her home. I believe they had hoped the marks would kill her, but instead, they just linger."

I turned to the voice, shocked to see Ilyan sitting right by my head, his back arched so he could meet me at eye level.

"Broth... er?" I was surprised when my voice cooperated, even though it was almost agony to get that one word out.

"Yes, her brother. Not me, thankfully, but I might as well have been responsible; she was spying for me at the time, after all." His voice sounded so angry and upset, the blame he felt still ravishing

.

through him.

"Broth... brother?" I tried again, desperately hoping Ilyan would understand my meaning and explain more.

"No, Joclyn, I am not her brother, but I am a friend."

I arched my back to get a closer look at Wyn again, the movement sending a violent spasm through my spine. I groaned in pain as it shot through me.

"Why... spy?" My voice strained, the words leaving me gasping, and my throat burning.

"Why was she spying for me?" Ilyan reworded my question, and I nodded my head, letting my back slide back into a more comfortable position.

"It's complicated," he said simply. "Wyn was spying on her father, her brother and their boss for me quite some time ago. She inadvertently saved me from a sticky situation and so I asked her to do me a favor."

"How... marks?" My words crept out, each one hurting.

"Wyn's kind—the Trpaslík—are a vicious race who punish traitors cruelly."

I opened my mouth to question further, but he cut me off.

"I would really prefer that you not worry about all this right now. You need to heal, and the faster the better." He must be irritated again; his accent was getting stronger and causing his consonants to turn into Zs and Vs.

"Please?" I wasn't begging. The words were coming a bit easier now, my voice stronger and laced with irritation.

"You're going to want to keep your back straight if you want it to heal properly." He spoke simply as he smoothly changed the subject, like healing on a couch was the obvious thing to do.

"Hos... hospital," I whispered, the rough movements sending sharp pains through me.

"I can't take you to a hospital, Joclyn," Ilyan answered my

mostly unasked question softly. "They will be searching for you at hospitals."

His hands wound under the pile of blankets I had been placed under, pushing and pulling my body to straighten my back and bringing my head back to look at him. I called out as he moved me, each shift in weight sending pain shooting through my body.

"Besides," he continued, "I can heal you much quicker." He winked at me mischievously as he finished aligning my back, causing the pain to stop. He kept his palms flat against the skin on my back, sending that familiar warmth through me.

"What...?" I tried again, frustrated when I could still only manage one agonizing word at a time.

"What am I doing?"

I nodded my head, pain shooting down my back.

"Healing you."

My eyes must have bugged out of my head. That one statement had opened up a floodgate, and every unanswered question and unexplainable occurrence over the past few days begged to be expanded upon. Everything flashed before my mind in quick succession as they tried to fit themselves together; my mind flashing like a badly animated short.

"How?" I breathed out, not sure if I was asking Ilyan or my mind the question. Luckily, Ilyan answered.

"Your father insisted that he told you."

My head snapped to him, another jolt running down my spine; I ignored it.

"He promised me he would find a way to explain it all when he gave you the birthstone. I assumed he did, but he seems to have disappeared since then."

I should have cared more that my father was missing, and I probably would have if we had had any sort of relationship. However, my mind couldn't see beyond that one piece of information that fit everything together: the objects flying around my kitchen, the sensation of flying, surviving a broken back and who knew what else, even Ilyan healing me with his hands. My father wasn't crazy. He wasn't deranged. He had told the truth.

"Magic," I said, more to myself than anyone else.

Ilyan nodded solemnly before replying. "I am sorry to have to tell you this way. I had hoped we would be able to gain your trust a bit more before telling you all that was going on."

"Magic," I repeated strongly. My teeth clenched in surprise and anger as my stomach spun in a threatening manner. The warmth of Ilyan's hands grew and the wave of nausea subsided.

"Yes, Joclyn. Magic."

I didn't know how to react. Should I be relieved, excited, frightened? Instead, everything absorbed into me, and my breath picked up in short, staccato puffs as I tried to cope with the onslaught.

"I wish I could make this easier on you. You are probably very scared."

Ryland had said that in my dream, but he also said he knew. I felt my panic surge as my need for answers grew.

"Calm, please, Silný," Ilyan whispered. The warmth increased again and I found myself falling asleep, whether I wanted to or not. "If you can stay calm, I will explain a bit to you right now. Can you do that?"

I wasn't sure, but I wanted to try. As the tired feeling in my body began to subside, I tried to keep myself calm, and my breathing even. Ilyan watched me, his hands still resting on my skin.

"The mark on your skin," he began, his voice calm and even, "is called a kiss. Although it really isn't a kiss at all, it's more like a poisonous bite. When the kiss—or bite—was given, a strong poison entered your bloodstream and changed you. It took the latent powers that you already had and enhanced them. We call those who receive this kiss, a Chosen Child.

"Now, not everyone has to go through this change. I, for example, was born with my magic. It is as natural to me as breathing. You, however, as with all humans who are lucky enough to receive a kiss, have to endure the change to bring the magic into your body."

"Not human?"

"No, Joclyn, I am not human. Although I do not differ much from your kind, I am part of a race known as the Skřítek. We are an ancient people who were once very plentiful; now there are only a handful of us left, only about four hundred."

"Scree..." I tried to say the word, but my tongue knotted around it. I needed to know more; my mind couldn't stop placing him inside a spaceship, but that didn't seem right. After all, he had told me he had been born in Prague, but now I was wondering if he had told the truth at all.

"Yes, Joclyn. Skřítek. Think of me as the gatekeeper for the birthplace of magic—the well in the earth where the powers within you originated."

I wanted to nod, but couldn't. Instead, I just looked at him, wide-eyed.

"As you know, the change a human must endure as they become one of the Chosen is very painful. The longer the pain, the longer the recovery, the more powerful is the magic." He paused and I could tell he was gauging how I was handling everything he was telling me. I tried to keep a straight face, even though I was still panicking just a bit.

Part of me still didn't want to believe him. If I had been able to string more than a few words together, I would have been rebutting him at every turn. As much as I wanted to argue, as much as I didn't want to believe him, I still couldn't get the images of the balls of light colliding in my kitchen, the flying refrigerator, or the sensation of flying out of my mind.

"How long?" My throat burned again as I spoke, my vocal chords cutting off before I could complete my question.

"Your father says you were in the hospital for about six months, which is one of the longest I have heard of."

My heart beat uncontrollably. The longest? What was I, some ultra-powerful freak? Ilyan shushed me quietly as his thumb traced circles in the skin on my back. I wished I could shy away from the touch. It was something Ryland would do.

"Now, this could mean nothing. Most children focus and begin to use their powers days after awakening. It has been a bit longer than that for you," he said darkly. I just stared at him.

"A kiss," Ilyan continued, "is given by a Vilỳ to human children who already have a natural ability. A Vilỳ is a dark creature that most closely resembles a small, winged dinosaur; although their faces are more human. They are brightly colored and almost seem to glow, making them easy to find."

The flash of blue, the glitter of wings; I remembered seeing both before the pain had hit. I had seen the little creature right before he bit me. I hadn't been paying close enough attention; I didn't know what I was seeing. If I had known what it was, would I have recognized it? Would it made anything easier? I doubt it.

"Vilỳs have not been seen in more than two hundred years, which is why, when your father found me in Prague, we came right to you. We would have taken you with us right then, grabbed your mother and ran, but there was a complication."

My forehead furled; I hoped that my silent question was obvious for him. He only stared at me though, his blue eyes deep and troubled.

"What... complication?" I tried to keep my face calm; I wanted to know more, but was afraid he would stop.

"In all things in life, there is a good and a bad, a light and a dark." He paused and I couldn't help but realize that his voice had deepened. The change scared me. "Your kiss is one of those things that possess a dual nature as well. My life has been consumed by this purpose; in many ways it is the sole reason I stay on this earth. Myself, and all those within my family, have spent our entire lives seeking out and protecting the Chosen Children who have been kissed by the Vilÿs. For centuries, I have sought them out and protected them..."

"Centuries?" I cut him off, although my voice was a squeak, but he still sputtered to a stop at my words.

"Yes, Joclyn, centuries. I am very old, much older than I appear." His lips turned up in a curious half-smile. "I wasn't lying to you when I told you I was born in the 80s. It just wasn't the 1980s."

"When?"

"It was in the tenth century, Joclyn." His voice was ashamed, like he was worried about my reaction. He had every right to be, too.

I struggled to keep my head, but after everything he had told me, what was one more impossible thing? I held my breath in an attempt to keep myself under control, unsure if I would be able to accomplish it. Thankfully, he continued anyway.

"The kiss on your skin is unique. There has not been a child who has been given this mark in more than three centuries. And the ones who had received their kiss before then have all but disappeared. This is why we had to come right to you. This is why we lied and hid; you are that important. You are the last of the Chosen Children."

He spoke as if he were done and had told me everything, but he hadn't. What about the bad side he had spoken of, what about the complications? I looked at him skeptically as I gathered strength to speak again.

"Bad side?" I said. Ilyan just looked at me before looking down at the couch. I waited for clarification, but none came. My heart skipped a beat in fear; was the bad side really all that scary?

"Complication?" I tried again, the longer word feeling like acid in my throat.

Ilyan looked away from me to focus on a spot on the blankets that covered me.

"There are those among my kind, and among the Trpaslík, who believe that the kiss is a gift, a sign of royalty. For four hundred years, they have systematically exterminated, not only the children who bare the kiss, but also the Vilys who are the sole reason the marks exist in the first place."

"Extermin..." My voice caught; I couldn't even bring myself to say the word.

"Yes, Silný, they kill them. The men who attacked you in your apartment were there for that reason."

I knew the men were trying to kill me—they had made that blatantly clear—but that wasn't why I found myself hyperventilating again; it wasn't why I found my vision fading in and out so fast my eyesight was almost a flicker. There were others who had wanted to kill me beside those men, and if it wasn't for Ryland, they would have. If it wasn't for Ryland knowing about the mark, and what it meant, they all would have succeeded.

"Ryland," I gasped, my weak voice shaking even more.

"I am not sure we should go over this right now," Ilyan said.

"Ryland!" My strong voice bounced angrily around the room. Wyn said something, but I didn't bother to look to see if she had woken this time. I didn't dare let my eyes leave Ilyan. Ilyan sighed and looked hard at me as my breathing and heart rate continued to increase in tempo.

"Wyn's brother is Cail. Wyn's father is Timothy. They both

follow the man who gave the extermination order for the children who bear a kiss on their skin; the man who bears the first kiss ever given—Ryland's father, Edmund LaRue."

Somehow, I knew; I had known from the beginning. I knew from the moment Ryland saw the mark on my skin. I knew when I saw his own mark, standing out so vividly on his back. I knew, but I simply didn't want to see it. I didn't want to accept it.

My breathing reached a rate that couldn't possibly keep me conscious. I looked into Ilyan's pained face for only a moment more before my vision went black. The warmth from Ilyan's hands filled me at an alarming rate, his magic seeping into me and allowing me to slip into sleep.

CHAPTER
19

THE SUNLIGHT STREAMED INNOCENTLY IN through the open window, saturating the faded carpet and white walls with the golden light of morning. A light breeze blew through the open patio door, bringing a sweet smell of flowers and grass into Wyn's living room. My face was warm and felt swollen as if I had been crying the entire time I had been asleep, which I wouldn't doubt, given the reason I was sleeping in the first place. I shifted my weight under the heavy blankets that covered me, surprised to feel only a slight ache in my joints.

My rested body and serene mood lasted only a moment until I realized the reason I had woken up in the first place. I could hear frantic yelling from the other room, the voices raised and lowered dramatically as they yelled at each other in Czech. Wyn and Ilyan were not angry though; they were panicked. The sound increased as a door opened and I watched Wyn walk out of the hall, a large bag draped over her back, an even bigger suitcase clenched in her other hand. The bags were so large in proportion to her body it looked like she would topple over at any moment. She caught sight of me staring at her and both parcels came crashing to the ground.

"Oh, thank all!" she sighed, her accented voice still sounding odd in my ears. She rushed over to me, placing her hand right against my cheek. I looked at her in confusion, still unable to take my eyes off her dark tattoos.

"Ilyan! She's awake." She looked at me sadly, realizing that I was looking more at the dark marks on her face than at her. "I would hide them, Jos, but it hurts too much and I need to be able to focus right now."

"Good," Ilyan's voice carried from the other room. "Is it hotter than before?"

Wyn removed her hand from my cheek and moved the heavy pile of blankets from off my torso. The removal of the weight increased the soreness I felt.

"Sorry," she cringed.

She placed her hand against my chest, pressing Ryland's necklace against my skin. My jaw tightened as the hot stone made firm contact. How could I not have felt that before? The ruby burned against me, making my whole chest feel as if it was on fire. The second Wyn released the pressure of her hand, the heat lessened, but I could still feel the necklace's intense warmth from within Ryland's sweater that they had placed me in.

"It's hotter," Wyn called back down the hall where Ilyan was.

I heard Ilyan swear in English before he appeared at the end of the hall, his hair pulled back into a pony tail and the knees of his torn jeans caked with what looked like dirt and blood.

"We are out of time. Get that stuff to the car; I'll be down with her in a minute."

Wyn obeyed, grabbing the large bags as if they weighed nothing and disappearing out the door.

Ilyan rushed over to me and stripped the top most blanket off the pile that covered me and laid it on the floor. When he removed the blanket, the aches increased just as they had when Wyn removed half of them a moment before.

"I'm sorry, Joclyn, but they have found us; we have to move now."

My heart plunged. I knew beyond a doubt who "they" were: Cail, Timothy, Edmund... Ryland. I kept my head about me this time, the magic-induced sleep seeming to have helped me cope with the reality of Ryland's association with the man who would stop at nothing to kill me.

"Ryland?"

"I don't know, Joclyn. He could be with them. He could be... I just don't know." Ilyan stripped the remaining blankets from over me, causing my body to tense with deep aches that overtook me.

"I am sorry, Joclyn. I would do this gently, but we really do not have the time. I had hoped to have your spine healed before we moved you, but Edmund has other plans." He kneeled down beside me and ran his hand down the right side of my face, his thumb resting on my mark. I expected a jolt or a pain like that which had accompanied Ryland's touch, but instead, I felt nothing.

"I need you to be as quiet as you can. I can't take the pain away right now; you need to be strong." He slid his arms underneath my body and I knew what he meant. My body wasn't as close to being healed as I had thought. With the heavy blankets gone, the aches and pains covered every inch of me. I felt like I had been thrown out of a third story window, which I had been.

I tried desperately to keep the majority of the sound in my throat as Ilyan lifted me and placed me on the floor on top of the blanket he had laid there. I lay like a rag doll, my body unwilling to move.

As Ilyan straightened me out, I caught a glimpse of fleece pajama bottoms—the same ones I had been wearing in my dream with Ryland. My heart caught, instantly aware that Ryland was right; it wasn't a dream. If it wasn't a dream, then what had happened to Ryland?

Ilyan wrapped the blanket around me tightly, like one does an infant, and then prepared to lift me. My body tensed as his hands began to slide underneath me.

"Ilyan," I pleaded, "I can't"

"You can, Joclyn. You have to. If we don't leave now, they will kill you. There are too many of them for me to fight on my own. You are the last of the Chosen Children; the last one between Edmund and his "perfect" world." He slid his hands under me and lifted me to his chest in one quick movement. I groaned as we moved, allowing too much sound to escape my lips.

"Do it for Ryland, Joclyn. He may need you soon."

I clenched my teeth. I thought of Ryland, the way he twitched and writhed as his father fought his way into his brain. Ilyan was right; someone had to save Ryland, too.

I turned my body into Ilyan as he ran out the door of the apartment and down the stairs toward the small parking garage that sat below the complex. I kept my teeth clenched as my body jostled around, my hands wrapped around the blanket. I focused on my tensed muscles in an attempt to ignore the sharp pains.

I could tell when we entered the garage; Ilyan's footsteps changed to a flat gait that echoed around concrete walls. He walked straight to the black Mazda he always drove, the rear driver's side door opening on its own before we even reached it. He leaned over and placed me in the center of the back seat.

"How many," he asked Wyn who sat in the passenger seat looking stressed.

"At least a hundred, but they are spread out."

Ilyan reached around me and firmly placed the seatbelt over my shoulder and waist, placing large bags and suitcases around me in an obvious effort to stabilize me.

"You still need to be quiet, Joclyn." He placed his hand against the right side of my face, his thumb resting on my mark. I twitched away from the foreign, uncomfortable touch again. "It's more important to get us out of here alive than in comfort."

"For Ryland," I sighed, trying desperately to keep my mind focused.

"For Ryland." Ilyan slid into the front seat, and turned the key in the ignition, revving the car to life.

"Where is the strongest?" he asked Wyn as he backed the car out of the parking stall.

The force of the car's movement slammed me into the large bag on my left. I cringed at the pain of the impact.

"There are more bodies to the east, but the strongest power is coming from the north. That would be my guess as to where they are."

"To the north then." Ilyan's jaw clenched as he hit the accelerator and gunned us out of the dark parking garage.

The warm summer sun poured through the back window, and I leaned my head against the seat, letting the sunlight hit my skin a bit. It felt nice; if only this warmth wouldn't go away, I might be able to endure the pain.

"To the north?" Wyn asked. "You can't be serious, My Lord. We would be walking into their trap."

There it was again, *My Lord*.

"We are already in their trap," Ilyan reminded her with a growl. He flipped his phone open and pressed it against his ear. "Ovailia," he spoke the second someone answered the phone, "set a trail to the east; we are going to go to the north. Meet us at the second safe house."

Ilyan did not wait for a response; he simply threw the phone to the side and turned the car around a sharp left-hand corner, followed by a quick right. My body flung around in the back seat like a rag doll, each impact sending more pain through me.

"What do you suggest we do when we come face-to-face with Edmund?" Wyn asked in a panic.

"We run." Ilyan pressed the accelerator down all the way as we turned onto the large highway that cut its way through the city.

"Run?"

"Yes, Wynifred, we run. We fly. We save our lives. I can save the battle for later. There are more important things to face tonight." They turned toward each other as a silent agreement passed between them. Ilyan turned back to the road again and increased our speed. I sat in silence, listening to their quick conversation, their infectious panic creeping into me.

"How far?"

"About two miles."

"Find all the usable cars, trees, buildings; I need to know what I have to... dammit!" he swore, causing both me and Wyn to jump. The car decelerated, making my body lean forward.

"What?"

"They have a barrier up, so they can track us. Switch me places."

Wyn didn't say a word; she simply moved over to the driver's side as Ilyan moved to the passenger's side, the car never deviating a millimeter from the road.

"Pace yourself with as many cars as you can, and keep your speed steady," he instructed, his accented voice filled with insane determination.

"Are you going to try to break through it?"

"No, I am going to demolish it." Ilyan looked toward Wyn, his face filled with enjoyment or madness, I wasn't sure which.

Wyn nodded to him once before accelerating, the force sending me against the back of the seat, Ryland's necklace pressing against my chest.

The necklace was a white hot brand, flaming through me, the

warmth pulsing hotter and hotter like the beat of a heart. It was more than just heat though; it was pain beyond my own: hate, love, fear, and excruciating heartbreak. None of the emotions were mine, but with that one touch, they filled me; they destroyed me. I couldn't help it, the second it burned into me, my mouth opened in an agonizing scream. My voice ricocheted around the car, growing louder in the cramped space.

I heard Ilyan yell along with me as a bright light moved away from him through the window, only to explode against an invisible force that broke into a million pieces. As the wall broke, my scream continued, only silencing when Ilyan turned to clamp his hand over my mouth.

"You need to drive as fast as you can, Wynifred; they know exactly where we are." He removed his hand from my mouth, and I instantly clamped my mouth shut.

"I'm sorry," I said quietly "The necklace... it's in pain." I didn't know why I had said that, but the phrasing was right. The emotions that the necklace filled me with felt as if it was in severe pain.

Ilyan's eyes grew wide, his jaw clenching. He looked over my head sharply as he looked for something. I could see his clenched jaw pulse angrily.

"Fast, Wynifred; they are both here."

Wyn hit the gas, and we sped away from the cars we had been pacing with. All the cars became blurs as we soared by them, the black Mazda swerving in and out between the others on the highway.

"What do you think of your brilliant plan now?" Wyn grumbled as she cut in front of a yellow Hummer.

"Faster Wyn!" Ilyan screamed.

The words had no sooner left his mouth than Wyn swerved to the left, barely missing another car. Only a second after she had moved the car, an explosion filled the space we had just left. I turned my head to the side, the red and white of the fire filling the air.

The explosion sent a panic through the cars and drivers on the highway. Half the cars pulled to the side of the road in confusion or curiosity as to what had happened, while the remaining cars sped ahead in a desperate attempt to outrun the fiery blast. All the cars began to drive erratically; they paced and swerved, several cars ramming into each other in violent collisions that filled the road with the sounds of grinding metal, and shattering glass, and the smell of smoke that masked the magical onslaught around us.

I watched them as we moved, the car swerving around each accident as we weaved our way through the masses. I could see the fear on the other drivers' faces; almost *feel* the palpable energy of the screaming men and crying women. I wanted to scream at them to run, beg them to find a way to get far away; they were all getting hurt, many of them dying, because of me.

My mother had died because of me, too. Her life had been stolen, just like all the others. I pulled away from the thought only to catch a short glance of a screaming woman that froze my soul. Was that how my mom had felt before she died?

Wyn swerved again, this time sending me into the corner of the suitcase. I forgot everything else and yelped out in pain as my breath was knocked out of me from the impact. She moved the car and another explosion hit the road, sending bits of asphalt against the side of the car. The residue of the blast pelted us, a large piece slamming into the side window near my head with a resounding crack as the glass shattered.

"Ilyan, do something!" Wyn screamed as she swerved once again to escape another explosion.

Ilyan hesitated before raising his hands above his head in silence and then placing his palms flat against the top of the car. His hands glowed bright blue as the roof of the car ripped apart in a loud explosion that ricocheted through the enclosed space. I screamed as the pieces of metal ripped and curled away from the car and into the remaining highway traffic. The hot wind of summer flew into the now topless car, whipping my hair haphazardly around my face.

Ilyan turned and placed his feet firmly in the soft seat of the car. He stood, his torso extending out of the top of the car as he faced what I could only assume were our pursuers. The wind caught his hair and whipped it around his face. The violent nature of the flying strands matched his face perfectly; his eyes were set in a dark, stoic blue, his jaw set in an oddly patronizing smile. There was so much power and determination that I couldn't look away from him.

"Hold on tight, Jos," Wyn screamed from the driver's seat. "All hell's going to break loose now that they know he is here."

I looked up at Ilyan whose smile had increased tremendously as he raised his hand to the side and sliced it through the air.

The car vibrated as a large, abandoned dump truck skidded across the road, rumbling violently in the opposite direction. The truck followed the span of Ilyan's hand as it swept behind us before a large pulse of light left Ilyan's palm. The light must have collided with the truck, as only moments later, our car rocked to the side, an explosion violently pushing it around.

Wyn swerved the car to the left, cutting over two lanes. Ilyan swayed, but stayed atop the seat, shifting his feet to compensate for the dramatic movement. He raised his hands above his head again; his palms open to the sky, his face toward whoever followed us. At first, I thought nothing had happened, but then I saw the flock of birds, their path changing to reflect the movement of Ilyan's hands. The stoic V of the birds was thrown apart as he moved his hands. A rush of wind sped above the car as they made their way toward our attackers, whipping through my hair on its way. It tugged at the bag I sat next to, the destructive force shredding the plastic.

Ilyan moved his hands again, this time to the side. I felt the wind rush past us before it picked up a small sedan that had been abandoned at some point in time. The car lifted easily into the air, the large metal frame spinning like a leaf in the wind. It hovered there until it zoomed away to crash into something or someone behind us. I jumped as the noise of the collision hit us, the sound echoing around the speedily emptying highway.

Ilyan smiled at the impact, his face alight with enjoyment. "There he is," he growled, and he lowered his torso for only a moment to speak quietly to Wyn. "You'll need to be on your toes. You know your father's temperament better than I do; Timothy is going to play dirty."

"You just keep yours under control, and we may escape this mess we are in," Wyn responded forcefully.

Ilyan laughed wildly at her before standing again, facing our attackers.

Wyn slowed the car briefly before accelerating again, her driving sending us barreling through empty lanes and around frantically driven cars. Ilyan only laughed at the movement of the car, his body swaying gracefully as we swerved.

His laughing continued as he waved his hands above him. I watched his actions in confusion as a large van came into view, maneuvering through the air above us. My heart jumped at the sight of the family still trapped inside. Ilyan had only been using empty vehicles as ammo, but someone else had thrown more than a vehicle at us. Someone else had thrown people. My anxiety lessened as Ilyan set the van down at the side of the road, and hopefully, into safety. He didn't waste another moment before sending a massive explosion toward our attackers.

Ilyan lifted his hand again, his eyes taunting the enemy behind us. His hand flexed, sending long strands of violent color from his fingertips, like electricity. The sound of explosions and grinding metal penetrated the air so completely; I could not tell what was going on.

Wyn swerved out of the way to avoid yet another explosion, but the tires still strayed into the broken road. Bits of asphalt flew into the empty cavity that was once the roof, littering me with small burning rocks.

I could hear Wyn's quick erratic breathing from where I sat, and I could hear her whispers as she spoke to the empty air around her. She spoke to Talon; she moaned his named as tears streaked down her face. She was trying to be brave, but her heart betrayed her. She knew there was no hope; she knew we were going to die.

Part of me knew she was right, and sadly, I was okay with it. I wanted to see my mother again; I wanted to apologize. As much as my heart ached and screamed for my mother though, a much bigger part knew I could not leave Ryland. I needed him, just as much as he needed me.

Ilyan sent another round of ammunition flying past in a steady stream of large rocks, small cars, and everyday mundane objects. Ilyan had grabbed everything he could with his mind and launched it away from us like weapons.

He lifted his hands again as a large, brilliantly-red, ball grew from his hands, shooting away from his palms like a bullet and pushing him back inside the car. The sound of the explosion rolled through me, the power loud and angry. My body called out in pain; my voice moaning and gasping with each movement. I remembered what Ilyan had told me; we had to escape alive and not in comfort. He had also said there were too many for him to fight alone. I looked to his crumpled form in the passenger seat, my heart sinking.

His face no longer held the joy, the solid determination, that it had held a moment before. Ilyan's face was screwed up with panic, a bead of sweat dripping down his forehead. Wyn swerved blindly to the side in an attempt to escape another explosion, the front of the car nicking another of the escaping vehicles.

"Take Joclyn and run, Wyn. Get back to Talon. I will hold them off as long as I can." Ilyan gripped Wyn roughly, his voice a panicked command that made my stomach flip.

"You'll never make it out! I can't... can't let you."

I could tell how much it cost Wyn to say the words, to actually be willing to not make it back to Talon.

"Don't worry about me; I can do a lot more when I don't have to worry about keeping others safe."

I twisted myself in the seat, my body screaming out in agony as I moved. Behind our speeding Mazda, a line of black SUVs followed, each one large and foreboding. Their gauntlet herded everyone down the highway, moving us into certain death. In the center of the line, speeding in front of all the others, was a bright yellow Lotus.

My heart stopped beating, my breath caught, and I felt the tears of panic splash down my face out of nowhere.

"Ryland." Had I meant to say it out loud, or simply speak to him in my mind? My voice caught in my throat, but the reply was right in my ear.

"Run, Joclyn. Stay with Ilyan." Ryland's voice was a whisper, but clear as day. I whipped my head to the side, devastation filling me to see nothing but the gray bag. I looked back to the Lotus, desperately searching for his dark curls.

"Ryland." I lifted my hand and placed it on the glass of the back window. The firm, smooth surface of the glass was hot under my touch. It felt like the burn of the necklace that still pressed against my skin.

I focused on the warmth, on the heat, the image of his face floating into my line of sight. The warmth grew, both in the necklace and in my hand. It moved into me, the heat seeping into every part of my soul. I pressed my hand harder into the glass in my desperation to see Ryland. At the increased touch, the glass shattered under my hand.

A million pieces scattered across the trunk of the car, over the road. I didn't have time to look at it; I couldn't be surprised. Only a moment after the glass shattered, the road behind us shifted. I screamed as the asphalt heaved itself into a giant pile, the earth moving to lift it upwards toward the sky, into a mound. The cars began to move up the increasing mountain for only a moment before they were hidden behind the large pile of asphalt, stones and earth that spanned the freeway.

I spun around, my body aching, to face Ilyan. I expected to see him standing with his hands extending out, but instead, he remained inside the car where he had fallen, his eyes wide and staring.

"Drive, Wyn." His voice was calm and awed.

I flipped my head back to the mound of earth and back to Ilyan, wincing at the pained movements.

"What happened, Ilyan?" I asked quietly.

He just looked at me. The answer was clear on his face—he didn't know.

I turned my body around, looking toward the distancing earth pile. Behind that pile, somewhere, was Ryland. I lifted my hand to my necklace, the warmth receding. The heartbeat of scorching heat left it, leaving only a slow throbbing. I held it tightly again, still staring back out the window.

"Did I do that?"

"I'm not sure."

"You're not sure?" I rounded on him; how could he not know? I stared into him in a panic, my throat burning, my body aching.

"I will know soon, Silnỳ."

"When?"

"Soon." He reached forward and placed his hand against my cheek. "We will be home soon and then I will know everything. And, I will tell you. I promise."

"Home?"

"Joclyn, I'm sorry, but I can't let you know where we are going quite yet."

I felt the warmth of Ilyan's magic flood through me, the numbness moving through my body and into my brain. I turned to see the last of the city flash past me before my vision blacked out and Ilyan's magic put me to sleep again.

CHAPTER 20

"J UST WAIT. YOU WILL SEE what I mean."

"I don't have time for this; can't it wait until later?"

"No, Ovailia, it can't. If he—"

"Fine."

I felt the depression of the bed as someone sat down near my feet. A bed. The more I woke up, the more I could tell it was a bed. I could feel the soft and hard combination of a spring mattress made far too long ago, and smell the musty stench of blankets left too long in storage. I opened my eyes, trying not to move.

It looked like I was in an old hotel room; the décor was something out of the sixties. The wallpaper was faded and peeling in places, but still had the obvious brown-on-orange striped pattern that was popular then. An orange, angular lamp sat on a darkly varnished table, a hard plastic chair pulled up to the side. The look of the room explained the musty smell of the bed and the blankets; they all must have been here since the day the hotel first opened for business.

Although the shade to the window near the table was open, the light filtering into the room was dim and filled with the blue light of dusk. Even with what came in through the window, there wasn't much light, which was further diminished by the dark color scheme.

"Ugh. More commercials. I don't know if I can wait any longer." It was the woman's voice I had heard before. It was deep and nasally. She was irritated, and by the sound of it, she was irritated all the time. Her voice held only a subtle hint of an accent, as if she had been trying to get rid of it for far too long and had only partially succeeded.

"Ovailia…" Wyn pleaded. I could pick Wyn's voice out now, accented or not.

"You have another minute, Wynifred; that is all. I hate human news; it's so boring," Ovailia's voice drawled out angrily.

I felt the bed move as someone shifted their weight. I just held still. I wasn't sure I wanted to let them know I was awake. Ovailia did not sound like someone I wanted to meet right now anyway.

"Here it is!" The sound on a television they had been watching was turned up, and someone shifted their weight again.

"We have a further development on the kidnapping of sixteen-year-old Joclyn Despain, who has been missing for twelve days. And in the murder of her mother, fifty-three-year-old Angela Despain."

Murder.

I thought of her still body spread over the kitchen floor, her beautiful, yellow nails. Ilyan had said it before, and I felt the same destructive force move through me now as it had then. The dilapidated house that contained my soul ripped apart with a violent explosion that rushed over me in a torrent of depression so deep, I was drowning in it.

I was barely able to stabilize myself amongst the flow that swirled around me. I did though; I caught my breath and found a hand-hold somewhere deep inside. I was stable, but empty. I could tell automatically that this pain, this emptiness, would never leave me.

"Ryland LaRue, who was last seen with the young girl, and continues to claim his innocence in her disappearance, has stepped forward in a press conference this afternoon, offering a reward for information leading to her safe return." The sound cut out as a video clip was loaded.

"Good afternoon, ladies, gentlemen, and members of the press."

I sat the second I heard his voice. Ryland, the hand-hold that I clutched onto deep inside me. His voice felt like an electrical current that shot through me. The blankets tumbled down around me as I sat, my body surprisingly not protesting the quick movements. The two women at the foot of the bed did not register my actions; they, too, were focused on the TV screen. I was vaguely aware of them; Wyn with her short, auburn hair, and Ovailia with an absolute sheet of sleek, honey blonde that fell well past her hips and cascaded over the grungy brown bed spread.

"I would like to address you today..." My ears did not hear another word. The sound of his voice faded away into the air around me.

At first glance, he looked like the Ryland I had always known, the Ryland I had always loved; dark curls falling over his face, strong jaw, strong body, bright blue eyes. However, once my heart stopped seeing and my mind was left to linger, I instantly felt the tears come.

He had been beaten.

His left eye was swollen and tinged with an ugly purple, a large gash ran from his cheek and down across his neck before disappearing underneath his shirt. A few more deep purple bruises were just visible from underneath his hair and around the collar of his shirt. Although he gestured with his left hand, his right and dominant arm hung loosely at his side. I could almost see the pain in his eyes, the strain in his face. I recognized the same pain in me, the same entrapment I had felt over the last few days as my body ached and tried to heal. He was in agony.

Then, he flinched. It was so subtle I almost didn't catch it. His left arm moved toward his chest and then out again. I reached toward the image on the screen, my heart calling out to him. The bed lifted as Ovailia stood and took a step closer to the screen.

"You see it, too?" Wyn whispered.

I tried to focus on what Ryland said, but I couldn't; my heart beat too hard in my chest. He seemed fine, until another twitch, this one bigger, caused him to stop. He paused and lowered his head, his chest heaving as he breathed. The clip played for only a second more before cutting back to the announcer and then the TV shut off.

"How much time does he have left?" Wyn asked.

I saw Ovailia's mane of hair shake, her shoulders sagging.

"A week, maybe two, if we are lucky."

I didn't flinch at Ilyan's voice, even though it was so close to me. He stood to my side, beyond my line of sight. I stayed still, my arm still extending toward the television screen.

"Why would he do something like that?" Ovailia snapped. "And to his own *precious* son, too." The words dripped off her tongue like poison.

"It wouldn't be the first time he has hurt his own children, Ovailia. You should know that better than anyone."

I turned toward his voice, my arm finally dropping down to the bed. He stood at the side of the bed, his back leaning against the ugly brown and orange papered wall.

"But if he only has a few weeks before his mind is lost..." Wyn began, her unfinished thought fading into the steadily darkening room.

"It's true then, everything he told me in the dream." My voice was so quiet, my throat burning as I spoke. I looked to Ilyan who raised an eyebrow at my question. In my peripheral vision I could see both Wyn and Ovailia whip around to me in surprise.

"What dream, Joclyn?"

I looked at him skeptically, second guessing myself.

"He came to me... I thought it was a dream..."

"What dream?" Ilyan repeated.

I felt a heavy panic creeping through me, the reality of what was happening hitting me hard.

"When you held me under the water, Ryland was there. I thought it was a dream..." My voice gained in intensity as the panic continued to grow.

"What did he say to you?"

My fear rose, knowing exactly what was going on. I knew why he was twitching, what was happening, because Ryland had told me.

"His father... he is deleting his mind. Edmund's killing him, isn't he?" I looked hard at Ilyan, my panic demanding the answers I desperately needed.

"He's not going to kill him."

My heart swelled in relief, until Ilyan's tone, his desperation, sank in.

"A Vymäzat is when someone uses their magic destructively on another person. In essence, they delete, or partially delete, that person's mind. They remove all memories and personality. A Vymäzat creates a shell of a person that can be molded to become what the one who uses the magic wishes them to become. In Ryland's case, Edmund will not kill him; instead, he will delete all of him and turn his body and magic into a weapon." Ilyan's voice was so deep, it almost didn't sound like him.

"No! We need to save him." I went to remove the covers from me, fully intent on running to his aide; but my head swam so uncomfortably, I was sure I wouldn't be moving anywhere soon.

"I don't know if that's possible, Joclyn. There is no known way to reverse it," Wyn said.

"What else did he say in your dream?" Ilyan asked gently, pulling my attention from the other two.

"Only that..." I paused as I replayed the dream in my head, trying to pick out important pieces of information. I stopped as I recalled him writhing on the ground, my memory vividly showing me the small mark on his back. The mark he had kept hidden from me. My breathing picked up again.

"He had a mark like mine on his back."

Ilyan only nodded in acknowledgment at me.

"Why did he have a mark?" I said to Ilyan in a panic when it became obvious he knew and wasn't going to provide me with an explanation.

"Do you remember when I told you that Edmund and his servants have been hunting the Vilỳ, and that it is the Vilỳ that gives a kiss?"

I nodded, waiting for him to continue.

"Well, Edmund captured them and siphoned off their poison for years and kept it, so that when his next child was born, he could create a child with such a large amount of magic that no one could defeat him."

"Ryland?" It was obvious who he was talking about, my stomach turned in worry or excitement at just saying his name.

"Yes, Ryland. He injected him with the poison when he was two. He didn't awake from the injection for eighteen months... it's a miracle he survived."

"How do you know this?" I asked, trying to ignore the bile churning its way up my throat.

"It doesn't matter how he knows, little girl." Ovailia's voice was ice against my back.

"But you said I was unconscious for—"

"And yours remains the longest *natural* awakening. Ryland's mark was forced, and therefore, an unnatural anomaly," Ilyan cut me off.

"Where were you in this dream?" Ilyan changed the subject as he came to sit next to me on the bed. I shifted away from him a bit, feeling uncomfortable with how close he was.

"I don't know. It was all white. Ryland said it was some sort of shared consciousness."

Ilyan smiled almost knowingly at my words, while Ovailia and Wyn gasped in unison.

"A Tòuha?" Ovailia exclaimed. "How is that possible?"

"What is that?" I asked "A Tòuha?"

"It is exactly what Ryland told you it was," Ilyan commented quietly. "A Tòuha is a place where your minds can go and be together, no matter how far apart you are in distance. It is normally only reserved for those who have gone through the Zêlství, which is why it is so surprising that you shared one with Ryland."

"Zêlství?"

"He means bonded," Wyn translated the word from Czech for me. "You would refer to it as a marriage."

My jaw dropped.

"Marriage?"

"I had a feeling your connection with Ryland was stronger than any of us thought after you raised the highway into a mound when we escaped." Ilyan's eyes dug into mine sharply.

"I did that?" I asked.

"Yes, but not on your own," Ilyan continued. "Ryland helped, too."

A pin could have dropped and it would have sounded like a herd of elephants. I could only stare at him, my jaw dropped in awe.

"You don't mean... the necklace?" Wyn asked, her voice almost a squeak of nerves.

Ilyan nodded in response to her question, his focus still on me.

"What necklace." Ovailia scowled. "What have you been keeping from me, Ilyan?"

Ilyan finally released me from his gaze to stare down Ovailia with hard eyes.

"I keep from you whatever I deem, Ovailia."

Ovailia wilted under his sharp gaze.

"You will have to excuse my sister," Ilyan's voice was impregnated with something akin to diplomatic anger. "She forgets her manners from time to time."

"Or on a daily basis," Wyn grumbled under her breath.

Ilyan chuckled at her comment while Ovailia only growled.

I probably should have been more shocked, given how fuzzy my mind was when Ilyan told me that Wyn was not his sister. Looking between Ilyan and Ovailia right then, I felt supremely stupid for ever believing that Wyn and Ilyan were siblings in the first place. Wyn was so short and darkly colored; she looked out of place between Ilyan and Ovailia with their tall, fair beauty. So much was alike between them; their high cheek bones, the shade of their eyes, and the golden color of their long hair. Ovailia's features were refined, her high cheek bones and cat-like eyes giving her the look of aristocratic beauty. Still, somehow, her attitude ruined it and turned some of her striking elegance into rubbish.

"Since you have chosen to keep things from me, do you wish to enlighten me now?" Ovailia waved one of her hands impatiently to the side, her long fingers extending like a dancers.

"Show her your necklace, Joclyn."

"What does any of this have to do with my necklace?" I asked, clutching the ruby tightly through Ryland's sweater.

"You are going to have to tell her, My Lord," Wyn spoke, her weight shifting on the bed to face me.

He stood and began to pace, only moving a few steps in either direction as he ran his hands through his hair in agitation.

"Ilyan?" I asked after I could take no more of his uptight movements. He stopped at my voice and came to lean against the bed, his face only millimeters away from my own. I flinched back out of habit.

"The necklace is more than just a gift; Ryland has infused it with his own magic as a way to keep an eye on you, to protect you. Every time you have ever felt it grow warm, it signals to him that you are in danger."

I nodded, remembering his sudden appearance at the Rugby field, and his apparent knowledge of my fight with Cynthia.

"But I am afraid it inadvertently became more than that. You see, the entire time you two have known each other, Ryland has been infusing you with his magic—to calm you, to heal you, to protect you, to comfort you."

I nodded before looking down at my lap. "The warmth," I sighed. "I pushed you out the first time you tried to heal me because Ryland's m... magic..." I struggled to get the word out. "It had just left me and I was scared."

"The day we went to the fire pit," Wyn interrupted, her voice low, "he healed your hand after you hit him, he used his magic to calm you when you were jumping over the fire, and you... you used his magic to help you climb the tree."

"What?"

"When you climbed the tree," Wyn continued, "you drew his magic off him and used it to sharpen your senses. It's why you are so fast. Why it feels so natural."

"Ryland did it all without knowing that you possessed your own unharnessed power," Ilyan continued. "So the more your magic mingled, the more they became dependent on each other, the more they became one. When Ryland gave you the necklace, he made it so that his magic would always be close to yours, and with that, he inadvertently sealed your fate. He permanently fused the magic, and in turn, your lives together."

"What are you saying? That Edmund could infiltrate my mind as well?" I couldn't keep the panic from seeping into my voice. I needed to save Ryland, but now it wasn't just him—it was me as well.

"I do not think it will come to that," Ilyan said. "Mostly what this means is that you can draw off each other. In essence, your magic cannot survive without his and vice-versa."

"In the apartment," Ilyan spoke solemnly, "it was Ryland controlling his magic through the necklace that saved you. In the alley, it was his magic that was taking the pain away. He consciously saved and protected you, even though his father was torturing him at the very same time."

"Torturing him? But in the dream he looked okay... Why does he look like he has been beaten, Ilyan? What's happened to him?" My thoughts strung together before settling on the brutal image of him that still flooded me.

"He *has* been beaten, Joclyn; possibly more than the television images show us. They can cast a spell on him, make it appear that he is not as injured as he is," Wyn spoke plainly, the truth cutting me.

"What worries me the most," Ilyan added, "is that Edmund is not allowing Ryland to be healed, or even allowing him to heal himself. He is kept in pain to weaken him, so that he doesn't fight back."

"Pain?" I asked, remembering my first assumption that he looked like I had felt the last few days.

"Yes, Joclyn, agonizing pain. Almost the same type of pain you felt when you first received your kiss. He feels that every second of every day and must live with it."

"But he didn't look like that... in the dream, I mean."

"That's because you were seeing with your heart." I turned to Ovailia's acidic voice. "If you had taken the time to see with your mind, you would have seen the true extent of his injuries. Then perhaps we could know with more certainty how much time he has left."

"Enough, Ovailia," Ilyan commanded, but I couldn't take my eyes away from her.

"So, Ryland is dying inside. His father is trying to *delete* his mind. So when you say he has maybe two weeks—"

"I mean in a week, maybe two," Ilyan whispered, "Ryland will be no more. He will only be a shell to be manipulated by his father."

I clutched my necklace, pressing the cold stone against my chest. I felt my heart beat wildly against my fingers. Once again, the mark had destroyed everything, everything I needed and wanted within my life. However, this time I knew the truth; the mark had truly given me the power to get everything back, the power to fix it.

"I will save him." My voice was quiet, but still confident. I knew I would do whatever it would take to save Ryland, to honor my mother, to change my life.

"I know," Ilyan whispered.

I turned to him, unsurprised to see that wild anticipation and crazy confidence he had had in the car. It wasn't the joy I had originally mistaken it to be, though.

It was power.

CHAPTER
21

*I*LYAN HAD EXCUSED HIMSELF A short while later, saying that there would be a council in an hour, and he needed to prepare. Ovailia had followed close behind him, her nasally voice whining about something I didn't understand. The second the door had closed, Wyn rushed to me, flinging her arms around me in a tight bear hug.

"I am so sorry, Jos, so sorry. If we could have gotten you out earlier, this never would have happened. If we..." Her voice caught and I could tell she was crying. I returned the hug, my arms hesitantly wrapping around her.

"I wanted so badly to just run away with you the night we watched the movie at the apartment, but someone had caught sight of Ilyan that morning, and he didn't want to risk being followed or trapped. If only we had..." She jabbered on and on, and even through the accent, I could tell she was the same old Wyn. Hearing this bit of normalcy made me smile. It took the edge off the desperate panic I felt with Ryland's situation, and the crushing depression over my mother. I sighed deeply and leaned into her, grateful for the emotional support.

"Can you forgive me?" she pleaded, pulling me away from her to look at me. Her eyes were so off putting; the all-encompassing blackness of them, combined with the dark tattoos, made her look ominous. I moved my hand up a fraction of an inch, as if to touch her skin, but put it down again. The movement didn't go unnoticed.

"I know I look a little... odd. You'll get used to it. It took me a hundred years to come to terms with my new face, so take all the time you need." She smiled widely at me, but I could tell it still made her a little sad.

"A hundred years?"

"Yeah, I am a ripe old lady. I was born in about 1795 and received the marks on July tenth of 1867."

"1795?"

"Yeah, and exiled before my hundredth birthday. That's why Ryland didn't recognize me; we've never met, and I highly doubt Timothy ever spoke of me after he marked me. So in a century or so you can tell me if you think they suit me or not."

"Wait, what? A century? I can't possibly live that long."

"All magical beings possess some realm of immortality, Joclyn. But it's kind of contingent; if you don't use it, you die. So, I guess, no, you won't gain your immortality unless you actually start to use that magic of yours."

I had accepted the fact, almost without question, that Ryland and Ilyan, and even Wyn, had and used magic, almost without question. In the back of my mind, the idea that *I* really possessed a magic of my own still felt like some kind of joke.

"But you won't be living until the world ends unless your back is healed. I apologize in advance."

Wyn lifted my sweater and placed her hand firmly on my bare back and instantly began to spread her magic into me as she checked my spine. I shuddered involuntarily. Her magic felt like ice inside my veins; it was the polar opposite of the relaxing warmth I got from Ilyan and Ryland.

Ryland.

"Will Ryland be all right?" My question was that of a child, and I knew it. I needed answers; I needed to know exactly what was going on so that I knew how to save him.

"He will if we get to him in time."

I shivered, my shoulders jerking uncomfortably. I wasn't sure if my jolt was due to Ryland's fate or to the icy magic that was moving through me.

"Sorry," she whispered. "The magic of a Trpaslík tends to be very cold. Of course most of my kind use their magic to kill rather than to heal, so that may be why."

I could almost hear the sarcasm in her voice.

"A Trpaslík?"

"Yes. Once, a very long time ago, my kind were the keepers of the fire magic."

Ironically, I shivered as the icy cold of her magic continued to move into me, chilling every part of me.

"Sorry, I'm almost done."

"Why is your magic so cold if you used to keep the fire magic?"

"I was told as a child it was taken from us by the Skříteks, and in the absence of heat, we froze. But I don't believe that anymore. Everyone here is a Skřítek; I am just the odd man out."

"A Trpaslík."

"Yep."

"So why have different names at all, if you all look so much like humans?" I asked.

"It relates to our magic. Skříteks are the keepers—or the warriors—of all magic. They were once a powerful army that kept balance over the rest of us, but have since been almost driven to extinction. The Trpaslík are destructive by nature; our magic relates more to earth elements, and we can control them at will. Vilÿs were the givers of emotions, and kept the humans from their vices. The names relate to what we do, not who we are."

"Then why do you still call yourself a Trpaslík if you no longer live with them?"

"Because I am destructive above all else." She grinned menacingly. "Trpaslíks are very good at making things explode. I'll show you sometime."

I couldn't help the shiver that spread up my spine. She enjoyed that reaction and smiled even more.

"Well, your back feels fine." Wyn jumped off the bed and flung the covers off me. I still wore the mysterious fleece pants and Ryland's sweater. I sat and picked at the soft fabric. Thinking of Ryland had made me edgy, like I needed to go run a marathon. My soul called for him, begging him to be okay, to wait for me.

"Broken back, huh?" I asked quietly.

"I know, hard to believe, isn't it? It actually broke in two places. Right here," she placed her hand at a spot right between my shoulder blades, "and here." Her hand slid down to rest a bit above the small of my back. "If it wasn't for Ilyan, you would have died."

I only nodded. Ryland had saved me, too. The images of Ryland's beaten face and my mother's broken body filled me. I felt my heart constrict again in its futile attempt to control the waves of emotion behind the dam I had built. I tried to push the heartbreak away; I needed her to be proud of me, wherever she was.

"Are you okay?"

I could only nod, my emotions moving far too slowly back behind their fortification.

"Where are we anyway?" My voice broke uncomfortably at the attempted subject change. I obviously couldn't handle thinking much about my mother just yet.

"This is one of our safe houses; it's an old motel that Ilyan bought and remodeled in 1968, hence the décor. We call it 'The Motel' strangely enough. Most everyone has updated their rooms, but this one and a few others have kind of been left alone."

Wyn helped me to swing my legs over the side of the bed, her hands assisting me to stand. My spine creaked, and I inhaled sharply as pressure was placed on it. Although the sensation was uncomfortable, it didn't hurt. It felt like I had never stood on my legs before.

"Come on," Wyn coaxed. "I want to show you something."

Even though stiffness had replaced the pain, I still needed help to walk; my legs needed to be reminded how to do it. Wyn helped me, step by step, as we moved slowly forward, stopping after a few steps when Wyn turned me to face the window.

The window opened to a beautiful courtyard that was surrounded on all sides by other rooms. It was full of flowers and vines that covered stone paths and beautiful wrought-iron patio furniture. And in the middle of it all, stood a giant tree. I had never seen one so large. It wasn't a pine tree like the massive redwoods; it almost looked like an oak. Its broad leaves stretched up and out, covering the courtyard in a relaxing canopy of quivering leaves.

"It's beautiful."

"I know. The view in Prague is just as nice, too. You will see it when we get there."

"Get there?" I couldn't help the panicked edge that crept into my voice. I couldn't go anywhere without Ryland.

"Prague is the city where all magic originates; it's where we live. I am sure we will go home after we get Ryland out." She smiled sadly as she answered my unasked question. I couldn't help but feel the waves of uncertainty she was broadcasting, like she didn't think rescuing him was a possibility.

"When do we go get him?" I could feel the jittery feeling coming back.

"That's what Ilyan is in council right now to decide, Jos." She moved some of my hair behind my ear, and I fought the urge to yell at her, not because she had touched me, but because I felt the need to leave to save Ryland right then. It bothered me that this need to rescue him had come on so strong, so fast.

"Can we go for a walk?" I asked the first thing that had come to my mind, hopeful that my anxiety would dissipate with the movement.

"Ummm, yeah. You are not allowed in council, and everyone else will be there. So, we can both go sit in the courtyard and wait for Council to be released, or we can go get some food in my room."

It didn't take much thought to decide which I wanted. I would probably never be in the mood to meet new people. The thought gave me an overwhelming urge to pull the hood of the sweater up over me and hide, but I fought it.

"Food sounds great."

Thankfully, the hall outside the room did not stink so much of the sixties. It had been covered in wood paneling, but painted a nice cream color and carpeted in a plush Berber that helped it to look much more modern.

As we reached the end of the cream-colored hallway, I noticed that only this hallway was covered in the lightly colored paint and carpeting. The new hall we approached was a deep green and had hardwood floors. Right at the transition, Wyn stopped and turned to a man I hadn't noticed. He stood tall and still, right at the entrance to the hall, his focus down the hall ahead of us. At Wyn's approach, he turned to her, but said nothing.

"Tell his lordship we have gone to my chamber. The Chosen Child has requested a meal and he is welcome to join us when Council concludes."

The man clicked his heels together, and Wyn bowed before

turning and guiding me down the green hallway in the opposite direction. I looked back at the man to see him still against the door frame.

"What was all that about?"

"I hate talking like that," Wyn said. "I am so much younger than everyone else, and they all get stuck up on rules, regulations and traditions. I'm lucky I have you; now we can be the irritating rule breakers together." I looked at her sharply; she hadn't answered my question. She sensed my gaze boring into her and stoically kept her vision forward.

"Wyn," I pleaded.

"Okay, they get stuck up on tradition, right? You have to address Ilyan in a certain way, bow to Ovailia in a certain way. You have to use the right verbiage in order to be properly understood," she sighed.

"Address Ilyan in a certain way," I repeated in a whisper. My Lord. His Lordship. "So, Ilyan is like your ruler."

"King," Wyn corrected. "King of four hundred people, yes, but still king."

My chest seized at the new information. Of course it made sense, but now I couldn't stop worrying about how I had acted around him, and if I would get in trouble for it.

"Considering they are the last of their kind, they take it very seriously. Well, everyone except Ilyan anyway," Wyn said.

"Does Ilyan not take his role seriously?"

"Not really. You'll see what I mean soon enough, though. Here we are." Wyn turned me toward a door that had been painted a green so dark it was almost black. In the middle of the door were two handprints, one small and bright purple, and the other large and dark red. She smiled before pulling me into the brightly decorated apartment.

I couldn't help but smile, too; the room was so Wyn, it was

infectious. The bright bubbly colors made the last of my anxiety evaporate. A large king bed covered with a squishy leopard-print comforter occupied most of the space. The bed had an intricately carved footboard, but instead of a headboard, a gigantic Styx poster covered the light, yellow wall. Wyn guided me to an oversized, upholstered, purple chair that sat in front of the window that overlooked the courtyard.

"Food," she chanted and bounced away to a half-sized refrigerator that sat next to the bathroom door.

"I like your room,"

She turned and smiled at me.

"It's so bright and fun," I said.

"Thanks! It's probably a little too much, but out of all the time periods I have seen, I could live in the 70s and 80s forever." She sighed as if caught in a silly memory and then turned back to the fridge.

I couldn't help but laugh. I wasn't even alive in the 80s; but from what I had seen, it probably wasn't a time that I would have wanted to have participated in anyway.

"I probably don't have much that's edible for you." Wyn had buried her head in the fridge, her voice coming back to me muffled. "Talon doesn't keep this thing very well stocked when I am gone." Her head emerged from within the tiny fridge, her arms laden with a few things.

"Talon? Do you share a room or something?" I had almost forgotten about Wyn's boyfriend.

"Uhhh... yeah... I'm over two hundred years old, remember? I like to sleep with my husband as much as anyone."

My jaw dropped just as Wyn giggled and looked down. She was so much like a bubbly teenager, it was hard to think of her as quite literally old and, I guess, married.

"So," she placed the containers on the table next to me, "we have Maso, which is kind of a casserole made with berries, and lentils. This is Listy, which is a leaf stew made with root vegetables. Or, I found some cheese that I think Delia made a few months ago."

"Leaf stew?" I asked, poking at the containers. My stomach flipped. I hoped better food appeared soon; I didn't think I could live on leaf stew and lentils for very long.

"I made the same face about the food you eat, too," she said. "We are all vegetarians and most of our food dates back before even Ilyan was born, when all the earth were hunter/gatherers." She shoved one of the smaller containers at me with a grimace. "Try the Listy; it's closer to what you would normally eat, so you might like it."

I looked down at the contents of what Wyn had just handed me, and bile rose in my throat. It looked like someone had shredded the branch of a tree and boiled it with leaves, carrots, potatoes and tomatoes. Wyn was already chowing down on some purple goo. I could already tell this would take some getting used to.

CHAPTER
22

THE LISTY DIDN'T TASTE AS bad as it looked. As long as I didn't look at what I put in my mouth, I could almost imagine it as a really thick meat stew. I didn't know how long I could last eating leaves and carrots, though. As much as I loved a good vegetable, I missed meat already and I was only one meal in.

Wyn finished two containers of food in the time it took me to finish my one. The entire time, she talked about how much she had missed normal food. I let her babble; the majority of what she said washed over me as noise.

My anxiety had not left yet; I was still far too restless for Ilyan's return. I needed to know when we were leaving.

I ate another spoonful and forced down the gritty leaves again. I was surprised that I wasn't starving. I was hungry, but not ravenous like I should have been. According to the news, everything had happened almost two weeks ago; meaning the half of a chili-cheese burger I had at Ryland's house was the only thing that had sustained me for so long. I asked Wyn and she waved it away, saying it was all part of the healing process.

I had just set down my empty container when the door swung open and a very tall, very muscular man burst into the small space. Wyn squealed and jumped up, practically throwing herself at him. The man grabbed her as she wrapped her legs around him, his face moving to nuzzle her neck. I couldn't help the stab of jealousy that rushed into my stomach at seeing such raw, heartfelt emotion.

Talon was large, so large that seeing the two of them together looked uncomfortable. He had slick, light-brown hair that was cut a bit shaggy and the same refined features that I had grown used to seeing on Ilyan. Beyond the straight lines of his face, there was little resemblance between the two. Talon almost looked like a barrel-chested football player, grown and stretched too tall. His arms were large and cylindrical, his legs long and slender. It was disproportionate, but looked good on him.

He finally pulled away from her, the surprise obvious on his face at seeing me sitting there. It took a moment for recognition to set in.

"Sorry about this," Talon said in an airy voice that didn't really match his size. "Wynifred has spent most of her time with you, so I haven't seen her much." He tried to remove her again, but she still stayed tight. Finally, he accepted defeat and went to sit on the bed and allowed her to stay positioned on his lap.

"I'm Talon, by the way," he said

"Joclyn." My voice was barely above a whisper.

"So, Joclyn, you seem to be all that anyone is talking about now."

I could tell Talon meant his comment to be just a conversation starter, but the way he looked at me made me uncomfortable.

"Why?" I asked, alarmed.

"Well, last of the Chosen Children, and all that." He flung his hand mindlessly to the side.

"Oh." My shoulders slunk and I looked down to my lap.

Talon laughed, a big booming sound that fit his body better than his voice did. My head snapped up to see Talon and Wyn, who had finally emerged from her hiding spot, both looking at me.

"Jos prefers to hide, Talon. She doesn't like to be noticed."

"Well, she will just have to get used to it then," Talon said. "She's the talk of the town! Finally, someone who can beat the socks off old Edmund!" He gave the air two rough punches with his hands, jostling Wyn around.

I felt the color leave my face.

"Talon, you can't say that," Wyn scolded as she detangled herself from her husband to sit next to him.

Talon opened his mouth to argue, but I cut him off. "It's all right, he's probably right anyway," I sighed. "After all; if I'm going to save Ryland, I might as well knock the socks off somebody." I felt my shy resolve melt away at the thought of saving Ryland. As much as I wanted to stay hidden, I wanted to save Ryland more.

As if on cue, a loud knock sounded on the door, followed by a deep voice announcing Ilyan's arrival. Wyn rolled her eyes, but Talon only laughed again, nudging Wyn as if preparing for some great joke. He got up from the bed and moved to the door in two strides, throwing it open and instantly going down on one knee, his head bowed in reverence. Even in this extreme position, I could still see the wide smile on his face.

"My liege, I bid you welcome to my humble home. It is an honor to welcome you into my presence."

Ilyan walked in, looking thoroughly un-amused, and shut the door behind him.

"Get up, Talon. You look ridiculous," Ilyan scolded. Talon jumped up and clasped Ilyan's arm tightly, his white teeth flashing.

"Sorry, Ilyan, I just didn't want our guest to get the wrong idea."

Ilyan turned away from Talon to face me, his smile widening just a bit as he passed Talon to kneel before me, taking my hands in his. I wanted to pull away from the close contact, but I didn't.

"Are you all right? Are you in any pain?"

"I'm fine. A little stiff when I move, but nothing hurts like it did."

"Good, I'm glad to hear it. I had hoped to keep you in bed for longer, but it seems I need to make things like that an order." He smiled before turning to Wyn who wilted a bit under his gaze.

"I am sorry, Ilyan. I couldn't stay in that room another moment. It's so dark and musty. Besides, I hated the 60s," Wyn grumbled and folded her arms.

"Yes, but my mother loved them."

"Your mother?" I asked, my voice catching on the word. Odd, since I wasn't even talking about my own mother.

"It's okay," Ilyan said. He had caught the heartbreak in my voice and brought his hand up to rest against my cheek. "You will get used to the pain you feel now. It will become part of you, eventually. I promise. But in the meantime, it's okay to cry." His voice became so low, I was sure that Wyn and Talon couldn't hear him. I nodded numbly at him, and he smiled, finally letting his hand drop from my face. My body loosened gratefully at the end of the contact.

"Now!" Ilyan announced, jumping up and clapping his hands together. "The Council has decided that it is worth the risk to go and remove Ryland from within Edmund's grasp."

"What are you saying?" I asked, not daring to hope.

"That, on the night of his graduation party, we will be going into the mansion and bringing Ryland back with us. We have to get to him before the Vymàzat completes itself. I know how to stop it, but only before it completes, so that's the key." My heart swelled at the renewed hope, my body's restless energy seeping into me again.

"But his party is more than three weeks away," I said in a panic.

"You are forgetting that you have been healing and unconscious for the past twelve days. We have eight to prepare."

"Eight days?" Wyn asked.

"Yes, which means we have eight days to get Joclyn ready to go and to be able to marginally defend herself. A Vymàzat is powerful magic, so I need someone who can keep him in his right mind for as long as possible. The strength of Joclyn's connection with him is unparalleled; meaning, you, Joclyn, are more likely to be able to do that than anyone else."

"Me...? Go into the mansion...?"

"Yes, Joclyn. You must be willing to do anything it takes to save him. How far are you willing to go, Silnỳ?"

I looked up to meet his piercing blue eyes, so full of confidence.

"I would do anything to save him." I was shocked at the confidence I suddenly felt. I had never been one to hold my own, to stand up to someone. I had practically hidden from Cynthia McFadden for years. Now, knowing I had a chance to save the one person who was the most important thing to me, my confidence felt more secure.

"Good," Ilyan said.

Eight days. Eight days and I would be back in the mansion I had practically grown up in. A shiver ran up my spine, but not in a good way.

"But... the mansion... it burned down," I said, suddenly panicked that we wouldn't be able to save him after all. "I saw it; the whole third floor was in flames."

"I can only assume that much of the damage was repaired or contained magically. Either way, the party will be held in a different part of the estate."

"Wait," Wyn's voice was loud and panicked from behind Ilyan. "You say you need her to defend herself; you can't possibly mean you are planning to center her, are you?"

"That would be the natural choice, yes," Ilyan responded as he stood.

"Now?" Wyn said.

"Yes."

"You can't, Ilyan."

"Don't worry so much, Wynifred. Joclyn is a very strong girl, I think she can handle a little bit of centering," Talon said.

"It's not Jos I'm worried about," Wyn grumbled behind clenched teeth.

"What exactly are we talking about?" I interrupted, becoming more and more confused by the minute.

"He just wants to center her, Wynny."

"What's centering?" I tried again, hoping this time to get an answer.

"Right now your magic is spread all over your body," Ilyan provided. "It's hiding in your muscle tissue and in your blood stream. When we center magic, we collect it all and bring it to one central place, making it usable. Right now, you can't use your magic because it's spread out. It's been spread out for so long, it doesn't really know where it's supposed to be; so for you, it will probably hurt much more than it's supposed to."

"Great, more pain," I moaned.

"Not that much pain," Talon provided with a smile. "So no reason to worry, right, Wynifred?"

"I told you, I am not worried about her. I am worried about Ryland."

"Ryland?"

"Ryland?" Talon echoed me. "What does he have to do with any of this?"

"Joclyn and Ryland have undergone the beginnings of a Zêlství, Talon." Wyn provided gravely. Talons jaw dropped. "If he is as weak as I am thinking, then centering her might well kill him."

"No!" I stood in alarm, but my legs almost instantly gave out and I tumbled back down to the chair. Ilyan was at my side in a moment, his warm magic plunging into me.

"It's all right, Joclyn. We are not going to hurt Ryland."

"But, Wyn said—"

"I think I have found a way around that," Ilyan interrupted me.

"How?" Wyn demanded angrily.

"We will use the drevo."

"Again?" Wyn exclaimed. "So soon? What if the magic rejects her?"

"I don't think it will."

"But what if it does?"

"Wynifred." Ilyan ended their conversation with one word. "Please go draw a bath."

"I can't use the tub in her room, Ilyan; it hasn't been cleaned. I—"

"You can use mine, Wynifred."

"Yes, My Lord." Wyn curtseyed and exited. Talon followed her, but not without clapping Ilyan hard on the back. Ilyan flinched before turning back to me.

"A bath? The same as before?" I asked once the door closed behind them.

"Yes, so please, try not to fight us this time."

Ilyan helped me to stand and guided me out the door and down the hall, one arm wrapped around my waist, the other holding tightly to my hand. I was grateful for the extra help, no matter how uncomfortable his proximity made me. The small amount of walking to and from Wyn's room had winded me, and I wasn't sure I could walk without his help.

We turned into the cream-colored hallway, Ilyan nodding to what I now assumed to be a guard.

"You will be staying with me in my corridor for the time being. I would like to have you close, just in case anything happens." He smiled at me. I tried to return it, but couldn't. Being so close, and having someone want me so close, was uncomfortable.

"This room is yours." He nodded solemnly to the door to the left. "And don't worry; we will strip it of brown and orange by morning. This room here," he nodded to the door directly across the hall, "is Ovailia's. I would say to stay out of her way, but you will find that to be an impossibility soon enough." I got the distinct impression that his sister was more of a bother than I had originally thought. We came to the end of the hall, which housed three different doors; one directly in front of us and two at either side.

"These doors here all belong to me, irritatingly enough, and you are welcome any time." His hand fanned across my back as he led me through the door directly in front of us. I drew into myself at his touch; I don't know why it made me so uncomfortable. Ilyan had found me, saved my life; but in some weird way, it felt disrespectful to Ryland to even let him touch me.

The room had been decorated in much the same way as the hall, with cream walls and cream carpet. Tucked into the corner, next to a window, was a giant bed with a white bedstead and white comforters, a large squishy divan nestled up against it. The room was so white and airy that even with the dark light of evening, it still felt comforting.

I could hear the sound of water running from one of the side rooms, the burning wood and mint smell stronger than I remembered. My body tensed-up, the memory of being held underwater still strong and terrifying.

Ilyan rubbed my back comfortingly as he led me to the bathroom, which was only just smaller than the entire brown and orange room. The walls and floor were covered in a white tile that brilliantly reflected the light from a large crystal chandelier that hung from the center of the ceiling.

Wyn was swirling dark blue water around in a huge, claw-footed tub, the color fading the more she moved the water. A small hand-carved wooden box sat open on a marble sink top, revealing the contents of what looked like chunks of dirt, weeds and bark.

"What is that?" I asked, my mouth going dry.

"It is the drevo. It is a mixture of bark of the Pristÿat tree, dirt that comes from the standing stones in Scotland, and the leaves of a Vzkrí," Ilyan explained.

I nodded. "I am just going to pretend I understood what you just said."

"The combination, along with the water, creates an amazing healing property. It can heal and repair anything."

"Even broken backs?" I asked with a smile.

"Even broken backs. But, it does more than that; it also cleanses your soul."

"Why...?" I tried again, "How is this going to work?"

"The hope," Ilyan began, "is that the healing magic, the drevo, will bypass you and pass directly to Ryland so that we can center your magic without harming him. And, if we are extraordinarily lucky, it will heal him as well; which may make the difference in how strong we find him to be in a week."

I nodded and stared between the now crystal-clear water and the box of mud. I had to do this; it would be gross, but I had to— for Ryland; it was becoming my mantra.

Ilyan left and allowed me some time to undress and wrap up in a towel. I felt odd standing in the middle of this gorgeous bathroom in only a towel. I took a deep breath and moved my head forward, allowing my hair to fall around my face.

"I can do this," I sighed to myself.

"Yes, Jos, you can. You ready?" Wyn said.

She stood by the tub, offering me a hand. I took it shakily and stepped into the incredibly warm water. I let the towel glue itself to me as I sank down into the warmth, thankful for some semblance of modesty.

The water felt just as thick as I vaguely remembered, like stepping into a vat of warm hair gel, but without the stick. I sighed and closed my eyes as I leaned against the side of the tub, feeling the warmth move into me. A moment later, Ilyan returned.

"How is it going?"

"The water seems to have accepted her; so far, so good."

"Joclyn." I opened my eyes to look at him. "I don't know how this is going to work, but if it opens up another connection, another Töuha, between you and Ryland, you can't let him touch you, okay?"

"Why not?" I asked, suddenly worried.

"If his father breaks in when you are in contact during a shared consciousness, he could use your magical connection to track you down. He could follow the pull of your newly-awakened powers to find you. A connection like that could put everything in danger. Do you understand?"

I nodded my head before leaning against the tub and closing my eyes.

"Open your mouth."

I obeyed, but didn't look as Wyn placed the bitter, gritty drevo on my tongue again. I closed my jaw around it tightly, fighting against the reflex to spit it out.

"Ready?"

"MmmmHmmm." I felt Ilyan's wide hand lay flat against my collar bone.

The warmth of his magic swam into me, the heat stretching to every corner of my body. It stayed there comfortably before his hand moved me under the water. I fought the temptation to gulp in air as he pushed me under. The warmth of his magic gained in intensity as I lay there, under the water, my lungs beginning to protest the lack of oxygen.

Ilyan's magic continued to increase until it grew into a pain, my lungs adding their own throbbing in their panic for air. My eyes snapped open again, just as I was about to pass out. I didn't see Ilyan and Wyn.

I saw Ryland's bedroom, I saw Edmund sharpening a knife, and I saw a lot of blood.

CHAPTER 23

I SAW ONLY A FLASH of the bedroom before I was dragged into the white space again. I stood frozen, in the middle of the large room, not daring to move. My hands flexed at my sides, every part of me on high alert. I heard a scuffle and a whimper, followed by a pained sob. I spun around at the sound, my heart plunging to see Ryland curled up in a ball on the floor, his body naked except for a pair of boxer shorts. His hands gripped his curly hair tightly, his knees pulled up to his chest. He sobbed as his body writhed.

I ran to him, but as I got closer I couldn't help but think that something was off about him. Just seeing him curled in a ball on the ground, he looked smaller, leaner and less muscular. I had almost reached him when I stopped short, remembering that I couldn't touch him. He cried out in agony again before reverting to his tortured ball.

"Ryland!" I called out, lifting my voice above his screams.

"Stay away!" he yelled, his voice panicked and high pitched. "Don't hurt me! I can't take any more."

I gaped at him, his body looked completely fine. Everything was smooth and perfect. Except for his boxers. I looked at what were obviously blood stains, some of the pools of red still wet and glistening.

Edmund, sharpening a knife.

My heart caught and sputtered, my stomach threatening to turn out its contents. What had Edmund done to his son? Ovailia had said I could see how he really looked by seeing with my mind and not my heart, but when looking at the wet pools of blood, I wasn't sure I wanted to see.

"Ryland," I kept my voice even.

"Don't hurt me!" He curled himself into an even tighter ball, his joints turning white from the tension.

"I am not going to hurt you, I promise."

"You will hurt me! Everyone always hurts me!"

"I won't hurt you. I want to keep you safe."

His whimpering and terror lessoned, but his body stayed wrapped in a ball.

"Everyone hurts me," he repeated, but his voice wasn't as terrified.

"I won't; I promise."

His body unwound from within itself, and he moved his hands from in front of his face to peek out at me. His blue eyes pierced me from behind dark lashes. He removed his hands all the way, looking at me from the ground where he lay.

I tried my best to stifle a sob. The boy that lay on the ground was definitely Ryland, but not the Ryland I had shared a cheeseburger with, not the Ryland I last saw. I looked into the face of a much younger Ryland; a Ryland who I stole cars with and snuck into his parent's pool in the middle of the night. He couldn't have been older than sixteen. He looked at me in confusion, the lack of recognition evident on his face. My heart plummeted.

"Who are you?" he asked, his voice catching in between tears.

"Joclyn," I answered honestly. "Don't you remember me?"

"Joclyn?" His face screwed up in fear. "You're too old to be Joclyn."

I guess he was right; if he was sixteen, he'd remember me at about fourteen.

"It's me, Ryland. I promise. I just look a little different." I gave him a little smile and his body relaxed a little more.

"How do I know it's you?"

"Do you remember when I was ten and we stole the car? Or when I was eleven and we snuck into the swimming pool, and you tried to do a flip and split your head open on the diving board?" His body began to relax with each memory I shared, so I kept going. "Or how about when we first met and you said that my eyes—"

"Looked like diamonds," he finished for me.

"Yeah."

"So, it's really you?"

"Yes."

"And you're not going to hurt me?"

"Never."

He unwound himself from off the white floor and sat up, looking around with wide eyes.

"Where are we?"

I followed his gaze, wondering how to answer him; I wasn't sure what to say or how to handle this. Ilyan hadn't mentioned anything about lost age to me.

"A special place only we can be—"

"Where no one can hurt me?"

"You're safe with me." I sat down near him, but far enough away I wouldn't be tempted to touch him. He looked at me skeptically for a minute before sliding his legs around and bringing his knees to his chest; the movement left a giant smear of blood behind on the ground. I couldn't take my eyes from it.

"Why do you look so old?"

I forced myself to look away from the blood and focus on his face.

"Magic," I stated simply. I felt like I was walking on eggshells, trying to figure out what to say. Although, at sixteen he would know everything, so much more than I even knew now.

"Magic? What magic?" His voice gave him away. I knew him far too well to know when he was covering something up.

"You told me about the magic, Ryland. You told me about your kiss." I had apparently chosen to say the wrong thing because he instantly began to panic, his arm flinging around to cover the mark on his shoulder.

"What kiss? I have no kiss; he took it away from me!" His voice was high and screechy again, the panic ricocheted off the white walls.

"The kiss, Ryland. The mark on your shoulder. You showed it to me…" I tried in vain to keep my voice even, but I knew it didn't work.

"He took it away from me!" Ryland screamed again like he hadn't even heard me. "He called me unworthy! I'm unworthy to bare the kiss. See. See! It's gone. All Gone!"

Ryland removed his hand from his back and shoved it toward me, the fingers stretched out in manic desperation. I looked at the hand, at first seeing nothing but white calloused skin, until it began to fade and change. I felt the change in me as my heart rate increased, and my vision shifted. The fingers were no longer white and beautiful; they were covered in blood. My mouth dropped in a panic as I looked at the smears of dark red.

I couldn't stop the part of me that wanted to see the real Ryland. I couldn't stop the desperate need to see him as he really was, and so my eyes lifted to his face.

Ryland sat on the floor in front of me, his dripping hand still extended toward me. The bruises from the press conference were darker and stood out vividly on his face and neck, many appearing where there were none before. The gash that ran down his face was wider and swollen in an angry red. Blood and sweat had matted his hair, causing the curls I loved so much to droop. Bruises and cuts covered his torso and chest, some oozing green fluid, and even more of them, a deep shade of blue. His right arm hung lifelessly to his side, trails of red flowing freely down the limb, over his fingers, and onto the floor.

I screamed and scrambled away from him. My hand flew to my mouth in an effort to cover the sound, but it was too late; the damage had already been done. Ryland screamed at the same time, and flung his younger body down to the ground, back into his ball. The action revealed his back to me, and I futilely fought the scream that rose in my throat. The shoulder where his kiss once lay, faced me, revealing an ugly red hole where Edmund had dug the mark out.

Ryland's cries filled my ears and pierced my soul in a way I couldn't ignore. Through my tears, through my shaking body, I crawled across the white space to him. My hands hovered uselessly over his body as Ilyan's words echoed in my ears. At that moment though, I didn't care. I wrapped my arms around him as he had me so many times before, and I gathered him onto my lap. His frame was so small; it only caused my tears to flow more. It took a moment for his body to relax and his arms to wrap around me. I slid my arms over his back, the warm wetness of his blood spreading over my skin.

I just sat there, holding him and shushing him. We sat like that, the smell of blood and tears swirling around us. Eventually, he untwined his body from mine and moved away, lifting his red hands to cup my face. I looked into his young eyes, my heart breaking with the reality of what was happening to him.

"I love you, Joclyn."

I balked. His face was young, but his voice was mature. My tears turned to sobs as I lifted my hand to his face, his own blood leaving my handprint against his cheek.

"Ryland?"

"I love you, Joclyn, but I can't stay here. I have to protect you." His hand slid over my skin to cover my eyes, and I knew when I opened my eyes again he would be gone. So I didn't open them.

"I love you, Ryland." I spoke the words to no one. My voice caught and I repeated it to myself over and over as I sank to the ground and savored the memory of his touch, his voice, no matter how brief the contact had been. I sobbed and moaned until the blackness took me and the connection gratefully ended.

I WOKE UP SCREAMING.

I sat up, kicking the covers off me aggressively as I looked at my hands and arms, in search of the blood I knew to be there. I panted and scrubbed and screamed. I barely registered that someone was there with me until a warmth began to spread through me, the panic receding. I let the warmth take over me, let it calm me down. Although it wasn't the warmth I really wanted, it would do for now.

My mind became clear as I continued to stare uselessly at my hands, part of me still wondering where the blood had gone. I was like Lady Macbeth, scrubbing and clawing madly at nothing. *Out Damn Spot. Out, I say!* Except this wasn't a play, the blood was real; it just wasn't on my hands anymore.

"Calm... Joclyn... calm." Ilyan's arms wrapped around me as his magic left my body. He pulled me to his chest, his hand running down my hair. "I'm here; it's okay."

I wanted to pull away from him; I wanted to run to Ryland. I grasped for the necklace, desperate to bring back the connection, desperate to see him again. Ilyan grabbed my hands and steadied them, his warmth moving into me again, the force of it weaker this time.

My screaming subsided into a low sob that racked through my chest. I forced my gaze away from my hands, surprised to see Ilyan's bedroom and not the brown and orange of the room I had been given. Ilyan clutched me to him as I continued to cry, grateful that my tears were finally leaving.

"What happened, Joclyn?" he asked when my crying had passed enough I could finally talk.

"Ry... Ryland... he is in pain... so much pain."

"Another Tòuha? What happened, Silnỳ?"

"I saw him; the bruises, the cuts... the blood. Ed... Edmund cut out his mark." I felt Ilyan's arms tense around me, his breathing increase in what I could only assume to be anger. "He was young... he didn't recognize me. Why didn't he recognize me, Ilyan?" The panic came back, that desperate edge creeping into my voice.

"Oh, Silnỳ, his mind is being deleted. He remembers less and less each day. Did he remember you eventually?"

"Yes, and before he left, I could have sworn it was him, that he wasn't sixteen-year-old Ryland anymore; that it was really him. That he wasn't sixteen-years-old anymore." I felt Ilyan's body relax a bit. "Is that good?"

"It means that all of him is still there, that he is still fighting."

"Why did he look so young then?"

"Because as much as he fights, he is still losing the battle. The longer he fights it, the older he will look in your Tòuhas. But when he forgets you completely, when he is only a child, then it will be too late."

Ilyan's words had a sharp edge that cut through me; it broke the dam I had made deep inside and let every single pent-up emotion and fear out in a tidal wave. I began crying uncontrollably again, but I didn't want Ilyan to take the pain away and put me to sleep with his magic. I needed to feel it. I cried and clung to him as I let everything out.

I howled over the death of my mother, the image of her lifeless body, vivid and vibrant. I cried at the memory of our lunch, the last time we were together, and how I had given her everything that she wanted; the daughter she had always wanted me to be.

I sobbed over the loss of my normalcy. I balled up against Ilyan as I thought about the changes in my life, the drastic differences that had occurred within such a small amount of time.

I screamed with the agonizing pain of a broken heart; my voice wailed as it broke and bled in my throat. I felt my heart break into a million pieces as everything hit me simultaneously, for the last time. Every memory of Ryland flashed by, and although I wanted to smile and laugh, the memories only hurt. Hurt that I could not have him; hurt at how much everything had changed.

Through it all, Ilyan just held me, his wide hands rubbing my back. He shushed and cooed and sang to me as I cried, and all of it made me want to cry more, because his weren't the arms I craved.

When it was done, I knew it was done. I knew I was stronger than the pain now.

"Why would he do that, Ilyan? Why would he cut the mark out?" Ilyan moved my hair away from my face, his finger lingering on my own mark. I jerked my head away, not wanting such an intimate touch from him.

"Do you remember when I told you the kiss is more like a poisonous bite? Well, the kiss itself is caused by a pool of poison. If it's cut out, you release the poison into the person who bears the kiss."

I gasped and the tears came back again.

"Will it kill him?"

"It can, but I think Edmund only hopes to weaken him further, and gain control over his magic that much faster."

"Why? Why is he doing this?"

"A punishment probably, but also to increase his control. Edmund has always viewed Ryland as a weapon, and now he sees the best opportunity to use him as such."

"We will be too late, won't we?"

Ilyan's face made it clear that he didn't know. Our eyes locked together in some silent agreement that we would try, but I couldn't shake the feeling that trying wouldn't be enough anymore.

Ilyan would say no more; he simply laid me back down in his bed and put me to sleep with his magic. I was probably more grateful than I should have been, considering all I dreamed about was chasing a bloody trail through the golden hallways of the LaRue mansion.

CHAPTER

24

THE FOLLOWING MORNING, I REALIZED the downside of the white-on-white scheme of Ilyan's room. The moment the sun began to creep over the horizon and the gray light of dawn had begun to fade away, the room became supercharged with light. The beams of golden sun shone through the window that Ilyan had pushed his bed up against. They bounced around and increased in brightness as the white walls and carpet reflected them back. Once the light had infiltrated my troubled sleep, I sat upright, sleep leaving me much quicker than I would have liked.

I was still in Ilyan's bed, still in Ilyan's rooms. I felt uncomfortable and scared. I shouldn't be here. Not only was he some sort of king in this place, he was awfully friendly.

I sat there trying to plan some form of escape. Even if I made it out the door, I wasn't sure I could remember which door led to the brown and orange room. I was having trouble focusing; a subtle buzzing was taking over my body, causing my mind to bounce around. It felt like the warm heat I had always felt from Ryland and Ilyan, but more alive, more electric. I brushed off the feeling, trying to focus on my escape again. The buzzing under my skin grew steadily, making me feel jittery and anxious.

I threw the blankets away from me, intent on just storming down the hall in the hopes of at least finding Wyn, when a loud grunt issued from the foot of the bed, followed by a large thump that shook the room. I looked toward the noise, terrified in my jittery state, that some explosion had gone off. Instead, I was treated to Ilyan yelling, or perhaps swearing, in Czech before he crawled on hands and knees into the bathroom, slamming the door behind him.

I stared at the door in bewilderment; I wasn't sure whether I should laugh hysterically or not. I could hear him thump around in the bathroom, random foreign words filtering through the ivory-colored doors. I sat up, fully intent on making my escape when Ilyan's thumping and yelling was joined by another voice, from someone running rapidly down the hall toward me. My heart sputtered as the door flung open and a very agitated, while still perfectly poised, Ovailia burst through the door.

"What in heaven's name..." She froze at the sight of me, her eyes bugging out of her head as her jaw worked mechanically in place.

Seeing Ovailia there with such a terrifying look on her face sent the energy into overdrive as it buzzed and vibrated through me. I grabbed the covers and pulled them up to my chin, realizing too late that that was probably not the best action to take. Ovailia's jaw only dropped more. I looked down; I was wearing one of Ilyan's light colored, button-up shirts... great.

"This isn't what it looks like," I said, desperately hoping she would believe me and not question any more. After all, I had absolutely no idea what I would say. I needed Ryland.

The energy under my skin increased, and I felt a desperate need to get rid of it.

"What are you doing here?"

I opened my mouth to answer, but no words came out. I could feel my cheeks turning a deep shade of crimson. Ovailia rushed to the bathroom door without saying another word to me, her eyes never leaving my blush stained face.

The door to the bathroom slammed behind her and my head dropped into the white cotton blankets. Great. This was not the way I wanted to start my day. The yelling in the bathroom increased as Ovailia joined in the fray. I could make out the two voices distinctly, even though I couldn't understand the words they were yelling at each other. I was secretly glad I didn't understand Czech. I wasn't sure I really wanted to know what they were saying.

I jumped off the bed, heading toward Ryland's sweater that lay across the foot. I grabbed it and went to tug off the yellow shirt that Ilyan had dressed me in. My blush deepened and melted into an embarrassed anger at the thought of what state I had been in after the bath and exactly what I was wearing now. I froze for only a moment before removing the shirt and tugging on one of Wyn's band shirts that had been laid out next to Ryland's sweater. I pulled the shirt and sweater on, keeping a close ear on the argument going on in the bathroom, just in case someone walked in on me. I glanced around for my pants, my heart dropping at finding nothing, not even the pajama pants I had worn last night. I guess I would have to stay in the plaid shorts I had been dressed in a bit longer.

I tugged the sweater down in hopes of hiding what I could only assume were Ilyan's boxers. I pushed down my anger at being left to sleep here and thrown into such a situation; after all, how hard would it have been to just walk me down the hall?

I turned to make my escape just as Ovailia burst through the bathroom door, still yelling something angrily in Czech. She was followed close behind by Ilyan who was soaking wet with soap in his hair and a white towel wrapped haphazardly around his waist.

The sight of him supercharged my agitation, bringing the level of buzzing on my skin to new heights. I looked back and forth from him to Ovailia, who yelled angrily. Ilyan rebutted something before Ovailia stormed out, slamming the door behind her. Ilyan exhaled angrily before turning to me.

"Pants are in the closet." His accent was thick, and it took me a moment to register exactly what he had said. He waved his hand toward a door on the opposite end of the room before turning back to the bathroom. I immediately decided to forgo the pants and continue with my original plan to track down Wyn.

"Oh, and Joclyn," his head poked out from behind the bathroom door, "don't go anywhere."

I fumed angrily at him before he closed the door to go back to his shower. I rubbed my arms abrasively in the hopes of lessening the buzzing. It seemed to be working a bit, the motion also calming my heart rate. I breathed deeply as I made my way toward the closet, the buzzing now only a hum. My anger and frustration had never reacted this way, but then, I wasn't sure I had ever been so emotionally charged before.

Ilyan's closet was a strange place. It was as large as the bathroom, with clothes stacked floor to ceiling. There was little rhyme or reason to it, and it took me a bit to locate pants among the heaps of clothes. I dug through the stacks of designer jeans, grateful that none of these would fit just right. I wasn't in any mood to be noticed by a large group of people quite yet. I chose one of the only pairs that didn't have the perfectly placed tears that Ilyan favored, pulling them on over the shorts.

Finding a belt in the mess was surprisingly more difficult than locating pants. I held the pants around me as I searched through drawers and boxes that were littered around the large space. I carefully lifted a sheet that covered one section of the wall and stopped short.

Behind the curtain was a perfectly organized wall of clothes. Each piece of clothing hung on its own hanger, covered with a clear protective bag. On its own, it would have been surprising, given the lack of organization among the rest of the clothes.

It wasn't just that though; at first, I thought they were costumes. Each shirt was longer and would probably fall to the knee on an average-sized man. Given the lengths and the style, I would almost call them tunics. The light colored garments were cut from fabrics that I could automatically tell where expensive. I fought the urge to remove the bags and run my hands over the soft silks, touch the fine jewels and golden ropes that adorned each one.

I hungrily ran my eyes over the glittering stones, the deep colored embroidery. The sleeves on each piece were exaggerated, but I couldn't tell by how much, given how loosely they hung on the hangers. Claudius, Macbeth, Lear, Romeo. I could see these on-stage in a million different plays, but they weren't fake, like costumes; they were shockingly real.

"Pretty, aren't they?" I jumped at Ilyan's voice, my hand clutching my chest.

"You scared me!" I spun to him and balked. While now soap-free, he was still only dressed in a towel. I inhaled sharply and stepped away, hoping he hadn't noticed my reaction. His chest was strong and thick with sinewy muscles, but that wasn't why I had reacted. The skin across his chest was criss-crossed with hundreds of raised scars, like he had been whipped.

I shook my head and looked away. My skin buzzed as my agitation returned, coming in full force again. I wasn't as mad as I should have been to see him dressed in only a towel.

"Sorry, but you were looking at my private collection; you kind of deserved it," he chuckled.

"Private collection?" I let the sheet fall over the clothes again. "Sorry."

"Don't be. They are not a secret after all. I wear them to council." He handed me a belt he had removed from under a pile of undershirts; I would have never found it.

"Council? You mean the meeting you had yesterday?"

"Yes, it is an official meeting, so I have to look the part." He grinned, but it looked more like a grimace.

"You mean, like King?"

His face fell. He turned from me and grabbed a few items of clothing off the many disorganized piles.

"Not 'like', Joclyn, just King." He gave me a sad, little smile and disappeared behind a partition I hadn't noticed due to the large amount of clothes draped over it.

"So, do I need to call you 'My Lord' now?"

He flung the towel over the side to join the clothes already there, and I instantly looked down at my feet, turning my back to him in embarrassment and frustration.

"That depends on a few things."

"Like what?" I asked as he came out from behind the partition, still pulling his shirt over his head.

"Well, for starters, when we are together like this." I blushed, which only caused him to smile. "Just the two of us, I mean. Or with Wynifred and Talon, then, no. But around anyone else, then, yes."

I nodded my head in understanding, knowing I would mess it up.

"Why not Wyn and Talon?"

"Wynifred was not raised with us, so she forgets from time to time. Most of the time, I let it slide as she and Talon have undergone the Zêlství, but there are times when she probably needs to remember her place a bit more."

"And Talon?"

"Talon and I grew up together; it would just be weird if he started calling me 'My Lord' and bowing all the time."

"Were you not always king?"

"No, Silnỳ." His answer was definite, and strangely final.

I shut my mouth, sure he didn't want me to ask any more questions about his royal status.

"What does that mean?" I asked, hoping my change in subject was easy to follow.

"What?"

"*Silnỳ?*" The word sounded odd on my tongue.

He looked at me quietly, his eyes narrowed suspiciously.

"It means, 'little one'."

I only nodded at him. What an odd nickname.

"Now, what do you say to a little bit of training for that newly awakened kouzlo of yours?"

"Training?"

"Yes, that buzz in your fingertips? I think it's dying to get out."

I looked at my fingers; it seemed silly that I hadn't realized exactly what it was before.

"It's..." I stopped mid-sentence, the proper words not finding the right place.

"It's your magic, Joclyn. Perfectly centered and dying for you to learn to control it."

I looked up at him, stunned; the buzzing grew a bit at Ilyan's sly half-smile.

"I think it's waited long enough, don't you?" He left the closet quickly; I padded after him in bare feet, so that I could keep up. He nodded to the guard and kept moving. I finally caught up to him as he opened a large door that led outside.

"Now," he announced, "the real fun begins. What do you say to growing a tree?"

"Growing a tree?" I said, alarmed. "How is that going to help me save Ryland?" The buzzing grew as panic joined my frustration.

"It will help because then you will be able to use your magic," he chuckled, which only made me more upset.

"Growing a tree is not going to help me! How will I use that? Grow a tree and then go hide in it? That doesn't help anyone." I could hear the harsh edge of panic creep steadily into my voice.

"It helps us more if you know even a little bit of what you are doing than nothing at all." Ilyan's voice was still calm, and somehow, that helped to decrease my panic.

"So when will I learn magic that can help me save Ryland?" The buzzing grew more with the fuel from my stress. I felt like I was going to explode. I breathed deeply, trying to gain control.

"We have eight days, Joclyn. I can't possibly teach you everything in eight days. So we will be learning the basics." His calm voice was a whisper compared to mine.

"The basics? How am I supposed to do anything with the basics?"

"We will begin," he continued, ignoring my outburst, "with plant growth so that you can gain control of your power. I will then teach you how to control wind, and if you are very lucky, we may touch on energy fields."

"That's it?"

"Yes, Silný. I will teach you enough so you can go in, defend yourself if you must, and so you can run away when necessary."

"Run away?" My heart plunged into my toes, my voice dropping in tone as my heart rate increased in timber. "I thought we were going to save him."

"We are." He left it at that and strolled away from me.

"Then why do I need to know how to run away?"

"Because you will not be strong enough to fight any of them. You are going with the sole purpose of getting Ryland out, and that task requires you to run away. You must know how to run away from Edmund, from Timothy, and maybe even from Ryland."

I followed him slowly to the courtyard Wyn had shown me last night. I didn't know what to say; my anger had lessened, but now I felt somewhat worthless. All my life, Ryland had protected and supported me, and now it was my turn to protect him, and I couldn't do it. Even with all the power that I now had buzzing under my skin, I couldn't. There wasn't enough time to learn how to do that.

The courtyard in the middle of the motel was the type of place I would gladly waste days in. The large branches of the tree that stood in the center of the space reached far over us, shading most of the courtyard throughout the day. What light seeped through the canopy speckled the stone paths and grassy patches with pools of warm sunlight and golden color.

I sat in one of the sun bathed pools of light, Ilyan by my side as he gently taught me to stretch and bend my magic. At first, all the pent-up energy came out in a rush and I covered us with dirt as a small area of ground exploded rather than causing the flower to grow, as I was supposed to do. I was elated; if it was really that easy, then perhaps I had a chance to actually help Ryland after all.

After the initial use however, getting the magic out was a different story altogether. I could still feel it tingle and move under my skin, but I could no longer get it to move beyond my veins and into my control. The buzzing grew and swirled around inside as my frustration twisted into anxiety. Perhaps this was all just a pointless exercise; my magic had been hidden too long. My magic simply didn't know what to do and was just as stubborn as I was. It made me feel dead inside.

By the time the sun had cleared the roof of the old motel, Wyn and Talon had joined our group. They sat off to the side, a sleepy Wyn curled up against Talon. I was happy they were there, but grateful that they weren't offering their own advice. I didn't know how much more failure I could take anyway. After about three hours of trying, I slunk away and leaned against the giant tree that was shading us.

"I give up," I moaned as Ilyan came over and joined me.

"Don't be ridiculous. You give up and Ryland dies, simple as that."

I flinched at his brutal honesty, his stern voice cutting through me.

"Are you still going to give up?"

"No."

"Good. Now, I have an idea, but it involves breaking a rule. Are you okay with that?"

"What rule?" I wanted to agree, but I was apprehensive about what he was going ask.

"Just answer the question, Joclyn."

"Fine," I grunted at him, folding my arms across my chest. I could hear Talon laugh at me from across the clearing; it didn't do much to improve my mood.

I followed Ilyan back to the space where we had been working, my foul mood increasing as he invited Wyn and Talon over to join us. Wyn bounded over with a wide smile on her face as she barreled into me with a bear hug before settling in next to Talon.

"All right," Ilyan began, "I need you to take off the necklace."

"What?" I clutched it in a desperate panic; I couldn't take it off— I had promised Ryland.

"Don't worry; you can put it on the second we are done."

"Why? Why do I need to take it off in the first place? It's just my magic, right? You said it probably just doesn't know what to do."

"While that may be the problem, I think it is something else. I think Edmund's magic, that is repressing Ryland, is repressing you as well."

I heard Wyn breathe behind me, but I could only stare.

"But I thought you told me... you told me Edmund couldn't affect me."

"I thought he couldn't, but it looks like he might be able to. If that's the case, we need to get you using your magic so we can train you to block Edmund's barrier. Do you understand?"

I nodded solemnly before moving to take off the necklace. My stomach flipped around inside of me. Not only was Edmund hurting Ryland, but he was hindering me as well. I sincerely hoped Ilyan's guess would be wrong. I handed the necklace to Ilyan, who wrapped it up in a cloth.

"Now," Ilyan looked at me eagerly, "make the seed grow."

I exhaled deeply, flexing my fingers as the buzzing shifted into the tips of them. I closed my eyes and focused. I could feel the energy; I could feel what it wanted to do. I placed my hand onto the ground and felt my magic move out and into the ground. Everything shifted under my fingers and a loud popping noise filled my ears. Talon and Ilyan yelled out in irritation while Wyn laughed hysterically.

My eyes popped open. Instead of being surrounded by large craters or flames, I sat in the middle of long grasses and prairie flowers up to my head. I hadn't conjured all of these, had I?

I looked around in a panic before jumping to my feet. Ilyan, Talon and Wyn all sat in the same places they had a moment ago, except that now they were all covered in dirt and sticks. Wyn continued to laugh hysterically as Ilyan spat and wiped dirt out of his mouth and ears.

"Well, I don't think we have to worry about how strong your magic is, just how to control it," Ilyan said between dirt clumps.

CHAPTER
25

I WAS DEVASTATED THAT ILYAN WAS right, that Edmund's restraints had moved through the necklace into me. I didn't want to think about what Edmund could do to me if he knew about the necklace, about the connection. What worried me so much more was the thought that if Edmund's magic was restricting me that much, what was he doing to Ryland? I couldn't get the image of Ryland's blood-covered bedroom out of my mind; it added to my tortures.

"I can't believe it was that easy. Especially after all the trouble I had before," I spoke quietly to myself as I stared at my hands. I almost expected them to catch on fire.

"Evil overlords can do that to you," Talon said as he handed the wrapped necklace back to me.

I took the necklace and looked at it solemnly. I desperately wanted to put it on, but wasn't sure if I could, or even if I should. The thought of how much it hindered me, of what it was now beginning to mean, was a heavy, choking weight.

"Go ahead," Ilyan urged as he sat beside me again. "Put it on."

"Do you think I should?" I carefully peeled away the folds of fabric to look at the jewel nestled there, the fine silver chain circling around like a snake.

"Yes, I do. I want you to try something," Ilyan replied.

I removed the necklace from the cloth and carefully placed it around my neck. At almost the exact moment that the ruby touched my skin, I felt my magic slow down, the energy lose some of the wriggling nature that I was becoming used to.

"How bad is it?" Ilyan asked, and I knew what he was referring to.

"Everything slowed down; it almost feels like my body has become sludge."

Ilyan nodded his head in understanding.

"Your magic is very strong, Joclyn. I think you can fight through this. In fact, if you can master it, it might help everyone in the future, especially Ryland."

My head perked up. I leaned closer to him, even though my instinct was to move away. My dark hair fell around my face as I bent toward him.

"How, Ilyan? How do I do it?" I asked.

"I don't know. You will have to figure it out yourself." He smiled, and I had the distinct impression he did actually know what I was supposed to do.

"Can't you just tell me?" I pleaded. I needed to know if it could help me save Ryland.

"I would, but I have never actually witnessed something like this. I have ideas, but they will probably not work for you."

"Why not?"

"Well, Joclyn, because your magic is not developed. For example..." His voice had taken on that deep, commanding tone that I had heard in him the first moment I had met him, in front of the school.

I flinched away.

"...if I told you to try to perform a double barrier and reverse it, would you be able to do it?"

I just stared.

"Or, how about an extended growth spell? No. You would not know what to do. I could teach you all that in a month, maybe two, but not today, not when your knowledge of magic is so limited. You have to figure it out for yourself because you don't know all of the basics yet." He looked away from me with superiority.

Wyn rubbed my back sympathetically, whether because Ilyan had just put me in my place or because I looked absolutely forlorn, I had no idea.

I lay back in the grass, dejectedly. Of course, it couldn't be quite so simple. I looked through the grass to the dirt, my mind spinning as I tried to figure out what to do. I could feel the low buzz of my magic. I still felt the desperate need for it to get out, but no matter how hard I tried, it wouldn't come.

I flexed my fingers and placed the very tips in the dirt, digging them in a bit. The warm earth and the electric hum from within me combined aggressively, but the magic would not move. I had the foolish thought to cut my skin to simply let it out. While probably a very natural progression, the image of cutting my own skin brought visions of Ryland being tortured to the forefront of my memory.

I flinched at the image, wiping it from my mind. Then I paused; the image had instigated something. I could still feel the super-charged buzz as the magic released into the ground where my fingers touched it. I now knew what I needed to do, and although I sincerely didn't want to, I brought a vision of Ryland to my mind.

This time, I chose the gentle image of him placing the necklace around my neck. The beautiful memory caused my heart to swell, and with it, a tiny bit of energy expelled itself. It wasn't enough to do anything, but it was something. I felt the warmth of it leaving my fingertips before it subsided.

I tried again, this time remembering the first time we had climbed the trees and how he had gently coaxed me down and hugged me tightly. My soul flew at the imagery, the magic surging momentarily and shooting out of me, causing the grass to grow about an inch. It was more, but it still wasn't enough.

I sat up, staring at my dirty fingers in amazement. I had felt it; felt the change. I could have sworn I could almost feel the restrictive cover that the necklace placed over me shift. If only I could shift it enough to overcome it.

"What is it, Joclyn?"

My head snapped up to see all three of them looking at me, confused. I could tell they had just been laughing about something; Wyn's shoulders still stuttered, as if trying to restrain a latent laugh.

"It's... I thought..." I paused. No matter how much I was learning to trust Wyn and was growing to like Talon and Ilyan, I still wasn't sure I was ready to go into everything quite yet. "It's nothing," I finished lamely.

Talon turned away from me, returning easily to whatever conversation they had been having a moment before. Wyn stared at me a moment longer before shrugging and returning to jabber along with Talon. Ilyan, though—Ilyan continued to look at me curiously. The intensity of his gaze locked me in place, the familiar blue shooting into me, sending shivers up my spine.

I didn't like the sensation that his gaze gave me. My stomach glittered with the attention, while simultaneously shying away from him. I was thankful when he looked away, releasing me from my inner turmoil. I shouldn't be as comfortable with him as I was; I didn't want to be.

I threw myself back into the grass and focused on what should be my only thought: getting my magic under control so I could help save Ryland.

Last year, when the spring flowers had begun to bloom, Ryland had taken me up the mountain to have pie. We had arrived right at dusk, and Ryland had been quieter than usual during our trek through the forest. When we had gotten there, he had produced not only the pie, but a chicken dinner he had obviously bribed my mother to make; he knew it was one of my favorites. I could still see his broad grin as he produced the food, the memory surging my magic. I plunged my fingers into the dirt again as a small amount escaped. I pulled my attention back to the memory, desperate for more magic to find its way out.

I think it was that night in the mountains that I had started to fall in love with Ryland. After we had eaten and laughed and joked as we always did, we had chased each other through the forest with the water guns that Ry had brought along. I had snaked through the trees, unable to keep my giggling contained, giving Ryland more than one opportunity to soak me. My sneakers had squished as I walked, another sure give-away. I had caught sight of Ryland ahead of me and prepared to make my attack when a perfect circle of flowers caught my attention.

Purple pansies grew among the pine needles and forest decay in a dainty, four foot wide ring. It was such an odd flower to find in the forest, and the circle so perfectly round. I had walked around it slowly, something pulling me to stand in the middle of it, even though I was sure it was taboo.

"Go ahead," Ryland had said. Now, even a year later, his voice remained crystal clear in my mind.

My magic surged again, but none escaped.

I had stepped over the border of flowers slowly, laughing at the intent of this new game. Ryland had walked around me, hailing the king of the fairies and urging him to accept me as a gift and to treat me well, his voice barely able to contain his laughter. Ry had leaned down slowly and plucked one of the beautiful flowers, presenting it to me with smoldering eyes...

"How did you do that?" Wyn said.

I shot up, surprised at the garden of pansies that had grown around me. Ilyan and Talon had disappeared, leaving only Wyn to witness my amazing breakthrough. I reached out and touched the soft petals; they were almost identical to the ones from my memory.

"Ryland. Our memories together," I whispered, fighting the tears that still fought their way out from my extended visit with such beautiful memories.

"Really?"

I didn't dare look at her; I only nodded.

"You think of Ryland, and your magic can move? What do you think of? Kissing him, his rippling muscles...? What?"

My heart thudded as I looked up to her: I didn't know what to say. "No, nothing like that. Just him. Memories of him."

Wyn's shoulders slunk sadly. "Like kissing him?"

"No, Wyn," I whispered. "I have never kissed him."

She stared at me in shock; she almost looked scared. "Never?"

"No, never. I mean, we got close," I added, just in case she got the wrong idea, "but we never actually made the connection."

Wyn continued to stare at me with that strange look on her face. I ran my finger through the flowers again in an attempt not to look at her.

"Is that bad?" I asked when the silence had become too much.

"No, no, no." Wyn reassured me. "It's just that... normally to have a connection as strong as yours, you would have at least kissed."

I began to feel even more uncomfortable. I looked down into the carpet of flowers as the blush crept up my cheeks.

"Your souls must be connected," she sighed.

I couldn't help but hear that teenage longing in her voice.

"It's like you are meant to be."

I rolled my eyes at her, but secretly, I hoped she was right. At least then I would be able to save him.

CHAPTER
26

$\mathcal{J}$LYAN HAD KNOCKED LOUDLY ON my door at daybreak to command me to meet him in the courtyard in ten minutes. Even without being awakened by the bright sunlight in his room, I still wasn't allowed to sleep in. I didn't give him the benefit of an answer. Instead, I rolled out of bed, thankful for the disappearance of the ancient décor. The brown and orange paper had been replaced by white walls with a deep green stripe circling the ceiling. The lumpy bed with the ancient bedspread was also gone; a small, squishy, pure-white day bed in its place. The dark table and orange lamp were still there, but they didn't look as old as they had before; they looked almost chic. It wasn't really my style, but I liked it anyway.

I had opted to shower first, deciding that since I hadn't actually taken a real bath in a while and knowing that I could be in and out in five minutes, it wouldn't be a problem. When I stepped into the hot water though, I knew I was in trouble. The jets of steaming water hit my skin, and every muscle in my body relaxed into a comfortable jelly. I let the water flow over me in long rivers as it wiped away the grit and grime of everything that had happened to me in the last two weeks. Granted, the water was clear and I actually had no real dirt or grime, it still felt wonderfully cleansing and invigorating.

I stood there for longer than necessary, feeling the now-constant buzzing. After my success with the circle of pansies, I hadn't been able to accomplish anything else without removing the necklace, despite trying late into the night. Standing here without the necklace, I felt my magic surge again. I didn't dare attempt anything for fear that it would hinder any success later. I turned off the water and stepped out, knowing Ilyan would be upset with my tardiness.

Sure enough, without the sound of the water, I could hear Ilyan and Ovailia shouting at each other in Czech again, their voices carrying through my door. I was beginning to wonder if this was a daily occurrence.

I dressed quickly as the angry yelling continued, trying to pick out clothes from among the mismatched array of what had been brought over for me. I could tell that most of these clothes had belonged to several different people. I opted for a band shirt I was sure was Wyn's and a pair of baggy, gray pants. Thankfully, a pair of flip-flops near my size had been left for me, so I slid them on as I pulled Ryland's sweater over my head, his lingering smell still clinging to the fabric. I flung the door open, and the yelling stopped.

"Look who it is," Ovailia sneered in a sugary sweet voice. "Finally decide to grace us with your presence, did you?"

I looked from Ilyan to Ovailia in confusion. Ovailia kept her eyes glued on me, her lips pursed, while Ilyan had his jaw clenched and eyes narrowed toward no one in particular.

"Here I am." I tried to sound perky, but my voice fell flat.

"Wonderful." Ovailia walked away, her hair swaying ominously behind her. Ilyan followed her, beckoning me to follow.

My guard went up instantly. I wasn't sure I wanted to spend an hour, let alone a day, with the two of them together. My experiences with them so far had been less than stellar. Ilyan led us, once again, into the courtyard, but my heart plunged at seeing the thirty or so people who were milling around the large space. My hands moved to pull my hood up, but stopped half-way; I needed to be brave.

"Sorry," Ilyan said sheepishly. "I had hoped to prepare you for this, but I didn't count on your needing a shower." He grabbed my hand and placed it gently in the crook of his arm. It didn't escape my notice that his posture improved almost instantly. "'My Lord', remember." He smiled bashfully at me before leading me into the large courtyard.

Everyone stood and faced him. I couldn't help but feel that my baggy pants and sweater left me terribly underdressed for this. Even though Ilyan wore his trademark torn jeans and button-up shirt and no one else was wearing anything out of the ordinary, the air of the situation demanded something better. As we walked past each person, they would bow their head and lower slightly. Ilyan would return the bow with a slight head nod and sometimes say a name. Thankfully, by the time we made it to the tree, most everyone had returned to what they were doing previously.

"Is it always like this?" I asked quietly, noticing that several of the people continually looked over toward us.

"My Lord," Ilyan reminded me under his breath.

"Is it always like this, My Lord?" I asked stiffly.

"Unfortunately," he mumbled.

"It should be like this more often and handled with much more dignity, but my brother seems to think otherwise."

I jumped at Ovailia's voice. I hadn't noticed her standing there.

"Well," she continued after glaring me down, "now that you are here, should we continue?"

"Ummm... sure," I answered, unsure if I should be adding some form of a title to Ovailia's name. She acted like she was entitled to one, so I wasn't sure.

"Good. Now, Ilyan tells me you have mastered plant growth easily enough. Let us hope the same rings true for your command of the wind." She held out a heavy muslin cloth. I hesitantly removed the necklace and placed it in the folds. Ovailia wrapped it up tightly and placed it near some bushes on the ground. I looked at it, longing to put it back on, but knew it would only hinder me, and I needed to get control of my magic fast.

"Now," Ovailia continued, "the concept of manipulating wind is much the same as plant life. You must infuse the wind with your magic until you receive the ability to control it. It is through this control that you will be able to manipulate yourself and objects around you."

I just nodded my head numbly. I knew that should make sense, but I couldn't seem to wrap my mind around it.

"Think about how you move your magic into the plants and tell them what to do," Ilyan said. "It's much the same concept, except with wind, you can do more; move cars or buildings, fly."

"We *were* flying that night you saved me!"

"Yes, we were," Ilyan said happily. Ovailia however, cleared her throat.

"Sorry... My Lord," I added hastily.

"I want you to learn this skill, so in case anything happens this week, you will be able to get away and save yourself."

My heart plummeted at the reminder of my need to run away. I wanted to be able to save Ryland, not be a hindrance and only have to run away. I nodded strongly and focused on what was going on.

"All right," Ilyan said, "bring your magic to the front and release it into the air around you. I want to see if you can summon wind from nothing."

I focused intently on the air and felt my magic seep out of me like a slow leak, pleased when I felt the air softly move itself into a subtle breeze. I pushed more magic out, excited at the quick success. The more I released into the air, the bigger the breeze became, until it swirled swiftly through the courtyard, pushing into those who remained watching us and eventually knocking me into Ilyan.

"Sorry, My Lord," I whimpered as he set me straight again.

"Don't be. That was wonderful!" Ilyan was pleased. Ovailia looked anything but.

Ilyan grabbed my shoulders and steered me to stand right in front of the large tree.

"Okay, now, climb the tree," Ovailia snapped impatiently, ignoring my quick success. "Show me how you accomplish these tree races that Wynifred has told me so much about."

I felt excited for a whole moment, until I looked up into the tree branches. The tangled knot of the tree extended high above me; no matter how hard I looked, I couldn't see a way through. It was more than the impossibility of the branches though, it was the fact that I could fall. My hands moved to wrap around my back without my even knowing. My fingers spanned flat against, the fingers touching the places where broken bones and nerves had been only a week before. My painfully broken back had given me a fear of falling.

"You won't fall," Ilyan whispered in my ear.

"How do you know I won't?"

"I won't let you." His finger moved up to trace a circle around my kiss.

I tore my eyes away from the tangled branches to look at him, stepping away from his touch and feeling guilty.

"But there is no way up, Ilyan—My Lord."

Ilyan smiled at me softly before turning to Ovailia. "If you will excuse us, sister, I believe this lesson will not require your assistance today."

Before Ovailia could open her mouth to rebut, Ilyan had opened his hand, the necklace flying into his open palm from within the bush. Ilyan then took my hand and began to lead me out of the courtyard. Everyone looked surprised that we were leaving so soon, but they stood and paid their respects to him as we walked by, nonetheless.

Once we had made it through the door from the courtyard, Ilyan's pace increased until we had emerged on the other side through yet another door, this one leading to a wide expanse of untamed forest. I couldn't see a city or town; we were surrounded by hills of forest, misty mountains just visible in the distance.

"Now, do you trust me?"

The answer to the question was obvious. I did trust him; I just didn't trust how he acted around me sometimes. I knew that I couldn't let my fierce loyalty to Ryland get in the way of Ilyan teaching me how to save him, so I nodded my head.

"Good. Now, do you trust me to not let you fall?"

It took a moment for me to get my wits about me. As much as I was scared of falling, scared of breaking my body again, I knew that I trusted Ilyan. He would not let anything happen to me; of that, I was sure. I nodded once in agreement, and a wide smile spread over his face.

"Good. I am going to teach you to fly the way my father taught me. I want you to use the wind to launch yourself into the air, straight up. Can you do that?"

"No," I said, panic seizing me.

"I won't let you fall, Joclyn. I promise you this above all else, I will never let anything hurt you. I am only here to protect you."

"Okay."

"Now get down and prepare to jump."

I crouched down to the ground as Ilyan had instructed, my palms lying flat against the ground.

"Now call the wind to you," he whispered behind me.

I closed my eyes tightly, attempting to forget that anyone was there, forgetting my previous failures. I breathed out, letting my magic come to a boiling point under my skin. My magic moved away from me easily, stretching away and bringing the wind back with it. The warm tongues licked at my feet and the tips of my fingers. I moved it around, amazed at the control I had over it. It obeyed my every thought.

"Now, jump."

With one swift movement, I kicked off from the ground, the wind propelling me upward, my arms extending out, warm air whipping past my fingers. The sensation was amazing; I could have never guessed that so much freedom lay in this, in flight. My face rose to the sun, enjoying the warm rays and the breeze that moved across my skin. The feeling of the wind's soft touch brought back memories of a million car rides up the canyon and a million tree races. Even through the bitter-sweet memories, I smiled. Then the wind began to change.

I had flown too high. The air zoomed past me as I began to fall. I looked around desperately for a branch large enough to land on, my instinct from the tree races kicking in. There was nothing, not even a stem big enough to support my weight.

I had been here before. I had fallen. I had almost died. I screamed in fear and agony as gravity pulled me toward the earth again. My body tensed, preparing for the awful impact that waited for me below. Instead of hard dirt though, I felt strong arms. My body clenched further as I looked into Ilyan's face, his arms cradled around me as he propelled us upward. His wind moved around us as we flew toward a tree, a large branch stretching out before him as if welcoming us. Ilyan landed on the branch safely, his arms still wrapped around me.

"I told you I wouldn't let you fall."

"Thank you, My Lord." I moved away from him, careful to keep myself standing on the tree branch.

"I am just Ilyan now, Joclyn."

"Thank you, Ilyan."

"You are very welcome." He smiled softly. "Now, we are going to do it again, but this time I want you to focus on the wind. Set your mind on what it is doing and how I am controlling it. Do not let fear enter your mind. I will be here, always."

I nodded and closed my eyes, calling the wind again. The warm breeze came almost instantly, but it wasn't just my magic controlling the movements of the wind. Ilyan's magic intertwined with mine as the wind swirled around us. It was not my magic that eventually forced the wind to push us off the tree branch. Ilyan's magic surged, sending us flying into the air. My body tensed in panic as my feet lost contact with the branch.

"Relax your body; do not think of the movement you are about to accomplish." Ilyan's voice was soft in my ear as his hands moved to grip my waist. "Focus only on the wind. Focus on its movement, on its warmth. Focus on how your magic will bring it to you. And do not worry, Joclyn; I will never let you fall." With that, he threw my body into the air, the wind he controlled pushing me up and away from the tree.

I screamed for only a moment as my body left the security of his arms, terror grabbing hold of me. Before I could act on the fear, Ilyan was there again, his arms wrapped around me as he kept me safely against him, our bodies floating through nothing. He stayed there just seconds before throwing me in a different direction, spinning me through the air away from him.

As I twirled through the air, my magic moved away from me,

my calm body giving it leave from its prison underneath my skin. My magic mingled with Ilyan's as he controlled the wind that supported me, our combined magic flowing and dancing. I continued to fly forward as our magic worked together to guide me. Ilyan grabbed me gently and continued moving us through the open air.

As Ilyan threw me away from him again, I understood; all trace of fear was gone. I knew exactly what to do. I grabbed the wind that Ilyan had surrounded me with and pushed it another way, my body moving alongside it as I controlled it.

This was the feeling I got when I climbed the trees with Ryland; this supreme happiness and freedom. It was just as Wyn had said; I had used Ryland's magic to climb the trees, except now, it was my magic giving me those same feelings. Even though I missed Ryland's comforting warmth, there was something empowering behind doing it myself.

"Now catch me," Ilyan's voice called after me. I turned my head to see him speeding away through the trees in the opposite direction from where I was headed, dodging in and out of the high branches. I laughed happily before easily changing my course to fly after him. Ilyan moved swiftly, his powerful arms propelling him further, his wind racing him ahead of me. He moved with an ever-increasing speed as he changed his course several times. His smiling face continued to look back at me as I desperately tried to catch up to him. I followed behind, not making much headway before he changed his course yet again.

As he moved, I saw a path that would give me a straight shot right to him. I smiled at the idea of winning the game before plunging myself down into the lower branches of the tree. It was harder to move here with the branches growing smaller and closer together, but being out of sight gave me the opportunity to cut across a corner that led straight to him. I broke out of the lower branches, a rush of wind pushing me up to where Ilyan flew. I wrapped my arms around his neck, pushing him off his course, and slamming us into a large branch of a tree.

"Got you," I said.

I rolled onto the branch as my body began to register the effort that was involved in not only flying, but also propelling through branches. I leaned up against the trunk of the tree and looked at where we had ended up, my breathing ragged and forced as I attempted to catch my breath.

"Very good," Ilyan said. He leaned forward and placed his hand gently against my face. I stiffened as his warmth moved into me, moving right to my back. It spread comfortably down my spine, wiping away the small aches that had popped up from our impact.

"I didn't break my back again, if that's what you're checking."

"I know, but it's always best to double check." He smiled before removing his hand, letting his fingers trace the kiss again.

"Why do you do that?" I said, moving swiftly away from his touch.

"Do what?"

"Touch my kiss. It seems you take every opportunity to touch it."

He withdrew his hand. "I'm sorry. Does it bother you?"

"Not as much as it should, I suppose," I lied; it actually made me very uncomfortable, like he was touching me in an intimate way. "When Ryland touched it, I kind of blacked out. Why doesn't it do that with you?"

"Because you are not bonded to me, Joclyn. I am not your mate and so our bodies don't react."

"Mate?" I exclaimed, terrified.

"Yes, Joclyn. The Zêlství, remember? Everything just has a different name."

I nodded my head like I understood, but my stomach still spun.

Mate? I was sixteen, barely.

"So why do you keep touching it?" I asked, freaking out a little bit. "You don't expect the same thing to happen, do you?"

Ilyan laughed, which I should have been happy about, but instead it only made me feel really embarrassed.

"No, Joclyn, you don't have to worry about that. I am only here to protect you. It's just..."

"What?"

"It's just been so long since I have seen one, since my father... My father had a kiss just as you do, did you know that?"

"Your father? But I thought you were a... a... Skry..." Darn it, I had forgotten the word.

"A Skřítek, Joclyn."

"I thought you were a Skřítek?"

"My mother was. My father was a Chosen Child, just as you. So I guess I am kind of a half-breed," he said.

"A half-breed... who is king of the Skříteks?"

Ilyan nodded at my connection. "My father ruled over all magical beings for a time, many years ago. So, I guess you could say that I inherited the title."

"Your father was king? Of the Skříteks?"

"More along the lines of king over everyone. In that time, there was no true segregation."

"What happened to him? Did Edmund kill him, too?"

Ilyan hesitated, looking away and running his hands through his straight hair.

I instantly regretted asking the question.

"My father was the first person that Edmund destroyed," he clarified.

CHAPTER 27

$\mathcal{I}$ HAD SPENT THE LAST two days in the air, although it wasn't by choice. Ilyan had insisted that once I had grasped the concept, I perfect it. I knew it was all with the pretense of my need to escape, and it made me mad. I had perfected moving wind, even under the barrier the necklace gave me, for short distances. It wasn't enough for Ilyan; he insisted I do better. I should have been happy for his persistence in teaching me, but I wasn't. I wanted to be stronger, know more and actually be of use when we went to save Ryland.

I yelled and screamed at Ilyan, begging him to teach me something new, to show me how to at least defend myself, but he refused. He was adamant that I perfect my mastery of wind. He demonstrated ways I could use the wind defensively, and I learned them easily, my skills improving swiftly now. Moving around pebbles and benches wasn't enough for me, and I begged further.

I must have pushed it too far; about three hours ago, Ilyan had snapped. He said nothing, but the ice in his gaze cut through me, and I shrank away, running to my room to escape the onslaught I was sure I had unleashed, but it never came.

I sat in the windowsill that overlooked the courtyard with my head against my knees. I looked out into the yard, seeing nothing except a green haze as the setting sun streamed through the green leaves of the massive tree. I had come here when I had fled from Ilyan and had attempted to teach myself some form of defensive magic, but I had no idea what I was doing.

My magic had surged and crackled underneath my skin and between my fingertips as I tried to conjure something, anything that could be of use. Nothing happened in all the hours that I tried. My inability to conjure more than wind had only soured my bad mood further.

I had stopped attempting any form of magic when the news had come on a few minutes ago, my ears perking up at the sound of my name. It seemed I was still big news, and what was more, Ryland was giving another press conference—live this time.

I tried to keep my focus off the screen, terrified of the condition I would see him in, but my ears were tuned to it intently, my heart thumping in anticipation. The possibility of hearing his voice had electrified my senses. I grabbed the necklace from its resting place on the table, desperate to be close to him in any way possible.

"And now we go live to the LaRue estate where Ryland LaRue will be addressing the press."

I reluctantly turned my head to the screen, my heart beating in eager, yet terrified, fear. The "Live" icon lit up the bottom corner of the screen and I couldn't help but think he would be right there, standing on the steps of that beautiful house. My heart longed to be next to him. I clenched the necklace tighter as Ryland walked out of the door to the small podium that stood at the bottom of the front steps where the press had gathered.

I would like to say he looked like he had healed a bit, but I knew better. His right arm still hung lifelessly beside him, his right shoulder larger than the left one. His bruises appeared to be better, and the cut was almost gone, but he was twitching more than he had been the last time. Each jerk was so subtle that most people wouldn't have noticed it. Each twitch shot through me like I was being punched.

Ryland paused and shifted the papers in his left hand before looking at everyone in front of him. His bright blue eyes met the camera, and everything stopped. Ryland was terrified; I had never seen him look so scared. Seeing him there on the screen, shoved Edmund's magic-enshrouding blanket completely off me. My uncovered magic surged, the energy prickling my skin like a thousand needles. I expelled it from me, surprised to find it willingly going into the necklace that I still held in my hands. I looked at the ruby, reluctant to take my eyes from Ryland for too long. My magic flowing into the ruby had increased its warmth, the heat comforting against my skin.

"It's okay, Ryland. You can do it," I spoke softly to myself, wishing I could help him.

On the screen, Ryland shifted, but it wasn't the twitch of the Vymàzat; it was something different. His eyes met the camera again, and his mouth turned up in that coy, little smile that always caused my heart to skip a beat.

"Ladies and gentlemen, I have asked you to gather together today with the intent of addressing an assumption that has been prevalent among the press. This assumption concerns the disappearance of Joclyn Despain."

A twitch.

"Fight him, Ryland, please. Fight him for me."

He smiled again. "I know it has been inferred that I may have been involved in her disappearance." A bigger twitch. "And I would like to state again, that I was not involved with this tragedy in any way. I am proud to say that I love Joclyn Despain with all my heart, and her disappearance has taken an even bigger impact on me than she may ever know."

He looked right at the camera, his eyes shining with tears. "I love you, sweetheart."

"I love you, too." The necklace dug into my hand as my magic continued to surge into it.

"I know you do. And that's why I need you to listen very carefully."

I froze, focused on the necklace, on the warm heat that I instantly recognized as not being my own.

"You need to..." He paused when a twitch so large came over him that he had to hold onto the podium tightly, his knuckles turning white before he could raise his head.

"Fight him, Ry."

"I'm... trying... Jos... Stay... where you are... Don't come... Stay where you are..." He twitched so much that his head slammed into the podium. I could hear the press yell and call out in alarm in the background. He rose slowly, and I could tell he had lost. The blue from his eyes was gone, the pitch-black filling them once again.

I yelled in fear, the necklace falling to the floor.

"Ryland!"

"I'm coming to get you," Ryland's voice hissed angrily.

I screamed out just as the door to my bedroom burst open and Talon rushed in. He caught me right before I fell to the ground. I fought against his hold as I yelled, reaching toward the screen in vain, my voice echoing around the room. Wyn followed Talon in and grabbed a pillow from the bed and covered the necklace with it, her hands pushing it hard into the floor.

"What's going on?" Ovailia yelled angrily, her agitation at being interrupted apparent.

"Get Ilyan!" Talon yelled, his arms wrapping around me protectively.

"Don't you dare talk to me that way," Ovailia scolded, affronted.

"Get Ilyan, now!" he amended, his voice loud enough to reach over my screams.

Wyn came up beside us, her arms wrapping around me tightly, her head resting against my back. Her cold magic flowed into me, the iciness shocking me, my panic stopping immediately. She withdrew her magic, leaving my own residual warmth to boil through me angrily at the absence of the necklace around my neck.

"Thanks, Wyn," I whispered.

"It's okay. He's okay." Wyn's soft voice vibrated through me.

"Did... did you see?"

"Yes, we saw."

"Saw what?" Ilyan's voice was laced with worry.

I heard the door close and footsteps approach as Ilyan rushed over and pried me away from my friend's strong arms. He pushed his magic into me, concerned that I was injured in some way.

"I'm fine, Ilyan," I sighed as I moved away from him, breaking the contact with his hands. "It's just... I mean..." I stopped. I didn't quite know how to explain what had happened.

"Ryland spoke to you through the television, didn't he?" Talon said.

Ilyan's head whipped around to stare at me as I nodded. He exclaimed something in Czech before turning to face me head on.

"I need you to tell me exactly what happened, Joclyn. Everything. Don't hold back, not now." Ilyan grasped my hands tightly in his.

I jerked my hands away from him; I think he had hoped that the contact would give me confidence, but it only made me uncomfortable. I wrapped my arms around myself, hiding my hands from him in case he tried again.

I stayed that way until Wyn graciously took pity on me, although her comfort felt almost as unwelcomed as Ilyan's. I didn't want either of them; I only wanted Ryland.

"I saw him on the TV; it was a live press conference. Seeing him there... I could feel everything. I pulsed my magic into the necklace and then Ryland started talking to me... and then... he changed... and..." I knew I hadn't done a very good job from the beginning, but Ilyan didn't get mad or scold me. He simply began to pace the room, mumbling under his breath.

"Ovailia!" Ilyan yelled. She opened the door, obviously listening from the hallway the entire time. "Get me a copy of the press conference, as quickly as you can."

Ovailia simply walked away, leaving the door to my room wide open.

Ilyan continued to pace as Talon began filling him in on what they had seen on the press conference and how Ryland had begun to talk directly to me. I filled in the gaps on my end when needed, glad I didn't have to say much.

I couldn't take my eyes off the pillow that Wyn had used to smother the necklace. It called to me, my heart thumping at my need for it. Before I knew what I was doing, my hands were hovering over the pillow, desperate to remove it.

"Joclyn, don't." Talon's voice was stern, and I stopped moving.

"Why not? I just... Can I put it back on?"

"No," Ilyan said simply. "He may be possessing the necklace."

"He?"

"Edmund." Ilyan's voice was like ice.

"So he knows now?"

"I'll have to see the video to know for sure."

I nodded, my eyes rolling back over to the pillow involuntarily.

"If he has, will you teach me how to block him from the necklace, from controlling me?"

"I can try; it's probably going to be more difficult than you are assuming."

"What do you mean?" My body sank into itself, folding me into a crumpled mass as the weight of everything kept falling over me.

"It's like 1 said before, Joclyn; it involves magic you don't understand yet."

"But I can try?" I tried to fight the hopelessness of my inability. If only Ilyan had taught me something other than just how to fly.

"If anyone can figure out how to do it, 1 am sure it will be you."

1 nodded, but had no idea what he meant. I was sure it would involve some training that 1 had yet to receive, meaning the chance of getting my necklace back anytime soon would be slim to none.

"It's queued up in your room, Ilyan." Ovailia spoke from the doorway, making it obvious she did not want him to stay in here. Ilyan stood and dismissed her before walking over to stand next to me.

"May I borrow your necklace, Joclyn?"

I nodded and let him take it, although 1 did not move from my spot on the floor.

1 just sat in silence, staring at the carpet where the impression in the plush pile still marked the place the necklace had landed. 1 could hear Wyn and Talon shift and whisper behind me, but 1 ignored them stubbornly.

So, 1 could speak to Ryland through the necklace; 1 could connect directly with him. While the possibilities were exciting, 1 couldn't help worrying about the other half, about what Edmund could do to me.

1 was only vaguely aware of the whispered conversation occurring between Wyn and Talon. Their voices were like chicken scratches in my head, blocking most of my thoughts. I wished they would just leave; 1 wanted to be alone. I wanted to yell, scream, and figure out how to make things explode. The buzzing under my skin had reached an all-time high, and 1 actually felt like it might be possible now.

Just as I was about to snap at them and demand privacy, the door opened and Ilyan charged in, necklace swinging before him.

"I can wear it?"

"Yes. I think Edmund just went on a whim with his comment. I can't sense any consistent connection with Edmund; it's all residual through your bond with Ryland."

I took the necklace from him greedily, eager to put it back on.

"Just don't purposefully push anymore of your magic into it, all right?"

"Why not?" I spoke in a panic; not allowing me to push magic into it was hindering any exploration, any contact with Ryland. My heart froze uncomfortably in my chest.

"I just don't want you to get hurt."

"How could I...?" I began to ask the question, but Ilyan just shook his head unwilling to give me an answer.

"I'm leaving," he announced.

"What?" Talon and Wyn asked together.

"I will be back on Thursday, so everyone needs to keep preparing for Friday night."

"Is everything okay?" Wyn asked quietly.

"I am not sure; I need to check on a few things. But don't worry; I'll be back soon." He smiled sadly at us, his eyes lingering on me before turning to go out the door.

"Oh," Ilyan added, his head peeking around the doorframe, "I'm terribly sorry, but Ovailia's in charge." He winked before disappearing and I felt my insides plummet. I wasn't the only one.

"Great," Wyn groaned, flinging herself back on my bed. "There goes my week."

CHAPTER 28

"*A*GAIN."

I flinched at Ovailia's voice. I had never really liked her, but now, I felt something akin to pure hatred toward her. I grumbled and flexed my fingers, hoping desperately that the magic I knew was hiding inside me would finally come out. It was no use, my body was already exhausted.

Ovailia had awakened me early yesterday morning, pleased at her chance to train me since Ilyan had left the night before. She dragged me unceremoniously out to the courtyard and demanded I begin producing the energy orbs that I had seen Ilyan and Cail create. At first, I was ecstatic for the opportunity to learn something useful, but it quickly became apparent that she was going to be a relentless teacher. Ilyan had been kind and patient, even going so far as to make the lessons into games so that I could learn more quickly. Ovailia though, Ovailia demanded instant satisfaction and results without even bothering to explain what she wanted me to do first.

To make matters worse, she insisted I keep the necklace on and work through the barrier before even learning the new tasks. I had worked hard all day yesterday to break through the blanket the necklace put over my magic. I was exhausted. I had struggled for hours without meals, only eating a small amount of stew before crashing into bed and falling asleep.

I had planned to wake up early and practice without the necklace on, so that, if anything, I would be able to at least know what I was doing before I had to try to break through the barrier again. My plan was foiled by a loud knock on the door before the skies had even begun to turn gray.

I had answered the door reluctantly, my whole body hurting from yesterday. Ovailia had demanded I follow her right then, not even letting me get dressed. I had been trying to create an energy orb ever since, with no luck. I had watched the sun rise, the birds wake for the day; but nothing had happened yet.

I stifled a yawn before focusing again. I let visions and memories of Ryland be my focus, still, the barrier didn't shift. The blanket that Edmund had placed over my magic was as strong as ever.

"You're not trying hard enough," Ovailia scolded from across the courtyard. She sat stoically in one of the many wrought-iron benches, a pile of small pancakes sitting next to her. I looked at them longingly before turning away from her. My hunger was not helping me focus.

I bit my tongue to keep from responding to her and flexed my fingers again. I closed my eyes and thought deeply about the first time I had met Ryland in his kitchen. The memory made me smile, and the barrier shifted just enough to let all the pent-up energy out of me in a rush. My focus had been solely on producing the energy, so when my body finally complied, it didn't have any direction or purpose. The magic shot out in a rush, flying out of both my hands and knocking me to the ground.

"You finally shift the barrier and you can't even control your power. Pathetic," Ovailia's voice sneered wickedly across the courtyard; my smile of accomplishment vanished.

"Hey, I'm trying, okay?" I snapped as I jumped to my feet, rubbing my hip.

"You are not trying hard enough."

"I'm exhausted, Ovailia. You haven't allowed me to get enough food or sleep for the past few days! I can't even think straight!"

She stood with her eyes narrowed at me angrily.

I shrank back a bit before planting my feet defiantly. I didn't want her to think she was getting the better of me.

"And how do you think it will be in two days when you enter the LaRue estate to save the 'love of your life'?" she sneered. "Are you going to have your wits about you? Are you going to be able to think straight?"

Ice snaked down my spine at the reminder of how little time was left.

"Yes!" I yelled. "I know what I am doing! I have been in that house more times than you could ever manage."

Ovailia stared at me, and for a wild moment, I was sure that I had won, that she understood that I knew what I was doing. Then, she began to laugh. The tinkling sound could very well have been beautiful, but it was so full of mocking malice that it only made me angry.

"I know what I am doing," I repeated defiantly.

"No," she continued. "You have no idea what you are doing. You are going to be terrified; you are going to be a hindrance to us all. I'm just trying to make it so that you don't accidentally kill anyone."

I squared my jaw and lifted my head. I was beginning to wonder if hate was a strong enough word for how I felt about her right now.

"I am not going to kill anyone." I was confident.

"Oh yeah? What about your beloved Ryland. What if, when he

holds you, the barrier shifts just enough that your magic surges? What if you can't control it? What if you kill *him*?"

The mention of Ryland's name, combined with my anger and frustration, was a tidal wave. The barrier shifted aggressively off me. My pent-up magic began to surge under my skin, rippling over my body like the prickling fur of a wild animal. That's how it felt within me—wild. I clenched my hands in an effort to keep it inside. No matter how much I hated Ovailia right now, I knew she was right.

She sensed what I was going through, and her smile widened broadly.

"You can't even control it right now, can you? I don't know what Ilyan sees in you. There is no way you are the Silnỳ."

"What?" I whispered. She had used my nickname like a title.

Ovailia smiled at my lack of knowledge. "Ilyan hasn't even told you. He must not trust you with such valuable information, just like he doesn't trust you to save Ryland." Her voice was snide, condescending; it only increased my power more.

I aimed my hands at her just as the magical energy reached a breaking point. A stream of light and flame burst out of me, hitting Ovailia in the dead center of her chest. She flew through the air before landing and skidding against the long grasses of the courtyard, leaving a long trail behind her.

Part of me was worried for her, while another only cared if I was going to get in trouble or not. My magic continued to stretch out of me as I brought the wind up and lifted myself into the air, only to land next to her a moment later.

I was about to ask if she was all right when she slammed her hand across my face. The slap, combined with the angry magical pulse she had filled it with, sent me spinning through the air to land hard against a small bush.

"You stupid, little girl!" Ovailia spat as she flew at me. "You know absolutely nothing. You think you can just waltz in and steal your boyfriend and everything is going to be fine! You'll be lucky if you even leave alive." She raised her hand again, a large crack sounding through the clearing as the earth next to my head exploded.

"I can do this!" I detangled myself from the bush, desperate to move in case she aimed for my head next time.

"No, I don't think you can!" Her hand rose toward me again.

I dodged out of the way, the smell of burning wood filling my nostrils. The smell was so similar to Ryland; it filled my head and mind with him. The smell that I always dismissed as campfire was really the smell of magic; the smell of a million spells, a million burning targets, the smell of each nightly practice he had with his father. It was him.

I turned around to face Ovailia again. The images of Ryland causing my magic to crackle on my fingertips, the electric energy determined to escape any way it could.

"You are going to kill us all!" she growled, her hands rising toward me.

I swung my hands forward; the powerful electricity that shot out of my fingers combined with the wind I had already conjured and collided aggressively with Ovailia. The energy pushed her across the courtyard, slamming her body into the wall of the building.

I looked after her, watching her crumbled body slide down to the ground. I heard her yelling angrily at me in Czech, the furious anger dripping from her voice. I didn't wait for her to regroup. I took advantage of the temporarily-shifted barrier and launched myself off the ground.

I took off into the sky, my body flying away as fast as I could manage, terrified she would follow me. I made a beeline to the forest where Ilyan had taught me to fly and glided into the leafy canopy.

I shot through branches and flung myself around trunks and over small meadows before coming to a stop on a large branch of an old willow tree. I clung to the tree as I caught my breath, air pumping out of me in energized spurts. My breath was coming way too fast; my face stung with my over-emotional heat.

It wasn't fair. I was stuck training with Ovailia who had rung me ragged, belittled me, and was determined that I was too dangerous to help. Then, in the end, I only proved her right.

I slunk down on the bough of the tree, my legs dangling over the sides as I waited for my heart rate to slow down; but it wasn't my heartbeat I was feeling.

I pulled the necklace out from underneath my sweater, letting the ruby sit on the palm of my hand. It had the normal warmth from its constant contact with my skin, but I could have sworn the ruby was beating. I wrapped my hand around the gem, surprised to feel the throb of a heartbeat, the quick tempo not matching my own. I felt the beat; the tempo almost panicked and desperate.

Ilyan had asked me not to push anymore of my magic into the necklace, but I didn't care. I didn't even hesitate; I let my magic surge out and fill the ruby. I felt the beat of the necklace fill my mind, the rhythm echoing around my skull like a drum. I let it consume me as Ryland's warmth followed steadily behind it.

I let my magic surge again, this time pushing the magnetic energy out of me. It collided with the necklace, and I felt my body grow heavy, like my bones had turned to lead. I closed my eyes, calling out when I saw the white room that Ryland and I shared.

I spun around, scanning the white space for Ryland. Finally I saw him, a boy sitting on the floor only a few feet away from me. I could tell he was younger, and my heart sank to my toes. He wore clothes that were ripped and stained, each article sagging off his body, many sizes too big. He sat quite still, humming a song that I was sure I had heard him sing before. His hands moved as if he were playing with something, but as I walked around to see what it was, nothing was there.

He jumped back, clutching the invisible toy to his chest as my feet came into view.

"Who are you?" The bright blue eyes of a thirteen-year-old looked up at me; the blue, deep and heavy, like he had already seen too much of the world. "Are you my new nanny?"

"Yes," I answered hesitantly before moving to sit next to him. "My name is Joclyn."

"Joclyn?"

I nodded my head.

"I like that name. My very favorite friend's name is Joclyn. I call her my diamond girl." He froze. "But you must never tell her I call her that! Can you promise?"

"I promise," I said sadly.

"Good."

"Why do you call her that?" I asked, though I already knew the answer.

"Her eyes... they are beautiful." He smiled widely for a second before the grin faded to nothing. "They are gray like yours, but much more beautiful. They are almost silver, like diamonds." He looked at me intently before returning to play with what I could only assume to be a car. The toy and his actions were out of place for how old he appeared, but something else was off. I couldn't quite place it. He moved his hand around the invisible object, back and forth, back and forth, as he continued to hum.

"Do you know why I need a new nanny?" he asked, his focus not leaving the car.

"No, why?"

"I scared the other one too much."

I didn't miss the strong mocking in his voice.

"Oh, really?" I smiled. "And how did you scare her?"

"I told her what my father did."

"What did he do?"

He looked up from his toy to look at me

"Not going to tell you. You remind me too much of Jos. Besides, I like you."

"I like you, too," I conceded, "but you won't scare me."

"Yes, I would."

"Try me."

He sat back and looked at me closely, his nose scrunching up a bit. The look made me smile; he had stopped making that face when he was about fifteen.

"He made me kill my mother." His voice was calm and plain, but I didn't miss the pain behind it.

I controlled my reaction carefully, knowing he was watching me, even though I wanted to panic. "I am sure he didn't..." I stated what was in my heart, willing what Ryland had said to be false.

"Yes, he did," Ryland snapped, his voice hitting a higher octave. "He kept her locked up until I could control myself and then he made me kill her." He started to cry, and I instantly regretted making him tell me.

"Why... why... would he..." I couldn't finish. I wanted to run away; I didn't really want to hear the answer.

"I let out some of the Vilÿs when I was seven, so he locked her up. He doesn't want anyone else to be like us." He dried his tears and went back to playing with his car, his humming loud and broken as he cried.

"You're not going to leave me, are you?" He didn't look up, but I could hear the longing in his voice.

"No." I reached forward and ran my finger through his curls, the soft hair moving through my fingers. "I'll never leave you."

"What if I asked you to?" My hand froze. His voice had

deepened into that of an adult, his head still hanging down.

"Ryland?"

"What if I asked you to leave, Joclyn?" He looked up at me, his thirteen-year-old face looking strikingly like my Ryland, the Ryland of today.

"I can't leave, Ry."

"I'm sorry, Joclyn. But it's too dangerous now." His hands reached up and grasped my shoulders tightly, his small fingers digging into my skin through the sweater. With one mighty jolt, he pushed me backwards. The white room disappeared as it faded into trees and sky. Ryland's face continued to look down at me as I fell, fell away from him, fell out of the tree.

Wind I didn't control came out of nowhere and caught me, just as my hand hit the ground in a precursor to the impact. The wind ceased as I dropped the last foot, landing hard on my back.

I grunted as I sat up, rubbing the now sore spots that had been so recently broken. "Ow."

"Yeah, I'd say so," Ilyan spoke from behind me. "You're just lucky I was looking for you or that would have been much worse." He was smiling broadly, but his smile faded away as he looked at me. It was like he could see right into me and knew what I had just seen.

CHAPTER
29

"WHAT DID YOU DO, JOCLYN?" Ilyan asked, his voice sounded like my mother's.

I flinched. "Oh, you know; the usual. Got mad at your sister, threw her into a wall, and flew away."

"You're not the first to do that," he smiled, "but that's not what I am talking about."

"What are you talking about?" The cornered teenager reflex was coming on strong.

"What did you do, Joclyn?"

I backed away from him as he continually stepped closer to me.

"Pushed my magic into the necklace, even though you told me not to; shared a Tòuha with Ryland, who was younger, by the way, and told me all about how Edmund made him kill his mother."

Ilyan's face went from angry, to concerned, to furious as I spoke.

"Is it true?" I asked softly, hoping to deflect his anger away from me.

"Is what true?" he snapped.

"That Edmund made him kill his mother."

"Yes."

"Why?"

Ilyan pinched the bridge of his nose in frustration, his eyes screwed up tightly. "Edmund tortures his children, Joclyn." He dropped his hand to look at me. "He uses them to increase his power, to bend their will so that they only answer to him. He trains them to be destructive weapons and pawns in his little game. He holds no love for Ryland; he probably made him torture his mother as a way to break him, to teach him a lesson."

"Them?"

"Yes, Joclyn. Them. All ten of them."

I stared at him, my hands opening in a question.

"What do you want me to tell you? It's nothing good."

I could tell how uncomfortable the subject was making him; he was very edgy.

"I think I have handled quite enough to prove I can handle a bit of bad news." My voice was firm.

He sighed exasperatingly at me before turning away, his hand running through his long blonde hair.

"Ilyan." I wasn't sure if I was angry or worried. The way Ilyan was reacting, it was so unlike him. I could almost feel the waves of negative energy flowing off him. He spun around to face me, his eyes damp.

"He tortures them, Joclyn. He tortures them until he breaks them and then he uses them or he kills them. It's not a monarchy he is running here. There is no next-in-command. It is only Edmund and the children he gobbles up and spits out. He did it to Zetta; he did it to Markus, Drayven, Ovailia, Sylas..."

"Wait," I interrupted him, my heart clenching in my chest, "Ovailia?"

Ilyan breathed out deeply, his face looking like a cornered dog.

He looked away from me, his hand dragging through his blonde locks again.

"Ilyan?"

"Yes. Ovailia. He tortured my sister by making her watch as he killed her mate. He forced her to track down and kill her friends. She bears a scar from her neck to her tailbone where he cut away, bit by bit, until she agreed to do it." His voice was so bitter, so pained.

I reached out to him, desperate to comfort him, to make it go away. Then, my hand dropped; the awful truth of what he was saying hitting me hard.

"Your sister." My voice was a whisper.

"Yes."

"No!" I took a step back in horror.

Ilyan looked into me, that unyielding defiance I was used to, coming on strong. His eyes, so familiar, so much like Ryland's. I had been too focused on Ryland to put the obvious puzzle pieces together. I felt ridiculously stupid.

"No!" I repeated, but my voice had lost its shock.

We just stared at each other. I had no idea what to say. All my life I had hidden. I had moaned and groaned and whined about some stupid mark. I had let it ruin my life, and all the while, my best friend, the one person who meant the most to me, was being tortured every day of his life. Furthermore, it wasn't just him; it was the man who had saved me, it was his sister, it was seven others who had lost their lives. I could have cried; my body almost begged me to. Instead, I squared my shoulders and held it in.

"We need to save him." My magic surged beyond the barrier as I spoke.

Ilyan looked at me for only a moment before striding away from me. I ran up beside him, his pace winding me.

"We are going to save him, Ilyan, aren't we? He's your... your brother."

"We are going to try."

"Try? I thought this was a sure thing!"

Ilyan looked at me, his pace quickening even more. I wanted to ask him to slow down, but didn't dare.

"Edmund has increased the security around the estate. We will have to get through a lot more of his 'henchmen' than I had originally hoped. What I could glimpse of Ryland did not paint a pretty picture; he can barely move at times, and when he does, he twitches so badly that he can't accomplish much. However, the party seems to still be ready to go on as planned, which can only mean that we are walking into a trap."

I stopped in my tracks, remembering all of Ryland's warnings to stay away from him, to leave him alone. He was still trying to protect me, and here I was, preparing to stroll into the lion's den to save him. It was ridiculous.

Ilyan noticed I was no longer walking beside him and trotted back to get me, now dragging me by the shoulder beside him. My feet stumbled before I caught up to his pace again.

"Don't sulk like a child; we are still going in to get him."

"We are?" My spirits soared.

"Yes, I need you two together."

"Why?" I knew I needed him with me, but it seemed odd that Ilyan felt the same way.

Ilyan grunted and stopped walking right at the edge of the forest. I could see the door to the motel through the break in the trees. He pulled me around to face him.

"I saw the video, Silný. He risked everything to talk to you, to tell you how much he loved you. And I know you love him, no matter how hard you try to keep it hidden." He smiled sadly, his hand reaching up to cup the side of my face. I moved away a bit, but his hand stayed firm against my skin. "Your bond is the strongest I have ever seen, and I am becoming worried that if he dies, you may not be far behind. And I can't let that happen. Because I need you, too."

"*You* need me? Why?"

"I just do." Ilyan leaned forward and kissed my forehead softly. I felt dirty for letting him touch me that way and moved away from him quickly.

"Wynifred is waiting for you in your room. We leave in the morning." He left me standing in the trees, feeling grimy and guilty. I wiped my forehead angrily before storming toward my room.

IT WAS OFFICIAL; I HATED the smell of hair dye. It burned my eyes and nose, the ammonia smell making me sick. I shook my head a bit to get the smell out of my nose, but it was no use. It was burning off my nostril hair, which wasn't necessarily a bad thing.

"Hold still or I am going to dye your face pretty colors, too."

I said nothing, but let her move my head to where she wanted it. When Ilyan had told me Wyn was going to help me get ready, this was not what I had in mind.

I had arrived in my room to a very excited Wyn who was armed with a pair of scissors and a bottle of hair dye. Even though they could alter my appearance magically, it would be easily seen through by Edmund and his men, which meant they had to alter my appearance physically. I had tried to convince Wyn to do something simple, but she wouldn't hear of it. She said that I needed to stand out enough that no one would guess it was me. It didn't make much sense, but I didn't want to argue.

I had been sitting dutifully in the chair since Wyn placed me here, my eyes closed as I refused to see what she was doing. I bit my lip until it bled when she cut off all my hair. My head felt instantly lighter. I only felt a bit of it fall around my face and on my neck before she began to coat it with the thick, sticky stuff I was now being tortured with.

I huffed angrily in the hopes of showing my frustration, but regretted it instantly; my throat was now coated with the burn of the fumes.

"Oh, calm down, Jos. I am almost done."

"You better not have made me look terrible."

"No one will recognize you. That's for sure," she laughed.

"What does that mean?" Now I was worried.

"Nothing. Stop freaking out. You can open your eyes now. You have to wait twenty minutes for it to develop and you're going to look like a loon sitting still with your eyes closed for that long."

I opened them, letting my eyes get used to the sharp chemical burn. Wyn stood in the middle of my bathroom with a huge grin on her face as she began to remove her gloves that were covered with cherry-red hair dye. She had told me she was dying my hair red, but for some reason, I had pictured an auburn color like hers.

"Red? Wyn! That's red!" Wyn grinned at me evilly, flexing her one hand of still gloved fingers at me.

"And black," she provided happily. "It's kind of all blended and fun! You're going to love it!"

"Wyn! My hair was already black! Why did you dye it *more* black?"

"Really, Jos. Calm down. You're going to look *so* good," she squealed and went back to cleaning up, dancing to the Styx music she had playing on the stereo.

"I don't feel like I am going to look *so* good."

Wyn just sighed at me and cranked up the radio in an effort to tune out my complaints.

"Wyn!" I attempted to yell above the music.

She turned down the radio and looked at me skeptically.

"You're not going to keep complaining, are you?"

"No," I said. "I was just wondering what you could tell me about Edmund's other children."

She stopped dead in her attempts at cleaning up, her arms falling to her sides. "I am not sure I am supposed to tell you about that."

"It's okay, Wyn. Ilyan told me."

"What did he tell you?" Her eyes narrowed dangerously.

"What Edmund makes his children do. He let it slip that Ovailia was one of them."

She waited before nodding and leaned against the sink to face me.

"Edmund wasn't always like that, you know. Ilyan's father and mother were bonded about twelve hundred years before Ilyan was born; Ovailia was born about thirty years later. About two hundred years after that, he began to change. They have legends and songs and beautiful paintings of the love shared by Edmund—the bearer of the first mark—and Filare—the Skřítek he shared his life with."

"What happened? I mean, if he loved her so much, why did he leave her?" The eager light that had filled Wyn's dark eyes vanished at my question.

"Edmund saw a woman in a town called Farcina. He lusted after her. Timothy..." she spat the word with venom, "my father, convinced Edmund to take her, convinced him that he should be the only one to bear the mark. He left everyone. Broke all magical beings apart. Edmund planted the seeds of distrust and started a civil war that almost killed all of the magic. And while everyone fought among themselves, Edmund massacred the Drak in secret."

"The Drak?"

"The Drak were a people who were bred from the mud to be the Keepers of the Waters of Foresight. They were the only ones who could look into the black waters and see the past, present and future. There were stories that they saw a Chosen Child who would destroy Edmund, and stop the madness that he had created. I think that's why he killed them."

"You mean, like a prophecy?" I tried to keep the disbelief out of my voice.

"I guess you could say that, but they were really anything but. Ilyan was there to witness it. He told Ovailia, not knowing that she was being used as a spy. Because of what Ovailia told Edmund, he ordered the extermination of the Chosen Children."

"And Ilyan still trusts her?" I was appalled. The bubbling turmoil in my stomach at what I was hearing was making me sick.

"Yes. It's been several hundred years, so he must have a reason. After all, Edmund did almost destroy Ovailia."

"Does Edmund... Does he really make all his children do... terrible things... or he..."

"Kills them, yeah." Wyn moved over and sat down next to me softly.

"After Ilyan and Ovailia, there were Markus, Zetta, Drayven, Sylas, Gielle, Mym, Thom and then Ryland. After Ovailia, each one had a different mother, each one forced to do different things. Markus was murdered in 1480, Zetta has been missing since she was 130, Drayven and Mym fought with Ilyan for a while, but you can't always escape the shadows of your past. They eventually turned against Ilyan, and he had to fight against his own siblings.

"Edmund found and probably killed Thom, about thirty years ago. He was hiding as a college student somewhere in the US. One day, his letters stopped coming. We all ran out to find him, but we never did. Not even a body. That was when Ilyan commanded that everyone stay together at all times. I never met him, but the way Ilyan talks about him, he was very brave. They all are, or were."

My stomach clenched.

"He made Ryland kill his mother."

Wyn turned to me with her mouth open in shock. It took her a second to recover.

"I am not surprised," she said darkly. "Edmund made Ryland torture Ilyan, too."

"What?" I asked, the memory of Ilyan's scarred chest filling my mind.

Wyn looked at me guiltily for a minute, thinking she may have said something she shouldn't have.

"About three years ago, Ilyan was captured in Greece. Edmund could have killed him then, but he made Ryland do it instead, or rather try to; Ilyan is exceptionally powerful..." she faded out and I looked away, not really wanting to hear anymore.

Ryland was about thirteen in the Tõuha. Only years before that, he had been forced to kill his mother. About the same time, the bright red hand print had appeared on his face and we had fled to the mountain for the first time. Three years ago would have made him about fifteen, about the time we started breaking into hospitals and defying his father even more. Ryland had gone through all that, and through it all, he had smiled and never said a word. I felt the bile rise in my throat.

"I need a shower."

"You still have five minutes," Wyn protested, but I just waved her off. I doubted five minutes would make that much difference.

I was grateful it took so long to get all of the hair dye out. The bright red and dark black streams of color swirled around each other as they slid across the floor of the tub on their way down the drain. I watched the water as I thought about all the people Edmund had hurt, all the people he was still hurting. Strangely, I didn't feel like I wanted to cry; I just felt sick and angry. I fought the anger; I didn't like the way it consumed me.

The swirls of red against the tub began to fade as I thought of my mother, even though the pain of her loss was still an open wound. I thought of how Ryland had hugged her the last time I had seen her alive. I thought of our happy smiles and of painting our fingernails ridiculous colors. I thought of Ryland when we got lost in the cemetery, when we played in the fountain at the park near his house. Also, strangely enough, I thought of my father.

He had, in his own way, tried to save me, too. I thought of the good memories from my childhood, part of me wondering where he had disappeared to since giving me the stone. Even Ilyan had said he didn't know where he was. Before long, I was smiling. While the anger at what Edmund had done was still there, it no longer dominated me.

As I continued to rinse the dye out of my hair, it became apparent exactly how much Wyn had cut off. I wasn't even sure I had any hair left. The hair on the back of my head was all but gone; only short hairs, about an inch long, were left. The front half was longer, one side more than the other. I guess I needed some hair to cover the kiss.

I stepped out of the shower reluctantly, not really wanting to look in the mirror yet. I threw on my pajamas and went to find Wyn, a towel wrapped around my head, even though there was no point. I walked into the bedroom to find not only Wyn, but Talon, Ovailia, Ilyan and about seven other Skříteks as well. I wished I could run back into the bathroom, but the sight of Ilyan made me stop short.

He was dressed in one of the many perfectly-laundered tunics I had seen in his closet that first day. The shirt was long and white, with simple trim in deep gold and purple. A large gold medallion hung around his neck, reaching down his chest halfway. The shirt was cinched to him with a dark leather belt that matched the boots that came to his knees. The worst part was the intricate, jewel-encrusted gold crown he wore on his head. He looked like he was going to a masquerade party. I fought the urge to laugh, instead opting to stare at him, open-mouthed.

"Manners, Joclyn, mràvy," Ilyan scolded roughly.

I looked around me confused and then did the only thing that made sense, given the situation; I curtseyed.

"My Lord."

"Let me see it, Joclyn," Ilyan commanded sternly, his eyes glancing toward my hair line. I removed the towel obediently, feeling uncomfortable. I felt the two remaining clumps of hair swing forward, a chilled breeze tickling my neck.

Ilyan came forward and ran his fingers through my wet hair as he dutifully inspected Wyn's work. My hair was now so short, I could feel his fingers rub against my scalp. The touch sent a shiver down my spine, and my shoulders jerked up toward my ears. Ilyan just smiled at me.

"Good, Wyn. The darker, the better on the face, I think." He moved away from me, his small entourage following him to the door.

"We leave tomorrow at nine. Sleep well, Joclyn." His voice softened just enough to take away the tension that had formed in my neck. He motioned the others out and closed the door behind him, leaving Wyn and me alone.

"Tomorrow," I repeated.

My nerves and butterflies came back instantly; twenty-four hours and Ryland would be here. Safe.

I could do this.

CHAPTER 30

*A*FTER WYN HAD FINISHED WITH me, I didn't even recognize myself. My eyes looked like pools of black on a pure white face. Every time I opened them, the glittering silver of my irises flashed menacingly, the shimmering color surprisingly bright against the black. My lips were dark, too; the dark burgundy setting off the vibrant red that saturated the front of my hair. The severe cut was nothing near what I would have chosen for myself. It was almost like a reverse mullet; a short, boy-cut in the back and stark, straight, longer lengths plastered to my head near my face. The back was dark black that faded into the bright red framing my face.

Wyn had gone one step further by giving my body the persona to match my hair. She had insisted I place a small magnet in my nose that resembled a nose ring and had taken about an hour to draw on a tattoo with a ball point pen. The constant pressure of the tiny pen-tip against my skin had hurt, although not as much as I assumed a real tattoo would. After an hour of being drawn on, my skin had thankfully gone numb, and she had left me with an intricate spider web that stretched all the way down my left arm and across my back.

I wore what could only be described as "club clothes": tight black pants that Wyn had to magically get me into, matched with what my mom would deem stripper heels, and a lime green, loose-fitting, backless shirt. Combine the face and hair with the tight-fitting, revealing clothes, and it gave me the appearance of a popular girl on her way to the club. I felt a desperate need to appear more confident than I really was.

I still felt like the insecure, scared girl I had always been. I looked at myself in the mirror and tugged at my clothes, desperate for some sort of comfort. Standing there alone reminded me so much of my first day without my hoodie. I clutched my necklace, remembering how Ryland had been right there to support me that day, how he had only looked into me and told me how beautiful I was. I exhaled deeply, the memory heaving through me like caffeine.

After Wyn had placed the finishing touches on my disguise, about twenty of us met in the middle of the courtyard in preparation for leaving. I wasn't the only one who had changed my appearance. Ilyan had cut his hair short and dyed it brown. Talon had kept his hair long, but had bleached it white; from the back he almost looked like Ilyan. I got the distinct impression that was the idea.

I pulled and tugged at my clothes as I walked toward the group, not wanting so much of my body to be visible. We all gathered together and took off into the sky, following Ilyan to a small run-down conference center in a city I didn't recognize. He herded us into a small room, with the sole intent of holding a planning meeting.

Ilyan had been speaking nonstop since the meeting began; he wrote on an old chalkboard, separated us into groups, and spoke to each member of each group individually. I didn't understand a word; everyone was speaking only in Czech. I shifted my weight again, my body sore and stiff against the folding metal chair I sat in.

I looked around; luckily, I wasn't the only one who was uncomfortable. Wyn sat in the back next to Ovailia whose icy stare was penetrating Ilyan as he continued to lay out what I could only assume was the plan of attack. Ovailia had spoken up several times during the meeting, and although I had no idea what she was saying, her voice was still venomous.

Suddenly, everyone stood in succession, the quick movement startling me. I stood with them, but immediately regretted it as they all began to pull chairs together and sit down in smaller groups. I sat back down, hoping no one had seen my blunder, and focused on my strappy four-inch heels as I once again adjusted my clothes.

I just wanted to disappear, and this outfit did not give me that opportunity. I tried to pull out my confidence for rescuing Ryland, but it was no use; only nervous energy remained.

"So, did you enjoy the meeting?" I looked up just as Ilyan pulled up a chair directly in front of me. His hair was too off-putting; I couldn't seem to stop looking at it. It just made him look too much like Ryland would look without his curls.

"I suppose it would have been great if I had understood anything."

"Sorry about that. But don't worry, I'm here to give you the Cliff Notes." He leaned forward and my eyes drifted to his short brown hair again in an effort to avoid eye contact.

"Gee, thanks."

"We discussed our attack plan."

I looked up expectantly, but he just sat there staring at me.

"And?"

"That's it."

Two hours of sitting in a hard chair and they had discussed the "attack plan". Great.

"So what are they doing now? Planning the after-party?" I spat bitterly, but instead of laughing, Ilyan's face fell instantly.

"They are saying goodbye to their loved ones, Silný."

I peeked around him to see Wyn and Talon with their arms wrapped around each other, a few other pairs coupled off around them. Most of the others were quietly talking on cell phones. I sat back in my chair, my nerves jumping angrily.

"Are you saying goodbye to your loved ones, too?" My eyes floated to Ovailia who stood against the wall, her head bowed.

"Of course."

My stomach jumped at his response. I opened my mouth to say something, but closed it as my confidence wavered. Ilyan chuckled at my indecision and leaned back against his chair with his arms folded as if he was getting ready for a show. I determinedly looked away from him, but my eyes were automatically drawn to his hair again.

"Are you going to be looking at my hair all night, Joclyn?"

"No!" I responded, a blush at being caught rushing to my cheeks. "It just looks so weird on you."

"You don't look too bad yourself," Ilyan said, pulling on one of the long, red strands that hung down at the sides of my face.

"Don't remind me. My hair grows slowly, too; I am going to be stuck with this hairdo forever."

To my embarrassment, Ilyan laughed, causing several people to turn.

"What?"

"You can grow it back with your magic, Joclyn." Ilyan chuckled deeply at me, causing a furious blush to deepen against my cheeks.

"What?"

"Didn't Wyn tell you?"

"No!" My mouth hung open in frustration.

Ilyan only continued to smile. "No wonder you looked so depressed when I saw you last night."

Truthfully, I hadn't been depressed because of my hair; I had been more concerned about his wicked father, but I wasn't going to get into that right before we left to rescue his youngest brother.

I shook my head and slammed my bare back against the cold, metal chair. I tried to shift my clothes again, but there simply wasn't enough fabric.

"So... are you going to tell me what this attack plan is?"

He sighed before nodding once and then angled his chair so we could both see the group that was still shuffling around the conference room.

"Wyn, Talon, Evert and Glenna will be clearing the roof. Ovailia, Ferne and Nyse will be clearing the upper hallways. Adyl, Benton and Eber will already be stationed at the party. Delia, Iolo, Jevon and Evadne will be clearing the exterior; and Tace and Zilla will be our forward guard. You will be with me." He pointed each of them out as he spoke; my mind unable to connect faces with their unusual names.

"And what do we do?"

"Rescue Ryland," he stated quietly. "I need you to get him to leave with you. We will all serve as some form of a distraction and guard while you get him out. Once you leave, we all leave. The longer you wait, the more dangerous this mission is for everyone."

"Get him out, sounds easy enough," I sighed sarcastically, thinking my task sounded anything but easy.

Getting him to follow me out would be easy, as long as he was Ryland. If he wasn't Ryland, I wasn't sure what he would do. He had attacked me in the Tòuha when he had changed. If he did attack me tonight, I was not sure I was powerful enough yet to fight him off. Worse yet, what if I got him out as Ryland, and he changed once we left.

I sighed and sank into my chair a bit, feeling completely useless.

"I hope you're right." Ilyan's hands writhed; he seemed to be thinking along the same lines I was. "We will go in under Zmizêt and make our way into the main hall; that is where Ryland will be."

"Zmizêt?"

"Yes, it's a shield that can cause you to be invisible. Of course, if it works in the LaRue estate with the same effectiveness it did on you, then we are all in trouble."

"What are you talking about?" I asked, my face squished together in confusion.

"All those times you saw me in your school, I was shielding myself with Zmizêt. But it didn't work so well on you." He narrowed his eyes at me curiously. "I wonder why that is?"

I shrank away from him as his blue eyes flashed dangerously. Was I broken or something? I couldn't get my magic beyond my necklace, but I could see people who were supposed be invisible? Definitely broken.

"You're the king; you tell me." I wished I could move away from him a bit.

"Manners, Joclyn." Ilyan didn't even flinch as Ovailia came up beside him. I, however, got the full extent of her glare and had to fight the urge to run away.

"I hate to interrupt, but it is time to go."

"So it is." Ilyan stood and moved away, leaving Ovailia alone with me. I had hoped she would follow him, but instead, she stepped closer.

"I would like you to know, Joclyn; I am only doing this to save my brother. I have no intention of saving you. If you get cornered, you're on your own." She smiled acidly at me, waiting for me to respond. Her look reminded me of the way Cynthia McFadden would use to egg me on. I shrank away from her instinctively. She glared toward me for only a moment longer before striding out of the room. I slumped back down in my chair.

I had the excited nerves of an audition, mixed with the raw, icy fear of going into the unknown. I shook my head, emptying the thought of Ovailia's comment from the nervous strangulation that was taking hold of me. The room had emptied of everyone but me and Ilyan before he turned and gestured toward me.

"I am going to have to carry you to Ryland's house, if you don't mind?" he said as we walked outside to where the others had gathered.

"What?" I was suddenly appalled.

"It's a risk for everyone if you have liquid memories of how to get back to the motel."

"What do you mean? I'm not a risk," I retorted, remembering all too vividly Ovailia's words in the courtyard.

"If you are captured, I don't need your memories to guide them to the motel. Since I don't have time to teach you to perform a Zmizêt, I need to be in contact with your skin."

"And you have to carry me? Why can't we just hold hands or something?" I suggested, irritated by the idea.

"If you won't let me carry you, Joclyn, I will just put you to sleep."

I grumbled in acceptance before allowing him to cradle me in his arms. I wrapped my arms around his neck, worried that he would drop me. He laughed at me softly; I knew full well how ridiculous I was acting, especially considering that the last time he had carried me like this, I hadn't been able to move.

We all swept into the air in unison, Ilyan leading us to what I was sure was certain doom.

This whole week, I had been confident that this was a sure thing, that everything would go perfectly. Then, last night, Ilyan had shattered my little delusional fantasy. This was not going to be easy; it would be dangerous. What was worse—we might fail.

"You need to close your eyes, Silnỳ."

I obeyed him.

"What happens if we can't get him out, Ilyan?" I asked into the darkness.

"We will get him out." His voice was so determined, I could almost detect that maniacal power in him already.

"But what if..."

Ilyan's arms tightened around me, pushing my torso into him.

"We will get him; do not worry."

I didn't dare say anymore. I didn't really want to think about it, anyway; thinking of failure almost seemed like a curse on this whole venture.

We landed among the lilac bushes, azaleas and roses behind the kitchen door to the large estate. Ilyan put me down, and I opened my eyes apprehensively, surprised to see only Ilyan and the two he had pointed out as our "forward guard". The others must have already taken their positions.

I looked up at the building curiously, surprised to see nothing but pale white stone. I knew the fire and explosions must have spread to this part of the mansion, yet there was nothing damaged. Ilyan must have been right; they must have repaired the building magically.

Being so close to entering the mansion made me edgy and I found myself shifting my weight and exhaling more than I should. This gained me quite a few dirty looks from Tace and Zilla, but I didn't care. I doubted anyone could hear me over the noise, anyway.

Happy screams and catcalls filled the air from the pool beyond the bushes; the heavy beat of the music inside pulsed through the air and shook the ground. Ryland's graduation from high school should have been a happy occasion, not the site for a rescue mission.

I could feel the tension; the pulsing, magical energy flowing from each of us as we sat ready, waiting to pounce. The magic seemed to beat in time with the music that surrounded us; the longer we waited, the louder it grew. Ryland's necklace sat hot on my skin under my lime green shirt, the intense heat warning me that danger was nearby. I pulsed my magic reflexively, hoping that being this close to Ryland, to Edmund, would provide me with additional control. Nothing happened; Edmund's restrictive blanket remained a suffocating force over my ability. I swallowed hard, hoping that when the blanket slipped off me, I could control the pent-up energy it would surely release.

The four of us looked up in unison as a large, red blast lit up the sky above the manor. The excited squeals from the pool echoed the deep boom of the explosion. Tace and Zilla bolted out in front of us, their bodies breaking through the bushes to the open parking lot. I screamed out in surprise as Ilyan grabbed me and flung me onto his back before he followed their lead.

The door to the kitchen flung open in a burst of wind that carried all of us into the hustle and bustle of the elaborate space. The wind pushed over trays of food and plates, and sent napkins flying through the air. The resulting mess sent the kitchen staff into a panicked frenzy. We took advantage of the disarray as we sped through the kitchen without having to worry about the Zmizêt being ineffective. Even without the diversion and the cloaking spell, our speed would have made us invisible. I just caught a glance of Mette's frazzled face before we took off down the staff hallway that led from the kitchen.

Tace and Zilla continued in front of us, our pace quick and fleeting. We moved through two corridors before Zilla's pace reduced to a casual saunter. Ilyan and Tace followed suit, Ilyan moving us right up against the wall.

Only a moment after the change in pace, two small men I had

never seen before came around the corner to face us. At first, it was obvious they couldn't see us, but realization dawned on them as the Zmizêt seemed to fall away from our bodies.

Tace and Zilla did not wait; they moved so fast their bodies blurred. One moment they stood in front of us, and the next, they were directly before and behind the two Trpaslíks. Two dim flashes of light lit up the hallway before their bodies fell to the ground.

Ilyan rushed to their side, his face falling in alarm and frustration.

"Well, so much for stealth," he sighed. He turned to Tace and Zilla and spoke to them in Czech before the two went into action, moving and hiding the bodies in the many servants' quarters surrounding us.

"I need you to stay right beside me, Joclyn." He didn't look at me; he remained looking straight forward as he spoke.

Tace emerged from the rooms first, followed by Zilla who shook her long, blonde hair as she spoke to Ilyan. He didn't wait to translate; he simply grabbed my hand and towed me behind him as we ran from hallway to hallway.

The music continued to increase in volume as we moved through the estate. By this time, we had abandoned any attempts at stealth, although it probably wouldn't have mattered since the music became so loud that any noise we made was drowned out.

We almost made it to the connecting servants' hall when Tace and Zilla plastered themselves into the alcoves of the doorways; Ilyan towed me after him into another doorway. He kept me hidden safely behind him, his hand holding me against the door as he looked at what was going on in the hall. I heard a small yelp, shuffling feet, and two dull thuds before Ilyan released me from the small space behind him. By the time I made it to the hall, the two Skříteks were already hiding the bodies in a storage closet.

Ilyan held me back as we reached the door that would open up into the hallway that connected to the main hall before turning and speaking to the others. His lips moved as he spoke, but I could barely hear him, the overwhelming music drowning him out. Before he even finished speaking, Tace and Zilla exited from our hallway into another. My body tensed; I felt strangely unprotected without them.

"They are going in first," Ilyan yelled into my ear. "They will be watching you in the hall. Are you ready?"

I couldn't respond, my body tense.

Ilyan plunged us through the door and didn't slow down as we approached the ballroom that housed the party. The hall light dimmed as we got closer until we were moving through a faintly lit hallway, the flashing lights of the party reflecting out of the open door and onto the wall in front of us. I kept my gaze on the dancing lights, trying desperately to keep my head on straight while still focusing on the dynamic energy that was building under my skin.

Ilyan stopped abruptly before we made it to the main hall and threw me roughly against the wall. I tensed; this wasn't part of the plan, and the look on Ilyan's face suggested trouble. He pressed his body against mine, every inch of him, from his shoulders to his toes, pressed against me. His hand grabbed one of mine and restrained it above my head.

My body froze; this unwelcome invasion of my privacy sent angry surges of magic vibrating under my skin. I tried to pull away from him, but he held me roughly in place, his grip increasing. I looked up to him in a panic, just as he leaned forward to place his cheek against mine. My heart thudded uncomfortably.

"Close your eyes and pretend that this is natural for us." His voice was rough in my ear as he nuzzled his face into my neck, his warm breath running across my skin. I fought him, and his grip increased, his body pressing more firmly into mine. It didn't hurt, but the pressure was definitely unwelcome.

"Do you want to get us caught?" he hissed. "Do what I say. Someone is coming."

I let my lids drop over my eyes and raised my hand to cup his neck. My heart beat erratically as I felt the negative energy pulse toward us, heavy footsteps announcing the arrival of someone I didn't want to see.

"Keep them closed," Ilyan instructed as he moved his head, hoping to mimic the look of an intimate kiss against my neck. I screwed my face up into what I hoped was a pleasurable expression as the negative power hit its peak. Ilyan intertwined his fingers with mine and pushed against me harder, the ridge of the wall pushing into my bare back.

Ilyan didn't wait for whoever had passed us to get very far before pulling me beside him and leading me into the large hall.

I stopped in place. The main ballroom had been transformed into a night club. I no longer felt out of place with my hair and clothing. Flashing lights flickered and vibrated to the beat of the music, lighting the mosh pit as everyone moved together in some odd semblance of a dance.

I didn't have time to linger as Ilyan pulled me into the crowd, a hundred other bodies instantly pushing against us. He moved us deep into the writhing mass, enclosing us within it. The lights flashed and pulsed as the crowd danced and moved against everyone around them.

Ilyan pulled me into him, his hands fanning out on the bare skin of my back as he moved me against him in a seductive dance. I fought the urge to shy away from him. I cursed my clothes; he wasn't the only person who would be acquainting themselves with my body tonight. I felt sick.

"Remember to play the part, Silný. Rich, powerful. And don't touch him unless you know it's him. I don't need Edmund to be able to trace you." I nodded as he whispered in my ear, his hand moving up to cup my cheek for just a moment. "I'll be close by." He looked into me, his finger running the length of my jaw bone.

I looked up and screwed my jaw in defiance, my eyes opening in a seductive powerful way that I hoped fit the look Wyn had given me. I popped my hip and squared my chest, trying desperately to mimic the ridiculous movements I had seen Cynthia McFadden do every day of my life. Ilyan nodded once in approval before turning from me, leaving me alone in the crowd.

I couldn't let my nerves get to me. I kept my jaw tight, my other facial features soft and wide as I began to move through the crowd. I was passed from person to person as I made my way through the throng of tightly packed people. I mimicked the sensual daces as I moved against the bodies that pressed against mine in ways that made me blush. I never wanted to be in a place like this again. I was here for Ryland, and that was enough.

A hundred faces blurred together as they danced, each one with hooded lids and open mouths in some drugged-out ecstasy. I danced through bodies so carefully entangled I could never be sure exactly what they were doing. I skirted around couples who had fallen to the floor in a blissful madness that I never wanted to see again. I moved through them, hoping my alert face and body didn't give me away.

I had almost reached the edge of the wall of people when someone grabbed me around the waist and pulled me into them. My face fell out of place in fear as I whipped around, expecting some attacker. Instead, I looked into the face of Ryland's friend, Tyler. He held me tightly to him as he looked down in pompous ignorance. His face looked like all the others: glossed over and void of all normal expression. I moved with him for a minute, trying to plan my escape when he leaned down to nibble on my ear. I jumped back in repulsion, remembering all too well what Ryland had told me about private school boys.

"What?" Tyler yelled over the crowd. "Too dirty for you?" He placed his hands on my hips and moved me back to him. I screwed my face back into position and pulled his shirt to bring him to eye level.

"You have no idea." I let one eyebrow rise in what I hoped was an alluring way. "Get me a drink?" I asked and wound my arm through his, letting him lead me the rest of the way through the crowd.

I didn't feel comfortable attaching myself to one person, but if I was lucky, he would lead me right to Ryland. I tried desperately to focus on my character and not let my nerves sneak through to give me away.

I gave him a small smile as he thrust a drink into my hands. I could smell the alcohol before it even made it to my lips. Of course there would be heavy drinking; it made sense given the state that everyone was in. I lowered the glass and set it on the table next to us, I didn't need any distractions.

The raw magical energy that had been boiling under my skin shifted. I checked to see if the barrier was still firmly in place. Being this close to the energies that controlled me was sure doing weird things to my body.

"You okay, little bunny?" Tyler asked in my ear. My irregular magic had caused my cover to slip. I put the face back on as I leaned into Tyler in a poor imitation of what Ilyan had done to me, but I failed miserably.

"You wanna get out of here?" he asked. I cringed—wrong direction.

"Let's dance," I yelled and dragged him back toward the mosh pit. Luckily, Tyler didn't seem to object to my mixed signals; he must have been beyond drunk.

I led him deeper into the horde of people again, my body dancing to the thumping music. He danced behind me blindly, his free hand trailing over the bare skin on my back as we walked; I fought the urge to cringe against his touch.

We weren't going the direction I needed to go, but now I was faced with the bigger problem of getting rid of him. My big idea had backfired.

I had only moved a few steps when my magic shifted again, this time taking the constrictive blanket with it. My magic reacted hastily to the unexpected freedom, and it took all my strength to keep it inside. Ovailia was right. I was in trouble. I was running out of time. My magic lurched again, still shifting in the same direction. I took a chance and followed the pull. The music continued to thump through me as I danced with Tyler, moving us through the crowd, grateful he was drunk enough to be led along on my little game.

My magic surged even stronger as we reached the edge of the crowd, this time near the DJ table. Tyler grabbed me and pulled me toward him into a position I was not comfortable with. I pushed him away and began to dance on my own, hoping that the alcohol surging through his system wouldn't make him too possessive.

It did.

He came up behind me, grabbing me roughly as his hands snaked around my waist, lifting the front of my shirt. I jerked away from him, only to be pulled back against him aggressively. I could feel his fingers like claws against my back. Tyler attempted to get me to dance with him for a minute, but his fingers were starting to hurt me, and I fought him, pushing him away from me.

"Come on, baby!" he yelled, coming up to me again. "Don't fight the power." He smiled greasily and grabbed my forearm tightly.

I cried out in pain as I tried to fight him, but his hold on me only increased. "Let me go!"

"No, baby, not until you give me what I came for."

I gasped as he yanked my arm, pain shooting through my

shoulder.

"You're hurting me!" I pleaded as I looked around me in a panic now, desperately searching for Ilyan or someone willing to help me.

"Come on, I know you like it like that."

"Not with you. Now, let me go!" I yelled as I caught sight of Ilyan breaking his way through the crowd, his jaw tight in anger.

"What? You here to catch little, rich boy? He'll just murder you like he did his other little bunny." His fingers dug into me as he shook me, his words cutting deeply. I looked toward Ilyan; my heart plummeted to see him dancing again, staring dangerously at something behind me.

I turned myself roughly against Tyler's grip to see what Ilyan was staring daggers at. I guess my plight hadn't gone completely unnoticed. Ryland was striding toward me, his face screwed up in a more furious anger than I had ever seen.

Even with the anger in his beautiful blue eyes, his look made me feel like I was like coming home again. My body grew extraordinarily warm. I felt like I could fly away right then. I kept my energy and my desperate need to be with him under control, but just barely. My heart beat even faster as his blue eyes met mine. I could have run to him, if it hadn't been for the vice grip around my arm.

"You can have him," Tyler spat, his free hand punching me aggressively across the face.

I fell to the ground just as Edmund's restraints flew off me in a torrent. I screamed out against the pain, clutching my head in an attempt to keep the overwhelming power of my magic restrained under my skin. The pain in my cheek, the rumbling headache from the impact with Tyler's fist, were all but forgotten as I screamed out, my voice ricocheting off the smooth floor.

It was too much to focus on, restraining the magic and managing the pain. My chest was heaving with the power of my magic, my fingers flexing against my head. I focused on the floor as I yelled out deafeningly, the power moving deeper into me.

"Breathe deeply and push it into your stomach." Ryland's voice was like honey in my ear as he lifted me off the floor to hold me against him, his hands resting on my lower back as he moved me to dance along with him.

I followed his directions, not willing to look up at him quite yet, just in case I lost control again. I pressed my face into his neck, almost losing my focus at the intensity of the memories, the joy that his scent caused me. I refocused and pushed it all back into my stomach, focusing on the space behind my belly button.

"Thanks," I mumbled as the energy was contained. I looked up at him, focusing with all my might on the surplus power I now kept locked in place.

"I told you not to come." He looked around nervously, and I knew Ilyan was right. We had walked right into a trap.

I followed Ryland's line of sight, my stomach clenching as ten Trpaslíks came barreling into the large room. They stopped momentarily before the man in the lead directed them out like a fan. We were trapped. Ryland moved us into the crowd, lifting me off the ground to plunge us into the gyrating mass quickly.

"Ilyan said you wouldn't leave if it was only him."

"I wouldn't. But I can't leave because you are here, either," Ryland said.

"I can't just let Edmund take you away from me," I stated emphatically.

"Stubborn to the end." He looked down at me, his bright blue eyes sending a shock through my system. He reached over and placed his hand softly against my face, covering my aching jaw where Tyler had just punched me. I leaned into his touch, needing him to be close to me.

"Are you okay?" he asked softly, his hand growing warm as his magic filled me.

I could only nod as my magic lurched again; I jerked with the energy.

"Focus, Jos," Ryland whispered, bringing me to rest right against him. "Jeez, how long have you been awake?"

"A week," I whispered. It was becoming harder to keep the energy restrained.

"Ilyan's an idiot." He pulled me against him, his cheek against mine. My heart sputtered and I heard Ryland laugh deeply. I suddenly felt very uncomfortable, not being able to see him properly.

"I need to see your eyes." I pulled away from him, trying to keep my body moving in the odd dance.

"You don't have to worry about that, Jos; you've already walked right into his trap. You saw all the men that swarmed in here, and there are only about ten times more surrounding us." He smiled, trying to break the fear that gripped me, but it only grew.

"Besides," he mused, "he's already so far in that it's a miracle I can remember you at all." He smiled, but it was so sad, so heartbroken.

"You need to come with me," I begged. "We need to get out of here right now." I pleaded my case to him, but he said nothing. He only smiled sadly at me and pulled my body to press against his.

I should have fought him, begged him further, but my heart was lost in his touch, his smell. I leaned into him, my soul swelling with joy. He pressed his cheek against mine as we moved. He held me so tightly that it felt as if we simply could not get close enough. I welcomed the contact; it felt so right. I felt so whole in that moment; my magic so close to its other half, my heart beating right next to his. We slow danced among the manically dancing pairs, lost in our own little world.

"I'd sacrifice anything," he sang softly in my ear, the Frank

Sinatra song blending with the loud club music. His voice broke; I could tell he was crying. "Come what might..." I pulled my head away to look at him. The glistening tears streaked down his cheeks. "I will not let anything take away what's standing right in front of me."

I reached up, my fingertips softly wiping away the wet tears from his face. As my fingers traced the lines of his cheek, the bruises and cuts swam into view. I gasped as I saw him up close; his face, his agony, making everything that much more real. My hand flew to my mouth, my own tears falling down my cheeks.

"Don't cry," he whispered. "Please, don't cry."

"But, Ryland," I spoke through my tears, "what has he done to you?" The tears came fast and hard as I placed my hand against his face, the ridges of his swollen jawline hard against my skin.

"It's okay. You're here now. Don't cry." His voice was soft. He held me tightly and I felt the warmth of his magic surge into my back. As he had for almost every day of my life, he comforted me, even though he could barely move. Even through his pain, his agony, he helped me.

I let the magic in, pulling it into me. It filled me in a way it had never done before, as his warm tendrils blended and moved with my own, intermingling in a familiar way that I never wanted to lose. The energy inside me continued to build uncontrollably, my skin prickling as the surges fought their way out. I knew he felt it, too; his smile was so triumphant, so happy.

"Now, I can never leave you. No matter what happens, no matter where I go. You will always be mine."

"Forever," I whispered through the tears.

Ryland leaned toward me, his eyes boring into mine, searching me. In that moment, I didn't care about the hordes of people surrounding us. I didn't care about Ilyan frantically yelling at us to stop. I needed him like I needed oxygen. I closed the gap between us and pressed my lips firmly to his.

That's all it took for my magic to explode.

CHAPTER
31

I HAD BEEN WAITING FOR this kiss for months, dreaming of the way it would feel to have his lips against mine, our bodies pressed together. My fantasies weren't even close to the reality I was now experiencing.

A warm tingling began in my toes and spread rapidly at his silky touch. His hand trailed up my spine to get lost in my hair. My magic expanded; his, still intertwined with mine. Our magic bubbled together like a pot overflowing. The two separate powers became so infused that I couldn't tell where mine ended and his began.

He pressed me to him roughly, a deep groan issuing from the back of his throat. I sighed at the sound, the touch, the pressure. My hands wrapped around him, clutching at his hips and elbows in a desperate effort to be closer to him. He answered my call. I gasped as our magic became a white hot heat that rocked inside our bodies with a violent force. The white heat grew, his touch tingled, the kiss deepened. My body became limp in his arms as the magic within me reached a point I could no longer control.

Our combined energies exploded out of us in a blinding, white light. It was the same light as when Ryland had touched my kiss for the first time, but now, it had more force and energy. It whooshed out of us as the ground shook violently in an explosion of energy, fire and wind. Flimsy human bodies were flung away from us as a result of the blast, slamming them into tables and walls with such force that I couldn't imagine many of them surviving.

Ryland held on to me tightly as screams began to fill the room. Teenagers ran for the exits in a wall of people that clogged the doorways, which resulted in yelling and fighting as the drunken crowd attempted to escape. I didn't dare move from Ryland's embrace; he held me in place, his arms shielding me protectively.

"You couldn't wait to seal her to you until we had gotten you out of here?" Ilyan yelled as he ran through the crowd, his hair long and blonde again.

"You knew you weren't getting me out of here in the first place, Ilyan!" Ryland yelled back. I turned in Ryland's arms to see Ilyan approach us, his skin glowing with energy.

"Ha!" Ilyan laughed without any humor. "You always did underestimate everyone, Ryland."

"You walked right into his trap and you accuse me of underestimating! You..." He stopped abruptly, his body twitching violently.

"No!" I yelled, clinging to him; he twitched again, his arm flying away from me.

"He's close." I heard Ilyan mumble from somewhere behind me.

The Trpaslíks who had walked into the room before had begun disentangling themselves from the wreckage around us. I looked around in a panic as more of them began to appear around us; from beneath the rubble on the main floor, on the balcony that surrounded the large room, in front of every doorway. Tace, Zilla and the other guards appeared out of nowhere to encompass the three of us in a wide circle, each of them with their hands palm side up, prepared for an attack.

The Trpaslíks began to approach us, their steps slow and measured. They kept looking from one to the other, gloating as if they were overjoyed with the prospect of battle.

I clung to Ryland, scared for both of us. He twitched again, the violent motion sending him flying to the ground. I sank down with him, my hands hovering uselessly above him; it was like the first dream all over again.

"Fight it, Ryland," I pleaded.

"Get him out of here, Joclyn," Ilyan said as sparks flew from his fingertips.

I grabbed Ryland and hung on to him, a gust of wind swirling around us as I prepared to take flight. My wind vanished in fear as an explosion rocked the room. The main doors flew off their hinges, the large slabs of wood flying right toward us. Ilyan raised his hand and stopped them in mid-air before shoving them in another direction, both doors now flying toward the Trpaslíks who were approaching us. The screams of the teenagers who were still in the large hall increased as they watched what was going on.

"Well, well, well." I jerked away from Ryland at hearing that detestable voice, my eyes searching for him in the mass of people standing in the doorway. Edmund stood in the middle of them, his tall frame and shortly-cropped hair giving him an almost militant look. Next to him stood Timothy and Cail, both of whom looked pleased, anticipating the events about to take place.

I felt Ryland flinch again. I threw my body over him, foolishly thinking I could protect him.

"My prodigal son has returned!" Edmund clapped his hands together in joy, an ominously pleased smile lighting up his face.

"No," Ilyan interjected powerfully, "I just came to save my little brother."

"Ryland!" I yelled out as Ryland flinched in my arms again, the reality of it all jerking at my magic again.

"Oh, look!" Edmund called out joyously. "Little Joclyn came, too! What fun! You sure have grown up since the last time I saw you. So beautiful. Such a pity to destroy you, but then I destroy things all the time." He smiled cruelly at Ryland who jerked again, his voice calling out in an agonizing scream.

"No! Leave him alone," I pleaded with Edmund, but he only smiled at me like I was the most pathetic thing he had ever seen. Ryland jumped again.

"Fight it, Ryland, please," I begged him, my hands pressing against his back. I desperately tried to push my magic into him, not sure if I was succeeding. Ryland lifted his head to mine, resting his hand against my face.

"You're so beautiful. I always thought so... with those eyes... They are just like diamonds." Ryland's body jerked again, and he screamed out in pain, his body tensing and convulsing as he fought his father.

"Fight it, Ryland!" I repeated, but I barely got the words out before Ryland's hand shot out to wrap itself around my throat. He lifted me up in one swift movement, my feet leaving the ground as he stood.

His black eyes looked into me with a look of evil pleasure that did not match his face. He smiled his beautiful half-smile, but this time, it held no pleasure for me. I clawed at his hand as my lungs called out for air, my chest heaving as it attempted to inhale.

A ball of light hit Ryland's side, shooting him across the large room. His hand lost its grip on my throat, and I went flying, Ilyan's wind bringing me right to him before I had a chance to hit the floor. He wrapped his arm around me securely, his eyes never leaving his father's.

"Well, that was fun." Wyn came up to stand next to me, wiping her hands against her jeans.

"Wynifred!" Timothy's deep voice had taken on a panicked quality I wouldn't have thought to ever hear from him. I jerked my head around to see the panic evident not only on Timothy's face, but on Cail's as well.

"Isn't this a veritable family reunion," Edmund commented in a bored voice. "Didn't want to bring Ovailia, I see; didn't think she could handle being near me again?"

Ilyan smiled, that look of power covered his face as a visible wall of energy moved away from us, shooting across the ballroom and ramming into Edmund and his men. They all stumbled back a step; many fell clear to the ground.

"Oh, I'm here, Father. I just prefer not to get my hands dirty." Ovailia's voice echoed around the room from somewhere behind us.

"I'm tired of this," Wyn said, stepping forward one step before jumping in place. The whole room shook and shifted as pieces of the ceiling and balcony broke apart and tumbled down around us. Her action opened up a floodgate, and the ballroom began to explode in a torrent of energy. Wyn laughed happily as she continued to jump; no wonder she had said her magic was destructive.

I covered my head and dropped to the ground as chunks of marble and wood came crashing down, leaving a giant hole gaping in the ceiling. I dodged and weaved away from the falling debris until I slid under a large table, finding two trapped party-goers who were screaming frantically.

I looked up as Wyn clapped her hands; the wall behind Edmund and his men exploded, sending them all running in a panic. The room groaned at the loss of a supporting wall, the structure heaving as it was torn apart from the inside out. Wyn's explosion separated the Trpaslíks from each other. Edmund seemed to have completely disappeared, leaving his minions to do his dirty work. With the

Trpaslíks separated, Ilyan and his guard were free to pick them off, one by one. Wyn laughed before heading straight for her brother, Cail, her look of determination, terrifying.

She met up with him as he broke out from behind the rubble. She pushed her hands toward him, a magical pulse pushing him back down into the rubble he had just escaped from. Cail recovered quickly, jumping to his feet as he shot a fiery orb of energy her way. Wyn dodged it, but lost her footing. Without thinking, I sent wind to her and righted her before her brother could attack her again.

My actions caught the attention of three Trpaslíks who flung away the table I was hiding under, slamming it into an opposing wall. My head jerked up to see the three small men approaching me excitedly. I jumped to my feet, shooting three waves of fire toward my attackers. The burning orbs collided with them, sending them skidding against the floor. The fire burned their clothes and singed their flesh, but the weak, unfocused energy wasn't able to do much more than that, and they quickly continued toward me. I didn't wait for their attack; I exploded into the air and away from them, only to land clumsily in the middle of the floor, not having planned where I was going. I spun around wildly, hoping to get my bearings.

The whole ballroom was now madness and chaos. Explosions rocked the air. Wind and magic flew between fighting pairs, leaving paths of fire and destruction behind them. I watched as Talon swung his arms wide, a trail of fire spitting from his fingertips. Zilla wrapped electrical ropes around her opponents, causing them to fall to the ground, one by one. Ilyan then disappeared from one spot, only to appear across the room a moment later, hovering behind one of Edmund's retreating allies. He placed his hand lightly on the Trpaslíks head, causing him to yell out in pain before dropping to the ground.

Another explosion rocked the building, sending more debris crashing down from overhead. Talon appeared behind me, grabbing me around the waist and sliding me across the floor just as a boulder-sized piece of the balcony crashed down where I had been standing. He shoved me behind him as he shot light and wind away from us.

"Get Ryland and get out of here!" Talon yelled as he sent a table skidding across the ground, the hard edge slamming into the back of one of Edmund's men.

I took off toward where Ryland's body still lay, crumpled from the impact.

"Ryland!" My voice broke as I called to him. I reached out and grabbed his hand, pulling it up to my face. His touch triggered my magic and I felt it surge into him. I could feel it move inside his body, instantly moving to intertwine with his power. His head turned toward me, the knot in my stomach releasing at the sight of his blue eyes.

"Jos," he whispered my name, a smile trying desperately to form on his lips, "you came."

"Yeah, Ry. I did. Now we have to get out of here. Come on, let's go, just you and me." I tugged on his arm, but he didn't budge.

"What did you do to your hair, Jos? I always loved your hair." His eyes were fading out on me, focusing on something far behind me.

"Ryland! Come on; we have to leave now!" I clutched onto him and brought a powerful gust of wind around us; I felt my magic fade as we lifted off the ground a few feet, only to crash back down to the floor. I tried again with the same result.

"Ryland, I need your help." I was becoming desperate; he still didn't respond to me. "Ryland! Please."

"Do you want to go steal the car, Jos?" His voice slurred as it faded away, his eyes gently closing.

"Ryland, no, no. Ryland!" He didn't move, and he didn't react, he just lay there.

The prospect of losing him clicked something together in my brain. I was instantly consumed with panic-stricken desperation. I called his name over and over as I pushed him, prodded him and even slapped him across the face. He didn't react to any of it. My movements became more desperate as the seconds clicked by in my mind.

I could hear the yells and screams of the fight that surrounded us, feel the rattle of the building as it was rent with explosion after explosion. I stopped hitting him, stopped screaming at him; I just sat there, staring at him.

He could have been sleeping. The way his hair fell across his face, the way his arms lay lifelessly at his side. I watched him, expecting him to grumble something in his sleep and roll over the way he always did; my heart almost willed it to happen. I traced the dark purple circles of his bruise, let my fingertips run the length of the healing scar across his face. He was in pain.

My voice howled in agony as I fell onto him, my arms wrapping around him. My magic rushed into him, glad to be home. I felt it swirling within him, mingling with the flaring embers he had kept hidden inside himself. I cried into his chest, feeling the connection grow within our bodies. His arms reached around me, his strong arms clenching me against him.

"Ryland?" I pulled myself away from him, my magic pulling back into me as I moved. I looked up into his face expectantly; my hope shattered at the black eyes smiling back.

"You are exquisite, aren't you? No wonder this body seems to want you so badly."

My heart screamed inside my chest at the deep voice that came out of him. I wrenched out of his arms and scurried away, my feet slipping against loose rocks that littered the slick marble floor.

"What? Don't you want this body, too? You seemed to be desperate to have it just a second ago." His body uncoiled toward me dangerously, the shoulders squared and back straighter than Ryland ever held himself. He towered over me as I continued to slip in the rubble. The building rocked with another explosion and I lost my balance, landing on my stomach.

Ryland reached down as I slid around in a desperate attempt to find my balance, and his large hand wrapped around my neck as he lifted me up. I was being choked at the pressure, my lungs unable to take in breath.

"Hello, pretty girl," he sneered as he brought me up to face him, the depths of his black eyes staring back at me acidly.

I didn't have time to react before he shot a flame against my abdomen. The powerful surge collided against my stomach, burning away the lower half of my shirt. The strength of the pulse shot me away from him, flinging me through the air to land hard on the marble floor twenty feet away, the impact sending a painful jolt rippling through me. I sighed as I rolled over onto my back, my body protesting the movement.

I should be hurt; I felt a powerful warmth, smelt the burnt fabric, but there was no pain. I looked at my stomach in confusion. The bottom of my shirt had been destroyed; the skin below it was blackened like charcoal, but nothing more. I wiped away the black residue, surprised to see no wound. My stomach was intact, the skin pale and smooth beneath the ash.

A white orb collided angrily against my chest, sliding my body across the floor with the impact. My attention was pulled from my stomach as Ryland's new attack sent me slamming into the wall. I looked up just in time to see him land in front of me, another pulse already prepared to fling my way.

I knew I should fight him, I knew I should attack him as he was attacking me, but I couldn't bring myself to do it. I couldn't bring my magic to me with enough strength to defend myself from the Trpaslík, let alone fight or injure Ryland. The thought of purposely harming him set my heart into a flutter of pain.

I scuttled to the side, the attack shattering the wall behind me instead. Without thinking, I grabbed a table next to me and flung it at him. My heart sank as I watched it fly, terror gripping me at the impending impact. It had almost reached him before he swayed to the side, the table flying uselessly past.

He walked toward me, smiling wickedly as I continued to shoot objects in his direction. All my attempts were useless; the small pieces of what my wind could grab and carry were either dodged, deflected, or they bounced uselessly off his chest. I knew I needed to fight back more intently, I knew I needed to try, but my heart wouldn't let me.

"Throwing things with wind; is that the extent of your power?" Ryland raised both of his hands toward me; I could feel his wind build around me as he shot all the useless objects I had sent toward him right back at me, but with a much greater force and in a quicker succession. I shielded my head as the wall on either side of me was pelted with the arsenal. Plaster and small rocks flew into my hair and bounced painfully against my bare skin.

The onslaught ended, and I looked up toward Ryland, hoping to see his blue eyes staring back at me. Instead, I saw a table. The table I had thrown at him was coming back to me at full speed. My mind went blank as I watched it barrel toward me, its four legs spinning in my direction. I wrapped myself into a ball just a moment before it hit. The legs had sunk deep into the wall around me, the tabletop stopping right before it came in contact with my body, pinning me in place instead of crushing me.

Ryland took the last few steps toward me, stopping right in front of me. I shrank away from his acidic gaze, terrified to find that there really was nowhere for me to go.

He reached down to cup my face, his hand cold and unfamiliar against my skin.

"You know, if I could break you, I would keep you." He smiled as he leaned down, his eyes level with mine. "My own pretty, little pet."

He dragged his icy fingers against my lower lip, the weight of his touch pushing my lip roughly to the side. I couldn't rip my focus from him. His face looked the same, but he wasn't Ryland anymore. He wasn't the boy I had grown up with, the one I loved so deeply. My heart whipped back and forth as I fought my feelings. I had to get out of here before the monster in front of me did something that Ryland would regret. I knew I needed to fight—actually fight him. I just hoped that I wouldn't hurt him.

I placed my hands against the table that entrapped me, surging my magic aggressively into it, hoping that it would have the desired effect. While, not the explosion I had hoped for, the table did fly away from me, taking Ryland with it. He flew helplessly through the air, only to land twenty feet away, the heavy table landing on top of him.

CHAPTER
32

I JUMPED UP, DESPERATE TO escape from the monster that had possessed Ryland's body. I ran only a few steps, my body preparing to launch into the air before a dead weight hit against my back, pushing me back down onto the floor. I tried to fight it, but couldn't budge against the power that held me in place. I looked toward where Ryland had landed; fear now gripping me as I saw him approaching, his hand rising to aim in my direction.

An energy stream of blue waves shot over me, ramming into Ryland's chest and stopping his progress. He only sneered at its sudden appearance, as if the powerful magic was no match for him. The magical barrier lifted off me and I rolled onto my knees, surprised to see Ovailia standing with her hands extended before her. My mouth dropped in shock at her perfectly poised figure, her cold-set eyes. She didn't even acknowledge my existence; she simply stepped over me as she approached Ryland.

I didn't dare look back before turning to run. The ground around me exploded and shook. I bobbed around, desperately attempting to avoid the fights and explosions around me before jumping into the sky. I sped through the air up onto the balcony that encircled the large room. I landed swiftly and continued moving, looking for a doorway or an alcove where I could hide.

The balcony below my feet shook, and I dropped to the floor, terrified it was about to collapse. It continued to shake as I lay still against the dust-covered carpet. I cautiously moved myself toward the edge to look below me. The floor of the ballroom was chaos. Colored explosions shook the air as unguided objects flew around and collided. Tracks of color and power flew from hands as the two sides fought relentlessly against each other.

Snakes of red surged from one Trpaslík, only to collide with one of our group whose name I couldn't remember. The red tendrils wrapped around her as she was slammed aggressively into the floor, her screams only barely audible over the sound of battle. I scanned the crowd, looking for anyone I knew. Ovailia was running, her direction taking her right out the door in pursuit of someone. I kept looking, happy to find Wyn still alive, battling back-to-back with Talon against her own brother. I reluctantly looked away from her in an attempt to find the person who was responsible for this whole charade, but Edmund had vanished.

Ryland was walking determinedly toward Ilyan who had caught sight of him, but was still engaged in another fight. I watched as Ilyan dashed from one place to another, lightning shooting toward the small Trpaslík he was dutifully fighting. The Trpaslík was no match for Ilyan, who swiped his hand before him and sent his enemy flying right into a group of trapped teenagers who had taken refuge under the stairs.

Ilyan turned and faced his brother, his hands moving roughly to either side, sending every bit of rubble that lay uselessly on the floor up into the air and toward Ryland's advancing form. Ryland yelled and called out in pain as he was pelted by the array of ammo, the force of the attack causing him to slide away against the floor.

Ilyan did not wait for him to recover; his hands moved again, producing what could only be explained as a chain of magical energy.

The links of power crackled and sizzled in front of Ilyan, the bright white light, shining throughout the room. Ilyan pushed the chain toward Ryland; it wrapped around him, restraining his movements. It was only just visible before his body seemed to absorb it. Ryland moved his hands up in a counterattack toward his brother, but I didn't see anything further. A large crack sounded in my ears as a heavy body landed directly to my left.

I spun around with a small scream. A well-dressed man with a neatly-trimmed beard was hovering near me, his sneer barely visible through the brown hair. My heart clenched in fear at what could have been Timothy's twin. I backed away from him, careful to keep my body from falling off the unstable edge of the balcony.

The tiny man said nothing; he only laughed as he raised his fingers and snapped repeatedly. At each snap, small explosions shook and shredded the ground around me. I squealed and screamed in panic as I was littered with sparks and debris from the explosions. The Trpaslík took another step forward, his hands still raised menacingly.

I flung my hands toward him, his body flying away from me as my attack hit him square in the chest. He hit the floor, came to a standing position, and began to advance, more explosions rocking the floor with each step he took toward me. I raised my hand again, sending a weaker wave toward him. He stepped back as it collided with him, but recovered quickly.

I did not wait to find out what his intentions were. I rolled off the balcony, sending my body flailing into the fight below. I had only fallen a few feet when I caught myself, my strong wind catching my spinning body as I moved myself toward yet another portion of the steadily deteriorating balcony.

I only made it halfway across the large space before a large mass landed on my back, dropping me down to the floor of the ballroom like a boulder. I crashed hard into the marble floor, my back instantly clenching in pain. I screamed out as I fought to get away from whatever had landed on me, surprised when hands shot out and enclosed my wrists.

"Thought you could run from The Master did you? Stupid, little half-breeds." The Trpaslík who had attacked me on the balcony pushed me down onto the floor, his legs straddling me as he restricted my movements.

I clawed and fought and threw any little rocks I could at him, but it was no use. He batted away my pathetic arsenal before clasping his hands on either side of my face as I had seen Ilyan do to someone else only a moment before. I screamed out as I felt the heat growing in his hands. It continued to build until it felt like a fire was burning inside my skull, its raging power boiling inside of my head. My vision blacked out as the pain grew, as my screams increased. Then it was gone.

The Trpaslíks weight left my hips as he fell to the side, his lifeless body slumping onto the cold floor. I sat up, my vision returning. I didn't wait to find out who my savior was; I simply turned and jumped, taking off into the air again. My fear had supercharged my magic, and I slammed into the balcony on the opposite wall, unable to stop myself in time.

I panted as I stood, my back seizing in pain. I ran forward, toward a door that would lead me out, my left leg dragging a bit. If I could just get to the door, I could make it to the large, second-floor balcony and escape as Ilyan had wanted me to. I didn't make it far before another body landed in front of me, the body unfolding to face me.

"Cail," I gasped.

"Awww, you remember me. How sweet. Probably not as well as

I remember you." He raised his hand to me and a bright red light flew toward me. He didn't let it build as he had before; I had no warning this time. I leapt to the side, my back flattening against the hard wall. The red ball erupted right where I had been standing, sending out the wood and stone of the wall in a splintering explosion. Cail looked at me and smiled.

I raised my hand and released the prickling energy in a rush. It slammed into him, but the energy wasn't strong enough to do any damage. He laughed as he straightened out to face me, while I turned and went to launch myself off the balcony again.

My feet had just left the ground when Cail's wind intercepted me and slammed me back, hard against the wall of the balcony I had just left. The wind continued to move around me and hold me in place, my shirt whipping around.

"You and your mother," he mocked as he walked toward me, his steps faltering as an explosion from below shook the room. "You are both such fighters. Why can't you die easily? But, you know it's going to end the same way, don't you?" He came to stand right next to me and I cringed against him, my body unable to resist the pull of his magic.

"You both end up dead." He placed his hand against my stomach, his palm against my skin. I could feel it grow cold as his magic entered me before beginning to warm as he generated a ball of energy. He formed it inside of me, the weapon building underneath my skin. I screamed out as the warmth turned into a burning heat.

"Let her go." Ryland's powerful voice filled the air as he landed roughly on the balcony beside us. He leaned against a large pillar, his body obviously weakened as he continued to fight his father's invasion of his mind. His body twitched uncomfortably, but his eyes were back to a bright shade of blue.

"Really?" Cail mocked, the heat continuing to move and grow

inside of me. "You think you have enough energy to fight me?"

"I don't..." Ryland panted, "but she does."

The ball of fire within me grew to a tumult as my energy drained away, filtering out of my body. I could feel my magic move into Ryland, the power increasing as our magics intertwined with one another, growing stronger with their union. My magic drained as Ryland shot a ball of intense golden light toward Cail. The impact sent him flying, his body tumbling off the balcony into the fight below. Ryland collapsed to the floor, his body twitching as he sank.

With no wind to hold me up, I fell roughly to the ground as well, the heat from Cail leaving a terrible pain in my stomach. I crawled to Ryland, placing my arms around his neck when I reached him. He twitched again, and I forced his face up to look at me, thankful for his beautiful blue eyes.

"How did you do that?" I panted, the pain still lingering in my belly.

"I can do anything with you." He tried to smile, but it was only a grimace.

Ryland reached forward and placed his hand on the skin of my stomach exactly where Cail's hand had lain. I felt my magic swell and grow as Ryland pulled it toward him, stopping it right before it left me to join him. The warmth stayed there and took the pain away almost instantly.

"How...?"

"Anything... with... you..." He twitched again, his whole body was shaking, but he refused to take his eyes off me.

I reached my hand forward; he grabbed it, pressing my fingertips to his lips.

"Love... you... always..." His shaking became uncontrollable as his eye color began to fade. I watched in agony as Edmund took over.

"No!" I clutched his hands desperately. "Don't leave me!"

"Always." His voice was broken and wispy in my ear as he pulled my hand against the side of his face. He pressed my fingers roughly to him, his grip tightening in his fear of losing me.

"No!"

Before the change could complete, the balcony shifted and collapsed. I held tightly to Ryland's hand as we were thrown over the edge, our bodies tumbling toward the fire-filled conflict that raged below. I swept wind to us, hoping the weak energy would catch us before we landed hard against the floor; instead, the wind flung us into a heap in the corner.

My body was entangled with Ryland's as we collided with the wall, but I wasn't there for long before Ryland grabbed me and shot me away from him in a surge of wind and energy. My body slammed into another wall, and I felt my back pop. There was no agony with it, so I stood, thankful that it had not broken again. I steadied myself just as Ryland landed in front of me, a wave of energy slamming into my stomach. I felt no pain; only pressure as the energy surge pushed me back, trapping me in place.

"Hello again, little pet," Ryland sneered as he walked toward me, his black eyes shimmering wickedly as he laughed. I cringed away from his advance, but my body was restrained again by his magic.

"Not going to try to attack me with your weak magic?" Ryland was right in front of me now. He leaned intimately close to me, one hand resting on the wall beside my head. I could feel his breath against my face; feel his hip as he pushed it against me. He smiled wickedly, and I felt the bile rise dangerously in my throat.

"That's okay; I have another idea." His voice was a sickening purr.

His hand moved into my line of vision, his fingers twiddling together, small sparks flashing from the surge in his magic. The sparks he produced continued to grow as his fingers rubbed together wildly. In only a moment, a small dagger appeared in his hand, the small silver blade glinting wickedly in the magical light that flashed and pulsed around us.

"You love this body, don't you, little girl?" He smiled wickedly. I couldn't look away from the dagger that spun between his fingers. "You love the way it looks, the way it makes you feel." He pushed his hip further into me; I gasped in pain at the pressure.

"Well, this body, it loves you, too."

The dagger stopped spinning and my eyes flew to his with a glimmer of hope. It was pointless.

"But I don't," he said.

I didn't even see the movement; I was too consumed with looking at his face. One minute there was no pain, and the next, the pain had moved beyond me. I screamed as the tiny dagger began to dig its way into the skin that covered my heart. I felt the warmth of my own blood drizzling down my chest as the dagger slowly worked its way into my chest, deeper and deeper, toward my beating heart.

"That doesn't hurt, does it?" Ryland's voice was so joyous; he enjoyed watching my agony as he tortured me.

"Ryland!" I screamed his name, my voice finding form as the pain grew. "Fight him, Ryland!" The evil imposter who restrained me only laughed as he dug the knife deeper into my skin.

"Sad. I don't think he can hear you."

"Ryland! It's me. It's Joclyn. Snap out of it, please!"

He only laughed with increased malice. I screamed again, feeling the blood pool around the waistline of my tight pants.

"Ryland!" I panted between screams, calling to him, desperate for him to make a connection. "Remember the tree... the old guard... at the hospital... Remember when we... ran away..." I screamed and panicked as the pain increased. He only laughed as he looked at me through the depthless pit of his black eyes.

"Remember when you kissed me..." I tried one last time before my voice broke; my mind too dizzy and confused to focus properly. My head slumped down; I focused on my own heartbeat, hoping that Ilyan would find me, that someone would see me, before it was too late.

"Joclyn."

My head rose slowly to see him—Ryland, blue eyes and all—looking at me. I couldn't bring myself to say anything; I just looked at him. His eyes looked me over, stopping in a panic when he saw the dagger that still remained in my chest, his hand and my skin covered with wet, sticky blood.

"Oh, God, what have I done?" he asked as he released his magical hold on me and I fell into his arms. He held onto me tightly as his magic surged into me; I felt the warmth fill me all over as the dizziness retreated and the flow of my blood seemed to stop. I looked up at him carefully, the obvious request lining my face.

"We have to get out of here," he whispered, not waiting for me to respond before he exploded into the air, my body still pressed tightly against his.

We didn't even make it past the hole in the ceiling before the entire process was reversed. A gust of wind I knew neither of us controlled pushed against us in the opposite direction, dragging us back down to the destroyed floor below.

Ryland's arms went limp and I tumbled out of them, heading down toward the ground, fast. My fear of falling only lasted a moment before Ilyan's wind grabbed me and pulled me, soaring across the room, straight into his arms.

"It's time to go," he hissed in my ear.

I turned from Ilyan, searching for Ryland. He stood across the room from us, his body tall and still as he looked intently in our direction, his eyes back to the colorless cast. He didn't move; he didn't flinch; he stayed still, just as his father commanded him to do.

Edmund's hand was placed on Ryland's shoulder, the fingers curved aggressively as they dug into Ryland's skin. Edmund seemed to taunt us from across the room, his stance just willing us to come and attack him. I knew we would lose if we tried, but I did not want to accept it.

"Ryland!"

"We can't take him, Silný," Ilyan said. He wrapped his arms around me as he pulled me away from them.

"No!" I yelled out in a panic, reaching for Ryland.

"I can't get him away from Edmund and get you out of here safely, Joclyn. You are my number one priority now. We have to go." Ilyan grabbed me tightly around the waist, and jumped us back. Edmund had just released Ryland's shoulder and Ryland was now advancing toward us surprisingly fast.

"No! I can do it! I can save him!" I don't know what made me say that; I knew I couldn't. My heart beat wildly as I fought against Ilyan's arm; my body, my heart, desperate to get back to Ryland.

"I can do it! Let me go!" Ilyan held me tighter as I fought against him, my hands clawing uselessly at his strong arm.

Ryland kept advancing as Ilyan restrained me, the members of the guard surrounding us again in an attempt to escape together.

"Ryland. Ryland!" I screamed until my voice broke, my mouth filling with the taste of blood. "Let me go! Ryland!"

Ilyan tightened his grip and I felt us take off into the air, the wind blowing against my skin as Ilyan took me away from the one person I wanted, the one person I needed.

"Ryland." I continued to fight, not caring if I fell. I needed him.

I fought Ilyan, calling Ryland's name in a desperate hope that he would change back, that he would see me and follow me. Our eyes locked as Ilyan flew me through a wide hole in the roof, the night sky swallowing us up and taking me away from him.

Now, I knew it was too late. His eyes faded to blue just as we passed beyond the roof of the building, but Ryland only looked at me in confusion, no trace of recognition on his face.

No matter if I came back, no matter how hard I would try, it was too late now. Edmund had erased every part of him.

CHAPTER
33

$\mathcal{I}$ WATCHED THE FIRE THAT had embraced the building; I watched the purple and green flames lick the roof and reach their slinky arms up to the sky. I saw the red and blue flashing lights of the emergency vehicles that surrounded the mansion, the hordes of people who came, either to watch or to huddle around the ambulances in panic. I watched as the bodies became indiscriminate specks and the flames became tiny orbs of colored light. I watched as the building became nothing more than a colorless speck in the midst of the city lights. I watched as it all disappeared into the blackness of a starless, moonless, hopeless night.

Through it all, I cried; my heart calling to Ryland as he disappeared from my life forever. I clung to Ilyan as my chest was wracked with sobs, my breathing ragged and broken. I drenched his shirt with my tears and any other gross secretions that joined my broken heart. He didn't seem to care.

Ilyan held me close to him as he flew us through the air, his arms holding me securely. In the back of my mind, I knew that he was singing to me. I could feel the rumble of his chest; hear his deep, comforting voice in my ear. But I didn't know what was being said, though; I didn't understand what the words meant.

"Teď tiše, moje malá. Upokoj se, buď klidná. S novým úsvitem se svět změní. A když se změní, uvidíš, jaký bychom měli být, ty a já." He sang it to me slowly, over and over.

My tears slowed, but the pain didn't go away. I had lost everything. My father had left me, only to disappear shortly after renewing contact. My beautiful mother had been murdered, a casualty of the war I had been thrust into. Moreover, my best friend, the new love who was so ruthlessly torn away from me—his mind had been erased and all memory of me had been stolen from him.

I was only vaguely aware when Ilyan landed. His arms loosened as he attempted to lower me down, but I held onto him tightly, my heart terrified of losing one of the last things I had. I clung to him like a terrified child, locking my fingers together in a panic.

"It's okay, Silný." He tried to release my arms again, but I only held on tighter.

"No!" I wailed into him, clinging to him. "Don't leave me."

"I am not going anywhere. I will be right back."

I felt his magic surge through my blood stream, and my body instantly relaxed. I sank to the ground, my eyes only barely registering Ilyan's retreating footsteps. I looked around myself, not really taking in the dirt, dried leaves and pine needles.

I had barely registered where I was—the fire pit—before Wyn kneeled before me. Her pants were torn and covered in dirt, the brightly-colored 'Queen' t-shirt burned and ripped at the hem.

"He's gone." My voice broke with my tears.

"I know." Wyn's voice wasn't condescending, or comforting, but my heart still rent open to hear it from someone else.

"I failed him, Wyn." I sank down further, my body falling

forward into Wyn's lap. She wrapped her arms around me, her head resting on my back. I felt her warm breath against my skin, her tears falling like dripping ice against me.

"It's all right, Joclyn. We will get him back."

I sat up, throwing Wyn off me, my blood heating to a sudden boil.

"Get who back, Wyn? He's gone! There is no more Ryland! He's gone!" I screamed as loud as my sore and broken voice would let me. It was probably a good thing Wyn's battle-worn face already looked like someone had punched her or I probably would have.

"I was supposed to save him, and I failed. I was supposed to protect him from his father, and I couldn't. He's not there anymore!"

"He has to be there, Jos. He loves you so much, he—"

"Loved me. The Ryland who *loved* me doesn't exist anymore. I lost my father because of a stupid mark! My mother was murdered because you people cursed me! And now I have lost Ryland, the one person who meant the most to me!" I felt that uncontrollable anger seeping into my soul again; the desire to fight and yell and scream hit much stronger than it should have been.

"Enough, Joclyn." I heard Ilyan's commanding voice flow over me; Ilyan's magical barrier freezing my emotions in place.

I felt the anger vanish, leaving me with the soul-crushing sadness of my heartbreak. I sank into the ground, my body curling in on itself. I ran my fingers over the dirt as I looked to the tops of the trees I had climbed so many times.

"It's okay, Ilyan; she's just hurt. She doesn't mean what she's saying." Wyn's voice was tiny; I could barely feel her hand against my shoulder.

"I know, Wyn." There was a pause and I heard Ilyan exhale deeply, his magical restraints peeling off me a bit. "It's time to go. You and Talon are going to carry the tail of the western evacuation and go home through Los Angeles."

"And Joclyn?" Wyn's voice was hesitant.

"Joclyn will be going into hiding with me. Ryland marked her, the Zêlství is complete. I am not sure if Edmund is going to use their connection to track her down or not. Until I know for sure, she is staying with me."

"Then I am staying with you, too." Wyn's voice was forceful, but sad; I couldn't imagine what it had cost her to say that, to commit to leaving Talon. I unwound myself from my cocoon of pity to look at her, my heart melting.

"You can't leave Talon, Wyn." My voice was soft and broken. "I left Ryland, and now he is gone. Please, for me, stay with Talon."

Our eyes locked as she reached forward to take my hands. A million thank yous, a million emotions passed between us before she stood, our hands extended between us in a last goodbye.

"I'll see you soon," I whispered. She could only nod. The phrase "going into hiding" did not bode well for quick reunions.

She squeezed my hands before turning away from me and then she and Talon took off into the inky night sky.

"It's time to go, Silnỳ." I looked up at Ilyan, surprised to see tears falling down his own cheeks.

Ilyan didn't expect me to stand; he leaned down and lifted me securely into his arms. He didn't cradle me as he had before, but held me against him in a bone-crushing hug that took my breath away. He pressed me against him as we soared into the air, the wind whipping his hair and what was left of mine around us. My emotionally drained body sank into him, a few soothing lines of his calming melody sinking into me before I fell fast asleep.

I woke up the next morning in a gray apartment. The walls were gray, the curtains were gray. It was an ugly gray palette that I had no interest in seeing. I rolled over and pulled the covers over my head, trying to block out the light. I breathed deeply, but it came out ragged and torn. I had cried all through the night.

"Did you get everyone out?" Ilyan's voice was calm and even. I could tell he was on the phone by the way he switched back and forth between Czech and English.

"We made it to the third safe house. I made everyone go before us, so they all should be safe."

I rolled over to lie on my back, throwing the blanket away from me. As I moved, the necklace shifted onto my skin; I had almost forgotten about it.

"Yes, get everyone to Prague. I will start the evacuation on my end. The more of a trickle we can form, the safer everyone will be." He came around the corner, surprised to see me awake.

"I am still keeping her with me, Ovailia; we have a lot of work to do and she is safer with me." He snapped his phone shut and leaned against the wall.

"How are you doing?" he asked, his voice tentative and quiet.

I looked at him before turning away, fixing my eyes on the ceiling.

"I'm sorry, Joclyn." His voice was deep and soothing, but I brushed his condolences away. I just wanted to be mad. "Everything will be all right, Silný."

I just nodded at him; I didn't trust myself to say anything polite.

"We are going to be staying here for a week, maybe two, so make yourself comfortable. But please, stay inside. It's not safe to go out right now."

I nodded again, my head falling to the side, looking blankly at nothing. Ilyan smiled sadly at me before leaving, calling behind him his plans to take a shower. I heard the door click and desperately hoped there was another bathroom I could hide in; somewhere I could lock the door. Judging by the fact that I could see the kitchen from the bed I lay in, I wasn't holding out much hope.

I exhaled heavily, my voice shaking at the action before beating my head against the pillow. My tears came strong, my heartbreak increasing the more I tried to ignore my emotions.

"I'm sorry, Ryland. I failed you."

I didn't want to be here; all I felt was an overwhelming sense of loss, of failure. I continued to bang my head against the pillow until my head began to ache, my temples throbbing. I focused on the pain until a new throbbing interrupted me.

The necklace was beating.

I sat up in one movement, desperately clawing at the fine chain around my neck. I didn't care about what Ilyan had told me; I didn't care about the danger. I just needed to see him, to know he was okay. I plunged my magic into the necklace, my efforts draining me. I closed my eyes as I fell back against the bed, the white room appearing before me.

"Ryland! Ryland!" I screamed the second I entered the open space.

"Yes?" I spun around, eager to face him, and saw nothing.

"Who are you?" a little voice asked.

I cried out, falling to my knees as my eyes came level with his. My heart broke as I looked at him. He was only a child, younger even than when I had first met him. My hand flew to my mouth as I sobbed, his blue eyes growing wide at my reaction.

"It's okay," his little voice was soft as he placed his small hand on my shoulder. "Are you hurt? I can make it all better; my mommy says I am very good at making things all better." He smiled widely, his mop of curls bouncing.

I just shook my head no.

"Are you scared then? I get scared sometimes. The cook, Marie, taught me a song about whistling that takes the scares away. Do you want to hear it?"

I shook my head no; there were fewer tears, now. I was gaining control, trying desperately to ignore the heartbreak.

"I'm... just... sad..." I choked out.

"Why?"

"I lost someone very important to me, someone I love."

"Who?"

"My very best friend."

"Oh." He paused and dug his toe into the ground. "I don't have any friends. You can be my friend if you would like." He was so eager, so much like he had been that first day when we had met.

"I would like that very much."

"I'm Ryland." He stuck out his hand; I took it eagerly, expecting something to happen, my heart breaking when nothing did.

"Joclyn."

"What a funny name," he giggled, his body shaking.

I couldn't even bring myself to smile.

Ryland looked at me with all the innocence, all the sparkly-eyed, new-world wonderment a young child has—a child who has known no pain and felt no heartbreak.

"You have very pretty eyes," he said softly. "They look like diamonds."

CONTINUE THE FIGHT WITH . . .

Eyes of EMBER

OUT NOW

ACKNOWLEDGMENTS

To those who inspired me:
Happy Birthday, Papa – I love you more than words can say.
For my Grandmother, whose passion for reading is infectious.

To those who supported me:
Julie Blaisdell
Wendi Fedderson
Annette Skoubye
Sheena Boekweg

And to those who created for me:
Rick Chianteretto of Dirty Boy Photography
Sarah at Okay Creations
Amanda and Carol of Natures Lace

And to the many more who have given me kind words,
warm hugs, and endless amounts of inspiration. There is not
enough ink in the world to thank you all.

Thank you for reading this little story that came out of my head. I
hope you enjoyed it

See any Editing mistakes?

As much as I try to make each book perfect, sometimes it just
doesn't happen. If you have found any editing mistake please feel
free to email me at contact@rebeccaethington.com with what you
found and where. I would love to send you some swag as a way to
say thanks!

ABOUT THE AUTHOR

Rebecca Ethington has been telling stories since she was small. First, with writing crude scripts, and then on stage with years of theatrical performances. The Imdalind Series is her first stint into the world of literary writing. Rebecca is a mother to two, and wife to her best friend of 14 years. She was born and raised in the mountains of Salt Lake City, and hasn't found the desire to leave yet. Her days are spent writing, running, and enjoying life with her amazing family.

After years of writing scripts for children's theatre company's across the country, Rebecca is happy to be making her debut into the world of fiction with Kiss of Fire, the first in The Imdalind Series.

Eyes of Ember, the second book in The Imdalind Series and Book Three, *Scorched Treachery*, are out now.

Rebecca will also be debuting book one in a new kind of paranormal/dystopia, *Through Glass*. Through Glass is told in bi-weekly novella's, many of which are out now.

Coming Soon From Rebecca Ethington

Of River and Raynn – The Catalyst
Of River and Raynn – The Sypher
Hit
Dawn of Ash, Book Five in The Imdalind Series
Through Glass Novella Series – Episodes 4-12

WANT ALL THE LATEST NEWS ABOUT IMDALIND AND
ALL THINGS REBECCA ETHINGTON?
Follow Rebecca

www.rebeccaethington.com

On Twitter:
@ RebEthington

On Facebook:
Facebook.com/rebeccaethington.author

On Instagram
http://instagram.com/rebeccaethington#

On Spotify
https://play.spotify.com/user/1280822781

On You Tube
http://www.youtube.com/channel/UCwKr4zggGMlbSzTqQGaYV
CA

CPSIA information can be obtained at www.ICGtesting.com
Printed in the USA
LVOW07s2328211215

467435LV00003B/448/P